# Make You Love Me

## L.A. SHAW

Make You Love Me

Editor: Brandi at www.mynotesinthemargins.com

Cover Design: L.A. Shaw - Canva

Formatting: L.A. Shaw - Atticus

Photo: Canva

To all the dreams we never thought were possible...

# Author's Note

Please Scan The Code Below For Content Warnings

# Prologue

*My Love,*

*Where do I begin?*
*I want you to know that you mean the absolute world to me. Filling even my saddest days with rays of sun. The way you hold me just right and know exactly what my body and mind need whenever you are near.*
*I can't believe it has been over 2 years and you still evoke butterflies every time I see you. I sometimes think I can feel your loving gaze even when you're not around.*
*Thank you for loving me even through my ups and downs and let's be real there have been more downs than ups lately. You have stayed by my side through the endless doctor appointments and treatments. Always smiling and making me feel beautiful and loved.*
*Even at my lowest, you empower me to be strong. You are my rock, which I am eternally thankful for.*
*But what about you and your life? I need to know that you will be okay even when I am no longer around. Living the life of a normal 18-year-old guy, with a future filled with endless possibilities.*
*Before you argue, I want you to know I have put some serious thought into this, and this is what I want for you.*
*I want you to be happy.*
*I want you to have a loving family filled with gorgeous, smiling children and the life you always dreamed*

*about. Owning your own shop, designing, and seeing your sketches come to life.*

*I won't be able to give you those things, of that, I am sure. You deserve the world because that is what you gave me every day, selflessly.*

*You have touched my soul with your love, and for that, I will always be grateful. I don't think I would have made it through this past year without you.*

*This is probably the hardest thing I have ever had to do. To tell the man I love with all my heart and soul that this is the end...*

*I know this will come as a shock, but I'm leaving town. By the time you read this, I will already be gone. Don't come looking for me... it's better this way.*

*Just know I've gone to live out the rest of my time, however long that may be, with a heart filled with your love.*

*I want you to wake up every day and feel my love surround you, even if I am not there.*

*You will get past this and find a girl who will love you for the amazing man you are. Because you deserve that. You deserve everything. I'm just sorry it couldn't be with me.*

*I'm doing this because I love you and I hope you never forget that.*

*Love Always,*
*Your Everything*

# Chapter One

*Lottie*

As I stare at my reflection in the full-length mirror, all I see are the numerous imperfections I've been critiqued about for most of my life. While I have come to terms with my body, being told that my thighs should be smaller and more toned, or that my belly should be a bit flatter with less jiggle, definitely chips away at your self-confidence. My ass, although big and round, is one of my favorite parts about me. Unfortunately, I've been told that it too could benefit from me dropping several pounds and inches. Ethel has repeatedly lectured me about my size, saying "Well-to-do men don't want their women to be too curvy and objectified, they want demure, dignified women by their side." Thankfully, I'm not looking to marry a rich well-to-do guy, they don't sound like much fun if you ask me.

It is what it is, and clearly my ass is not going anywhere anytime soon. So, to be perfectly honest, I'm not too mad at the cheeky cut of the costume I'm about to put on. It's all the other parts I'm sort of dreading. Ashley swears it'll fit, especially with the corseted back she designed. I obviously would have opted for at least one size larger, but she was in charge of designing the outfits.

Ashley has been my best friend since third grade, when she moved to our quiet New York neighborhood. She came into my life just when I needed her the most, right around the time my mother passed away. She was older than me by a year but that didn't change a thing. Ashley is like the sister I always wanted. There isn't a thing she wouldn't do for me and the same goes for her. We're frick and frack, tweedle dum and tweedle dee, thing one and thing two. You get the picture. We're inseparable, making us the dynamic duo, Tig and Bitty. I'm Tig because of my tig ol' bitties and she's Bitty, since she's just so damn tiny in comparison to me.

After Ashley graduated, she stayed local due to family obligations and work, so I'm thrilled she spends her time off with me down in Nori Beach.

Hence why I'm staring at this Playboy Bunny for this stupid-ass party I agreed to go to. I love her to death, but right now I'm seriously regretting this decision.

She's been hyped ever since we first heard about it a few days ago. Of course, some dipshit made it a costume party, and that was all Ashley needed to hear to get her creative gears turning.

"Girl come on, I want to see it!" Ashley bellows as she practically knocks down the door to my bathroom. All I've managed to get on are the fishnet tights. My hair and makeup are done, but I haven't worked up the courage to finish getting dressed.

"Um... I'm not ready yet."

"Oh, come on, you've been in there for an hour."

Turning back to the offending corset, I let out a defeated sigh. "Yeah, yeah, I'll be out in a minute." There's no point in faking sick at this point, right?

Ugh! This was a stupid idea. I mean, who has a Halloween party in June anyway? Nori Beach, North Carolina, is a well-known destination around the country. Families from all over come and spend their summers at their lavish beach houses that line the coast. With rich families, there are always over-the-top parties thrown by their spawn trying to one-up their fellow neighbors.

Don't get me wrong, I love it here and I'm thankful my family has a summer house that has been in the Richmond family for generations. The only downside is that I'm left with the She-Devil herself in an enormous house with nothing much to do.

I don't have many friends down here. I personally think most of the teen population here are a bunch of snobby assholes. Therefore, I keep myself busy during the weekdays, taking walks on the boardwalk and laying out on the beach with a book in my hand. My weekends are usually filled with more of the same or hanging with Ashley when she's here.

Luckily I've avoided Ethel Richmond since arriving last week. Living with her brings on a whole new meaning of nitpicking. First, let me start by saying that Ethel is my grandmother on my mother's side, but she thinks that phrase makes her seem too old and lacks the proper respect she rightfully deserves. Yeah, she's a real peach. Second, she will be the first person to highlight your flaws and harp on them until you make the adjustments she deems appropriate. I've lived with her constant critiques for most of my life and you could certainly blame my body shaming habits on her. Honestly, I can't stand being around her for extended periods of time, but she's one of the few family members I have left, so I do what I can to keep the peace. Which means I'll be keeping myself busy this summer and our interactions to a minimum.

This party will be fun, or at least that's what Ashley keeps telling me. I just need to get myself out there and make the best of it, leaving Ethel's critiques behind.

Tucking and fidgeting with this costume for the last time, I grab my phone and quickly send a selfie to Jonathan in hopes of spiking a little dirty talk from him. He's so straight-laced and proper. Totally not my type normally, but Ethel doesn't seem to like him or his family much, which just makes me want to hang out with him more.

He's nice and all, he's just so serious, always on point—Mr. future President. I like to have fun and be young, and it's like pulling teeth to get him to relax. I'm trying desperately to loosen him up a bit. *Let's see if a little skin does the trick.*

Opening the bathroom door, I see Ashley sitting at the edge of my bed on her phone. The clicking of my heels on the hardwood gains her attention and her head pops up. "Holy shit, Babe! You look so fucking hot! I knew this design would work perfectly on your shape." She whistles at me as she stands. I immediately blush at her attention and fidget my hands.

"Tig, I'm serious... you're a knockout. I cannot wait to see the attention you get tonight. We're going to have these Nori Beach guys drooling all over us." She takes my hand and twirls me around. Like I said, she's awesome at being a hype girl and I definitely feel more at ease. Her enthusiasm is contagious.

Ashley hands me a shot of who knows what to help calm my nerves. We raise our glasses and cheers. "Fuck it... here goes nothing," I murmur to myself as I take it down.

"Did you send Mr. Stick-up-his-ass a pic of how fucking hot you are? I bet he doesn't even know what to do with it. Probably thinks his phone will get confiscated with such deplorable im-ages on it." She laughs so hard she snorts, imitating a man with ramrod straight posture and a snooty-looking face. I literally burst out laughing. She's so ridiculous sometimes.

I smack her arm when I regain my composure. "That's not very nice Ash. Jonathan's not that bad."

"Ha! That's one way of putting it... besides, do you even like him?" She raises one eyebrow in question, handing me another glass of who knows what.

"I mean... I guess. I don't know," I mutter into my drink.

"Oh, come on babe. You should absolutely, without a doubt, know if you're into someone."

"I guess you're right. I honestly think I'm trying to make it work just to piss Ethel off. The look on her face when I brought him to dinner was priceless. Made me think if I held onto him for a bit longer—"

Ashley interrupts, "You can't string him along just to piss off Ethel. As fun as that may be, it's not fair to him. Although I'm not sure if he even has emotions, he's such a robot."

"Ugh, I guess you're right." I glance at my phone to see if he's responded to my sexy selfie. Nope, nothing. "I'm supposed to see him soon. I guess I'll break it off, even though we both agreed to just have fun this summer."

"Set him free girl," she fake-sings into her fist. This girl has definitely been pre-gaming without me. I smile and down the rest of my drink, holding my glass out for another.

"That's my girl!" She smiles and glances back at her phone. "Okay, our Uber should be here in about ten minutes, so let's have another one before it gets here." I nod, accepting my fate. Ashley beams as she pours us another shot of liquid courage.

\*\*\*

We pull up to the elaborate iron gates that precede a long stone driveway. Ashley squeals in excitement as they slowly open and our car creeps closer to its destination. The sprawling historic home is decked out top to bottom with Halloween decorations, and it looks like there's a haunted maze set up on the grounds. We come to a stop and Ash grabs my hand, practically dragging me out of the car.

We approach the steps just as the doors open, allowing the thumping bass to travel outside. Several people spill onto the stairs before us, just barely missing a collision. Still holding my hand, Ashley sidesteps the drunken masses, and we make our way into the home. We spot the bar set up on the opposite side of the room and weave our way through the crowd. I smile, hearing several guys whistle at us as we pass. Maybe this costume wasn't an awful choice after all. *Touché Bitty.*

I grab two beers from the ice buckets and hand one to Ash while she scopes out the place. It's quite dark in here besides the themed lighting and black lights. The space we're in is super crowded and it appears that all the furniture and most of the decor have been removed to protect it from the impending chaos that will ensue by the end of the night. Because let's be real, some shit always goes down by the end of the night.

We spot an opening on the dance floor and make our way over there just as "Essence" by Wizkid starts to play. My body takes the reins as the heavy beat pumps through my system, along with the shots we took earlier. Ashley and I love to dance. It's probably why we like parties so much. If there are good beats playing, we will start a dance party just about anywhere. If I'm being honest, it's so freeing to just let go and move to the music. I'm not thinking about what's wrong with my body, who I should or shouldn't be hanging out with, or what responsibilities I'm ignoring. I just let it all go.

We like to make a show of it out on the dance floor. Our surroundings disappear and we both vibe with one another, feeding off each other's energy. My insecurities about the damn costume are long forgotten, and I am truly having a great time.

Several songs later, Ashley swigs her beer and leans in to speak. "Holy shit babe, we're drawing quite the audience." I peek over her shoulder and take notice of the crowd surrounding us. I give her a sly smile as I turn my ass into her, drop it down low, and slowly work my hips up. When I stand up, she grabs my hand and I spin her around. Just as she's about to complete her turn, her elbow is grabbed by someone dressed as the Joker. A very tall and jacked Joker. I wish I could see his face beneath all the face paint, but damn, his presence is overwhelming. She side-eyes me, silently asking if it's okay if she dances with Mr. Tall, Dark, and Jacked. I give her a knowing smile and take my tipsy ass back to the ice buckets. My beer has been empty for quite some time now, and a girl needs to maintain her buzz.

Grabbing another beer, I make my way out the back doors that are right off the kitchen. If I know Ashley, she'll be busy for several songs, so I have a few minutes to cool off. I find a secluded spot on the massive back deck and lean against the railing. It's a beautiful night out. The bright stars light up the sky and I can't help but get lost staring at them.

I startle out of my daze when I hear high-pitched screeches coming from the garden to my left. It takes me a few moments to realize I'm standing right next to the spooky maze I saw earlier.

Laughing to myself, I take a long swig of my beer. Silly girls, purposefully going into a haunted maze so they can be coddled and cling on the arm of some guy. I've never been one for spooky walks or haunted houses. Not because I'm scared, but because I would physically harm someone who jumps out at me even with a fake weapon. I don't like things popping out at me. It triggers my inner warrior and I physically lash out with strength I forget I possess.

I once accidentally knocked out Ashley's older brother Micah. We were in her room, deeply engrossed in a horror movie, when he jumped out of the closet with a mask on, scaring the ever-loving shit out of me. He thought it was absolutely hysterical. I, unfortunately for him, did not. My immediate response was not to scream, no that would be too typical, but instead to punch the masked offender square in the face. Not only did he crumple like a pile of fallen bricks, but he ended up with a broken nose and two matching black eyes. Needless to say, he no longer tries to pull pranks on me, even if he is a foot taller than me now.

"What's so funny?" is whispered softly into my ear, causing me to jump to the side and swing my arm around, making contact with whomever just whispered to me. "Ouch."

I eye the offender as he rubs his arm in his... Batman suit. "Serves you right. Seriously, who sneaks up on someone like that?"

"You were over here staring into space with a big smile on your face and I couldn't help but ask what was so amusing. I didn't realize you were going to go all Cobra Kai on my ass."

I laugh as he jokingly continues to rub his arm. "I'm surprised the bat suit didn't withstand the blow."

"I mean it's just a suit, and technically, Batman has no real superpowers. He's just a normal guy, after all." He smirks.

"Yes, this is true, but he is definitely still one of my favorites." I beam up at him. Have I mentioned how deliciously tall this Batman is? He's at least a foot taller than me. "I wanted to be a superhero too, but my better half got the final say, so here we are." I wave a hand at my outfit for emphasis.

"No shit. Hugh Hefner is walking around here somewhere without one of his bunnies?" he jokes while fake-looking around for an old geezer in a robe.

I hit his arm again. "No jackass! My friend Ashley wanted to be bunnies and I couldn't let her be one by herself. Certainly not among this crowd."

"So, there is no Hugh?" he asks, leaning against the railing, putting his body on display.

Yes, I know he's in a Batman suit and his mask is covering most of his face, but from what I can see, he's sexy as hell. Thick stubble peppers his strong jaw, and his body certainly fills out the suit he's wearing. *Mmm, he looks delicious.*

"No, no Hugh."

"So then, how does a bunny lose her partner-in-crime and find herself outside all alone?"

"She's busy dancing with a Joker... Hey, wait a second... Do you have a sidekick as well? Awe, did you and your friend dress up as the Joker and Batman?" I tease him.

"Listen, before you get all cutesy on me. It was my idea to be Batman first, then that fuckhead jumped on my shit and said he was going to be Joker." He puts up his hands, defending his honor as a badass.

I bust out laughing at how much the idea bothers him. "No worries, dark crusader, your secret is safe with me."

He makes an exaggerated gesture of relief and smiles a megawatt panty-dropping smile. *Holy hell!*

"Thank fuck. Wouldn't want to ruin my street cred and all."

Shaking my head, I turn back towards the maze and stare out into the unknown. I feel the heat from his body as he comes closer to stand behind me. Then I smell him and oh damn, why does a hot guy who smells good automatically make you question your inhibitions? This guy is drop dead gorgeous and if I'm not careful, I could easily do something reckless.

"You never answered my question. What was so funny before?" he whispers in my ear with that deliciously smooth southern accent of his. Tiny goosebumps erupt on my arms from his breath on my neck.

He situates himself against the railing with his back to the maze, pulling a joint from his pocket and lighting it. He takes a few hits, then passes it my way.

"Well?" he says, gesturing to the joint and looking for an answer with the one word.

Taking the j from him, I take a long drag, letting the smoke fill my lungs and exhaling it out in one smooth breath. I'm no habitual smoker by any means, but when you live in the world I do, it's a welcomed escape. I think my skilled hit surprises him, considering he raises his eyebrows and nods his head respectfully before taking it back.

"I was laughing at how ridiculous haunted walks and houses are." He stares at me with a confused look on his face. "Okay, let me rephrase that. How ridiculous girls are when they go through them. All damsels-in-distress and shit. Quite pathetic if I'm being honest."

To further prove my point, we hear another ridiculously loud screech from the maze.

I motion with my hand in the direction of the noise. "Exhibit A."

"Never thought of it like that," he says as he turns around. We're now standing side by side, looking out amongst the home's massive yard. The essence of his cologne wafts in my direction and I inhale deeply, trying to hold on to its intoxicating scent.

He continues, "I always thought people enjoy them because of their body's reaction to the thrill of it all. The adrenaline pumping through your system generally leads to one, if not all of the F's in life." I look at him with a puzzled look on my face. "Fight, flight, or fuck," he adds.

I scoff at him. "Well, we've seen my body's reaction, and I certainly go for the fight in that scenario."

"Oh, I've seen it alright..." he says in a much lower tone as his gaze peruses me from head to toe.

My eyes widen and my breath hitches as an image of him grabbing my rounded hips, pulling our bodies so close together that our limbs interlock, flashes through my head. My body heats at the thought of his beautifully sculpted body dominating all of me. His mouth devouring mine. His hands groping and kneading my soft flesh. His teeth leaving reminders of his ownership, and for some reason, giving up that control to this complete stranger doesn't seem scary to me. I know it should, considering I don't have a lot of control over much in my personal life, but with him, it feels... Safe.

Needing to snap the fuck out of my fantasy, I take the joint from him again, only this time our fingers connect, eliciting a buzz that radiates through my hand. Shocked, I let out a small gasp at the strange feeling. My hands won't cooperate, and I drop the j, letting it fall to our feet.

Batman bends down and picks it up, chuckling softly. "What's your name, little bunny?" *Little?* Did he just call me little? I don't think anyone has ever called me 'little' in my entire life.

He steps closer and arranges the joint in his fingers, raising it to my lips to assist me in taking my next hit. My hands get all clammy and my body heats from his close proximity. I brace my hands against his chest to steady myself, unsure of what in the hell is happening to me. I feel his muscles tense up for a moment, then relax under my touch.

"Everyone calls me Lottie," I say in a shaky breath just as his fingers make contact with my lips. I take another long pull, then lean my head back and away from his hand, letting the smoke slowly drift out of my mouth.

"Mmm," he says while licking at his lush lips. The desire to pull his plump bottom lip into my mouth is overwhelming.

"That's a gorgeous fucking name..." His hand gently sweeps the hair off my face and tucks it behind my ear. I practically melt into his touch.

"Wha—what's yours?" I stammer, unable to recover. Geez, *Lottie, get your shit together, girl.*

He smiles down at me "Greyson. Well, actually..."

"G, what's good?" An unknown voice breaks the trance we've been in.

We both startle and turn to face the intruder, who is none other than the Joker waltzing up to us with Ashley on his arm.

***

## *Greyson-*

This girl has me in a fucking trance. I didn't even hear my cousin Trent, until he was right here, yelling in my ear.

I noticed her and her little friend putting on a show earlier. I have never been speechless over a chick before, but this girl Lottie... she is something else entirely.

For starters, her body is seriously... fuck man, it's unbelievable. I have always been one for more curves, but this girl's curves are like something straight out of my dreams. She is stacked in all the right places and her face... her face is fucking beautiful.

When she was shaking her ass on the dance floor, I had to come outside before I did something stupid. I was about ready to growl at every motherfucker in there and tell them I saw her first. Even if she had no idea who I was. See? Stupid. Hence why I'm outside.

I can't stop staring at Lottie as her friend asks if she's okay with her ditching the main party to hang with Trent.

Apparently, she can't keep her eyes off me either.

The friend stops her conversation and looks at us both before she excitedly says, "Wait! Oh shit. Did we interrupt something here?"

Lottie quickly defends, "No! You know I have a—"

Her friend cuts her off and says, "Well, you two keep eye-fucking each other, so I just assumed."

Lottie's face immediately blushes at the comment. I think this girl is more innocent than she appears to be.

She lowers her voice to speak to the other bunny at the same time Trent whispers in my ear. "They are both fuck-hot, man. You good if I head upstairs for a while? Nathan is keeping his eye on things in the house, so you and Stacks are good to do your thing too."

"Stacks..." I guess I did call her that before I knew her name. It fits her perfectly. Her tits, and damn that ass. I've been rocking a semi ever since I saw her in that fucking bunny outfit.

"I don't think my night will end quite like yours, but I'm good either way," I say.

Honestly, I just want to get to know her more. Of course, I want my hands all over her. What dude wouldn't? But there is something about this chick, I can tell. I wouldn't want to just hit it and quit it.

Fuck, I feel so far off my game just by being this close to her.

With a cocky smirk, Trent says, "You mean someone might turn *THE* Greyson Rexwood down? No fucking way, man."

My summers here with Trent typically consist of us hooking up with random girls. Trent may have regulars because it's his hometown, but I never double-dip here in Nori Beach. I am always upfront with them about it being a casual, one-time thing for me, and that never seems to deter them from attempting to get in my pants. He isn't used to me wanting to hang out with girls for any reason other than sex. This feels different, though.

Ignoring him instead of hitting him back with a cocky response, I direct my attention to Lottie. "You want to chill with me while these two go fuck each other's brains out?"

The stacked bunny blushes. This girl is an enigma. She can pull from a j like a pro, and has a body built for sin, but she shies away when the conversation turns too sexual, yet she looks at me with lust in her eyes. *I can't figure her out just yet, but I'm damn sure going to try.*

She pulls me out of my thoughts. "Sure."

Lottie turns around toward her friend, who whispers something in her ear and then pecks her on the cheek. It's easy to see these two are thick-as-thieves.

Before letting her friend leave, Lottie says, "Just come find us in a bit or I'll send in the rescue squad." Then she gives Trent one last warning look as she walks my way.

*She's even cuter when she's trying to be all intimidating.*

Trent pulls Ashley away as he responds to Lottie without taking his eyes off his prize. "I'll take good care of your girl, trust me." Of course, the asshole then looks our way and winks as he walks off.

Taking that as my cue, I grab Lottie by the hand, pulling her towards the guest house. To my surprise, she moves her hand so that it interlocks with my fingers.

Looking back at her beautiful face that's covered with a sweet, shy smile... I can tell this girl is too good for me, but fuck me, does her hand in mine feel so right.

\*\*\*

Thirty minutes later, somehow, I'm even more impressed by Lottie. She is literally whooping my ass playing *Call of Duty*. Thirteen-year-old me would have already come in his pants.

"Fucking Juggernaut got me!" she yells while throwing down her controller, her New York accent showing more with her frustration. She seems to typically be well-spoken and calm but when she gets excited her words lose their "R's" and she starts using her hands a lot.

I've been out of lives for a few minutes so I'm just staring, taking in all her competitive glory. Realizing I find her amusing, she starts laughing. "What? Thomas would give me shit right now if he knew I let that happen."

As soon as Lottie saw my PlayStation, she told me about her neighbor, Thomas. He got her hooked on *Call of Duty* when she used to babysit him.

According to her, they formed an unlikely bond over video games and pizza. Even though he is fourteen now and doesn't need a babysitter anymore, they occasionally meet up to game together when she's back home in New York.

Yeah, back home in New York. A long-ass way from North Carolina. She's here for the entire summer, so maybe this won't be the last time I see her.

"Well, I won't tell him. But speaking of Thomas, how about we order a pizza in honor of him?"

She squeals, "That's the best idea. I'm starving! Now the question is... what kind of pizza guy are you, Batman?" I like that she keeps calling me Batman even though I'd changed out of the costume almost immediately after getting to the pool house, smiling at how she soaked up every inch of my face like she was committing it to her memory when I took off the mask.

"Well, I'll eat anything, but since you asked, I was going to order from this spot Trent turned me on to. That high-class fucker got me a pizza with barbecue sauce as the base instead of regular pizza sauce and I've been hooked ever since. I dip it in some ranch and it's the best fucking thing I've ever tasted... so far."

I can't help it; she's too tempting. I can't say I haven't thought about tasting her multiple times tonight. The thought of seeing her come apart on my tongue. *Fuck Me.*

Of course, she catches onto the suggestiveness in my comment and a pink hue takes over her cheeks, but she rolls with it quickly.

"I mean, you'd probably catch a lot of shit in New York for that kind of talk, but I have to admit that actually sounds amazing. I'm down, let's get it."

I grab my phone and place the order for delivery. She speaks up again and I notice she put the pillow from the couch over her stomach now that she's sitting back.

*Don't hide from me Stacks... every inch of you is sexy as fuck, down to the soft curve of your stomach.*

"This bunny outfit was cute and all for the party, even if Ashley had to threaten me, but I wish I had some extra clothes. This thing is uncomfortable."

"I can't say I've minded seeing you in this outfit, but I would love to see what you look like in my clothes, too." I love how her cheeks flush even more. "Do you want one of my t-shirts and some shorts? I think I have some with a drawstring, they'll still be big, but you can roll them up."

She looks shocked by my forwardness, but then it changes to a smile. "That would be perfect. Will the clothes smell like you?" Then she slams her hand over her mouth as I chuckle.

"I hope them smelling like me is a good thing."

She lowers her chin and nods, still embarrassed, "It is but that was a weird thing for me to say. You just smell so damn good. I can't think straight."

I gently tap my knuckle under her chin to gesture for her to look up at me. "Don't hide from me or hold back what's on your mind. I like that about you, you don't seem to have a fake bone in your body."

She chuckles, but it's more sadistic this time. "Well, you haven't seen me being paraded around by my awful grandmother yet."

I walk to my room and gesture for her to follow me. "How the hell could anyone mistreat you?"

She shrugs her shoulders with a smirk. "I know, right?"

I go over to my dresser and grab some clothes. "Go ahead and change." She hesitates for a moment before reaching for the pile. "You have me looking forward to seeing you in my clothes, so you can't let me down now." I hand her the clothes and nod my head towards the ensuite bathroom.

Lottie hands her phone to me, unlocked, and says in an unsure voice, "Thank you. While I change, would you mind adding your number?" I grab her phone with a smile, and she continues, a smile now spreading across her face, "I'm having a lot of fun and don't have many friends in Nori Beach. Most people here are stuck-up assholes. Since it doesn't seem like you're one of them, and we're both here for the summer, I just figured we could hang out again."

*Friend-Zoned... for now.*

I don't respond, just do as she says and add my info to her phone. Shooting myself a text because I'm not leaving the ball in her court. I want to see her again.

As she's coming out of the bathroom, I notice she has a text. Handing her the phone, I say, "Jonathan texted you." I try not to sound agitated because I have no right and I don't even know who he is.

She opens the message and reads it to herself as she lets out a little gasp. Her face immediately changes, and her entire body deflates.

"Ughhh speaking of awful assholes. Why I put up with this shit is beyond me."

"Who is he, and where can I find him?" She looks at me, confused. I clarify, "So I can kick his ass for putting that look on your face?"

That puts a small smile back on her face. "Glad to know you're the guy to call if I need a body buried, but no, don't worry about it, he's no one. No big deal."

I soften my voice. "Tell me Lottie. What did he say?"

Lottie looks at me curiously but gives me her phone.

**Jonathan:** *Seriously, Lottie you look like such a disgrace. What were you thinking? I thought you* *were going to a beach party, not a plus-sized party at the playboy mansion. Cover yourself up. You look like a slut.*

My blood is boiling. I scroll up to see what she sent him before he responded.

When I look at the picture, so many emotions hit me. One—jealousy that she sent this picture to that motherfucker. Two—lust because damn, this girl is Fine with a capital F. Third—rage. Homeboy really does want to die.

I gather my thoughts together to speak because I can't imagine how she must feel after receiving a text like that, even if it is complete bullshit. She looks so defeated right now, withdrawn, with her chin down in embarrassment.

"Chin up Babygirl." Using my knuckle again, I'm going to fix that chin-down problem.

"I would ask who he is again, but honestly, it doesn't matter because there is no excuse for how he just responded to you. Fuck that dude, seriously, Lottie. If I was lucky enough to get a picture like that from you, that definitely wouldn't be how I'd respond."

She swallows before saying, "How would you respond?"

I'm not holding back because damn it, I want this girl so badly, and I want her to know it.

"You look sexy as fuck, and I bet every dude that saw you in that costume wishes they had you. But guess what, they can't have you because you are MINE, at least right now you are."

She stares at me with her mouth slightly open in shock at my forwardness. "I wish I was the lucky motherfucker who you thought of when sending that picture. Then, I could tell you how badly I want to put my face right between those perfect tits of yours and lick every exposed inch of you before ripping that bunny suit off and getting to what I really want... that sweet pussy of yours."

She gasps. "Oh, wow."

Dropping her phone to my bed, I grab her by the waist and pull her towards me so she can feel what my imagination is doing to me. There is no resistance on her end, only rapid breathing and blown-out pupils.

*Friend-Zoned my ass.*

"I've had all night to think about it. Ever since the moment I saw you walk onto that dance floor, my imagination has been running wild with the things I want to do to you and this tempting body of yours. Now that I've gotten to know you a little more, my want... no, my need for you has only increased."

"Greyson" her one-word moan has me moving to crash my lips down on hers just as a very distinct sound comes from Lottie's phone several times in a row and she jumps back. "That's Ashley, I need to check it."

Hating that it ruined the moment, but watching her intently check her messages from her friend, I see the immense loyalty she gives to those she loves, and I respect the hell out of that.

With a worried look on her face, she says, "I need to go. Ashley needs me. Thanks for a great night. Sorry I'll miss out on the pizza."

*Oh hell, what the fuck did Trent do?*

"This isn't over. When can I see you again?"

A little smile plays on her lips. "I can't believe you're real," she practically whispers before she turns to run out.

"Text me!" I desperately say.

Desperation is an emotion I've never felt when it comes to a girl, but damn if I don't feel that watching her hurry out of my front door.

# Chapter Two

"You should have worn the peach skirt set I laid out," Ethel mutters from the seat beside me.

"It's a wool suit, and it's summer... no way in hell was I putting that thing on. I would die of heat exhaustion." Not to mention the fact that the thing was so fricken ugly it looked like something a senator's wife would wear, not a soon-to-be eighteen-year-old.

"Oh please! You're being dramatic, Charlotte. You would have looked better in it, instead of looking like..." She waves her hand in my direction with a displeased look on her face. Don't get me wrong, she always has a displeased look on her face, but this one is a bit extra like she just smelled something horrid.

I roll my eyes at her dramatics. I chose to wear a white maxi dress with a macrame detailing on the top. It's super flowy and comfortable. Plus, my tatas look great in it, and I honestly don't care what Ethel has to say about it.

"How are things with the Waterbury boy, Jonathan, right?" Ethel asks as our car comes to a stop.

"Great, he's coming to visit soon." The lie slides right off my tongue. I will not give her the satisfaction of knowing our relationship is probably over.

I take a quick glance at my phone, checking to see if Jonathan has responded to my latest text. We haven't spoken since the other night. I thought he'd be turned on by my costume. Unfortunately, it seems like it had the complete opposite effect on him. *Oh well, I knew it wasn't going to last.*

He's just not the one. Not the one that makes my heart pulse when he's near or gives me butterflies in my stomach when I see his name. Not the one that can make my body melt from his touch... *like Greyson's touch did.* I get shivers just thinking about him.

I've enjoyed Greyson and our quick texts over the last few days. They're not extensive by any means, but that doesn't stop the giddiness I feel when his name pops up on my phone.

"Are you even listening to a word I'm saying?" Ethel barks as we get out of the car. *Oops.*

"I'm sorry what?" I smile genuinely, trying to avoid the lecture on how listening is a great quality men look for in a wife. Blah, blah, blah.

"Charlotte, you can at least pretend to be paying attention. I said take a sweater to cover up your chest. Your dress is inappropriate and shows way too much skin for my liking."

"Unfortunately, Ethel, I do not have a sweater with me because it is ninety-two degrees outside."

She scoffs and adjusts her Chanel linen jacket. "Come on then, we're late for our reservation."

I trail behind, silently cursing her out in my head. Ugh, why must she be the most infuriating person I've ever met?

We walk for several minutes along the boardwalk, somewhere I never thought my grandma would visit in her lifetime. We finally stop in front of a spot a lot of locals flock to, The Shack. It's a fun tiki bar-themed place with amazing food and crazy drinks. Again, so outside of my grandmother's normal stomping grounds, I think she may have fallen ill.

She spins to assess me one more time before we enter. "Will you stop dragging your feet, and stand up straight, you're slouching." Nope. She's feeling just fine.

Following her inside, I'm still in utter shock that this is where she made reservations for lunch. Usually, lunch entails boring-ass meals at her country club surrounded by helmet hair-styled old women. Each wearing matching Chanel suits and so much expensive perfume you can almost taste it in the air. Almost like it's a sport, these women are interested in nothing more than meddling in their family's lives and being catty bitches towards one another.

The hostess greets us both and then shows us to our table. Handing over our menus, she informs us our server will be with us shortly. My head is buried in my book-sized menu when I hear a throat clear. I look up and eye a very sexy guy in a tiki shirt. A very sexy guy indeed, except I personally think this one looks better dressed as Batman. "Greyson?" I ask in utter shock to see him here.

By his stunned expression, I can tell he's surprised I'm here as well. Greyson recovers quickly and beams at me. "Lottie, it's great to see you again."

"So crazy! I didn't know you worked here." I hear Ethel make a noise, bringing my attention back to her. "Oh, I'm sorry G, this is my gran—Ethel. This is Ethel Richmo—"

"Nice to see you, Mrs. Richmond," he interjects before I can finish getting her full name out.

"It's nice to see you too, Greyson. How do you know my Charlotte?" She eyes me inquisitively.

"Wait, a second... You two know each other?" I blurt out in surprise.

"I'm from Richmond Hills. Everyone knows of the infamous Ethel Richmond," Greyson explains, with an indifferent look on his face.

Based on his response, it appears Ethel's well-known, but maybe not well-liked, which doesn't surprise me one bit.

"Yes, I've run into him several times at my Country Club," she adds, completely disinterested. "But please, do share how you two know each other."

"I met her this past weekend at my cousin's house." He beams a megawatt smile at me. "We had a really good time." He adds a wink for emphasis.

Geez! I bet he is totally giving Ethel the wrong idea. I chance a look in her direction to gauge her reaction, only to see that she's actually smiling at him as he speaks. What in the actual fuck? Ethel is smiling... not only am I surprised that her face can still form a smile with all the Botox and fillers it has, but also the fact that she still possesses the ability to show emotion.

I'm rendered speechless and turn my attention back to the huge hunk-of-a-man in front of me. Our eyes meet and I can't help the butterflies that take off in my stomach. I dip my head to hide the blush rising up my cheeks.

"Well, ladies, what can I get you to drink?" Greyson asks.

"Ah yes, I would love a bottle of sparkling water and lemons for the table please," Ethel responds.

He turns his attention to me, silently asking for my order.

"Uhm, I'll have a sweet tea—"

"You'll have the sparkling water, dear. Remember it's summer, which means fewer clothes to hide behind," Ethel chastises while glancing distastefully at my dress.

Oh my god, no she didn't.

Utterly mortified, I glance at Greyson and see his jaw tick.

"Sparkling water is fine," I say with a tight smile.

He nods at us and leaves the table to get our drinks.

"Well, that was awkward," I mutter in Ethel's direction. When she doesn't answer, I peek to see her dissecting the menu.

I would love to say I'm surprised by Ethel's comment, but who am I kidding? This is Ethel Richmond we're talking about. I just hope Greyson doesn't feel the same way.

"Here you go. A bottle of sparkling water and lemons, and a glass of sweet tea," Greyson says as he places our drinks on the table.

Ethel shoots daggers at him as I place my straw into my drink and take a long pull, savoring its delicious flavor.

I sneak a smile in his direction to show my appreciation. He nods his head with a sly smirk on his face, as if giving me a silent confirmation that he likes my curves just the way they are.

*Oh, I'm in trouble with this one.*

Thankfully, we finish our meal with no more awkward instances. Ethel filled most of the silence, gossiping about her friends and their grandchildren back in Richmond Hills. I didn't have to say much except for the occasional generic responses to make it appear that I gave a shit.

She's currently on the phone, chatting about a big event she's hosting this fall. It gives me time to relax and enjoy the rest of my tea while I steal glances at Greyson every chance I get.

My phone buzzes on the table with a notification from Jonathan. I take a peek at it, debating whether I want to even read what he has to say or not.

"Are you going to answer him?" A gruff voice comes from behind me.

I jump at his sudden appearance.

"Geez, you scared the shit out of me," I breathe out.

Just then, Ethel ends her call shaking her head while grabbing her things and putting her phone in her purse. Greyson is looking at me like he wants to say more but doesn't. He just drops the check on the table and turns to leave.

"Oh, Greyson." Ethel stops him mid-stride. "I hate to burden you, but I must run; I have James waiting for me with the car. Would it be too much to ask for you to take Charlotte home for me? Of course, I would do it myself, but I need to be across town in ten minutes and—"

"No! Ethel, I'll call an Uber. No need to inconvenience him," I say, trying to hide my embarrassment. I've always been a burden when it comes to Ethel.

"I'm off in thirty minutes." He turns his attention to me. "If you don't mind waiting, I'll take you."

"No. Honestly, I promise, I'm fine. I can figure it out." I shake my head, grabbing my phone, I quickly swipe away Jonathan's notification, and open up the Uber app.

His hand covers mine and gently lowers my phone to my lap. Once my phone is down, Greyson uses his hand to raise my chin so our eyes meet. "I got you, Lottie, it's no trouble."

"Oh perfect!" Ethel exclaims and hands Greyson her credit card to cover the check. "I'm going to scoot out now. Charlotte, just bring the card home with you. Greyson, it was a pleasure running into you."

Ethel grabs her things and hurries out the door. What was that all about? Where is she going that's so important?

She didn't mention she had anything to do after lunch, but then again, she doesn't really share any information with me, especially her whereabouts.

I look to Greyson, who is still staring at the exit with his fist clenched and jaw locked.

"I'm so sorry she dropped this on you. I appreciate your offer, but I really am okay with calling an Uber."

He side-eyes me. "Will you cut it out, I told you I got you. I'll drive you home. Now, go sit your pretty ass down at the bar. Nathan will get you a drink while you wait. I need to finish my side work."

A Virgin Tiki drink later, and I'm in deep conversation with Nathan and his girlfriend, Berkley, who took a seat next to me while I waited.

"Oh, you'll have to come with us sometime. It's a lot of fun! I usually just lay out and tan, but it would be so nice to have another girl there for once," Berkley says excitedly.

"Where are we going?" Greyson asks from behind me, lightly placing his hands on my shoulders.

Turning in surprise, I smile at him. "Berkley was just telling me about Nathan's boat."

"I think we're going out soon, maybe even tomorrow. I'll let G know the details," Nathan says from behind the bar.

Greyson leans into me, whispering into my ear, "Are you ready to get out of here?"

"Sure."

"Aiight, I'm out and I'm taking this fine ass with me," he says as he helps me off the bar stool. "Bye, Berkley... Later man!" He nods his head towards the couple.

"Bye guys. It was so nice meeting you!" I wave my goodbyes.

"Bye, hope to see you soon," they both say in unison.

He guides me out of The Shack with a hand on my lower back. The contact sends tingles up my spine.

We walk in silence for a few moments before I speak up, saying the thing that's been on my mind since Ethel and I got here. "What are the chances that you're from Richmond Hills?"

He snaps out of his silent bubble and eyes me curiously. "Yeah, small world, I guess. Still can't wrap my head around the fact you're Ethel's granddaughter."

"Ha! I know exactly what you mean. I guess by only seeing her once a year, her wicked ways haven't rubbed off on me." I laugh, trying to make light of the fact that Ethel is evil.

"So, what do you want to do?" Greyson questions, changing the subject.

"Oh... Please don't let me keep you from any plans. I feel bad enough having you drive me home."

He stops walking to face me. "Lottie, let's get something straight. I don't do anything I don't want to do. So, if I say it, I mean it." He eyes me, assessing my understanding, placing his hand on my cheek. "Please, tell me what you would like to do."

"I um—I wouldn't mind walking around a bit, maybe play a game or two. I haven't made it to the arcade yet this summer," I reply.

"Attagirl... lead the way." He motions for me to walk.

I smile to myself as we head towards the beckoning, flashing lights of the arcade.

Hours later, we're walking out laughing loudly while Greyson carries a ridiculously oversized stuffed pink unicorn.

"I can't believe you won that." I laugh while he repositions the pink monstrosity over his shoulder.

"Hey, what kind of gentleman would I be if I didn't? Besides, I saw you eying this thing the moment we walked in the door." He quirks his lips to the side, forming an adorable half-smile.

*Geez, was that a dimple? Mother have mercy, this man is dangerously handsome.*

"Well, thank you very much, sir. I love it!" I giggle back.

Feeling my phone buzz in my purse, I take it out, seeing three notifications from Jonathan. Oh, so *now* he wants to talk. His timing sucks.

"Still haven't dumped the douchebag yet?" Greyson says from beside me, clearly eyeing my phone from his vantage point.

"Ugh, no. To be honest, we haven't talked since Saturday night. But I plan on it..." I trail off at the end, muttering more to myself than him.

"No one needs that shit in their life. From the looks of it, you already deal with enough," he says meaningfully.

"That obvious, huh?" I sigh, lowering my head in defeat.

He frees one of his hands and lifts my chin. "Never let anyone make you feel like you're not good enough. Keep your chin up, the world will treat you differently."

"Thanks, Greyson," I say, staring into his blue eyes. They search mine like he has something more to say, but instead, he nudges my shoulder with his. "Come on Stacks, let's get you home. Don't want your grandma to think I kidnapped you."

*What did he just call me?*

"Why did you just call me that?" I question, bracing myself for his explanation.

Greyson smiles. "Because the first time I saw you I thought damn, look at that perfectly stacked ass. Then you turned around with those," he says, pointing to my chest, making heat flare in my cheeks. "And a flawless face to match. It was obvious you were stacked in all the right places."

His words bring heat to my core. I have never had a guy, especially one who looks like him, speak so positively about my body. Yes, men have ogled me but to have someone like Greyson who isn't actively trying to screw me talk to me like this definitely builds my confidence up a few notches.

"That wasn't what I was expecting." Smiling up at him, I add, "But I like it. Thank you for being a guy who knows how to appreciate a girl with curves."

Nudging my chin up with his knuckle so he can stare into my eyes, he says, "Anytime... they deserve to be fully appreciated."

Not quite sure how to handle his compliments, I nervously look down at my phone. It's almost six p.m., and I've been having so much fun, I've lost track of time.

"Oh! I didn't realize what time it was. I'm sorry I took up so much of your time."

"Stop that right now. What did I say about that shit?" He looks at me, a bit annoyed. "Lottie, I enjoyed today, and I want to hang out again soon. Would you want to go out on the boat this week?"

"I'd love to," I say before I can even digest the fact that he asked me out.-

"Good," he says as he grabs my hand with his free one.

As we walk back to his pickup truck, I can't help but giggle at the fact that this gorgeous man, all muscles and squared jaw, looks absolutely insane holding a bright pink unicorn on his shoulder. But the smile on his face tells me he couldn't care less what people think of him. It's so refreshing.

*I think I could learn a lot from him.*

\*\*\*

Greyson helps me out of the truck and grabs my unicorn out of the back. Walking me up to the front door, he hands me my prize.

He leans down and kisses me on the cheek, lingering for just a few moments before he steps back and looks at me. The steady butterflies in my stomach are in full force right now.

I open the front door and turn as he says, "Goodbye Lottie, I had a great time."

"Me too. I'll talk to you soon." I smile as I close the door behind me.

Bracing myself against the closed door, I let a girlish squeal loose.

*This summer might not be so bad after all.*

# Chapter Three

Greyson

Taking Nathan's boat out is normally one of my favorite parts of summers in Nori Beach, but I have to admit the previous times don't hold a candle to today.

Last night I was barely in the guesthouse door when Nathan texted me, telling me to pick up Lottie and meet him at the marina by ten in the morning.

That gave me the perfect excuse to text Lottie, even though I just dropped her off. I don't think I have ever messaged a girl this fast, I know for a fact I've never initiated it, never had to.

> **Me:** *You down to go on Nathan's boat tomorrow with him and Berkley? He just texted and said for us to meet them at the marina by 10 in the morning.*
> **Stacks:** *Yes, definitely. They both seem really cool. I've never gotten to experience Nori Beach from a boat. I'll have to see if Ethel's driver knows where the marina is, but just in case, will you send me the address??*
> **Me:** *No need. I'm picking you up. Be ready by 9:45.*

*Stacks: Okay, Mr. Bossy pants. See you tomorrow.*
*Me: See you then pretty girl...*

Once we are settled on the boat, we make our way out to our favorite fishing spot. Berkley takes Lottie up to the front of the hull, where there's a section of cushions for them to lay out on.

It isn't long till Berkley encourages her to relax and get her tan on for the ride out. When the coverups come off and I see the display of backside perfection from Lottie in her cheeky black bathing suit, I swear I've never been more thankful for Nathan's girlfriend than I am at that exact moment. The way the bottom sits up high over her hips, accentuating her round ass and curves even more.

I can tell she's worried about the way her bathing suit fits her body because she keeps tugging at it just as she did the first night in the bunny costume.

I wish I could make her see how damn sexy she is.

Lottie must feel my eyes on her because she looks back towards where I'm standing beside Nathan.

My eyes peruse her exposed skin, taking in her curves. I find myself licking my lips at the thoughts running through my mind. When our eyes meet, I make no effort to hide my attraction. Winking at her, so there's no doubt in her mind about what I think of her in that bathing suit. Fucking sexy.

That earns me a little shy smile.

I don't like that her head has been filled with bullshit most of her life. This girl deserves more. If the only thing I am good for this summer is making her realize how fucking perfect she is, then I'll be happy with that.

Watching her get so excited over our up-close and personal look at the wild horses on Shackleford Banks is priceless. She just can't get over how beautiful they are. Her megawatt smile rivaled the sun when I told her you're allowed to camp on the island they inhabit.

I explain to her the horses were brought over by the original settlers and have been on this small island, and others along the Carolina coast, ever since.

Now, watching Lottie practice casting her fishing rod out into the ocean has me as confused today as I was yesterday when I found out who her grandmother is.

Ethel Richmond's name is well known around my home-town... "Richmond" Hills—for fuck sakes.

Ethel's reputation precedes her, as does her last name. Every-one in our area knows who she is. Most people smile and wave, but few like her.

The main thing I know about her is she's rich as hell and owns the fancy-ass country club where I occasionally do pool work with my boy Ford.

But her granddaughter, on the other hand... She's nothing like her.

Once I clarify we aren't just fishing for sport, she jumps right in, even wanting to learn to bait her own hook.

A little yelp from her draws me out of my head as she says, "Oh shit, I think I got one."

I notice her rod jerk a little bit, but she regains control and holds steady.

I jump into action and move right behind her, holding onto her hips instinctively. "Damn girl, I think you're about to get the first catch of the day." Seeing the pull of her reel, it must be a good-sized fish. "It looks like a big one. Just hold it steady."

She looks up at me with a huge smile on her face, proud of her accomplishment.

"Ahhh who knew fishing was so fun? This sucker is heavy, though. I don't want to lose him," she says, looking at me again with an anxious expression.

I reassure her by placing my hand on her back. "I'm right here. You can do this, but I promise I can quickly grab the rod and reel if you need me. Just say the word." I take hold of her elbow. "Now slow and steady... you got this, Lottie."

That seems to give her the boost of confidence she needs, and she focuses on her task, doing the damn thing.

I should not be turned on watching a girl catch a fish, but I can't fucking help it.

Earlier I offered her my Dri-fit long sleeve fishing shirt to put over her bathing suit instead of her nice coverup.

Yes, that bathing suit was sexy as fuck, but seeing her so happy and carefree while wearing my shirt has all kinds of shit stirring to life inside me.

Right as the fish comes to the top of the water, I immediately recognize the colors. It's a huge Mahi-mahi. Lottie reels it in close, as I quickly pull the line and wrestle it into the boat. The smile on Lottie's face is contagious. Nathan cheers from the back of the boat and Berkley comes up to snap some pics.

Standing there with the fish in between us, I can't help but lean down and give her a quick kiss. "Hell yeah Stacks, you did it!" Looking a little stunned, she takes her free hand and lifts it to her mouth before she says, "Today has been amazing, Grey."

"And to think we're just getting started," I say with a wink before turning to handle the fish.

Nathan comes to help me with the Mahi-mahi and throws it in the fish cooler. I smile as I look at the girls, who are celebrating Lottie's first catch by cracking open some cold ones and dancing around. This boat has the best sound system on the water and we're blasting anything from Kane Brown to Jack Harlow and everything in between.

Nathan speaks up from beside me, "Now this is *Reely* living."

His corny ass uses a play on words in reference to his boat's name.

"Yeah brother, I'm starting to see that."

Nathan looks like he wants to say more, so I bite. "What's on your mind, Nate?"

"It's just good to see you smile and open up with a girl. I know you weren't celibate last summer by any means, but I also never saw you actually hang out with any chicks. I definitely didn't see your grumpy ass smile as much as you have today."

That makes me laugh. "Yeah, I won't lie. The minute I saw her, I wanted to fuck her. But then I talked to her, and I realized she wasn't that type of chick and that I didn't want it to end after just one night."

He pats me on the shoulder and looks over at his girl as he moves to the captain's chair. "I know the exact feeling. When Berkley moved to town last year and flipped my world upside down, I knew I'd do anything to have her. I know some of my friends don't get being tied down to a girl when we're still young, but I really don't give a fuck, and neither will you. When you find the right one and she consumes your every thought, you'll realize you don't want to live without her. Plus, all those friends are jealous as fuck because I get pussy way more than they do."

Personally, I've never thought that about him and Berkley. They have a lot of fun together and he is the same person when he's with her and when he's not. Why would you want to give up something that feels so right?

"Yeah, they sound like dumbasses. It's not like that for me. I've just never had a girl keep me interested beyond sex... Until now," I say as I look over at Lottie with her long brown hair blowing in the wind as she listens intently to Berkley.

"That's what I'm saying brother, I see that, and I just don't want you to let her slip away. You deserve it, man," he says as he starts getting the boat ready to head to another spot.

I nod in agreement. "I don't want her to slip away either, but this is unfamiliar territory for me, and she lives in New York. That's a long ass ways away."

"Yeah, but y'all are both here right now, aren't you? There's a reason for that." *Point made.*

There's no doubt in my mind there is a reason.

We continue to fish for a bit more, but nothing's as exciting as Lottie's Mahi.

We decide to take the scenic route back to the marina. Lottie is currently snuggled into my side while she chats with Berkley, who is sitting across from us as Nate captains the boat home.

Pulling her even closer, I whisper to her, "You feel so good in my arms, pretty girl."

She looks up at me with those need-you eyes as she says, "It feels like I'm right where I'm supposed to be." She shyly looks back out to the ocean as I kiss the top of her head, not able to help myself with this girl.

Seeing that we're approaching one of my favorite spots in Nori Beach, I point it out to Lottie. "I need to get you on the back of my bike. Maybe we can take it for a ride over there for a sunset this week. It has the best views in town and is typically a locals' spot." Lottie nods enthusiastically as she checks out The Lookout and its surroundings.

My aunt used to take Trent and me there when we were younger.

Speaking of that punk, I couldn't convince him to come fishing with us today. He's still mad at me since I threatened him to not push Lottie for answers about her friend who ghosted him.

If she wants to talk to him about it, she will on her own, not because he pressured her.

Pussy-struck ass. Plus, he said he didn't want to be the fifth wheel when all he can think about is the girl who keeps running out on him.

We're cruising for a bit before Berkley speaks up, "Ooo you can see the *You've Got Mail* mailbox from here. That's another local secret The Lookout holds."

That seems to interest Lottie. She looks over to the mailbox and then back at Berkley. "What is a mailbox doing in the middle of a beach cliff? Do people put things in there?"

"Yes, it's really neat. People put letters in there for others to find. Sometimes just random ones not intended for anyone in particular. People also put used books in there and use it as a book exchange. Basically, it's a free for all. I discovered the author Meghan Quinn that way because I found her book *The Dugout* in there."

Lottie squeals, "Oh man, you know the Towel Brigade, too. Aren't they perfect?" *Towel brigade? I don't even want to know.*

"Yes, girl!!! Yay, someone else I can gush to about romance books."

Nate chimes in, "Are you talking about your book boyfriends again Babe?"

She giggles and says, "Lottie, we'll talk more about that later."

Book boyfriends, huh? I guess that's better than real boyfriends. *Fuck that Jonathan douche.*

Lottie must remember our original topic as she says, "That is so awesome about the mailbox though. I definitely want to see that in person. I am not afraid to admit I'm a hopeless romantic thanks to my mom, and that mailbox just makes me believe in love even more."

This would normally be a conversation I would zone out on, but with her, I find myself storing every little detail in the back of my brain.

***

We help Nathan and Berkley clean up the boat and unload everything. Nate agrees to clean the fish and have us over this week for dinner so we can all eat the fresh Mahi Lottie caught.

He also assures her that the majority of our fish are going to the local shelter for their Friday fish fry.

Lottie gives them both hugs goodbye and thanks them multiple times for extending the invite today.

She takes my hand in hers as we walk, just like she did that first night we met. I lead her to the passenger door of my truck, opening it up for her to hop inside.

Before getting in, she leans into me and gives me the best hug I have ever received.

When she pulls her body off mine, she looks me in the eyes. "I've been coming here every summer for most of my life, and I have never experienced Nori Beach like this. Thank you so much, Grey."

She is too damn sweet for me, but I can't help wanting to taste her. Leaning down towards her beautiful makeup-free face, I kiss her mouth.

Thankfully, she opens up easily for me. Our tongues sliding over each other and igniting something intense between us. I feel her whole body shiver in my hold. Gripping the back of her head as she claws at my chest, our tongues continue colliding with each other in perfect rhythm.

There is nothing in the world like this kiss. It makes me want to give up everything, tell her all my truths, and hope that she'll still want me.

# Chapter Four

Greyson

*Thick, Creamy, and Tan.*

Lottie's thighs in those cut-off shorts are a fucking distraction, which is probably why I am getting my ass handed to me in putt-putt. Her flowy shirt may hide some of her irresistible curves from me, but those shorts are giving me the best view. I can't stop staring as she lines up to most likely sink another hole-in-one.

Missing this time, she stomps her foot and looks at me with a little pouty face.

*Damn, why is she so cute?* I want that bottom lip between my teeth.

"Chill, Tiger Woods, you're still beating me by a long shot. How are you so good at this, by the way?"

She laughs as she moves down hole twelve with her putter in hand.

"Well, I might have hustled you a little bit," she says, looking back at me and catching me staring at her ass again.

Walking her way, trying to distract her. Since this hole took me four shots, I lean into Lottie's ear. "I'm listening Stacks... how did you hustle me exactly?"

Her breath catches a little before she says, "Don't be mad, but you know how I told you I haven't been to mini golf since I was in elementary school? Well, I may have left out that I go to the *actual* golf course with my great-grandfather and his buddies every Saturday morning back home." She lets out a little mischievous giggle.

Of course, as she finishes, she drops the ball in on her second attempt and does a little victory shimmy.

"Mad... I'm relieved to know I'm being beat by a professional. Seeing as how the loser has to buy ice cream and I would never let you buy on a first date anyway... It's only right that you win," I say, taking my knuckle to her chin and gently nudge for her to look at me.

I notice she doesn't hold her head high enough and it really bothers me. I find myself doing this gesture with her often in the short time we've known each other and hating the people in her life who have made her second guess herself.

For someone who normally couldn't give two fucks about getting to know new people, with Lottie, I want to know everything. Hence my next question.

"So, are you really close with your great-grandpa?" I just can't seem to stop myself from touching her. As we walk toward hole thirteen, I put my hand on the small of her back.

"Yes, actually, they're my guardians... well, he is now. My great-grandmother passed away last year, so it's just been the two of us lately."

*Where are her parents?* I think, but don't ask because I want her to tell me on her own. Surprisingly, she does.

"I lost my mom when I was in the third grade, and I never knew my dad. My mother was very close with her grandparents, my Gigi and Papa, and since she was young when she had me, they were still at a capable age to care for me. There was always bad blood between my mom and her mother, Ethel, so I only ever really saw her at the holidays or during the summertime... here." She gestures her hands around her, referring to Nori Beach.

I thought me and the boys had it rough growing up, but damn, even with all the money in the world, I see the loss and devastation she's had to endure in her short life.

Fuck, thinking about her being in pain feels like a crack to the sternum.

"I can tell by the way you talk about your great-grandparents that they're special to you. If Ethel is their daughter, what the fuck happened to her?" I say, recalling how she treated her at The Shack the other day.

That gets a laugh out of her, which I find she does every time I insult her asshole grandmother.

"Honestly, I have no clue. My mother was an angel on earth and my great-grandparents are both amazing people. I think money and greed turned Ethel into a very malicious person long before I was even born." I see she's fidgeting with the charm bracelet on her wrist... another thing I plan to find out more about.

Before I can respond, some dumbass interrupts us. "Yo, are you two going to hit the damn ball or what?"

I turn around to look at the chump and give him a look... *You're fucking with the wrong one, brother.*

"No, but I'm going to shove this club up your ass if you don't change your tone. How about you ask nicely, seeing as how it's a slow night and we didn't realize anyone was behind us," I say, standing my ground with my arms crossed.

Between the look I'm giving him and my words, he flipped his script real quick and clammed up on me. I know I'm a big, broody looking son of a bitch. *Don't bother me and mine, and I won't mess with you.*

"We are taking our time, so why don't you guys go ahead of us since you seem to be in such a rush." I hear Lottie say to the prick as she steps back, making room for them to pass. Thankfully, the jerk listens to Lottie, passing us quickly and quietly. They even skip ahead to the next hole.

I like how she handled that, not meek and timid. She was direct, but still polite. That seems to fit her personality. She's self-conscious in some ways, yet confident in others. *Perfectly her.*

"You're way nicer than me. Hope I didn't scare you, but we clearly didn't see them behind us, and I don't do well with people catching that tone with me for no reason."

She leans up and gives me a quick peck on the cheek. "No, actually, quite the opposite. I'm not used to anyone standing up for me like that. I like how protective you are."

Relieved that my assholery didn't scare her off. I'll show her I can be charming too... *at least for her.* "You know how in the movies the guy always gets behind the girl and shows her how to swing a bat or a club or whatever."

She nods her head, looking at me curiously.

"Well, I was thinking since the roles are reversed in this scenario and you're the expert, maybe you could help me with my putt. I promise to rub my ass on you and everything."

She bursts out laughing as she moves behind me to attempt to reach around and grab my putter. She can't even reach my hands once they're extended.

Now both of us are laughing. "I don't think we're going to be starring in a romantic comedy anytime soon. Also, no offense, but you don't seem to be the type to watch rom-coms, so tell me what ex-girlfriend..." she pauses and swallows thickly, "or current girlfriend, has you watching them?"

"For starters, my boy Ford has a low-key hard-on for chick flicks, so he makes us all suffer through them. I ain't going to lie, some of them are catchy as hell. And second, there is no girlfriend. I would have kicked her to the curb after the way you made me feel at that party, anyway. It wouldn't have been fair to her."

She looks at me shyly with a sweet smile I don't deserve.

Nodding my head towards the hole we're on, I say, "Let's finish this game before another jackass comes along."

***

Two hours later, after getting my ass handed to me in putt-putt and grubbing on some seafood at The Shack, Lottie and I are sitting on the beach in between her grandma's house and my place.

This girl is something else. Unlike anyone I have met. Her kind and smiley personality is just what my grumpy-ass needs.

Honestly, I'm not the type of guy to hang with chicks. They normally get theirs and I get mine, and then we part ways. The girls back home know not to even attempt to get more out of me. They see me as a fun rebellious phase that meets all their criteria. Tattoos—check, motorcycle—check, football player—check, asshole—check. I've never minded before because I love to fuck without the strings attached. But with Lottie, I like that she doesn't see me that way. I don't want to just tick all the boxes on her rebellious bad boy fuck list. I want to be more to her.

Lottie's had me hanging onto every word she's said since the moment I met her. She isn't surface-level like a lot of rich girls I know. I could see that a few days ago on the boat over the excitement she had for all the new things she was discovering about Nori Beach. Even more when she made sure we planned to eat the fish and not just catch them for sport. Lottie said if we weren't going to eat them, then we should leave them for someone who needs it. Her face lit up when Nate told her he normally takes about half of the smaller fish he catches to the shelter in town. A few local guys do that, and the shelter holds a fish fry on most Fridays. Once she heard that, she was grabbing the rod and insisting I show her exactly how to use it. Nate promised he would take all the other fish we caught that day to the shelter if she would let him cook the Mahi for us one night this week. Lottie liked that idea. The fact this girl, who has probably never wanted for anything in her life, genuinely cares about others who don't have that luxury makes me like her even more.

Pulling us out of our comfortable silence, Lottie says, "So I told you a bit about my family earlier. Tell me about yours."

"My dad raised me pretty much on his own... Well, with the help of my grandparents and like fifteen other bikers." She looks at me with confusion, so I continue, "My dad is the President of the Rebel Knights motorcycle club, his chapter is in Richmond Hills."

"Oh wow, I knew you rode a motorcycle, but I didn't expect that. That's actually so cool. I'm probably going to sound dumb saying this but the only information I have about motorcycle clubs is what I saw on *Sons of Anarchy*... but what exactly does your dad's club do or are they just a bunch of guys who get together and enjoy riding bikes?"

That makes me chuckle. "Well, they for sure aren't on a *SOA* level, but they dabble in some slightly illegal things. Where do you think I got that good-ass weed from?" We both laugh at that statement.

"Mostly it's a brotherhood made up of guys who, yeah, enjoy riding bikes, but that's not all they do together. For instance, we own and operate the best motorcycle repair shop in the state. They have several other businesses, but also do a lot of community outreach and charity rides. My dad is the best man I know and honestly so much more than a dad to me." I rarely talk this much, especially about myself, but I want her to know everything there is to know about me.

*Well, maybe not everything.*

"Earlier you mentioned your mom had you when she was young. My dad had me pretty young too, so he always says we grew up together. He says I taught him as much as he taught me over the years. I have two ride-or-die best friends that have had my back as long as I can remember, but nothing tops my relationship with my dad."

"That's so awesome. I feel like my mom and I would have been like that if she hadn't died when I was so young. I'm very thankful for my great-grandparents though, they have given me an incredible life and more love than imaginable."

"I hate that she was taken from you, babe. I bet she was incredible, like you."

Her eyes hold so much emotion as she says, "Thank you, she really was something else." Lottie looks down at the bracelet she's been twirling around her wrist.

I reach out to touch it. "Was this hers?"

She nods her head. "Yes, it was one of her most prized possessions and sadly, I never got to hear the story behind where most of the charms came from. But I know she never took it off."

Noticing one charm in particular I say, "Did you know seahorses mate for life? Fun fact I learned last year in biology."

"Yes, I do actually," she says with a sad smile, staring mindlessly at the charms around her wrist. "The person who gave her this was very special."

The emotional moment is broken by her phone ringing. She pulls it from her pocket and quickly places it face down on the blanket I brought with us. She's ignored several phone calls throughout the night. Once when I first picked her up and again at The Shack. I haven't liked the look on her face when she glances at it, so now curiosity is getting to me.

Nodding my head towards the phone, I tell her, "You know you can answer that if you need to."

"No, I think I'm going to have to block him because even though we broke up, he keeps calling and harassing me. His ego can't believe that the fat girl broke up with him."

Realizing she's talking about that douchebag Jonathan, I grab the back of her head and bring her closer to me so our eyes are at the same level.

"First off, never ever call yourself fat in front of me again. I don't think you understand how perfect you are. Let me put it to you like this... yes, girls have gotten my attention before, and no, I'm not a virgin, but my dick has never had an immediate reaction to someone based on their mouth-watering curves. I promise your body is what my dreams are made of. Don't even get me started on this face... you are perfect."

In the moonlight, her hazel eyes have turned as dark as the ocean tonight. My girl is turned on, but I'm not finished.

"Secondly, let me put a stop to his punk ass. Please give me the word and I'll call him right now..."

On cue, her phone vibrates again. Silently praying it's him, I reach down to flip the phone over and love that his name is 'bitch boy' in her phone now. I look to her for an answer.

Without words she swipes to answer the call and hits speaker phone.

"Hello?" His pretentious voice sounds annoyed.

I nod to her because I want to see what he says. "Hey, what do you want Jonathan?"

He huffs out, "What do I want? You know what I want, Lottie. You can't break up with me knowing you'll find no one better. Please... with a stature like yours, you should be thanking me for dating you, especially since you won't even put out."

*Fuck that, I've heard enough.*

Picking the phone up with rage coming out of my pores, I spit out, "Listen up motherfucker. Don't ever speak to Lottie like that again. Actually, lose her number while you're at it. If I find out you so much as speak her name again, I will personally take my ass to New York City to beat yours."

"Who the hell is this?"

"Someone that knew from the moment they saw Lottie what you obviously never figured out. Now she's moved on so you should too." Hanging up the phone and tossing it back down, I look at her and notice she's looking at me with an emotion I'm not sure of... amazement maybe... appreciation. Possibly both.

"Never let a man, or anyone for that matter, speak to you like that again, okay?"

Watching her closely, she nods and sits up on her knees getting closer to me.

"That's the second time tonight you've stood up for me. I think that earns you a kiss. What do you think, handsome... can I kiss you?"

I lick my lips and before I can even respond, Lottie leans over and touches her mouth to mine. She pulls back all too quickly and, looking down, seemly shy about her forwardness.

I take my knuckle to her chin. "Chin up Babygirl."

As soon as she looks up at me, my lips are on hers, devouring every spark, every taste, every moan.

I can't help but pull her onto my lap and thank fuck, she doesn't pull away in the slightest.

I know she can feel my hard dick pressing into her and to my surprise, she starts grinding down into me. I grab handfuls of her ass, trying to pull her as close to me as possible.

Pulling my lips off hers, needing to taste the rest of her, I move down to her neck, nipping at it with my teeth. Lottie must like what I'm doing because she lets out a moan that has me on the verge of begging her to give me everything.

My need to touch her is only increasing with her little moans. I pick her up off my lap and place her in front of me on the blanket. Moving up to my knees she follows my cue when I press my lips to hers again in a searing kiss. Kissing, licking, and sucking as we're both on our knees... bodies pressed to each other.

I reach to undo the button on her shorts and stop kissing her to ask, "Is this okay?" She looks up at me, swallows hard, and nods eagerly.

*Thank fuck.*

I move my hand to her unbuttoned shorts and down into her panties until I reach her sleek, warm pussy. "Fuck Babygirl, you are so wet."

"Greyson, you make me crazy. Please touch me." I let out a groan because damn this girl does me in.

Not hesitating, I slip one finger inside her. "Fuck Lottie, you're going to squeeze the life out of my dick... you're so tight." She moans and starts twisting her hips, grinding her clit onto the palm of my hand.

"Grey, holy shit that feels good." I add a second finger to get her ready for my dick. Lottie lets out a little gasp.

"It's okay baby," I say while placing a gentle kiss on her lips, continuing to move both fingers in and out. "See, look at you. You are going to take my cock so well."

That has her increasing her movements again. I take my thumb to gently circle her clit and Lottie's eyes roll to the back of her head.

Her moans and my panting breaths are drowning out the waves crashing in the distance.

*She's close.*

With my free hand, I pull her head towards me and whisper in her ear. "Come... It's going to feel so good. Let me hear it." I lick and nibble on her ear. "I can't wait to have my tongue on this sweet pussy of yours."

With that, she completely lets go, and I'm unable to take my eyes off her as she comes undone.

*What a fucking sight.*

I whisper into her ear, "Let's take this somewhere else. I want to see you, taste you, fuck you. Whatever you'll let me do. I've wanted inside you since the moment I saw you."

Leaning back so I can see her face, she looks so turned on but also shy all of a sudden. "You good? We don't have to do anything else tonight. You just make me so fucking hard and needy for you."

She shakes her head. "No, no, it's not like that. Trust me, I feel the same, and you don't know how bad I want all that too. I just... well, I'm a virgin, so I just need you to take it slow with me, please."

*A virgin. How did I not see that coming? I guess I never really gave it much thought.*

Grabbing her face to make sure she is getting me, I say, "Lottie, if you chose to give me something so special, I want it to be completely on your terms and only when you are ready. You say the word, and I'm all yours."

***

I've been lying in my bed in the pool house for two hours and I still can't seem to get Lottie off my mind. I have never enjoyed foreplay more than I did when she came on my fingers while moaning my name through the salty air.

When I got home tonight, I went straight to the shower to jerk-off to memories of that moment. The way she looked, the way she felt... the way she came.

But it's not even just the sexual need I have for her that's keeping me up, it's the way she makes me feel. The hold she has on me in such a short time is hard to explain. I felt it from the moment I saw her. Initially I thought it was just my undeniable attraction to her, but I've quickly realized there's more to it. I'm drawn to what's inside her. I don't mean inside her pussy because, yeah of course that too. I mean inside her heart, her mind, her soul.

She's taking over my mind.

Reaching over to my nightstand, I grab my cell and fire off a text to her.

*Me: Can't fall asleep...*
*Stacks: Oh no, you okay?*
*Me: Mind won't shut off...*
*Stacks: Aw, want to talk about it?*
*Me: Yeah, it's a big problem I've been having lately. You see, there's this girl.*
*Stacks: Oh yeah, do tell :)*
*Me: Well, she's driving me fucking crazy.*
*Stacks: ...*
*Me: She's all I can think about.*
*Me: She's the first thing that pops into my head when I wake up and the last thing on my mind before I close my eyes at night. Shit, she's even a star player in my dreams.*
*Stacks: What's so great about this girl?*
*Me: I've only known her for a few weeks and the list just keeps growing.*
*Me: Her curves and those pretty hazel eyes that hold kindness. That beautiful smile she gives me that's brighter than the sun. The sweet demeanor she shows me and everyone around her. How she can be a classy lady but then turn around and hit a joint while whooping my ass in video games. This girl can bake a cookie that will melt in your mouth, cause it's so damn good. And when she came earlier tonight it was music to my ears.*
*Stacks: She wishes she could see herself through your eyes.*

*Me:* That's one of my top priorities... to make her see.

*Stacks:* I can one hundred percent confirm that you have been on "This Girl's" mind every waking minute since she met you.

*Me:* Good...I plan to stay there.

# Chapter Five

"You still haven't touched him yet?" Ashley chastises over the phone.

"No, I—I haven't really had the opportunity. I mean, his hands have been all over me, but I haven't touched *it*. Only through his clothes."

"Girl, you've been with him basically every day for the last two weeks, and you're not at all interested in what his peen looks like?" she questions.

"It's not that I'm not interested... I just, I don't know. I guess I'm nervous."

"I get it, I do. I don't mean to pressure you or make you feel bad. It's just the way you've been talking about him... guess I'm just surprised you haven't," Ashley adds.

I don't understand my own hesitation. I really like Greyson. He's kind, attentive, and so fricken' hot. Not to mention his bossy side. Gah... I love it. When he's all assertive and takes control of the situation, I swear little hearts shoot from my eyes.

"I don't know what I'm doing with him. I know he's experienced, and I don't want to embarrass myself," I tell her, knowing damn well it's also because I'm self-conscious as hell about my body. I've seen his Instagram. I know the kind of girls he hangs out with; here's a hint, they certainly don't look like me.

"Tig, you have nothing to be embarrassed about. You are absolutely stunning inside and out. Do you not recall the way guys were drooling over you at that party?" she reassures me.

"Ugh... I know, and he's never once made me feel bad aboumad looks. In fact, I think he's quite obsessed with my curves, if I'm being honest." I laugh, recalling how his hands rarely leave my round hips when we're together.

He hasn't even seen me with all my clothes off yet. The most skin he's seen is me in my bathing suit. But his hands have certainly had their fair share, he's touched every part of me with those skilled fingers of his. He lets me take the lead when we're together and I'm thankful he hasn't pressured me for more.

"Girl, he'd be a fool to think otherwise. You know if I ever switch teams, you're my first conquest," Ashley teases.

"Who are you kidding? You're not switching teams anytime soon. Especially not after the way Trent gushes over you since you guys started messaging back and forth. How is that going by the way?"

"Yeah, I don't know if I mentioned how much I appreciate what you did. Friending Trent on Instagram has definitely been entertaining, to say the least. We chat basically every day, but you know..." Her words trail off at the end.

"Ugh, I know, babe. All you can do is make the most of it while you can. I knew you were going to be a stubborn ass, so I took the first step for you... and you're welcome," I say, hoping she'll see that she can't put her whole life on hold.

"Shit, I have to get ready for work. I love you Tig! And remember to touch his peen and report back to me. Don't be afraid, maybe hop on the Hub and watch a few videos for inspiration. You know what... scratch that, you read enough smut. I'm sure you have an idea of what you need to do."

"Haha, love you too, Bitty. I'll keep you posted." I giggle as we hang up our call.

I finish getting myself ready by throwing my unruly hair into a high ponytail. I check myself out in a mirror to make sure I'm comfortable with the way everything fits. I have on a cute high-waisted pair of bike shorts and matching sports bra with an oversized t-shirt over it.

Greyson mentioned we're going to "work up a sweat" today when we talked earlier. Makes me a bit intrigued that he didn't clarify in what way, but I figured this outfit is cute enough.

> **Greyson:** *I'll be there in 10. Bring your sexy ass and a bikini. We're going swimming afterwards.*

Bikini...Ha!

> **Me:** *Okay, I'm ready. Should I bring some snacks and drinks?*
> **Greyson:** *Lottie, you are the snack... but bring whatever you like. Have any more of those delicious cookies you made? I'd love some of those if you have 'em.*
> **Me:** *I'll pack us some goodies. See you soon.*

I can't stop the smile that spreads across my face as I head to my closet to pack a bag. I wonder what he has planned for us.

I lace up my sneakers and gather my stuff to head out. Greyson should be here any moment. I'm practically skipping out the door when Ethel enters through the main entrance.

"Where are you going and dressed like this, no less?"are the first words out of her mouth.

"Hi to you too Ethel... Greyson is picking me up in a minute."

"Will you be gone all day?" she questions. Where is this coming from? I don't think she's ever shown an interest in my whereabouts.

"Uh, I think so. I probably won't be home for dinner, if that's what you're asking."

"Oh, don't be silly dear, I have plans for dinner. Then I will be gone the rest of the weekend. I just wanted to see if this Greyson boy is doing right by you."

*Huh? That's weird.*

"Yeah, he's been really kind. I'm having a good time hanging out with him," I respond hesitantly.

"Oh, that's excellent. I'm glad to see you're making new friends in the area," she says with a smile on her face.

What the hell is going on? This behavior is so unlike her. She hasn't mentioned Jonathan once since Greyson and I started talking. I'm not sure if she's figured out we're over yet, but I'm not offering that information either.

"Uh, yeah... Sure is nice to have someone to spend time with." I make a dig at her, referring to the fact she's never around. Not that I would spend my spare time with her, but making some sort of effort would be nice. I am her only granddaughter.

"That's great dear, have fun." She pats my shoulder and continues strolling into the house, completely ignoring my sarcasm.

Moments later, I hear the rumble of Greyson's motorcycle making its way up the driveway. I smile inwardly. This is the first time he's taken me on his bike. He's made references to it, but I haven't seen it yet.

When he pulls up in front of me, it takes me a moment before I can pick my jaw up off the ground. He is sex on wheels on this thing. My god. His large frame straddling the bike does crazy things to my insides. His devilish smirk coupled by his freshly trimmed beard doesn't help the state of my panties, either. *Yep I'm touching his peen asap.*

"Get on Stacks, we're going for a ride," he says while reaching for a spare helmet.

I hold up the bags, silently asking where I should put my stuff. Realizing he'll probably need to help me, he swings his leg over the bike to dismount, placing the helmet on the handlebars.

*Damn, he is beautiful.*

His tight black t-shirt hugs his massive biceps, bringing attention to the sleeve of tattoos on his left arm. Greyson's wearing a pair of distressed jeans that fit his muscular frame perfectly. You can tell these jeans are naturally distressed and not store-bought by the indent of his wallet and the natural wear pants get from hard work. Knowing this only makes him that much hotter in my eyes. The fact that he's not afraid to work with his hands and get dirty, unlike most of the guys I'm used to.

I finish checking him out as he approaches me. His blue eyes lock onto mine, and I swear I think I sway just a tad as I mentally swoon. Still unable to form logical sentences, I hold out the two bags for him to stow away. He chuckles at what has to be a shocked look on my face. My cheeks are probably red as hell too. Taking the bags, he places a kiss on my cheek and walks away with a sexy swagger to his step.

I shake my head to try and break the spell this guy has on me. By the time I come to, he's already back on the bike with my helmet in his hand. He's wearing that cocky-ass smirk I'm growing to adore.

Placing the helmet on my head, I ask, "So, where are we going?"

"Oh, you'll see. But first we're going for a ride. I need to feel your gorgeous body behind mine, straddling my hips."

My cheeks instantly flush.

"Uhm..." I look at him hesitantly. "I've never ridden before. Do I need to do anything in particular?"

"Nope, just hop on, hold on to me, and follow my body's lead. Don't worry about the rest," he says with a sinister smile.

I can't help but think he's insinuating more than just riding on the back of his bike. For the first time, I'm not afraid of what he's suggesting. After my pep talk with Ashley, I'm actually excited to see where this adventure takes us.

We drive around aimlessly for at least an hour all along the coast. It's breathtakingly beautiful to see the shore like this. Fresh air blowing in my face, the roaring strength of the bike between my thighs, and my arms securely holding onto his sides. He definitely did this on purpose, knowing what a turn on it would be.

Pulling off at a small overlook, he parks the bike. He skillfully gets off then helps me do the same.

"Come on, I want to show you something," he says in his bossy tone.

I'm trying to steady my shaky legs. I certainly wasn't prepared for the weird feeling I'd have in them after our ride.

Reaching for my hand and lacing our fingers together, he chuckles. "The feeling will subside shortly. Don't worry, we can take it slow."

I let out a deep sigh. *Does he know every word from him sounds like a hot af invitation to jump his bones?*

"Okay, lead the way handsome." I wink at him.

He leads me down a trail through the cliffs. The surrounding woods are serene and there are patches of beautiful wildflowers.

"How have I never seen any of this before is beyond me," I say out loud, not necessarily to him.

"Lottie, you've been hiding in that castle of yours for too long." He chuckles at the face I make in immediate response to his words.

"You know damn well I'm no princess. If that's what you're alluding to," I huff out.

"Well, castle or not, it seems like there are a lot of new things I can show you, pretty girl," he says with a devilish smile and the most mischievous face I think I've ever seen.

"I know you're different, Stacks. And trust me, it's a relief." We continue to walk along the path as he speaks. "I've lived in Richmond Hills my whole life, surrounded by the disgustingly rich folks who have everything they could ever want or need and the hardworking ones who count the days till their next paycheck. And let me tell you, you're not like any of them. You are so different, but in a damn good way... The way you handle yourself shows your elite upbringing, all while being so down to earth. You're unfazed by getting a little dirty and roughin' it with me. Some princesses I go to school with wouldn't be caught dead doing half the shit we've done. Just makes me appreciate you that much more."

He slows his pace to a stop and turns to me. "You're something special, Lottie. I hope deep down you know that."

I can't help but lean up on my tiptoes to wrap my arms around his neck and take his lips with mine.

"You really know how to make me believe you," I whisper with our lips still close enough to land a soft kiss after.

After several hours and working up quite the sweat hiking, Greyson informs me we're going back to his place to swim. Trent is in New York visiting his brother, and we'll have the place all to ourselves.

We pull up to the side of the pool house and I can't stop the excitement that thrums throughout my body.

"Come on, let's get changed. The pool is calling my name. I'm also dying to see you in a bikini," Greyson says with a wink as he helps me off the bike.

"Ha! The fact that you think I even own a bikini is comical." I laugh at him as we head inside.

He stops abruptly, and I practically crash into his back. He spins around with a surprised look on his face. "Lottie, you're fucking gorgeous. I would give anything to see your fine ass in a bikini. Your body drives me absolutely insane." With that, he grabs a healthy handful of my ass and kisses me deeply.

"Come on," he growls as he resumes walking. I can't help the blush that creeps up my cheeks as he re-adjusts himself.

Walking outside, I find Greyson already swimming in the pool. I might not have worn a bikini, but I did choose a very revealing one-piece. Similar to the one I wore on the boat, but this one is practically a thong, and my tatas look fantastic. Normally, I wouldn't be caught dead in this particular suit, but the way Greyson stares at me like he's a starved man gives me the confidence boost I need.

I step to the side of the pool and take off my coverup. The moment it hits the ground, Greyson stands still, devouring every inch of me from head to toe with those intense blue eyes.

"Fuck me," he moans as he runs his hands through his dark, wet hair. He quickly makes his way to the stairs.

"Is it cold?" I ask, dipping in my toe as he climbs out.

"You're killing me in this thing, babe," he says with that growly tone of his, sending a wave of heat between my thighs.

I can't help but bite my lip and take in his dripping wet body. *Holy shit!*

His arms look huge with his hands tugging on his hair like that and the way the water cascades down his chiseled chest and abs has me dying to lick each and every drop. *What is this guy doing to me?*

"If you don't quit lookin' at me like that..." He starts but doesn't finish his train of thought. Instead, he leans down and lifts my body into his arms, wedding style. "Hold your breath," is the only warning I get before he jumps into the pool.

Coming up for air, he wraps his big arms around me, and I instinctively wrap my thick thighs around his solid body. This feels so right, being here in Greyson's arms.

We stare at each other for several moments, neither one of us wanting to disrupt whatever this is charging the air around us.

He leans in to place a gentle kiss on my lips. His arms tighten around me, and I can tell he's struggling to keep himself in check by the tensing of his body beneath me. But I no longer want him to be gentle. I'm not a fragile little thing.

I lean up in his hold and deepen our kiss, grinding my body on his while we devour each other's mouths. I feel Greyson's very hard and very thick erection rub between my legs as he grabs hold of my ass.

Walking our entwined bodies towards the pool wall, I softly whimper, and he groans into my mouth.

"What are you doing to me, pretty girl?" he asks as he grinds his covered erection against my center once more, eliciting a loud moan from deep inside of me.

I don't have words to describe what he's doing to me. Especially not when I feel his lips traveling down my neck, nipping and kissing a trail to my collarbone.

"I'm dying to taste you. I don't know how much longer I can wait," he murmurs into my neck.

Greyson looks extremely confused when I push gently on his chest so I can break free of his hold. I decide I want to show him how good he makes me feel. To clear up any confusion, I reach my hand down with a confidence I wasn't aware I had and run my palm against his large bulge, gently stroking him over his swim shorts.

Greyson's breath shudders at my tender caress. His hands go to the tied strings at his waist, undoing them, but leaving the decision to pull his shorts down to me.

My hands grip his waistband, and I slowly maneuver them down his form. His hand goes to my wrist and my eyes shoot up to his.

"Don't think you have to do this if you don't want to baby. I'm more than happy to play with you if that makes you more comfortable," he says with earnest eyes.

"Do you not want me to?" I ask him, lowering my chin now, second-guessing myself.

"Lottie, look at me." He lifts my chin, giving me a kiss on the lips. "There is nothing I want more than for you to pull my cock out. I just want to make sure that's what *you* want to do."

Nodding at him. "I just—I don't know what I'm doing. I thought you stopped me because of that." His dick twitches between us at my words.

"Fuck, do you not see what you do to me?" With that, my hands join his at the waistband of his shorts and pull them down.

My hand grazes his soft flesh with slight hesitation, and his body shudders once more at my touch. He grabs my face and kisses me. "You're the most beautiful thing I've ever seen."

Greyson gently raises his body so he's now sitting on the inner ledge of the pool, which also means I'm face-to-face with his very large and very thick erection. My eyes go wide at the sight of him naked in front of me, and I can't help but lick my lips. I gently wrap my hand around him and slowly stroke it up and down.

A few moments later, I ask him, "Is this right?"

He groans and leans back, placing his hands behind him on the pool deck. "Yes, Lottie. Fucking perfect." He stares at me through hooded eyes, and I have never felt sexier than I do right now.

A little bead of liquid forms at the tip of his cock, and I lean down to taste it. I hear him mutter from above me, but I can't make out his words. Wrapping my lips around his hard length, I slowly take him into my mouth.

I've read enough smut that I know what I should do, so I keep one hand around Greyson's cock while my mouth moves along him. Feeling his large hand tangle into my hair as I move the two in sync with one another spurs me on even more. I lock eyes with him, savoring the way he feels.

"You look so gorgeous with my cock in your mouth," he says as he strokes my hair. I can't help but squeeze my thighs together at his words. I am so turned on that the pressure alone might be enough to get me off.

I love the sounds coming out of him right now. This strong, almost impenetrable man is coming undone under my touch, and there is nothing hotter.

"Fuck, baby. Keep that up and I'm going to come down that throat of yours." His words only turn me on even more. There's no way in hell I'm stopping now.

Another minute later and I feel his body tense and he's groaning something along the lines of "don't stop... about to come", but I'm not really paying attention to his words. I'm too focused on his face and how utterly masculine and breathtaking he is when he lets it all go.

Once he stops twitching, I give the throbbing head of his cock one more swipe of my tongue as I stand up. I'm not even fully standing before Greyson is pulling me in for an all-consuming kiss.

"Stay the night with me," he finally says as we break apart.

I giggle. "That good, huh?"

"Babe, that was mind-blowing. I just want to spend the rest of the night returning the favor," he says as he tucks a loose strand of my wet hair behind my ear.

I lean into his hand.

"I can't tonight... but I could tomorrow. Is Trent gone all weekend?" I question. I could sleep over tonight knowing damn well Ethel isn't around, but I need to unleash all of today's events on Ashley and mentally prepare for a sleepover with Greyson.

He scoops me up and twirls me around in the pool. "He's gone for the rest of the weekend. You're mine tomorrow, all day and night."

What I wouldn't give to be his for more than just tomorrow.

# Chapter Six

Greyson

My Ol' Girl has kept me busy all day. I have washed her, shined her up, and now I'm cleaning out the carburetor. My teal blue, 1963 Ford F-100 Stepside pickup truck is an eye-catcher, but she didn't get that way overnight.

My Grandpa, who used to be the President of the Rebel Knights, loved his motorcycles, but this truck always held a special place in his heart.

When I was younger, he started working to restore it and from the time I could hold a wrench, we had a weekly date with "Ol' Girl", as he called her.

Although I would much rather still have him here, I was honored that my Nana gave me his truck when he passed last year. She said he wouldn't have wanted anyone else to have it.

My Grandpa taught me restoration and my dad taught me how to fix just about anything on a bike. It's in my blood and I love it. Now I'm excited to take our family's shop to the next level and teach my old man and his guys a few new tricks.

Even while I focus on my truck, my mind is constantly full of thoughts about Lottie. I feel like a kid on Christmas Eve anticipating my date with her. I planned something special, and it's the first time I have ever done anything like this, which has me more nervous than I want to admit.

I also keep reminding myself that tonight I have to show some self-control. All I can think about is Lottie's mouth on my cock yesterday in the pool, so I've been rocking a semi all fucking day. By far one of the sexiest moments of my life.

Her mouth full of me.

Those beautiful eyes looking up at me for reassurance.

Full tits spilling out of her bathing suit.

Wet.

Gorgeous.

Fuck, I think I'm in over my head.

I hear my phone ring in my pocket and thank God because I need a cold shower after letting my mind go there again. I take the rag off my truck to clean my hands before reaching into my pocket.

Seeing "Pops" on the caller ID has my dick rapidly chilling the fuck out.

"What's up, old man?"

"Who you calling old, punk?" His voice brings a big smile to my face. We both chuckle and he continues, "I miss you, my boy. What you up to?"

"Working on Ol' Girl, it was time to clean out the carburetor." I turn around to lean against the truck.

"He would be proud of you for taking such good care of her. You working this weekend?"

"Nah, I'm off actually." Cringing a bit because I know what's about to come next.

"Well, why the hell didn't you come home? I figured you were working like usual, even though I told you that you don't need to work so hard. I will help you out, son. The machine is a smart business move on my end as well."

I knew he would go there. "I know Dad, but you've done enough for me and the business. You've also taught me how to be self-sufficient, and I want to do this on my own. I want to contribute to the shop myself and not just have everything given to me."

"And I'm so proud of you for that, buddy. I don't know how I got so lucky with you. The guys are excited about you getting the CNC machine and taking the courses to learn how to use it. They think we're about to be Orange County Choppers and get our own show or some shit."

That has us both laughing again.

I've known from a young age that I wanted to follow in my dad and grandfather's footsteps and work on bikes. As I got older and learned more, I realized I wanted to get our shop into doing custom work. So, for the last year, every bit of cash I've made has gone into a stash. I'm saving up to buy the equipment needed in order to do that kind of work at our shop and to pay for the pricey courses that will develop my skills and designs. The special machine can streamline production and bring in revenue the club never imagined possible. It will make it more efficient to design and manufacture parts for bikes, which will allow us to do more customized work than we can take on at the moment ever before.

I know my dad can afford to help me and I love that he supports me the way he does, but like I said, he's done so much for me already. He stayed when she didn't, and he has sacrificed every day since.

One day, I'll also want to pursue being a prospect in the MC. The Rebel Knights are my family, after all. But for now, we have an understanding that I will follow my dreams first and decide when to join on my own terms. That is very important to him, me seeing all my dreams fulfilled, especially since he didn't have much choice in the matter when he was my age.

"Well, ya never know. We may be even bigger than them one day. I can see it now, Rebel Knights Choppers."

"I hear ya boy!" He pauses and then circles back to the weekend. "So if you ain't working, what's got you staying in town? Trent throwing another party?"

"No, Trent's actually in New York this weekend with Trevor." Leaving out the part about him chasing after Ashley. I didn't disclose that part to Lottie, either. He said he wanted it to be a surprise and telling Lottie would have absolutely ruined any chances of it being kept secret, especially if it involved Ashley.

"I'm hanging out with Lottie, my... friend. Actually, I'm taking her on a date tonight. Kinda nervous, which I would only ever admit to you, but you know I don't do this shit."

"Wow, she must be something else if you're taking her on an actual date."

Thinking of her pretty face, I say, "She really is Pop. Like nothing I've ever seen."

"In that case, stay there and take her out any chance you get. I felt like that once... I'd give just about anything but you to go back to those days."

Even though I didn't grow up in a home with two loving parents. My dad has always made it a point to tell me how love should be. He always says how great it is to have someone who is "Your person, your anchor in life," to always hold on to, no matter how rough life gets. I know he had this once and I sure hope one day he finds it again.

He continues, "It's about time you stopped fucking with girls that don't mean shit to you. Not every chick is like your mom, Greyson."

*I love you Dad, but why the fuck do we have to bring her up?*

The thought of Lottie leaving me to be with some guy who fits in her family's tax bracket has my blood boiling. Would Lottie do that to me? I just have to remind myself not everyone is like my mother, a woman who cherished the green over her family.

"That woman doesn't affect my decisions. But seriously, no other girl has ever held my interest like Lottie does. Speaking of that, I need to get going so I can finish the truck up before it's time to go grab her."

"All right my boy, have fun. wrap it up and treat her right. We miss you and love you."

"Love you too Pops. I'll see you soon. May even have to bring Lottie to meet you," I say as I hang up.

My dad is the toughest motherfucker on the street, but he loves like no other. He is loved as much as he is feared. He has never once made me question his love for me, but it never gets old hearing his stern voice get all soft towards me.

He has instilled a lot of himself into me.

Don't mess with anyone I care about, and we're straight.
Loyalty is everything.
If you are in my circle, I will die for you.
Completely devoted to the ones I love.

Lately, that circle and devotion seems to be growing by one sweet, curvy, brunette beauty.

# Chapter Seven

I'm a ball of nerves as I throw everything imaginable into my overnight bag. This is really happening. Holy shit.

Honestly, this thing between Greyson and I almost feels too good to be true, but I am enjoying every minute with him. He makes me feel important, like he latches onto everything I say and do. It's something I haven't felt in quite some time, to be honest.

One would probably say I'm a bit jaded when it comes to forming close relationships with people. Between my dad leaving before I was born, to my mother passing away when I was eight, I have a tough time with deep connections. Let's be real, everything is so temporary in this life. It's only a matter of time before something happens and loved ones disappear, so why bother?

Don't get me wrong, I've always felt loved being raised by my great-grandparents, but there was definitely something missing. And now that it's just my Papa and me, I've been feeling some sort of way lately.

Ashley has been the only constant outside of my great-grand-parents. She's the one I run to for everything, always giving me her fair and honest opinion. Never one to judge or turn up her nose. I'm so thankful for her and her family. They arrived in New York when I needed them the most, and they've always been there for me when I need them.

So, after chatting into the wee hours of the morning with Ashley, I think I'm ready. Ready for anything that could possibly happen between Greyson and me tonight. My cheeks flush with the thought of Greyson's large body over mine, whispering filthy words that set my body on fire.

Not sure how my mom would feel about me losing my virginity. These are the times I wonder what our relationship would be like. I honestly think I would have felt comfortable enough to open up to her about it. After all, she lost her virginity at sixteen... well, according to her journal, she did.

Going over to my closet, I reach behind my coats to the built-in shelf where I keep my mother's box of her most-prized possessions.

Gigi passed down my mother's keepsakes when I was entering my freshman year of high school. She figured I was old enough to take care of them, and that my mother would have wanted me to have them.

There were a ton of things inside the box, from concert ticket stubs and mix tapes to journals and love notes. All giving me a small glimpse into the teenager my mother was. I cherish every-thing inside her keepsake box as if it was some fortune-filled treasure chest. To anyone else, this box might seem like the contents of a teen's junk drawer, but to me, these items are irreplaceable. Just like her charm bracelet that I wear daily, everything this box contains helps me keep her close.

Her notes and journals have become a source of comfort. At first, I felt wrong reading them, but then I realized she wanted me to have this. Wanted me to learn everything I could about her. Not only does it make me feel closer to her, but it has also inspired me to start my own journal. It's a great form of self-care to write out all your feelings. I wonder if that's why my mom started hers?

Her first journal starts about the same time she meets the great love of her life. I know the particular entry I'm looking for because it's actually my favorite. While it spoke of her love and the loss of her virginity, it spoke of me as well.

*Dear Journal,*

*I gave away a piece of myself last night.*

*I gave it away to the guy who makes my knees weak and my toes tingle with just one look.*

*I gave it away to the best person in the whole world, and I couldn't be happier.*

*I know everyone says we are young, and my mother thinks this is just a rebellious phase for me, but honestly, I don't believe that for one second. I have always been mature beyond my years. I know without a shadow of a doubt that the way he makes me feel is unlike anything else I'll ever experience in my lifetime. My Twin Flame... the great love of my life!*

*He was so perfect, so gentle, so attentive, but so sexy and domineering. Yes, it hurt but I can't wait to do it again. The connection I felt with him during it was unbelievable. I honestly didn't think I could love him any more than I already do.*

*I know we are taking a risk having sex before marriage and, as my mother likes to remind me, "No prestigious man will want someone else's hand-me-downs." She does not like that I'm with Smitty, and she makes sure to remind me that he could never provide me with the life I deserve as a Richmond. But again, I couldn't care less. I want it all with him and no one else.*

*One day, if we are ever fortunate enough to have a daughter, I will always fill her head with love and inspiration. I will not care who she loves as long as they make her feel protected and treat her like she is more precious than life itself. I may be 16 and in no way ready for a baby, but I do know one day I can't wait to love a child unconditionally, the way a mother should.*

*We will prove my mother and the rest of town wrong one day, many years from now, when they realize those "young and dumb kids" are still together and living life for happiness, not for money and greed.*

*He is the best thing that has ever been mine and I don't want to ever give that up.*

*xox,*
*Leah*

Leaning back against my pillows, I hold the journal tight, fighting back the tears.

Oh Mom, how I wish you were here.

I wonder how much different my life would be if she were still around. Would we have stayed in New York, or come back to North Carolina? Would Ethel be more involved in our lives? Would I have met Greyson? Sadness rakes over me at the thought of not having him around. Geez, get it together, you've only known him for what, a little over two weeks. For some reason, with him, it feels like longer, like our paths were meant to cross.

Thankfully, my phone chimes with a notification, and I don't have much time to dwell on all the thoughts coursing through my mind.

**Greyson:** *Hope you're ready for me, pretty girl. I'll be there soon.*
**Me:** *What do you have in store for me?*
**Greyson:** *Oh, you'll find out soon...*

\*\*\*

"I thought you said you knew how to cook," I smirk at him as we enter Greyson's kitchen. He follows behind me, carrying the bags of food the delivery man just dropped off. While he places them on the counter, my eyes take in the array of food containers.

"Little do you know, I'm the next fucking *Top Chef,* but for tonight, I got us dinner to eat somewhere special," he says from the other side of the kitchen, his large body leaning against the fridge with his muscular arms crossed over his chest. I can feel his eyes roaming over my body. I wore my favorite spaghetti strap romper for this reason. Ashley, of course, helped me pick it out while on FaceTime. She told me it makes my tatas and ass look fantastic.

"Okay handsome, let's go then... I'm getting *hangry,*" I say before I lean up on my tiptoes to place a quick kiss on his lips.

Grabbing the bags full of food, we head back to his truck, and he follows me to the passenger side to open my door for me. I instantly blush. I don't think I'll ever get used to him doing that. No one has ever opened the door for me, well, besides Ethel's paid drivers.

I hoist myself in and watch as he walks to his side. He has such swagger when he moves. Everything he does is so damn hot.

He looks at me from his seat with a frown on his face.

"What?" I say as I adjust my clothes, making sure nothing is spilling out.

Without warning, he leans over, wraps his arm around my waist, and pulls my body across the bench seat. Settling myself right against him, my legs are straddling the gearshift. His hand rests on my thigh, lightly stroking my skin.

"That's better. You were too far away over there. I've been dying to touch your skin since you walked out of your house in this sexy-as-fuck outfit."

I smile as Greyson shifts the truck into reverse. His hand immediately returns to my thigh afterward. He continues to do this for the entire ride, his hand never leaving my skin for an extended period of time.

By the time we pull up to the Lookout, I'm so turned on I think I might combust. I don't know if he realizes what his seemingly innocent touches do to me. One look at his smug-as-hell face tells me he's all too aware of what he's doing. *Cocky bastard.*

Greyson grabs our food and a blanket, then steers us away from the main area, taking us down a trail that leads to an opening lower along the cliffs. When we walk into the clearing, I recognize it immediately. The *You Got Mail* mailbox is right in front of us with its flag up. Excitement fills my veins at the thought of what could be inside it.

I look at Greyson and see him setting down our things on the blanket. I make my way over to the mailbox, eager to see what's inside, pausing just for a moment before opening it.

"Go on Stacks, open it up." I feel his warm breath as he whispers into my ear. His body is so close to mine.

I quickly pull it open and see a lone envelope inside with 'Pretty Girl' written across it. I look back up to Greyson with wide eyes and he smiles down at me and nods his head to say go on.

My heart is beating so loudly I fear Greyson can hear it. I can't believe he set all this up. How long has he been planning this? Calm down, Lottie. I take a deep breath and pull out the

envelope. Why am I so damn nervous? *Oh, I know why. Because he is trying to own my freakin' heart with this little surprise.*
With shaky hands, I rip it open and read.

*Lottie,*

*I hope like hell you have enjoyed the last two weeks with me like I have with you or else I'm about to make a fool out of myself.*

*I've never been quick to get too close to anyone... just ask my friends and family. I keep my guard up at all times. But YOU, Lottie, are single-handedly bringing those walls crashing down. So much so, that the thought of not having you in my life scares the shit out of me. Don't even get me started on how I feel about the thought of you seeing another guy.*

*I look forward to our days together, hanging out and getting to know every single inch of you. I want to know all your likes and dislikes, what turns you on, and even what pisses you off, so I'll be sure to do it every now and again because you're so damn cute when you're mad : )*

*Lottie, before you, I had never felt this uncontrollable desire with anyone. No other person has ever consumed my every thought, even my dreams, the way you do. You have me so caught up in my head when I'm not with you. I honestly don't fully comprehend everything I'm feeling when it comes to this thing we have.*

*I think I'm falling hard and fast and I don't want it to stop.*
*Yours,*
*Greyson*

I quickly reread the note once more, unable to form a response to how amazing his words make me feel. It's as if he took every single one of my hopes and fears and wrote them as his own. How does he always know what I need to hear?

Unable to contain my emotions, I throw myself at Greyson. Jumping into his arms, I wrap my legs around him and kiss him deeply.

"All of it!" That's all I'm able to get out in between our frantic kisses. I hope he understands what I mean. All of it—all of the emotions, needs, desires. I feel it all.

I'm frantic to touch his skin after such revelations. The fact this brute-of-a-man has poured his heart out has me ready to give him all of me. I'm all over him, our hands eager to touch every part of each other.

He breaks away abruptly, and I go to protest, but then hear a muffled conversation from people walking the trails nearby. We're not hidden by any means, which is unfortunate because I would love to have Greyson on top of me right here, right now. The voices get louder, and I know our private moment is over.

He leans in, resting his forehead on mine. Slowly trying to calm our hunger for each other. "There's nothing I want more than to continue what we've started here." He adjusts his very large bulge in his shorts for emphasis. "But I want to take my time with you, pretty girl."

I look at him for a few moments, memorizing the angles of his face and the look in his eyes. It's something I never thought I'd be fortunate enough to have. I thought I would somehow be roped into a relationship of convenience or a business deal by the She-Devil. Never one for true love because that is without a doubt what I feel for him.

"Come on. Let's eat so we can get back and I can satisfy those hungry eyes of yours," he says, grabbing my hand and walking us to the blanket he's laid out.

Snuggling myself up to him, holding on to his arm with one hand while my other hand hangs interlaced with his, I say, "I think you might be the most perfect man I've ever met." I gaze up at his gorgeous face as we stand at the edge of the blanket.

I notice he flinches slightly at my words. Does he not realize how perfect he is?

"Babygirl, nobody's perfect."

"Okay, you might be right, but I think you're perfect for me," I say with a big smile. I want him to know just how much I feel for him.

Intoxicating smells come from the containers he's opening and my mouth waters. He catches me staring and smiles.

"Mangiamo!" he says with an attempted Italian accent as we both sit.

I can't help but laugh.

"This smells so fricken good," I say, reaching across the blanket for a dish.

"It's from a small little spot my aunt loves. She takes Trent and me there often. The owners are an older couple who moved here from Brooklyn. They make the best fucking food I think I've ever tasted."

"Mmm," is all I'm able to get out, too busy devouring the shrimp scampi dish I have in my hands.

"This food reminds me so much of my favorite Italian spot in the city. I'll have to take you there when you come visit." I smile at him as he takes a big bite of his chicken parm.

"Can't wait. Especially with Trent going to NYU in the fall, we'll have to."

We finish our meals and clean up in what feels like minutes. I'm not sure if it's because we're both starved or because we're anxious to get back to his place. Either way, I can't help the tingles that take over my body as the truck headlights illuminate the pool house as we approach it.

After placing our dinner bags on the kitchen counter, I feel Greyson's large body behind me. His hands come to rest on their favorite spot, right on the curves of my hips.

He kisses my neck and I tilt my head to the side, allowing him easier access. I moan softly when his kisses become a mix of licks and bites. I can feel him hardening behind me as he grinds himself against my ass.

"Please," I pant. "Please take me, Grey."

He pauses for a moment. "Are you sure?"

Am I sure? Is this what I want? I don't take long because I know damn well my mind was set on this long before I even read his heartfelt letter. He's everything I want and everything I need.

"I've never been more sure of anything in my life."

That earns me a growl from Greyson as he spins me around and lifts me from under my ass so my thighs can wrap around him.

"Fuck baby..." he says while staring into my eyes. I swear I can get lost in those stormy blues of his. There's so much to be said swimming in his gaze, but we can save that for another time. Right now... right now, I want this man all over me.

He walks us to his room and lays me out across his bed. Taking a step back, he just stares.

Several moments later, he finally speaks. "You're the most beautiful thing I've ever set my eyes on, Lottie Richmond."

Geez, this man, I don't think my heart has ever felt this full.

He rips off his shirt in one quick motion and is kneeling between my thighs moments later.

"Let's get this off of you..." He helps me sit up to slip off my romper, which leaves me in my bra and panties.

"Fucking gorgeous," he says as he leans in to kiss me.

# Chapter Eight

*Damn, nothing could have prepared me for this.*

Looking at Lottie right now has me about ready to explode. With her curves on display and knowing what she's about to give me, I can barely stand it... the need I have for her is bone deep.

*She's breathtaking.*

I've heard that term before and always thought it was just an exaggeration of words, but looking at Lottie in this moment, feeling like she's the air I breathe... I know the term is true of its meaning.

Taking both of my hands to the sides of her face, she bends her head back to let me drink her in. I never knew I enjoyed kissing so much until her.

Kissing was always a means to an end, but with Lottie, it's different... because she's different. I know after tonight, I'll be ruined for anyone else.

She groans in protest as I pull my mouth from hers. Readjusting my very hard dick in my pants, I say, "I can't wait any longer to look at these tits of yours. Just seeing them spill out of your bra is driving me crazy." I move to reach for the back of her bra, but she beats me to it.

The light pink Double D bra falls to her lap.

Staring with no shame, I have never seen a more perfect rack before.

I don't say it aloud because I don't want her thinking about my previous ways, but fuck me. I knew they were big, but seeing them and her hard, pink nipples—her tits are even better than any fantasy I've imagined over the last few weeks while getting myself off.

Needing them in my mouth, I gently push her down on the bed. Touching my lips to the crook of her neck, I kiss all the way down her chest to in between her breasts.

Panting, Lottie begs, "Please Greyson." I lean over to take one nipple in my mouth, swirling my tongue around it, sliding my hand up to her left nipple and tweaking it while lightly biting the other. She lets out a loud gasp when my teeth connect.

When I pull my mouth away, she groans in frustration until she realizes I'm making my way further down. "Be patient pretty girl," I say as I reach to pull her panties down.

"I need you G," she whispers.

Kissing the top of her smooth pussy, I respond with, "I know baby, trust me. I'm going to take care of you. I love seeing you so eager. "

With that, I lean in and give her one long lick from bottom to top. Lottie's back arches off the bed. "Fuck Grey," she moans as I continue to lick her.

"I want you to come on my tongue before I take you. I have been dying to taste you and it will get you good and relaxed for me. Can you do that for me, Lottie?" She nods eagerly.

When I go back between her legs, I take my tongue to her clit and make small, continuous circles.

She starts to writhe under me to the point where I have to hold down her curvy hip to keep her in place. Cussing more than she ever has in my presence, I can tell she's getting close. I want to edge her a bit, so her orgasm is explosive.

Pulling back for a second I see her protest but silence her with a kiss and then say, "Don't worry I'm going to let you come, pretty girl."

Slowly I drag two of my fingers down to her dripping, swollen center. "I'm going to use my fingers to loosen up this beautiful tight pussy."

Starting with one finger slowly, in and out, loving the flushed look on her face... She's ready for more.

I push a second finger in and start working her at a steady pace. Leaning back down to put my tongue on her clit. I feel her clench around my fingers and I know it's coming. Focusing on her and trying not to lose my load in my pants I continue doing the exact same thing.

"Yesss Greyson, yesss! Ahhh—fuck baby!" Hearing her come and call me baby has me dying to be inside of her.

I shift my eyes up to watch her as she comes undone, keeping my mouth right where it is while she rides it out.

"Fuck Lottie, I need to be inside you. Are you ready for me Babygirl?"

She surprises me by sitting up and reaching for the button on my shorts. "I was ready the minute I felt your beard between my legs. Please, I need you. I need this..."

Grabbing Lottie's hand to stand her up, I pull the comforter back and nod for her to lie back on my sheets. I kick my shorts and boxers off, revealing my rock-hard dick. Lottie's eyes widen like it's the first time she's seeing it.

Moving over top of her I say, "I hope you know how much *this* means to me... you mean so much to me, Lottie." Without letting her respond, I take her lips in mine and say even more with this kiss than I can with my words.

Lottie kisses me back with so much emotion. I have never felt this much want and complete need just from a kiss. I reach down and grab my cock, sliding it up and down her wet pussy. She breaks our kiss to watch me move through her folds. Moaning, she says, "Keep doing that—yes. God, that and my taste on your lips has me ready to come again." I chuckle when I feel her body twitch slightly.

With my hand still on my dick, I move to her opening and press the tip slightly in.

"Relax Babygirl, I've got you." Even as wet as she is, Lottie still tenses as I break through her barrier. She squeezes her eyes closed, pushing through the initial pain.

"This first time is such a special gift; it means the world to me. I'm sorry it's uncomfortable for you." I lean down, peppering kisses all over her face. "But I promise, next time I'm inside of you—Fuck…" I shudder as her tightness grips my cock. I need to take a moment before I embarrass myself.

"I'm okay, Grey, I promise. This means everything to me." She pauses and her eyes relax as she opens them to look at me. "It's easing off," she says as she looks down at my dick entering her pussy, moaning.

That has me looking down as well, and I can't lie, seeing her blood on my cock sets off something primal inside of me.

I pick up my pace but still take it easy on her. Soon, I will fuck every inch of her in every way known to man, but tonight is about so much more than that.

Getting more comfortable, she leans up to me as I instinctually go to her. Our tongues and lips collide, but our eyes stay open and on each other.

Something happens. I don't even think I can put it into words. Feeling it in my heart… No, in my soul. I know I'm inside of her, but it somehow feels like a piece of her just implanted itself in me.

"I don't ever want this to end," she says as I pull back, not sure if she means this moment or us in general.

*Me either baby, me either.*

Grabbing her full breasts with my free hand, I whisper, "Fuck Lottie, I can't get enough of you. I want to touch every inch of you every second of every day." She moans my name as I caress her.

"Grey, I—this is all so much. I didn't expect all—all of this," she says as she rubs my chest. Hearing the implication of her words has me twisted up even more.

"Neither did I. This is unforgettable... you are unforgettable, Lottie."

Her body is writhing underneath me. I know this feels good to her, but I also know she is probably too sore to come from her G spot. I'm struggling to hold it together. "Fuck baby, I'm going to come. I've been hard for you since the moment I met you, so I'm lucky I made it this far."

Stroking her, in and out. Storing every single detail deep in my brain. She reaches up and pinches her pretty pink nipple. Seeing her touch herself does me in.

I come deep inside her. I don't think I have ever come so hard and long in my life.

As I come down from the high, I look down at the sexy girl underneath me... her hazel eyes are still blown out. Lottie is panting. Those beautiful tits of hers are rising and falling quickly. Her long brown hair is the epitome of sex hair, all over the place, and her plump lips have sweat glistening above them. My girl is literally oozing sex appeal from her pores.

Lottie speaks up in a husky tone. "Fuck Grey, seeing you come was the hottest thing I have ever seen in my life, and feeling you release inside me... I didn't think I could be any more turned on, but you've proven me wrong again."

Her words have me ready to go again. But another thought pops in. Fuck, I was so into her I didn't use a condom.

"Babygirl, please tell me you're on the pill. I was so caught up I didn't even think. Fuck, I'm sorry."

She reaches up and tenderly strokes my cheek. "Don't worry, I'm on the pill. Ethel insisted I start it a few years ago."

"Never thought I'd appreciate that woman, but thank fuck, because I don't think I could stand ever using a condom with you."

She giggles, then shifts her hips beneath me.

Knowing her clit is sensitive from her earlier orgasm, I shift my body off hers and place my thumb to it as I suck on her nipple and nibble, remembering she enjoyed that earlier.

She lets out a moan that is more like a plea. My girl wants to come again.

"Hold on baby, I've got you."

I take my hand that is between her legs and move two fingers down further, where I feel the evidence of my orgasm leaking from her.

Now I am officially hard as a rock again.

I can't help but massage it around, using it to lubricate her clit, and continue rubbing her, bringing her closer.

"Oh Greyson, that feels so good. Yesss... please, just like that."

I keep my attention on her sweet spot. Knowing by the way she is wiggling beneath me and muttering unrecognizable words, she's getting close.

Her legs start to press together, and I know better than to stop the rhythm of my fingers.

Within seconds she is squeezing her beautiful thick thighs and I feel her clit pulsing as she moans my name long and loud.

She lays there so relaxed, and sexy as fuck... so MINE. I swoop down to pick her up, and kissing her again, I say, "Thank you for giving me that. I don't deserve you."

Lottie places her hand on my face. "Don't say that G, you have opened my eyes to so much about myself. I wouldn't have wanted to give that to anyone else. No one else could ever compare to you. I want to see myself the way you see me and because of you, I'm getting there."

Words have never meant so much to me. A sharp pain hits me deep in my chest. This girl is turning me inside out.

"Let's get you in the shower baby because after that it's time for you to pop my cherry."

She looks at me with a curious smirk on her face. "And how exactly am I supposed to do that, sir?"

"You get to take my snuggling virginity. I've never slept in a bed with a girl, let alone held her, but I'm ready to spoon the fuck out of you."

She giggles as I put her down and says, "That makes me want to be your one and only snuggle buddy. Your first and last."

Reaching in to turn the shower on, I wink at her. "I think I'm okay with that."

First *and* last. Her one and only. If I can just convince her to keep me.

# Chapter Nine

The past month has been spent with either my brain or my hands on Lottie.

Ever since our first time together, Lottie has been my little feen. Not that I'm complaining, I sink myself inside her every chance she gives me.

When I'm not at work, she's with me, hell even sometimes when I am at work, she is with me.

Other than the occasional guilt trip from her grandmother to take part in one of her charades, Lottie spends all her time with me.

I can see a big difference in Lottie's confidence, and I'll be damned if I let Ethel tear it down any more than she already has. So, I was wary when she convinced me to do lunch with her grandmother at her house. No insults were made toward Lottie, which meant I kept my mouth shut and played along. I know Ethel has some ulterior motives up her sleeves, she seems to be a very calculated woman.

Lottie is free most weekends, since Ethel has to return to Richmond Hills for "business" often. Makes me wonder why she's gone all weekend when, in all actuality, she's really not *that* far from Nori Beach. Whatever the case, it gives Lottie the freedom to do as she pleases, including sleepovers at my place. My aunt thinks Lottie is the best thing since sliced bread and never gives me a hard time about her staying over.

I mean, I'm eighteen now, but at the end of the day it's her home and I respect her. Thankfully, she doesn't care because waking up with Lottie in my bed is one of my favorite things about this summer.

I find myself wanting to... no, needing to spend every second I can with her.

The week Ashley came to town, I thought I was going to lose my fucking mind. I had to share my time with Lottie, and I realized right then and there I don't share well. Thankfully, since Ashley put Trent out of his misery, we did a lot of double dating that week.

Lottie thrives off her relationship with her best friend. I gained a whole new respect for Ashley with the way she constantly boosted my girl up and just all around showed her nothing but love. I already knew how big Lottie's heart was by how she treats me and everyone else she meets. Shit, she even treats her asshole grandmother with respect. But seeing her with Ashley just reiterated how much love she has for those close to her.

I couldn't help but be a little jealous. Not that I don't want her to have that with Ashley, but because I also want her to have that with me.

I want us to be unbreakable, everlasting.

During Ashley's visit, Lottie planned a birthday campout for me on the beach. It was the best birthday I can ever remember having. She even let me bend her perfect ass over our favorite rock at the lookout while the fireworks burst across the sky in the distance.

The way she gives it as good as she takes it... Damn, I would've never believed she was a virgin a month ago if I didn't know any better.

Tonight, I'm cooking for her and we're having a little date night at my place. I've only had the opportunity to cook for her one other time this summer and that time I grilled more than anything, but I plan to show her what I've really got tonight.

I spent a lot of time with my grandparents after my mom left us. If I wasn't working on the truck or a bike with my dad and grandpa, then I was in the kitchen with my Nana. And if you ask any Richmond Hills Rebel Knight, no one cooks as good as Dot Rexwood. So, I called her up today and she refreshed my memory on everything needed to make the perfect fried chicken, mac and cheese, butter beans, and corn pudding.

The fact I'm taking the time to do all this just shows how far gone I am for this girl.

My nana was all excited and told me she was going to beat my ass if I didn't bring Lottie home with me soon. She said I better not be like my aunt who met a man in Nori Beach and never came back home. Nana acts like the beach is a thousand miles away. In reality, my aunt has always been good about coming home at least once a month to see all of us since it's only a two-hour drive.

Right after I put the corn pudding in the oven, my phone dings three times back-to-back. Thinking it's Stacks and hoping she's telling me she is running early, I rush to look at it. But it's not my girl, it's my best friends and this little "Bro Chat" that Ford started.

I give him shit for being needy, but in all reality, these guys are like brothers to me, so our daily texts put a smile on my face, which prior to Lottie, was a rarity.

*Nox: Hey Dickheads*
*Nox: G just saw your dad at the gym, dude's look-*

> *ing swole. You are never going to surpass him if you've been slacking like I think you have this summer.*
> **Ford:** *Yeah, he's gone and gotten himself all pussy whipped. He'll probably come home not knowing how to lift or fight since he can't make any time for the gym these days.*

Smiling, but shaking my head at these two. We live to get a rise out of each other.

My boy Nox is going to be a big deal one day in the fighting world. Ford and I get the unlucky privilege of helping him train. I love to fight too, but not to the extent Nox does. I hope like hell to be cheering from his corner in the UFC one day.

> **Me:** *Both of you shut the fuck up. I'll still knock you the fuck out Ford.*
> **Me:** *I have still been active... just in other ways.*

I know damn well they'll take that sexually, *which is also true*, but I'm still doing calisthenic exercises and swimming laps. I want to stay in shape for football and sparring at the gym. My coach is already going to bench me for at least the first game or two because I'm missing summer practices. I made a deal with my coach that if I came to camp with the team and promised to work out on my own time, he would still let me play this season. Luckily, we went to football camp the week before I met Lottie. I love playing football, but I don't live and breathe it like others. I came to Nori Beach so I could save my money for what I really want to do in life. Now that I've met Lottie, I'm even more thankful I made that decision.

> *Ford: Oh, I bet you have... pussy must be good if it
> has you coming back for seconds.*

I know he's used to joking like that with me, but I practically
growl, texting him back.

> *Me: Don't ever mention my girl's pussy again. This
> is so much more than that and I don't even give a
> fuck if y'all want to rag on me about her. Trust me,
> if either of you had a girl like her, you would feel the
> exact same way I do.*
> *Ford: Damn, it is true...*
> *Nox: See I told you Rex said his boy was in love.
> His sappy ass was all happy about it too.*

That sounds like my dad, but I'm not discussing this with them
before I've even had a chance to talk with Lottie.

My feelings for her came on so fast that until recently, I hadn't
even tried to decipher them, but I know, without a doubt, I am
in love with Lottie.

A week or two ago, when our fucking turned slow, and
our eyes wouldn't leave each other's, the words came out of
nowhere into my head. I held back saying them aloud because
I know she deserves more than just lust-filled words.

After thinking about those three words regarding how I truly
feel about Lottie... I know there's no question.

> *Me: I'm hoping to bring her home before school
> starts back up. I'll let you guys know so you can
> meet her. But you fuckers better be on your best
> behavior.*
> *Nox: Well you better hurry up, you only have a little
> over two weeks. We need to see this situation in*

*person.*
**Ford:** *Don't worry... I'll turn my charm all the way up and have her wanting to leave you for me. You know the ladies love this face.*

I shake my head even though he can't see me.

**Me:** *Not a chance in Hell Pretty Boy.*

Ford acts like he hates that nickname, but secretly we know the cocky fucker loves it. He's the most outgoing out of us three and the biggest player too.

**Me:** *Alright hate to cut this shit short but my girl is coming over soon, so I gotta go.*

I put my phone down because I know they'll give me a little more hell before cutting it out for the night, and I really need to get to cooking the rest of the food.

I miss those guys. I know Lottie will love them and vice versa. They may talk a lot of shit, but I know I can trust them with my life... and with my girl.

\*\*\*

# *Lottie-*

Walking into Greyson's pool house, I'm hit with the intoxicating scent of dinner. I don't even bother to knock anymore, that's how comfortable I've become coming over here. Thankfully, Trent doesn't mind either. Well, at least according to Grey, he doesn't care.

Trent's been a little down these past few weeks. Can't say I blame him. I know he and Ashley will work their shit out, somehow, but being the peacemaker I am, I've been trying to cheer him up with baked goods. Greyson complains when I come over with a tin, saying the guys are right and he won't be conditioned for football come fall. But let me tell you, his ass is the first to the cookie box when I arrive. They're both suckers for a standard chocolate chip cookie. Pssh... amateurs. Makes me feel good when I whip out some of the real tasty recipes and they go nuts for them.

I head towards the kitchen where Greyson is busy cooking up a storm. The music is loud and he's so enthralled with what he's doing, I don't think he heard me come in.

He is so damn handsome. My heart swells at the sight of him. How am I going to survive living so far away from him? Away from the man I, without a doubt, love with every fiber of my being? I've known it for quite some time, even before we first had sex. Being too afraid to scare him away with my overwhelming feelings had me locking them up tight. But I can't end this summer without him knowing how much he means to me. How much I want what we have to work, despite the distance.

I place the cookie tin on the counter just as Greyson turns around and smiles at me. In one swift movement, he picks me up in a hug and twirls me around.

"Fuck dinner. You look more tempting," he says, placing me back down.

"Oh stop. Damn, it smells so good in here." I playfully swat at his arm.

He's staring at me with a look I know all too well.

"Will you stop! You're insatiable."

I swear we bang like three times a day.

"Pretty girl, when it comes to you... it will never be enough."

Laughing and shaking my head, I walk over to the stove where several pots are. I want to see what's hidden beneath all these lids. I feel him approach behind me, his hands grabbing my ass.

"God, I fucking love this ass and these shorts... but this shirt has me about ready to take you on this counter." I blush as his hands travel up to my boobs and he squeezes. I'm wearing a simple tank top that hugs my body, not something I would have ever worn in the past.

"I've never felt comfortable wearing something like this outside of my own house." I spin around to face him. Peering into his eyes, I continue, "Being with you has helped me embrace my body. The way you look at me, the way you make me feel about myself... No one has ever made me feel the way you do. I—"

Just then, the loud kitchen timer goes off and I scurry away from the stove, but not before Greyson pulls me in for a deep kiss.

"There's nothing I want more than to see you smile every day, and to know I'm the one that's putting it there."

He turns to take care of whatever needs his attention. Jumping up onto the counter across from him so I'm not in his way, I can't help but admire Greyson's ass in his jeans as he moves around the kitchen. So plump and firm, it must look even better in his football pants.

Mmm, the thought of him all sweaty on the field... I'll have to make it to one of his games in the fall. *If he wants me there.*

"You're awfully quiet. What are you thinking about?" he says over his shoulder.

"How nice your ass probably looks in your football uniform," I say with no shame. That earns me a deep laugh from Greyson.

"You'll have to see me in action." He winks and delivers a devilish smirk.

"That's what I was thinking."

"Okay, food's just about ready. Want to grab us drinks? I set the table out on the patio already," Greyson says while pulling a dish out of the oven.

I grab a soda for him from the fridge and refill my water, then head out through the French doors that lead to the back patio.

A big smile spreads across my face as I set our drinks down. He's so fricken cute, I can't even.

Greyson has a vase of the most gorgeous shade of purple hydrangeas in the middle of the table. *He remembered.* I mentioned them being my favorite in passing one day and he actually remembered.

What did I do to deserve someone so thoughtful and attentive? I look up to the sky and send a silent thank you to my mom. She must have sent him to me, knowing exactly what I needed.

I head back inside to help bring out whatever else we need. But instead, I stop to throw my arms around him and take his lips in mine. I kiss him deeply and passionately. He's too damn perfect.

When we break away for air, I can't stop the words that fly out. "I love you Greyson—so much it scares me."

His eyes widen at first, but moments later his lips are crashing into mine once again. "You make my heart beat out of my chest every time I even think of you babe. You're everything I could have ever wanted. I love you too, Lottie, so fucking much."

Greyson's thumb wipes away the stray tear that has fallen on my cheek. "You're so fucking beautiful, I love everything about you." He leans down and kisses my nose. "I'm so lucky to call you mine."

We kiss some more, savoring the moment. With my arms around his neck and his lips all over me, I feel like I could stay like this forever.

"Babygirl, if we don't stop, I'm going to drag you to my room and all this cooking will be for nothing."

I respond with a childish whine and pout my lips.

"But don't you worry, I have something special planned for dessert," he says with that sly smile of his.

My body, already brimming with lust, is ready to say screw dinner and let's skip to the good stuff, but I know how hard he worked on this meal.

"Okay, handsome, I look forward to it," I say suggestively while grazing my hand over the semi tenting his pants.

"Fuck, I love you," he says as he swats my ass. "Now grab a dish and let's eat so I can devour you."

\*\*\*

Dinner was absolutely delicious. My man can cook!

Sitting on the patio was so romantic, he timed dinner perfectly with sunset and it was breathtaking to watch. There's something to be said about a Carolina sunset. The way the vast open sky takes on the vibrant colors of the rainbow and the way those colors deepen as the sun sets over the distant tree line, really makes you stop and just admire its beauty.

I sit there twirling my bracelet as I watch the last of the sun dip below the horizon, thinking about how happy I am at this very moment and how long it's been since I've felt this way.

The sound of Greyson's chair scraping the floor beside me grabs my attention. "What's going on in that pretty little head of yours?"

"Just thinking about how happy I am and what a fantastic summer it's been." I beam a megawatt smile at him. He smiles and pulls a small box from his pocket.

"I got you something..."

Looking at him with a surprised look on my face, I say, "What do you mean? You didn't have to get me anything."

"I've had it for a while now, actually, just wasn't sure of the right time to give it to you," he says as he hands me the small white box with a blue bow. "I hope you like it."

Sliding the lid off quickly, I'm excited to see what's inside.

I'm taken aback by a gorgeous silver anchor charm with a rope tied throughout it in the shape of an infinity symbol. "Greyson, this is beautiful. Thank you." I quickly clip the charm onto my bracelet, admiring its detail.

"I saw it one day and thought it was perfect for you... for us." He looks at me with love in his eyes. "My dad always said that one day I'd find my anchor in life. Something that's solid and true, giving me strength, no matter how rough life gets... You're my anchor, Babygirl, and I would be lost without you."

"Oh Greyson. I love you so much. I'll be your anchor just as you are mine. Always."

I quickly scramble from my seat to get to him. He pushes his chair away from the table, knowing all too well that I'm about to throw myself at him. Once I'm straddling his lap, I kiss him like I've never kissed him before, so deeply passionate and full of emotion. I'm grinding myself onto his hardness and feel swelling beneath me. He lets out a moan as I rock my hips.

"I love you too Babygirl, no matter how far, always." He kisses me gently, placing each of his hands on the sides of my face. "We will make this work, someway, somehow, we will make this distance thing work. There is no way I'm letting you go."

# Chapter Ten

Greyson

Sitting here beside my girl watching the sunset, I can't help but feel an overwhelming fear of doom. Long distance scares the fuck out of me. We currently have one week left of our time here in Nori Beach.

It's been almost two months. And damn if the time hasn't gone by faster than any summer in my whole life. I have no doubt that I can wait for Lottie, and I'll do whatever it takes to be with her, but I can't control everything, including how she will handle the miles between us.

Today, Lottie came to have lunch at The Shack while I worked the midday rush. Once I finished my shift, we came to spend the afternoon at the beach.

We've been out here swimming, relaxing, talking about anything and everything. I've been doing a lot of admiring, loving the fact she is feeling confident enough to wear a bikini. And let me tell you, she is wearing the damn thing, showing all those jaw-dropping curves.

Some guys, probably about ten years older than us, were gawking at her earlier as we walked down the beach. Until they caught my death glares and had enough decency to wipe the drool from their chins.

"We still have two more questions in our game!" Lottie breaks me out of my thoughts.

We've been playing an interesting game of twenty-one questions. It's been funny for the most part except for question number seven. "How many girls have you been with, and do you have a regular back home?" Everything in my brain screamed... Avoid, Avoid, Avoid. But I knew I couldn't, so I answered as honestly as I could without putting doubts in her head. "Do you really want to know the answer to the first part? And as for the second part... No, not anymore."

I hated how she dipped her chin after that, a habit of hers that we've broken this summer.

"Chin up Babygirl, like I said, not anymore. I would never give up what I have with you over someone who has never meant more to me than just a hookup. I promise you that. You have my heart and soul, Lottie."

That seemed to make her feel better. I hate that my past creates doubts for her, but I get it. I'm no saint and I have secrets that could ruin us, which is why the next question that comes is a tough one...

"Okay, so question number twenty, G, tell me your deepest, darkest secret," she says with an evil little smirk.

Not necessarily lying, but I am omitting my darkest secret for another deep secret that I've never discussed with anyone else.

"The year I got my license I went to Casen, a Rebel Knight's brother. At the time, he was a new prospect, and had just starting doing some PI work after leaving the police department. I begged him to get my mom's latest address but to keep it between us. Told him it would just hurt my dad to know and that I would do some free work on his bike in exchange for his time and silence." I take a deep breath because the past hurt me more than I like to admit.

"He got me the info a couple of weeks later. Surprised the hell out of me when I realized her address was only one town over from me, in Highland. I mean, I hadn't spoken to her in over nine years, and she was still living so close to me. It made me want answers that much more. So, I jumped on my bike and drove the twenty minutes to her place and I sure as shit did not expect to see what I saw." Knowing I need her, Lottie moves to sit in my lap and kisses my cheek.

"I pulled up to this huge mansion about the size of my aunt's place. I was shocked. My mom was just a club chick from the rough part of town. How in the hell was this huge house where she lived? My dad had mentioned she remarried a man with money, but I didn't realize how much money..."

The feelings of being that abandoned kid start to seep in again. *What mom leaves their son for fucks sake?*

My dad worked his ass off to make sure I grew up right. My family and the Rebel Knights helped us get through that rough time in our lives, but the hurt of being deserted by my own mother lives deep inside me.

"It was the end of the summer before school started back. I heard laughing and splashing coming from the backyard. When I went around back, she was sitting on the side of the pool while two boys, probably six and eight years old, played in the pool. There was another boy, probably around my age. He sat on the diving board with his feet swinging over the water. They were all smiles and happiness."

I remember my mind was going a mile a minute, like maybe she was their nanny or even a stepmom, until one of the little boys looked at me. Not only did he see me, but I also saw him. He had the same smile and dimple that I have.

"One of the boys spoke up when he saw me. 'Mom, who's that?' I was still standing there in shock. It took me a second to hear that he'd called her mom. She turned towards me and about jumped out of her skin. It had been almost nine years since she had last seen me, and I suspect she thought I looked a lot like my dad."

I pause until Lottie encourages me to keep going. "Did you talk to her?"

I nod my head. "Yeah, she got up and came over to me. Basically, she told me she missed me and how I could move there with her, my two half-brothers, older stepbrother, and her new husband. She kept saying how she could give me an amazing life now because she was loaded. I told her she was nine years too late and maybe if she had ever reached out, I would've consider it. I had just one question for her... why did she leave us?"

"What was her response? Either way, I know it wasn't good enough because how anyone could ever leave you... I will never understand." Hearing her say that makes me hopeful.

"She said she could never be "*Her*" and my dad would never truly love her. She wasn't enough for either of us and she knew that from the moment she trapped him by getting pregnant with me."

Lottie looks at me with confusion and I continue. "My dad was in love with another woman before he and my mom hooked up... my mom came along not too long after it ended. I don't think his heart was healed at all. He loved my mom as the mother of his child, but I don't think he ever gave her his full heart. I only ever saw my dad treat my mom with care and devotion. I understand that not being enough for her but still... she didn't have to leave me too."

Now that I'm older I do get my mom wanting every part of my dad, especially his whole heart. If Lottie could only give me half of herself, I don't know that I could deal either. My dad and I had this talk once he thought I was old enough. He tried so hard for me. I remember him saying he knew she deserved someone a hundred percent in love with her, but he never thought she would leave me because of his inability to.

He's apologized a million times over his broken heart causing me pain, but at the end of the day, he knows just like I do that my mother chose to leave not just him but me too... her flesh and blood. I think maybe she would have come back for me if she hadn't found someone with so much to offer. The greed got to her and became more important than even me.

I turn to her and look into her eyes, hoping she can see the hurt there, the distrust I still hold. "I'll never forget that sickening feeling of being left behind for an upgraded version of what she already had."

"Oh Grey, I'm so sorry." I see her eyes welling up with tears while she grabs my hand in hers. "There is no better version of you. You are the most amazing man, always so strong and protective. I knew your mom left, but I didn't realize there was so much hurt and turmoil behind it. I can honestly and whole-heartedly say it is her loss. You are an incredible human being."

*If you only knew.*

"Unfortunately, I've made mistakes in my past. Some I'm not very proud of, but *you* make me better. Lottie, you make me want to be the best man I can be for you. I want you to be proud that you are mine and I am yours."

"Greyson, you have no idea. Being yours has given me a better outlook for the future. It's terrifying to think about what happens when the summer ends, but I do know I never want to be anything but yours."

Pulling her face to mine, I kiss her long and hard before I point out to the water and say, "You could put that whole ocean between us, but even that won't keep us apart." Whispering in her ear I add, "Mine, always."

My chest aches with a memory of Lottie sleeping in my bed. Two nights ago, I woke up disoriented from the night before. I looked over and saw her lying beside me. Seeing the slow rise and fall of her chest immediately put me at ease. Until another emotion took over... lust. She was twisted up in my sheets, her perfect ass on full display with a tiny g-string in place. Long, dark hair covered most of her face and breasts, with just enough of a view to tease me. She had this cute little smile on her face. Lottie looked so comfortable, peaceful, happy, and completely mine. My morning wood turned to stone as my eyes roamed all over her. Feeling the extreme need to capture the sex goddess laying in my bed, I grabbed my phone and snapped a picture. Then I woke my girl up with her g-string pulled to the side and my face between her legs.

*I'm going to miss nights like that.*

"Yours, Baby," she says breathlessly. "I don't want this to end. I will come visit you in Richmond Hills every month and you can come stay with me in the city too. We can make this work. Grey, tell me you want that? Tell me we can make this work?"

"I don't ever want to give you up. I know it won't be easy but I'm right there with you, we can make this work." I pull her short frame to my chest and continue. "Nothing will keep me from you, Babygirl."

She cups my face. "You promise?"

"I promise you," I say right before sealing my mouth over hers. Sealing our words with this kiss because I feel it deep in my bones. She was meant for me.

\*\*\*

"I know the story about you inheriting the truck since Ol' Girl was so special to you and your grandpa... but what about your bike? When did you start to ride? How old were you when you got your first one?"

Looking over, I see Lottie's beautiful sun-kissed faced riding shotgun in my truck. She is so cute when she starts to get tired.

Her mouth doesn't stop moving, and she gets all giggly. The long day out in the sun definitely drained us both.

Before I can answer, she says, "I'm sorry. I just want to know everything I can about the guy I love."

Hearing her say that will never get old.

Messing with her, I say, "I know, baby, I just didn't know if we were playing Twenty-One Questions again or what?"

She backhands my upper arm from her side of the truck. "Oh shut up, Grey, you enjoyed every second of that game!"

"Ouch." I laugh. "Okay tough stuff, I'll answer more of your questions."

"The minute my dad saw I could maintain two wheels on a bicycle, he bought me my first dirt bike and I've been riding on motorized two wheels ever since. I got my first motorcycle when I was fifteen, between birthday money and side jobs. I was determined to buy it for myself. Luckily my dad's best friend Gunnar, gave me a sweet deal on a bike he was selling."

The memory has me chuckling. "Boy was his daughter pissed. She thought he was saving it for her, so she went out the next week and bought another club brother's used bike just to piss him off." Another important person to me that Lottie needs to meet. "His daughter's name is Frankie; she's like a sister, we grew up together. She's basically the girl version of me, so I have a feeling you'll love her."

Lottie snuggles in a little closer to me on the bench seat. "I love hearing about all your family and friends back home. Everyone seems so awesome. Hopefully, I can come down for a long weekend during the fall so I can meet everybody."

*I don't want to wait that long.*

"Well, actually, I've been meaning to ask you about that. The Rebel Knights are having a family cookout at the clubhouse next Saturday, during the day. Ford also said one of our football teammates is throwing a party that night so we could go back for the day and night. That way, you can meet everyone. Would you want to come with me?"

Taking my eyes off the road for a sec to look at her, I see a big smile on her face that quickly fades to sadness.

"Ughhh, I want to so, so bad, but Ethel already had me confirm some BS luncheon at her house with some people she needs to schmooze. Apparently, I have to do it before I go back home because she hasn't asked much of me this summer."

"Seriously Lottie, fuck her. You shouldn't be manipulated into doing her dirty work. Ditch her ass and come meet everyone. They're driving me crazy wanting to meet you."

Huffing again, before she says, "I know Greyson, but she's my mom's mother at the end of the day and some of the only family I have left. I promise the first free weekend I have back home I will be on a flight right to you and everyone you love in Richmond Hills."

Not satisfied with her answer but not wanting to be a dick because I know the loss of her mother and great-grandmother has been hard on her I don't press anymore.

"I'm so sorry G, I wish I could get out of it."

I remain silent for a few so I don't say something about Ethel I will regret.

Lottie reaches over, putting her hands on my chest, and looks up at me with those pretty need-you hazel eyes of hers. "Don't be mad, baby." Then her hands trail down my torso and towards my belt. "Let me make it up to you... please."

Knowing I would never say no to what she's offering, I decide I don't want to wait till we're home. We're approaching a side road I recognize ahead, and with her hand now down my boxers and on my dick, Lottie asks, "Where are we going?"

"Don't worry about it. You just keep doing what you're doing," I say as I pull into the old parking lot. This restaurant was popular when I was a kid, but several years ago, they moved to a beachfront location and this spot has been vacant ever since.

She huffs and tugs on my cock. "Ooo broody Greyson, I kinda like it. Even though you normally save that attitude for others."

I want to smile, but I decide to play it up a bit. "You haven't seen anything yet, Babygirl." Lifting my hips, I tug my pants down more to give her better access. "Now put my cock in your mouth."

Lottie's eyes turn black, and she literally moans before leaning down to do just as I said. She sucks me just how I've taught her this summer. So fucking perfect. Her eagerness plus her unashamed questions about what I like has made her an expert at giving head.

"You suck me just right," I say as I rub my hand down her back to pull her dress up, exposing her bathing suit bottoms before I pull it down. She helps by shimmying them off, but quickly gets back to sucking me.

Trailing my fingers down her ass crack until I get down to her slick, wet center, Lottie moans a "please" right as I stick two fingers in her pussy. In and out, back and forth, just like my dick in her throat.

Wanting her to come while she rides me, I push her up, letting my dick pop out of her mouth. "Scoot over. I'm going to move to the center, so you have more room to straddle me without the steering wheel in your back. I want you to ride what's yours."

She doesn't respond with words; my eager girl moves right away. "Take your top off while you're at it. I want to see those tits bounce with you."

Once she is bare for me, I pull her onto my lap and in one full thrust upward, she's seated completely on my dick. Lottie rolls her hips around in a circular motion to adjust to my size before she starts moving up and down.

"Fuck, your pussy feels so good," I moan out as she leans down to take my mouth in hers. Pulling me as close to her as possible, she continues to ride me while devouring my mouth. Lottie is so worked up and ready to explode, rubbing her clit on me in this close position.

I pull back enough to bite her bottom lip and move to her neck, licking up towards her ear and nibbling on her earlobe. I love the way every part of her tastes.

Grabbing her thick ass with my rough hands as I whisper, "Come on my cock pretty girl. I want to feel you so tight around me that I can barely handle it." Finding her perfect rhythm, I can see in her expressions and hear it in her moans she's about to let go.

Lottie's already tight pussy squeezes me like a vise as her eyes roll to the back of her head. Visions of her coming like this are never far from my mind.

"Fuck yes baby, I'm not done with you yet though..." I say as I move us towards the passenger side door and push it open. "Do you think you can stand for a second?" She nods her sated face.

Getting out of the truck with Lottie still in my arms, I stand her up but spin her around so she is facing towards the truck, giving me the perfect view of her ass. I push her upper back forward so her soft stomach and heavy tits are pressed down into the seat of the truck with that ass on display for me.

I spank her because I know she loves it, using it as a warning before burying myself into her.

Watching her ass shake while I slam into it from the back is a sight no man deserves, especially not me.

We both love this position. Lottie loves the angle and I love the view.

Seeing my dick get lost in her ass cheeks as it enters her pussy has me spreading her cheeks apart so I can see more.

"Fuck Lottie, why are you so perfect? Your body was made for me. You were made for me."

I can feel the tingle build in my balls as I get close. When Lottie says, "Harder G, fuck me harder." I'm pretty sure I start to go right there. Almost feeling guilty by how hard I'm pounding into her until I feel her start to pulse. She comes again as she screams my name. I make a rash decision to make a fantasy of mine come to life by pulling my cock out of her and shooting my cum all over her big, beautiful ass.

When I come back to, she pants, "Fuck, I think I had another mini orgasm when you came on me."

Welp, guess I don't have to worry about her being upset I got her messy. Fantasy complete.

Turning her around, I give her a loving peck on the lips. "That was so fucking hot. You know how much I love you, right?"

Lottie nods. "And I love you more than all the waves in the ocean... Does that mean I'm forgiven?" she says with a hesitant laugh.

"It's all good Babygirl. You know I can't stay mad at you for long."

*Or at least that's what I thought.*

*** 

Pulling up to Ethel's beach house, I'm ready to see my girl.

She said they should be done by late afternoon. Just in case they're still inside having tea or whatever the fuck rich people do, I decided to head out back to the gazebo that Lottie uses as her reading nook. Plus, that means I hopefully get to avoid Ethel.

I was pretty damn disappointed when Lottie told me she couldn't go home with me today because of some bullshit uppity lunch she had to do with her grandmother.

I hate Ethel using her like a pawn in the little games she plays. She is nothing but a puppet master, and I'm so ready for Lottie to get to the point where she tells her to fuck off. Even though Lottie's mom couldn't stand her own mother, I know it's still hard for Lottie to give up hope on Ethel because she doesn't have much family left.

I park my truck on the road and walk through the gate so I don't draw any attention to myself, heading around the left side of the house towards the backyard where the gazebo sits. I shoot Lottie a quick text telling her where I'll be when she's done.

Looking ahead, I notice two people sitting in the gazebo. A few more footsteps closer and my heart and steps falter.

Lottie is sitting there with none other than Jacob Roberts. That rich fucking prick. Her back is to me so I can't see her face, but they are way too fucking close for my liking. Then he leans over and brushes her hair back from her face. She doesn't lean into him, but she doesn't back away either. The smile on his face tells me this is no friendly get-together. This guy wants what is mine... I see black.

Willing myself to calm down before I beat the fucking shit out of this boy, I stop in my tracks. I can't believe she chose this shit over coming home with me.

This was her "dumb lunch"?

For something she wanted nothing to do with, she seems awfully content right now. I'm so fucking furious I can't see straight. How could she brush this off as if it was nothing?

*You know what*—Fuck. This. Shit.

If she wants to be with someone like that, then she can have him. I'm out of here.

Right as I go to turn around, I see her head pull back and she says something to him. Then her body turns in my direction, seeing me for the first time, and a look of horror takes over her beautiful face.

Our eyes meet for only a moment, and I feel like I'm going to throw up or rage out. I don't need this shit. Unable to cope with this situation right now, I continue to turn away and head towards my bike.

I hear her coming after me, but I refuse to give that prick the show he probably wants.

I need to clear my head before talking to Lottie. I know this is fucked up. I can hear her sounding more frantic each time she calls out to me, but she can't see me like this. And I sure as fuck can't talk to her when I'm this out of my mind with anger and jealousy, especially not with him around.

Lottie makes it around the front of the house as I'm almost to my motorcycle. She's yelling my name, begging me to stop.

I turn towards her and put my hand up. "No, Lottie." She surprisingly listens, stopping in her tracks and locking tear-filled eyes on mine.

Seeing her so upset has me ready to say screw it and go to her... until I see *him* as he comes up behind her.

I can't have this conversation right now. There's so much more that she doesn't understand.

"I just need some time. I'll call you later."

Tuning her out as she calls my name again, I jump on my motorcycle and get the hell out of dodge.

Fuck, I can barely breathe. The air feels like it's been knocked out of my lungs.

I am in this so deep, just seeing another man near her has vomit burning the back of my throat.

Logically I know she didn't do anything wrong, and she came after me not giving a shit what he thought, but still...

How long will it be before she decides he's the type of guy she really wants to be with? She lives nine hundred miles away for fuck's sake.

But I need her. I love her.

I also need a distraction to clear my head before I talk to her, and I know the perfect place to go for that.

# Chapter Eleven

Shit Shit Shit!!

"Greyson!" My last call to him is drowned out by the noise of his engine as his bike rips down the road.

I drop to my knees as a sob rips out of my throat. No, no, no. It's not what he thinks. I would never do that to him... I'm not his mother.

I hear Jacob's footsteps approach behind me.

"Charlotte, are you okay?" he asks as he crouches next to me, placing his hands on my shoulders. I flinch at the contact and quickly stand to distance myself.

"No! I'm not okay."

I dart to the backyard to find my phone. Needing to call him. He needs to know this is all a misunderstanding.

"I'm guessing that was him?" Jacob asks as if he couldn't already figure it out. His footsteps follow closely behind me.

I swing my body around, trotting backwards. I can't waste any time.

"Yes, that was my boyfriend, who clearly got the wrong idea from whatever it is he thinks he saw."

"Oh..." he says, looking a bit perturbed.

I turn back around as I approach the bench where I last saw my cell.

"What do you mean... Oh?" I question over my shoulder.

"I know—I mean, I didn't realize you had a boyfriend until you mentioned it. Ethel never said anything. Shit—I'm sorry."

I huff out as I shake my head. "Of course she didn't. To her, you and I are a match made in heaven."

I grab my phone and shoot off a quick text. Knowing he's on his bike, I won't get an immediate reply, but I have to try.

> **Me:** *It's not what you think... Please call me. I love you and only you.*

I look to see Jacob still standing nearby. Watching me with caution, like I'm some sort of bomb just moments away from detonation. Well, he isn't wrong.

"For what it's worth, I'm truly sorry, Charlotte."

Clutching my phone close, wishing for it to ding with a notification, I excuse myself from Jacob.

"Thank you, but I have to go. I'm sorry Jacob. It was nice to see you again."

I've been around Jacob a few times and he's never made me feel like he wanted me for anything more than a friend. So, when he touched me in the gazebo, I was a little stunned, to say the least. Hearing him say "Ethel didn't mention anything" has me knowing exactly who pushed him to try something with me. I knew her being okay with me and Greyson was too good to be true.

I don't even wait for his reply before I book it through the house and up to my room, avoiding Ethel and Jacob's family.

Hours pass and I only receive a single text response from him. Not a phone call, just one single text.

***Greyson:*** *I just need time to think.*

I know he's saying he needs some time to cool off, but how long is that? By now, he must have several unread texts and at least a half a dozen missed calls from me. How can he not even give me a moment to explain what he thinks he saw?

Ughhhh!

I yell my frustrations into my pillow for what feels like the hundredth time tonight. I'm exhausted. My stomach is in knots and my head is pounding. Not only from the fear that Greyson won't let me explain, but from the berating I got from Ethel after I abruptly disappeared while we still had guests.

Did she know Greyson was there? She went inside moments before it all happened. She must get alerts from the front gate opening. Geez, I know she's manipulative, but I didn't think she was this evil.

"Please answer your phone, Grey, please!" I pray to the sky above as his phone rings out and I hear his voicemail.

I lay there with bloodshot eyes staring at the ceiling. I'm mindlessly twirling my charm bracelet when I hear my phone vibrate from the nightstand. I look at the clock, it's ten o'clock at night. Maybe he just needed time to calm down.

I answer the phone quickly. "Hello."

"Lottie? Hi, it's Sally."

I sit up quickly. Why is she calling me at ten p.m.? Sally has been with us since I was a child. Gigi and Papa hired her when I was little to help around the house, so they could spend as much time with me as possible. She's been with us ever since. She's like a great aunt in a way. Always at family dinners and holidays. She doesn't have family here in the United States, so we treat her as a member of ours. She has her own living quarters in my great-grandparents' house, so she helps a ton with Papa especially now since Gigi is no longer with us and I'm in Nori Beach.

"Hi, Sally, what's going on?"

"Hun, it's your Papa... He just got taken away in an ambulance."

"What? What happened? Why? Is he okay?" I'm diving out of my bed to get clothes on, hanging on every word she says.

"They think he's having a heart attack. They took him to New York Presbyterian hospital."

"I'm on my way. I'll get there as soon as I can. Thank you, Sally." I hang up and frantically throw some things into an overnight bag. I stare at the large stuffed pink unicorn from our first date, if you could even call it that. Unfortunately, it's too big to take on the plane with me, so I'm forced to leave it behind.

I run out of my room and run into Ethel's, finding it empty. I make my way downstairs and hear muffled voices coming from the study.

I hear a man's voice as I approach the wooden double doors that are slightly ajar. I stand just outside the door to listen to what they're saying.

"It's not right, and you know it," I hear the male voice say.

"Oh please, James. It's inevitable," I hear the shrill of Ethel's voice. "I needed to make arrangements, and this is one of them. I can't let everything fall to shit, I have a reputation to uphold."

"This is wrong, you've gone too far," he says, and I hear footsteps approach the door. Shit.

I decide to make my presence known and knock on the door as it slowly opens.

I nod at Ethel and look towards James. "I need a ride to the airport." I then glance at Ethel. "Papa was taken by ambulance to the hospital. They think he's having a heart attack."

The expression on her face doesn't falter or show any emotion. Of course, it wouldn't. She doesn't care about anyone but herself. I don't think she shed a tear when Gigi, her own mother, died.

"Very well, James, can you please drive Charlotte and please make sure she gets on the next flight out?" she asks.

I'm in utter shock. She isn't coming with me?

"You're not coming?" I blurt in pure frustration.

"No darling, I have so much to tend to with the annual gala and all. Please keep me posted. I'm sure he will be just fine."

I have no words. She really is the devil. I don't have time to argue. My life is literally falling apart right before my eyes. Ethel is the least of my worries.

I turn to James, who is looking at me with care and concern. At least someone gives a shit.

"Okay, let's go then," I say as I grab my things and walk towards the door, not bothering to say goodbye to Ethel. What's the point? She doesn't care.

As I watch the streetlights go by, I grab my phone one last time, praying Greyson will answer. I have to tell him what's going on. I didn't even get to say goodbye.

The phone rings for several moments and just as I'm about to end the call, it picks up. I hear loud music and chatter in the background. Is he at that party he was talking about the other day?

"Hello!" I yell into the phone.

"Helloooo!" a slurred female voice responds.

I pull my head back to make sure I dialed the right number.

"Uhm, is Greyson around?" I ask, hoping like hell he's right there.

"I'm sorry he's busy, but who's this?" The voice picks up a more clipped tone.

"It's Lottie, his—" Shit, am I still his girlfriend? Yes, yes I am. We had a fight; we didn't break up. "It's Lottie, his girlfriend."

There's a moment of silence before she speaks. "Ohhh right, the heifer from the beach."

"Excuse me?" I blurt out. *Are you fucking kidding me?*

"Yeah, he told us all about you. His summer fling. This photo he has of you when your number calls was a bit of a shock. I'm surprised he went for a girl your size," she says that last part with a mocking tone.

My silence must make her feel bold because she continues spewing her venom at me.

"Honey, he's not your boyfriend. Greyson Rexwood doesn't do relationships, especially not long-distance ones."

"Can I please speak with him? It's really important." I need to tell him I'm leaving but don't want to feed into her, I know she's baiting me.

"Did you really think a boy like him would want anything more from a girl like you?" When I don't respond, she continues, "Oh, how sweet? You really thought it was more, didn't you?"

I can't believe this is happening right now. Is this really my life? A sob breaks from my lips and I try to muffle the sound with my hand, but she still hears me.

"You poor thing... You must know you were just a hole to keep his cock warm while he was away for the summer. Because let's be real, he would never want something like you long-term. He must have used up all his normal hookups in Nori Beach if he had to start fishing in the plus-sized pond."

"Who are you?" I don't even have words to respond to her, I just need her name. A name to give to a certain group of people I know can make this bitch pay.

"Me?" she feigns innocence. "I'm Amber, and yes, to answer the question. I'm his usual fuck."

"Fuck you!" I blurt as I hang up the phone, sick to my stomach. *What the hell just happened?*

I break down and let the tears fall freely. I've dealt with so much pain in my lifetime, but I have never felt this blindsided. Obviously, he went to that party, but why the hell won't he just answer his phone and why the fuck is he letting that bitch talk to me for him? My phone lights up in my hand. Looking down,

I see I have a message from an "828" number. That's G's area code. Quickly opening up the message, I instantly regret it.

It's a video and even though a big part of my brain is screaming, telling me I don't want to see it, the other half wins out with the need to know. My stomach sours even more because I have a feeling this is going to rip me to shreds.

Pressing play, my stomach immediately lurches.

I know that big frame, those mannerisms, even those grunts. He may not say anything like he does when I'm the one on my knees for him, but I know it's him and I'm guessing this is Amber with his dick in her mouth. Dropping my phone like it's on fire, I think I'm going to be sick.

I can't even form a normal thought right now. Numbness is what I feel. How can this be happening?

Greyson, with another girl, is etched in my brain now. This can't be real.

I think something heavy is pressing down on my chest. I need to get it off me so I can vomit. My hands are trembling uncontrollably. I can't believe he would betray me like this. That he would go to someone like *her* of all people.

I meet James' eyes in the rearview mirror.

"What do you need Miss Lottie?" he asks.

Answering through broken sobs I didn't even know I was crying, I say, "Pull the car over, please."

I can barely register anything happening until James comes around to open my door for me. My hands are on my chest, trying to soothe the overwhelming pain I feel as I get out of the car.

I immediately drop to my knees, feeling the tiny rocks at the edge of the pavement digging into my hands and knees as I hit the ground. James tries to help me stand, probably thinking I fell, but I push him off and then lean forward to empty whatever little bit of food I have in my stomach.

I stay there on my knees for seconds, minutes, hours, I honestly don't know.

I don't snap out of it until James puts a hand on my back and says, "Miss Lottie, your phone is vibrating. Miss Sally is calling you. We need to go so you don't miss your flight."

Hearing Sally's name and knowing that I need to get home to my Papa has me coming out of this surreal nightmare I'm stuck in.

Heading back to the car, James hands me my phone and shuts the door behind me.

I may have exited the car a broken, sad girl, but now I'm a broken, angry-beyond-words girl. Reaching for my phone, I block Greyson's number and the number of whoever sent the video. *Doesn't take a genius to know it was probably that raging slut Amber.* I don't want to hear a word he'll have to say when he realizes the big fucking mistake he made.

Fuck them both. They can have each other. I know I'm worth so much more than Amber any day of the week. So, Greyson can keep his stupid slut for all I care. I can find better. I deserve better.

My heart shatters a little with that lie I'm telling myself. I may not mean it quite yet, but I am determined to get there. Greyson may have helped create the strong, confident girl I was turning into this summer, but it's up to me to maintain her, and I most certainly will.

I slam my head against the seat's headrest and scream with pain and frustration as my heart feels like it's literally cracking into a million pieces. My screams eventually turn into quiet sniffles as the tears continue to fall down my cheeks. I cry, lost in a whirlwind of thoughts of Greyson and me. For everything I thought we had and just lost within a matter of hours. I cry for all of it.

Why? Why did you do this, Greyson?

Why did you make me love you if it was all for nothing?

# PART TWO

# Chapter Twelve

By lunchtime, I am sick of hearing about how smoking hot the new girl is. I know my friends are just trying to help pull me out of my funk. They think I can fuck Lottie out of my system, but what they don't get is she's anchored to my fucking soul.

The past month and a half without her has been pure hell. Luckily for me, I'm not the life of the party anyway, so only those really close to me know I'm struggling.

There's no getting Lottie out of my head either. No matter how pissed I am. Yeah, I was the dick who ran out on her before letting her explain, but I had to get away from there before I did something that would get me in serious trouble. Seeing *him* of all people anywhere near my girl had me feeling fucking murderous.

The next day, when I went back to Nori Beach to explain where my head was at, she was gone. Shortly after that shocking discovery, I realized she had blocked me on everything as well. The Lottie I love would have never given up on me so easily. Part of me thinks her evil-ass grandma had something to do with it.

*Despite that, why wouldn't Lottie have found a way to let me know something? Unless she found out my secrets and didn't want to hear my side of it. No... there's no way.*

I was, and still am, so confused. I want fucking answers.

Trent swears he knows nothing. Ashley told him if he didn't stop trying to fish for information about Lottie, she was going to cut him off. Which coincides with the middle finger emoji and the "Fuck off asshole" message I received back when I reached out to Ashley. I got Trent to agree to let me come up and hang with him the first weekend in November. Since that's the only weekend we won't have a football game, I can fly to New York after practice on Friday. Trent's older brother, Trevor, will pick me up because Trent said he has something going on that Friday he can't miss. I plan to talk to the Rebel Knights' PI, Casen, this week. If he can get me an address for Lottie's great-grandparents' house, that's the first place I'm going when I touch down at JFK.

I honestly wish I had done that weeks ago, but like with the death of a loved one, I went through the stages of grief. At first, I was in complete denial and kept thinking she was going to call me at any minute and explain what the hell happened. Then I was fucking pissed. This is when my dad, Nox, and Ford figured out something was seriously wrong. I was picking fights with everyone, trying to drink my weight in tequila, and harassing Trent about being a Judas-of-a-cousin for not telling me what was going on.

Recently I've been somewhere between that stage and just straight up depressed... a terrible combo. Thank God for football. If the coach hadn't threatened to kick me off the team with my continuous half-ass attempts of maintaining my spot on the D-Line, I probably wouldn't have gotten my head out of my ass. Football has been the distraction I needed. Plus I get to take my anger out on the field.

Ford slaps me on the arm, bringing me back to the present. "G seriously wait till you see the rack on this girl, and she has a fat ass." He fakes dying as he lays across the table, then continues, "She's beautiful too... probably the baddest chick I've ever seen."

I just smirk at his horny ass and shake my head, thinking to myself maybe she is, but he hasn't seen Lottie yet and I know for a fact no one holds a candle to her.

Amber huffs and rolls her eyes at Ford. Just her presence annoys me. She is one of the jock hoppers, the chicks that are always hanging around, just trying to be seen and hook up with us. No matter how many hints I try to drop about not wanting more from her, she still follows me around.

*Why did I ever touch this girl?*

I almost choke on the pizza I'm eating when I see the "fine-ass" new girl walk into the cafeteria with her food tray in hand.

*What the fuck?*

Ford gives me a knowing smile. "See G, I told you... baddest you've ever seen right? I knew she would be your type. All innocent but sexy at the same time." Amber scoffs and I'm stunned into silence.

I am utterly speechless right now with a million thoughts running through my head. My chest feels like it's caving in on me.

Lottie. *My motherfucking Lottie.*

What is she doing here?

My heart is pounding at the sight of the one girl who owns me. Now I'm even more confused. Why is she here in Richmond Hills? A little over a month ago, this would have been the best news of my life, but now, my gut turns with anxious thoughts. Did she move down here to be near *him* and live at her grandmother's house? I can't imagine Lottie wanting to live with her full time but then again, she does let Ethel control her like a puppet.

My fists squeeze to the point of turning white at the thought. I can't see her every day and know she isn't mine to hold anymore.

*If she is really with him, I will lose my shit. I will raise fucking hell.*

She's walking with Remi Kincaid, who was most likely assigned to show Lottie around the school on her first day. Lottie looks so damn good, almost too good, all eyes are on her. Looking every bit the Richmond she is with her perfect hair and clothes, and her head held high.

Something seems different about her though. She looks like she has lost some weight. Her curves look more accentuated than they were. Every inch of her was perfect before, why did she go and lose weight? The biggest difference I see in her is the way she carries herself. She has her head held high and all eyes on her as she walks this way to find a table with Remi.

Lottie glances my way but quickly avoids my stare. I know she saw me, but she doesn't seem to care, which just solidifies the fact she didn't come here for me. Not that she's given me any signs that she would have.

She waves to the table right beside ours and says something to Remi before they head towards the group of familiar faces. Lottie goes around to the other side of the table where I can see her even better. Although right now I'm wishing I couldn't. The big smile she gives Snow as he moves over to make room for her has all my pent-up anger surfacing to the top.

How the fuck does she know him? That greeting didn't look like one between two people who just met today. Frankie is also sitting at their table with her best friend Lucian. Remi walks to sit with a group at the other end of the table. I see Snow introduce Lottie to them and that guts me, I'm supposed to be the one doing that. Frankie is basically my family.

I sit there stunned, trying to count to ten in my head before I flip this fucking table over and claim her in front of everyone in this room. I can't take my eyes off her and it's like as soon as she realizes who Frankie is she looks right at me. *Could she feel me staring at her?*

Frankie's head turns to see what she's looking at, but I don't take my eyes off Lottie. It's still there, that undeniable thing we have. I can see it on her face—she's trying to fight it... us, but her guard slips slightly when she sees Amber, who has apparently decided to link her arm in mine that's propped on the table. I didn't even notice she had moved closer to me until I saw Lottie's eyes go to her.

Snow glances at me and then back to her as he says something that puts her mask back in place and has her smiling and laughing a little. Corbin Snow and I run in the same circle, we aren't close, but I have never had a problem with him... until right now as he soaks in all that is Lottie.

*Chill the fuck out Greyson, she's just making new friends... doesn't mean it's anything more. I want answers... Snow is the polar opposite of that rich boy Jacob.*

Ford is talking to Nox and the rest of the table about our home game Friday night and the bonfire afterward, but I can't seem to give a fuck about anything but Lottie right now. She's not even acknowledging me after everything we shared this summer and that fucking hurts.

*I need more of a reaction from her...even if it's a middle finger pointed in my direction. A month ago, we were making love and promising forever.*

Noticing she glances back my way after what feels like a lifetime, I decide that if Lottie wants to pretend I don't exist, I can play that game too. Taking advantage of the clinger next to me, I swing my right leg over the bench so that I'm now straddling it. Pulling Amber in between my legs. She shifts closer then looks up at me and I wink. I know I'm confusing her because I never give in to her attention-seeking shit anymore, but I need to see where Lottie's feelings stand.

I watch Amber cautiously because she's licking her lips and looking back at my mouth... Oh hell no. You give this girl an inch and she takes a mile. Movement in my peripheral vision has me looking away from her.

That's when I see Lottie get up and storm out.

It takes everything in me not to follow her. Yes, I wanted to see if she cared, wanted to see more of that jealousy I got a glimpse of, but now I'm feeling like an asshole for using Amber to get a rise out of her. *Shit, I didn't think this through. My head is all fucked up.*

I don't want her to think I moved on that fast. It's only been a little over a month. It may have only taken that long for me to fall in love with her, but it's going to take a hell of a lot longer in order for me to fall out. *If ever.*

My phone beeps and the name that pops up makes my heart drop. I guess she unblocked me.

> **Stacks:** *I see Amber still likes her position between your knees. Fuck you and your little fuck buddy.*

How does she know about Amber? And when did she start saying Fuck so much?

***

# Lottie-

The past month and a half has been hell.

My Papa passed away the day I returned to New York. Turns out, he kept me in the dark about a heart issue he had for many years. I barely made it to the hospital in time to say goodbye. Sally kept telling him I was on my way and to hold out a bit longer, and somehow, he did.

I was able to tell him I loved him and how grateful I was to have him and Gigi in my life. Through tears, I told him I will never forget how much they both loved me and that I will work hard to be strong and happy like I know they want me to be. He was unable to speak at that point, but I felt his hand squeeze mine. He knew I was there and shortly after, he closed his eyes and passed peacefully.

Now he's with Gigi and my mom looking over me while I figure out this thing called life.

My heart shattered that day. It hurt so badly knowing I didn't have anyone left in my family that truly loved me. I needed Greyson so much in that moment. How could he do this to us? I still love him with all of my heart and soul. I don't even know how to deal with this hurt.

Sorting through my Papa and Gigi's estate was time-consuming, but I'm thankful I could distract myself a little bit. It was sad but comforting looking through old boxes of things from when I was growing up. It was a blessing that they had all the proper paperwork in place because Ethel was MIA and I had no clue what the next steps were. A long-time family friend who was also their lawyer, was with me so he was an amazing help through it all.

I will never understand how Ethel can be so cold and detached. I still hurt every day from the loss of my mom and now both of my great-grandparents. But she doesn't even seem phased that her father just died.

The reading of the will was quite an eye-opener. It was the only event Ethel seemed to care about regarding her father's death. She might as well have stayed in North Carolina, because to my surprise, I was given everything. Every single property, including the Nori Beach home I love so much. Their priceless heirlooms, Gigi's extensive jewelry collection, their Manhattan brownstone, Papa's remaining shares of Richmond Steel... all of it. They left Ethel a note, not sure what it pertained to, but besides that piece of paper, she left with nothing.

Being as I'm still seventeen and unable to access any of my inheritance until my next birthday, I was left with no choice but to pack up my life and everything I grew up around and move to Richmond Hills permanently. I was forced into the home of my only surviving family member, Ethel. The fact that I'm the sole proprietor of the Richmond fortune, and moving into the house of the slighted Ethel, scares the shit out of me. Thankfully she has no control over my inheritance. I can only imagine the hoops she'd make me jump through to get it. Papa set up small weekly distributions until my birthday in January when all the funds transfer to me.

Not only will I be under her control for the next four months, but this move also puts me back in North Carolina, where *he* is. I'm already enrolled in Richmond Hills High School and start this week. *Fuck my life.*

I arrived at Ethel's on Saturday morning. James picked me up from the airport, informing me that Ethel was out of town and was sorry she couldn't be there. *Wow, what a shocker.*

Keeping myself busy, I unpacked and settled into my room. It's now Tuesday, school starts tomorrow, and I am going fricken stir-crazy. I open my laptop and search for a way to diffuse all of my nervous energy. I came across Lights Out, a boxing gym in downtown Richmond Hills. This should do the trick.

When Papa died, I was utterly distraught. I feared for my own health and made sure to get myself to a doctor for a checkup. Turns out, I'm in the clear, for now. I was told that a condition like his was something he developed later in life, and to make sure I looked after myself and my health.

The next day I joined the local kickboxing gym Ashley goes to. She was always raving about how good she felt both mentally and physically when she left there, so I gave it a shot. Best decision I've ever made. Not only is it helping me get through one of the hardest times in my life, but I feel stronger in mind and body.

My curves are more defined now. Even though that wasn't the initial plan, I'm not mad at the reflection I see in the mirror. I feel confident and sexy in a way only *his* words used to make me feel. Now, I feel it in myself. Not only do I feel good, but I know that if I can get through these past few weeks, I can get through anything, and that has given me more confidence than anything before.

Since Ethel doesn't live too far from downtown, I figured I'd walk to the gym. I toss on a large tee over my sports bra and biker shorts, grab my sneakers, and head out.

I've been a ball of nerves since the plane touched down on Carolina soil, so I need a way to recenter myself. It's not long into my walk that I approach the brick building. Large graffiti lettering reads Lights Out above the glass double doors.

Walking through the entrance, I let out a deep sigh. This is exactly what I needed. I approach the reception desk and come to a stop when I'm face-to-face with a strikingly handsome guy. He has bright blond hair that almost looks white and a beautiful set of ice-blue eyes. I can feel his gaze as he peruses my body. His full lips now have a smirk on them that only brings my attention to his strong, chiseled jaw. *Damn, they really do make them different down here.*

He doesn't say a word, just stares.

I clear my throat and initiate conversation. "Hi, I'm new in town and I was wondering if I could try out your gym."

"You certainly are," he says, as his eyes finally meet mine. *Uh, what?*

He stands from behind the desk and my god. Tall, pure, lean muscle is all I see. He may not have Greyson's muscle mass, but he towers over me even more than G did, which is saying a lot.

He walks around the desk and comes to a stop in front of me. Holding out his hand to shake mine, he says, "I'm Corbin. Most people call me Snow."

"Hi, I'm Lottie."

We stand there for several moments and I realize how awfully quiet it has gotten in here. Glancing around, I notice most of the activity has slowed down. I feel as if all eyes are on me... Or are they on Corbin?

As if noticing the change as well, Corbin turns to scan the gym. He must come to the same conclusion because in the next moment, his deep voice bellows, "Mind your own." Within seconds, the sounds of the gym roar back to life.

Corbin stands there shaking his head. I can't help but ask, "What was that all about?"

He smiles at me, popping a dimple on his cheek, and I swear I get a little flutter in my stomach. *Wow, that was unexpected.*

"Fresh meat... these hooligans aren't used to a knockout like you walking through these doors."

"Oh. Uhm... thank you," I stammer, not really sure how to respond.

"Come on Trouble, let me show you around," he says as he heads towards the main part of the gym. The inside of this place has a rustic brick look and it's in pristine condition. This is no hole-in-the-wall boxing gym, you can tell the owner definitely takes pride in it. Lights Out has an open floor concept, so I can easily spot the two sparring rings on the other side of the room. I continue to follow Corbin as he points out where things are around the space.

Walking past the guys hitting the bags, I immediately get that itch to join in. There is just something so powerful about letting out all your aggression and feelings on that big, heavy punching bag. It's become my own form of therapy.

"So, we have classes every day that are included in your membership. You will also have access to the rest of the gym equipment anytime you want it. Have you done kickboxing before?"

He stops in front of a guy going at it on the speed bag. "Yeah, I've been going several days a week for the last month up in New York. It's an addiction. I'm definitely interested in the classes."

"Sweet, well I teach a class on Mondays and Wednesdays at 4:30 and then also on Saturday mornings. I would love to see what you've got, plus the first three classes are free. You should come try tomorrow's class." Before I can answer he turns to the guy that finally took a break from hitting the speed bag. "This is Lucian, he graces us with his presence every now and again... Lottie here is thinking about joining us."

Lucian looks to me with a friendly smile. I notice his eyes don't linger on my body like Corbin's did. He stretches his boxing glove-clad hand towards me, I take the hint and give him a fist bump as I say, "Nice to meet you, Lucian."

"Same to you Lottie, are you new in town?"

I nod. "Yes, my grandmother is a local. I just moved here from New York. Do you guys go to Richmond Hills High?"

I bet they know him... *and her.*

Both answer "yes" in what appears to be practiced unison. I can't help but giggle at that.

Lucian speaks up with a smile on his face. "Swear that's never happened before."

Corbin turns to face him and asks, "Where has Em been? I haven't seen her scrawny ass in a bit."

Lucian laughs at that. "Scrawny or not, that girl scares the shit out of me." He looks to me to explain. "My sister Emerson has some sort of super-human powers. She's a tough little thing, she takes on guys in the ring that are almost double her size and weight. She's here almost everyday training." I can see the way his face lights up when he speaks about his sister, they must be close.

"She's one of the best students I have, she's been training since she was thirteen." Corbin beams in pride and a slight protectiveness.

Lucian turns his attention back to Corbin. "She actually hurt her wrist last week so she's taking it easy. The doctor insisted, otherwise you know damn well it wouldn't have stopped her." They both laugh at that.

"She sounds like a little badass, I can't wait to meet her." I smile at them, feeling at ease around these two.

"She sure is, and a pain in *my* ass too. But I love her to death."

"Does she go to Richmond Hills High too?" I ask.

"Yes, she's a junior," Lucian says, the smile never slipping from his face.

"Speaking of which, I actually need to head back over there for football practice. It was nice to meet you Lottie... catch you later Snow. See ya' tomorrow." He leaves us standing there as he heads to the locker room.

"We both have early release since we've already met our senior class requirements. I'm guessing since you asked, you're starting there?"

"Yep, I start tomorrow."

"Well good. I'm glad you came in, you'll know a couple of familiar faces now."

*If you only knew.*

"Yes, me too. I think I'll take you up on your offer about the classes. I'll get my ride to drop me off here after school tomorrow."

He smiles at me with his insanely perfect white teeth. "Actually, I can give you a ride tomorrow, if you want? I need to stay till the end of the day anyways. I have a group project meeting and then an appointment with my guidance counselor."

"Okay if you're sure, that would be awesome."

"Yeah Trouble, it's my pleasure. Now let's get you some gear and start this workout. I'm excited to see you in that ring."

A few hours later I leave Lights Out, happy I've found a place where I can work out my aggression.

I really enjoyed my time there. Corbin was very nice and stuck by my side. We really hit it off. Talking and getting to know each other came easily as we walked through the rest of the gym. I'm excited to take the bootcamp class he swears will kick my ass.

It felt weird to accept his offer of a ride so quickly, but there's something about him that put my soul at ease. From what I learned about him and his friends, I can tell he is a good guy. Lucian seems nice too. Hopefully, having met them will ease the stress of starting school tomorrow.

*Ugh, school starts tomorrow.*

Dread courses through me. My head is saying don't look at him, it will only hurt more. But my heart needs to see his face. I need to know if it was all a lie. If we were just a summer hook up that meant nothing to him. I am so scared to face tomorrow. I need Ash to give me a pep talk or some shit. I have to be strong walking in there, to *his* territory. And don't even get me started on how I feel about possibly seeing that bitch who helped him shatter me.

I know Grey and I are long overdue for a conversation, but I don't think my heart can take it right now. It hasn't even been two months since I lost my Papa. I'm too sensitive to deal with hearing Greyson explain why he ran into the arms—*and mouth*—of another girl just a few hours after seeing Jacob and I talking. What if he confirms everything I fear, and our entire relationship meant nothing to him? Everything just hurts. I only want it to stop.

Maybe I'm wrong. Maybe it's all a big misunderstanding... nope, definitely not. There is no mistaking Amber's lips around his cock and the sound of his moans. Those moans I know so well I hear them in my sleep. I did *not* make that shit up. I mean how the hell can someone *misunderstand* seeing a full-on blow job? Ugh!

Thank God for Corbin and Lucian. At least now I'll know two friendly faces in the hallways tomorrow.

# Chapter Thirteen

Tugging on my shirt one last time, I walk up the steps to Richmond Hills High. Feels real weird walking onto his turf, but this was not my doing. Ashley is always talking about fate and how things have a funny way of working themselves out. I sure hope she's right because right now I feel like I'm going to throw up. *Cut that shit out, you can do this.*

The main office is right off the school entrance and as soon as I walk inside, there's a cute, petite, dark-haired girl with glasses waiting.

She turns her attention to me. "Hi, I'm Remi! You must be Charlotte Richmond."

Catching me a little off guard, I stumble on my words. "Oh—Uhm, Hi. Yes, I'm Lottie."

"Ooh, I love the name Lottie. Super cute. Love that top too. I wish I had tits like that—" She stops the stream of words coming out by slamming her hand over her mouth. I giggle and smile. I like her.

Her comment makes me thankful for Ashley. We were up late last night FaceTiming. She gave me the pep talk I needed to see Grey again without losing it in front of a bunch of strangers. And she helped me decide on the perfect outfit for my first day of school. I didn't want to look like I was trying too hard, but I wanted to feel confident. My knotted button up with a lacy bralette and ass hugging jeans has me feeling just that.

"Shit, I'm sorry. Everyone tells me I talk too much and clearly, I don't have much of a filter," she says apologetically.

"No, it's totally fine. Actually, you remind me of my bestie in New York. It's quite comforting."

"Oh, thank fuck," she says, cringing slightly when she realizes she dropped an f-bomb in the middle of the principal's office.

"Okay, here's your schedule and locker info. I'm your student guide since I'm in a few of your classes. I'm going to show you around for the next two days so you can get familiar with this place. Now let's get the hell out of here before they fire me on my first day." We both laugh and she hooks her arm in mine as we walk out together. I can't help but smile. *Maybe Richmond Hills won't be so bad after all.*

The first few periods go by painlessly with Remi by my side. We had two classes together and now comes the dreaded lunchtime, where every senior in the entire school sits together and eats in one large room. Thankfully, Corbin is the first person I see when we walk in with our food. He's sitting at a table with a curly-haired girl, along with Lucian and a couple of others. He nods my way as his eyes take their time roaming over my body. I wave back, trying to hide the slight blush creeping up my cheeks. Remi sighs next to me, "Man, I would give anything to have someone look at me the way he just looked at you." She pushes her glasses up her nose.

"I met Corbin yesterday at Lights Out. We worked out for a few hours. I'm thinking of joining," I tell her, trying to avoid the fact that Corbin was blatantly checking me out.

"Oh no, not Snow, but God, yes, he's hella-hot. No, I mean Greyson Rexwood. He's basically eating you alive but also looks sort of angry. Like a sexy wolf on the prowl type of vibe," she says from beside me. I don't respond right away, too stunned by the sight of him sitting there with the bitch from the video. My heart twinges. I was right, I am so not ready for this.

"Right girl, I'd be stunned to silence too. Like he's super-hot. With his muscular football body and that whole bad boy, motorcycle club style," she says while nudging my arm a bit.

"Oh, yeah he's definitely handsome." Trying my best to sound indifferent while I shake this feeling of uneasiness away. *I can do this.*

"Where do you normally sit?" I question, silently begging to remove myself from the center of the entire cafeteria. I can feel people's eyes on us. *Geez, what is with these people down here? Why do they stare so much?*

"Over there, my friends are at the other end of Snow's table." She juts her chin in that direction. I take her lead and head that way. Of course, Corbin's table is the one directly next to Greyson's.

I'm greeted with Corbin's signature megawatt smile. He slides over, making room for me to sit, then introduces me to the curly-haired girl. I try to ignore the daggers I feel coming from Greyson's direction.

"Frankie, this is Lottie. She just moved here from New York."

"Hey girl, nice to meet you," she says to me with a beautiful smile. I also get a warm hello from Lucian who is sitting beside her.

Frankie? Is this Greyson's Frankie?

Looking up to him for confirmation, his eyes lock with mine. *Guess he was staring.*

Frankie's head turns, catches Greyson staring, and turns back at me. Corbin repeats the same motion moments later. I refocus my attention on the table trying desperately to ignore Amber's arm linked in Greyson's and how sick it makes me feel. *Why is he doing this to me? To us? I hate this so much.* I can feel Frankie's observant eyes on me. I refuse to make eye contact, I know she'll see too much, and I'm not ready for that yet.

I feel like my heart is going to jump out of my throat. Why does he have to be staring at me? It's bad enough the bitch is hanging onto him like a spider monkey, but seriously, does he want me to tear up in front of the whole freaking cafeteria?

Out of nowhere Snow chuckles to himself, as if he's in on some secret. Shaking his head, he says, "See I told you, you're going to be trouble." I can't help the nervous laugh that escapes, letting out some of the pent-up tension I'm feeling.

Fortunately, the conversation moves on and I'm trying my hardest to stay focused on the smiling friendly faces surrounding me and not the broody handsome-as-sin face I can see out of my peripheral vision. "There's a bonfire this weekend after the game. You should come. It'll be kick ass," I hear Frankie say from across the table.

Looking up I realize she was directing that comment my way. "Oh—yeah, sounds like fun," I reply, not really sure what I'm agreeing to. I need to get out of this room to clear my head. I was doing just fine when he wasn't smack dab in front of my face and sitting all cozy next to *her*.

Ashley is going to have a field day with this one. I can just hear her now, plotting all the ways we can discreetly get back at Amber for being such a bitch. Don't get me started on the list she already has for Greyson. She swore her allegiance and secrecy when everything went down with him. I know she still sees Trent, and I'm sure he was fishing for information for his cousin, but I'm confident she hasn't said a word. I trust her. Plus, she was so damn mad, I didn't want her hate for Greyson to spoil what she has going on with Trent.

The table is still discussing the plans for Friday night when I chance a glance in Greyson's direction. I've felt his eyes on me non-stop since I sat down, and sure enough, he's still staring at me. While our eyes are locked, he shifts his position and straddles the bench, causing his legs to open towards the bitch. He then grabs her waist and slides her so she's nestled between his thighs. When I see her look up at him, they're so close their lips could touch at any second—the thought of watching them kiss has vomit rising up in my throat. I need to get out of here.

I quickly load up my garbage and grab my bag. "I'm going to hit the restroom before my next class. Remi I'll catch up with you after. It was nice seeing you all... Can't wait for Friday," I yell that last part over my shoulder.

Once locked securely in a bathroom stall, I try to catch my breath. *Fuck him.* Here I was thinking maybe we could be civil and just coexist. Who was I kidding? Now I know for sure I didn't mistake what I saw in that video. *UGH!*

My hands are shaking with nerves and anger. Pulling out my phone, I do what I've been dreading since the night it all happened. Tears of rage blur my eyes as I unblock his number.

> **Me:** *I see Amber still likes her position between your knees. Fuck you and your little fuck buddy.*

I turn off my phone and put it into my bag, not wanting to see if he responds. His actions speak for themselves. I just needed to get that out, and now that I have, I can focus on starting to heal once again. My breathing begins to calm down as I stare mindlessly at the penned-up bathroom stall walls.

I'm so ready for this day to be over so I can take out these overwhelming feelings on a punching bag. Corbin said to wait for him by the main office. So here I am, just waiting as the crowds go by. I get a few inquisitive glances, but most are too busy chatting with their friends to notice me. Good, I'm done with today and people.

I see Frankie's hair over the sea of students, and I smile. That girl really has some bomb-ass curls. She spots me and heads over to where I'm leaning up against a windowsill.

She nudges my shoulder. "You know I know, right? Figured it out the moment I saw his face and how he was staring." I let out a deep sigh and close my eyes. I guess he's told them about me. "It's okay, you don't need to talk about it right now. I just want you to know I'm here if you need to talk."

"Thank you, I needed that," I say, trying to fight the tightness in my throat. I will not let myself shed any more tears for him.

"No problem. Oh, and of course, I would never say anything to him. Just like I won't tell you what he's told me. Just wanted you to know I'm here," I nod, totally understanding he's like a brother to her.

I look up into the crowd and see Greyson's sharp gaze zeroed in on us. He's heading our way with determination in his eyes. I don't think I'm ready to talk to him, especially not after that stunt he pulled earlier.

I don't think my heart can take any more of a beating today.

*** 

## Greyson-

The rest of the day drags by painfully slow, especially after the text she sent me.

> **Me:** *Are you fucking serious Lottie... THAT'S the first thing you say to me after a month of silence. And what the fuck are you talking about?*

I responded immediately but of course she has nothing to say. Each new period, I have my eyes glued to the door, waiting for Lottie to walk in, but no such luck. I'm determined to catch her alone. I want to know why she's here, and I don't want to hear it through the Richmond Hills grapevine or some damn text, but from her own mouth.

When the boys and I are heading to the locker room at the end of the day, I spot those perfectly thick hips of hers leaning up against a wall chatting with Frankie and know this is my chance.

Looking at the guys, "Y'all give me a few." I say as I take off towards Lottie.

Ford chuckles, "Well that didn't take long, I knew she'd be the reason you'd finally get your head out of your ass..."

*You have no fucking clue, brother.*

Ignoring him, I go towards her. My heart is beating against my chest like Travis Barker pounding on his drums. I have missed her so fucking much. Lottie looks up and sees me coming her way. Obviously trying to avoid me she excuses herself from Frankie and begins walking away, but I'm faster. Grabbing her arm, I turn her towards me. She tries backing away from me, so I use my size to my advantage.

"Not so fast, Stacks," I say as I back her against the wall.

She pushes against my chest. "Do *not* call me that, you lost that right."

Hating the tone she's catching with me, I growl back, "What the fuck are you doing here?"

"It's really none of your business but I'm waiting on my ride," she says with a blank look on her face.

"Don't be a smartass... you know what I mean. What are you doing in my town?" I growl, pointing to my chest. Unable to keep my temper in check, I ask, "Did you come here to be closer to your future husband hand-picked by your grandmother?"

"Again, none of your business Greyson," she huffs out at me.

I grab her hips, loving the feel of her curves beneath my grip.

"Did that rich prick tell you, you needed to drop weight? You still look hot as fuck Lottie, but I can feel it here," I say squeezing her hips. "And I can see it here," I whisper, grazing my hand across her waist as she inhales a shaky breath. "Tell those fuckers you're perfect. Don't let them get in your head, Lottie."

I don't care how bad she hurt me, I hate the thought of anyone pushing their warped ideas of what they think women should look like onto her.

She takes me by surprise when her elbows come down on my forearms knocking my hands from her waist. Creating a little distance between us, she moves off the wall and seethes at me, "I did this for me. I needed to take my anger out on something since I couldn't punch you. Kickboxing was the perfect way to do that. I needed to take control of my health and make some lifestyle changes after..."

"Trouble, you ready?" Corbin Snow interrupts and I could explode.

"Who the fuck is Trouble?"

He ignores me and smiles at Lottie who is now walking towards him.

"Lottie! Wait, we aren't done."

She turns back to me. "Yes, we are. You made sure of that."

Snow puts his hand on her lower back.

"Get your fucking hands off her," I say, moving towards them as that black fog starts to take over. Nox and Ford must have picked up on the tension because all of a sudden, they're both holding me back and asking what the fuck my problem is.

As I watch her walk through the front doors to the parking lot with Snow, I stop fighting them knowing they won't let me go.

I pull at my hair in frustration... *how did we get to this?*

Nox's head swivels back to me once he sees them go out the doors. "Oh, fuuuck."

*Great, I should have known his perceptive ass would figure it out.*

"It's her, isn't it?

I don't answer and then Ford says, "Wait, what?"

Nox continues, "I've only heard people call her Charlotte today but seeing how you just reacted to her leaving with Snow it hit me."

Ford catches on, "Shiiit... that's Lottie, *your* Lottie?"

I can't bring myself to say it because right now she's not mine and it seems like she is going to do everything she can to make sure I know it.

# Chapter Fourteen

This party is really something else. I knew it would be with the Chargers' big win tonight. Our team kicked some serious ass. My old high school didn't do football like they do in the south. The whole town basically came out to watch the boys play. It was an intense game, and I was happy to have Frankie by my side to fill me in on who's who on the team. Even though my eyes took in the entire field, they couldn't help but focus in on the player that has my heart skipping a beat. *Foolish thing, pining for someone who is no longer theirs.*

Not going to lie though, his ass really does look spectacular in his uniform. His tight pants and broad shoulders coupled with his new sleeve of tattoos have me crossing my legs. I wonder what theme he went with on this arm. I loved his forest-themed arm, tracing the intricate lines of the trees and moon, but now, with both arms covered in ink... gah! A girl can only take so much temptation.

I never imagined what my first High School bonfire party would be like, but I guess it would be something like this. We're somewhere in the outskirts of town in a clearing with massive trees surrounding us. There are dirt roads leading to this spot, so I'm assuming it's a regular hang-out. The fire is roaring, and music is blasting. People are drinking, laughing, and having a good time. I'm about three drinks in and for me, that's usually enough.

Yesterday and today went by surprisingly quickly. I didn't have a single run-in with Greyson and was only shoulder-checked by Amber one time. Of course, she feigned innocence when I said something, but I know I was her target. Does she feel threatened by me? She made it clear with that video she won.

Lucian dropped Frankie and me off here since she's a badass who drives a motorcycle—and I didn't want my driver to do it. It's bad enough I'm already hearing my name whispered around the halls. They know of my family, shit we go to *Richmond* Hills High School. I don't need to give them any more fuel.

I need to learn how to drive. Ashley's brother, Micah, tried to teach us one time, but that turned into a total shit show. Being raised in New York City means you're not required to have a license. Between taxis, Ubers, trains, subways, and buses, there's always a way to get where you want to go.

Ethel has been on her best behavior. She seems extremely preoccupied with who knows what, but she's been almost decent towards me. When I told her I was going to a party tonight, she just told me to have fun. *Have fun!* So unlike her, but I'm not complaining. She did ask me to join her for brunch on Sunday, which was a surprise. The fact she asked me and didn't demand it was a nice change. I'm still skeptical of her new-found disposition towards me, especially after the results of Papa's Will. I feel like we're playing a game. A game I don't want any part of, but it's her next move I truly worry about. I know she has something stewing in that calculated brain of hers.

I bop around the party, never straying too far from Frankie. I hope she doesn't mind. She seems more than happy to hang around me too. From what Greyson said about her, she's definitely a genuine person.

Ugh Greyson. Every time I feel a sense of normalcy or calm, reminders of him come to mind. It's not fair honestly. I swear I can still feel his scratchy beard along my neck and thighs. He played me, made me feel like a fool for believing him... for believing in *us*. I'm not in the right mindset to deal with him right now. I want to approach the conversation with a level head and not this heap of emotions I've been dealing with.

Speak of the devil. I see his blue eyes focused on me from across the fire, the flames creating magnificent shadows across his stupidly handsome face. Football must be bulking him up because I swear he's even bigger than I remember. His beard's a little longer and so damn sexy. He's here with his boys, Ford and Lennox, whom everyone refers to as Nox. I had a class with each of them this week and although Nox seems quiet, he was friendly. Ford, geez that boy is a handful. You can see why the girls fall at his feet. He could charm his way into anything.

While staring off into the distance, Frankie comes to sit next to me, bringing me another hard seltzer. We crack them open and cheers our drinks. I release a sigh as I lock onto Greyson's eyes once more. *So close and yet so far. God he is so beautiful it hurts to look at him.*

"You ready to talk about it yet?" I hear her say from beside me.

"Honestly, it's so screwed up I don't know..."

"Remember, I grew up in a motorcycle club. The shit I've heard and seen would blow your mind. I once walked in on my uncle getting a blowjob from two club whores, a sight I can never unsee. Try me."

"Wow, yeah, not the visual you want. Ok, well clearly you know Greyson and I had a thing over the summer. It was everything I could have ever dreamed of. He was amazing, so sweet and caring. The moments we shared were like straight out of one of my romance books," I say, trying to brace myself for what happened next.

She nods at me to continue as she takes another sip of her White Claw.

"So... one day he popped over as Ethel, my grandmother, and I were finishing up a luncheon. I was out in the back yard with her friend's son, Jacob. We were just hanging out, and he reached for my face in a more-than-friends type of way. I pulled away and told him about Greyson. He apologized, but it was too late. Greyson saw me with Jacob and just stormed off. He said he needed time and would call me later."

She looks at me intently. "Ah yes, I remember that night. He went on a bender. Definitely wasn't himself. It all makes sense now."

"Well, needless to say, I never got a call or text. I was a wreck. Then I got some devastating, urgent news and tried to reach him one last time in desperation. I had to go back to New York. My grandfather was in the ICU. That girl Amber answered his phone and was such a bitch I could barely respond. She basically alluded to her and Greyson being a thing and that I was a joke, and nothing I experienced this summer was real."

"I tried to ignore her words, but I was totally shocked. I didn't believe Greyson would ever do anything to hurt me like that, but then I received a text that changed my tone real quick. It was from an "eight-two-eight" number I didn't recognize, and it was a video clip of Amber giving Greyson head. I literally dropped my phone. I was so disgusted I had to pull over and vomit. Then a few hours later my world turned upside again when my grandfather passed away suddenly." I say that last part with a shaky breath, reliving the story has my mind a mess.

"Wow, that is some shit," Frankie says as she angles her body towards mine.

"Listen, I know I said I wouldn't share your side with him, nor his side with you. But all I can say is I highly doubt Greyson was with Amber that night. I was at that party, and he was so drunk off his ass he was practically sleeping on the couch. He lost his phone at some point too. I took him home with some help from the guys," she says, eyeing me intently.

"I know this doesn't change how you feel or what you saw, but I think you two desperately need to speak to one another. Oh, and Amber is a fucking bitch. She's been after Greyson's attention forever," she says while sipping her drink.

"Well tonight certainly is not that night, I'm too twisted up to have a logical conversation with him. I might jump him instead, he's so fucking hot it hurts." I mention that last part more for myself than her.

"He's definitely good-looking. Glad we grew up like siblings because the thought of anything more with that boy makes me cringe." She fakes a gag, causing us both to laugh.

"How about this... we forget about my tragic love life and get drunk," I suggest, lifting my can to her.

"Fuck yeah! That sounds perfect to me. Lucian said he'd pick us up. You're more than welcome to crash at my place if you want."

"Yesss! My goal is to forget my name, so I might take you up on that offer." I smile at her, thankful she's by my side.

"Do you mind me asking what's with you two?" I question, knowing the familiar look all too well on Lucian's face whenever he sees her.

"Ah yes, Lucian and I are best friends. Have been since the day he came to my rescue in elementary school. Not that I needed any rescuing, but he's protective like that. Anyways, we've never been more than that. I see the way he looks at me, but I don't know if I want to risk the friendship we have for more. But fuck, has he grown into one sexy ass dude." She smiles at me with that last part.

Thankful for her candidness, I say, "I'm sure it will all work out in the end."

"Shit, I should be telling you that." She laughs.

We sit in a much-needed silence for a few, both of us lost in thought. We sip our drinks and look out to the crowd. Noticing everyone is doing a line dance to some country song, I ask Frankie, "What dance is that?"

She looks at me like I have five heads and says, "Are you kidding me Lottie?" Standing, she reaches her hand out pulling me up. "Come on girlie, I'm going to teach you how to do the Copperhead Road. You're a southern girl now, it's a rite of passage."

Oooh this should be fun... I nod my head and take her lead. Grateful I have some people like her in my life here.

\*\*\*

## *Greyson-*

I'm sitting across the bonfire like a total creep just watching Lottie have the time of her life.

Stacks throws her head back so far in laughter her hair bounces off her ass. Long brown hair she curled my favorite way tonight, in big waves that remind me of the beach. She is making rounds, taking shots, and dancing with my friend. She keeps using her hands when she talks to Frankie. I bet her accent is strong and her words are missing their "R's" right about now too. *Fuck, she's adorable when she gets tipsy.* I knew those two would hit it off, I just never imagined I would be an outsider looking in. At this point I'm sure Frankie knows who Lottie is to me. I could corner Frankie and ask her to give me some answers, but I know her, she won't say a damn thing. Plus, I want to hear them from Lottie's mouth.

The music is thumping from the huge wireless speaker in the back of Clark's Chevy Silverado. He's one of my fellow linebackers and a big part of the reason we won our game tonight. This is his family's farmland, and we use it as a party field often. His older brothers started the tradition and we've helped Clark carry it on. It's the perfect spot, secluded and surrounded by trees.

There are over a hundred people out here, but my eyes can't seem to leave Lottie and all her perfection. She has on these tight-ass jeans with holes all over them. They hug her ass and show off her round hips in all their glory. Her top is cut short, revealing a sliver of her stomach above her jeans. It's long sleeve, black and shows off her new-found confidence. I am a jealous man watching all these douches drool over "The fine-ass new girl." I am also proud as fuck. Seeing Lottie hold her head high and own her beautiful body has me so happy. She finally knows how damn perfect she is. I just wish I was the man at her side as she flaunted it.

Taking another swig of the beer I'm babysitting, I watch her throw back the fifth of liquor she and Frankie have been passing back and forth. Her lips around that bottle has me thinking of exactly what those pretty pink lips and mouth are capable of. She's killing me, I miss her so fucking much. I miss her voice, her touch, her laugh... her pussy.

I want to work through this bullshit and make her mine again, but first I need to know that she won't put Ethel's stupid requests before me again. Especially not that fucker Jacob. I assume he's no longer in the picture, but I need to hear it from her. I will never allow another Roberts to fuck with my head again.

Lottie stumbles towards the bonfire and I'm on my feet before I can think twice. One of my teammates catches her before she falls. I can't hear what she says to him, but I hate the way his hands are lingering on her curvy hips.

Hands that are still there when I approach them. Before I can stop myself, I'm gripping his wrist to the point of causing pain judging by the grimace on his face. Greg quickly lets go as I pull Lottie into my arms. He looks at me with his brows furrowed. I level him with a stare and bluntly say, "Don't even think about it." Greg must be smarter than I give him credit for because he listens and backs away.

Lottie turns around and looks at me. "Grey... I knew it was you." And then she boops me on the nose. Actually fucking boops my nose. I can't help but smile because I'm desperate for any attention she'll give me at this point.

"How'd you know it was me?" I ask.

"I could feel you, and then I could smell you." She giggles. "How do you smell so good? It's not fair." She shoves me and moves towards Frankie, putting her arm around her neck and kissing Frankie's cheek.

*And now I'm jealous of one of my closest friends. Well jealous of her cheek at least.*

"You were right G, she is the best." She looks to Frankie, and I notice her face changes from drunk happy to drunk sad.

"He told me we would hit it off because you guys are a lot alike, but I know you will never betray me. Right, Frankie?"

*What the fuck... betray her? Where the fuck did that come from? Did her grandma get into her head to make her think that?*

Before I can comprehend what she's implying, Lottie is grabbing Frankie's hand and dragging her closer to Clark's truck. Everyone is crowded around, going wild to "Jackie Chan" by Tiesto and Post Malone.

I dash towards them. Frankie is closest to me, so I grab her arm. She lets go of Lottie and turns to look at me. With concern on her face, she pauses, and we both look to see Lottie joining Remi in the crowd. She doesn't seem to mind as the song changes and she starts 'walking it out' to "Walk it Talk it" by Migos. That has me smiling about a memory of this summer.

Lottie and Ashley have a thing for 2000s rap and hip-hop, so they know all the dances and like to add them into the new shit.

I know Frankie is watching me stare. She knows me well enough to know why I stopped her, so her next comment doesn't surprise me.

"Not tonight, G, but you two need to have a serious conversation." I nod my head, knowing she's right. Lottie is way too tipsy. I need to get answers about the cryptic things she's been insinuating. First that confusing Amber text, and now this.

"Frankie, has she told you everything?"

She looks weary. "G, don't ask me to get in the middle of this. I really like her, and you're like a brother to me. This conversation deserves to be between the two of you, which is basically what I said to her as well."

We both look Lottie's way to check on her and she's watching us. "I'm going to go over there with her. I'll watch out for her tonight, I promise." She pats my arm and walks away.

***

It's a few hours later and we're taking the party back to Frankie's house since her dad is staying at the clubhouse. *Doing God only knows what with my dad and some soccer moms who want a ride on the wild side.*

I don't move far from the girls at the bonfire, feeling the need to keep my eye on a drunk Lottie. When Frankie comes over and mentions some of them are going back to her house for a kickback, Nox and Ford jump all over that. Frankie and her dad live beside me, so I probably would go either way, but there's no question since I know Lottie will be there.

After several failed attempts of trying to convince Frankie they need to ride with me, I finally give up. She informed me that Lucian is already on his way to get her and there is no changing that girl's mind once it's set. We aren't super close, but I know he's good people and always has Frankie's back. Honestly, we would probably be tighter but I met him through Frankie and when she's around, his full attention is on her. He worships the ground she walks on, and I know he wouldn't do anything to put her in harm's way. He hangs out with Snow a lot, so I am so fuckin' glad when I see him pull up alone.

When we get to Frankie's, I decide to raid Gunnar's stash and roll a fat blunt since I'm not drinking. I know he won't care as long as I replace it. When I come back into the living room everyone's sitting around talking shit and passing around a bottle of tequila.

I can't help the pang of jealousy that runs through me as I see Nox laugh at something Lottie says. Nox is like me, he doesn't entertain people he doesn't like, and he definitely doesn't laugh at them. Seeing how easily she fits into my world is slowly shoving the knife full of regret, deeper and deeper.

Taking a long pull from the blunt, I hope the smoke will help settle all my racing thoughts.

Deep down I knew she wasn't like my mom because she despised Ethel for what the money and greed turned her into. But seeing her that day with Jacob had my mind all over the place. I needed time to cool down, but I never imagined she would up and leave without so much as a conversation. When I went back to Nori Beach the next day looking for her, she was gone... like packed up and gone. I was in complete shock and convinced myself I didn't know Lottie at all. Now seeing her like this, I'm back to square one, questioning every decision I've ever made. *Full of fucking regrets and wanting to go back to the time before that day ever fucking happened.*

Ford catches me standing back watching and yells, "Hey pussy, bring that blunt over here and share."

I walk my ass over to him, because I sure as shit can't smoke this whole thing by myself tonight.

"Oooo is that the good shit you had this summer?" Hearing her voice directed at me lights me up inside but having her regard me like just another guy she hung around with this summer pisses me the fuck off. I still take the opportunity to go over to her.

Pulling another long drag off the blunt, I lean down as she looks up at me with wide eyes. Touching my lips to her mouth as I hold in the smoke, I take my blunt-free hand to the back of her head to hold her firmly to my lips. She opens her mouth with the slightest moan, and I blow the smoke down her lungs. She inhales, taking it in further as I lean back to watch her.

Still the sexiest damn thing I've seen, she exhales pursing those kissable lips, her hooded eyes watching me closely. A low growl comes from deep in my chest as I hold myself back from kissing her fuckable mouth.

Everyone is silent as they watch us. Ford breaks the quiet moment. "Now that we're all horny as shit from that little stunt, can I please hit that blunt G!" I chuckle and pass it to him.

The party continues but neither one of us can take our eyes off the other. Someone decides to play Circle Of Death, which is a drinking game with a deck of cards where everyone gets even more fucked up really damn fast. I'm still not drinking so I just keep being the creep I am and watch Lottie.

She's having a lot of fun so when I come back from the bathroom and see her crying with Frankie in a corner, I feel the uncontrollable need to fix whatever has her upset.

Frankie leads her towards her bedroom and I follow them.

"This is just so hard being around him but not being his... I'm going crazy." Hearing her say this gives me hope even though her painful tone guts me. Frankie soothes her as she sees me and waves her hand for me to go away. I don't listen. Lottie lies down with her eyes already half-closed.

"Let me, please Frankie?" I whisper to Frankie as she starts to take Lottie's shoes off.

She surprisingly listens. "Okay G, only because I think she needs you and I trust you won't do anything stupid."

"Thank you." I nod back to her.

Frankie gives one last warning before she leaves. "I'll be back in a few minutes so don't upset her more or I will have to beat your ass." I give her a look that says "*I got this, now leave*" as I sit down on the bed beside Lottie.

Removing Lottie's shoes, I throw the extra blanket from the bottom of Frankie's bed over her. I brush the curls back off her face and kiss her forehead, lingering to soak up her scent.

She whispers "Grey... what are you doing?"

"Just tucking you in Babygirl."

But before I can continue, she sits up straight and starts to rip her shirt off as she slurs "It's so damn hot in this place." Then she giggles and says, "Or maybe it was all that tequila."

I smile at her drunk-girl conversation with herself until I get a front-row seat of her full tits spilling out of her bra. Fuck, have I missed this view. Gently running my index finger between her cleavage, not even realizing what I'm doing until she grabs a hold of my wrist and whispers my name almost like a plea. When she licks her lips, I know I need to snap out of this. She is way too drunk and when I have her again it won't be like this. Jerking my shirt off over my head and throwing it over her quickly before I do something stupid, I lean back and adjust my dick in my pants as she lifts the shirt off her chest and inhales deeply.

"Damn I have missed that smell," she says all dreamy-like. I wish she would give me an ounce of this sweetness when she isn't drinking. But these days that seems unlikely even if I don't really get why.

I smile at her and say truthfully, "I have missed every fucking thing about you pretty girl."

Sighing, she gives me a sleepy smile and says, "Tell me it wasn't all fake?"

That has my blood running cold. "How could you think that? Of course, it wasn't. It still isn't."

In a pained voice, she says, "You hurt me so bad, and now..." She lets out a deep sigh. "I'm so confused."

"You and me both Stacks. We need to talk when you're sober." She doesn't respond after that, so I sit and watch her like I've been doing all night. Reaching down to touch her charm bracelet, hope ignites even more in my chest from the sight of the anchor I gave her still in place. She may not be ready to admit it but somewhere in that heart of hers, I'm still there.

Her breathing is slow now. She's so peaceful, so perfect.

It takes everything in me to get up from Frankie's bed and move away from her. I know sober Lottie would wake up pissed if she found herself wrapped in my arms. So, I back away. Pulling my phone from my pocket, I shoot her a text so she'll wake up to it tomorrow.

**Me:** *Let me know when you're ready to talk.*

"I love you more than all the waves in the ocean Lottie Richmond," I whisper as I walk away, closing the bedroom door behind me.

# Chapter Fifteen

**Corbin:** *You know skipping out proves I'm right!*
**Me:** *Right about what?*
**Corbin:** *That you couldn't handle my class... it's okay to admit it. You wouldn't be the first.*
**Me:** *I will do no such thing. I killed it in your class on Wednesday, and you know it. To be honest, I thought you were a little soft.*
**Corbin:** *Soft... me? I'm the furthest thing from soft. But you know who is, the girl who drank so much last night I had to take her home instead of to class.*
**Me:** *Please don't remind me of the amount of liquor I drank. My head just stopped hurting.*
**Corbin:** *It's 7:00pm... lightweight!*
**Me:** *Ugh... Struggling... send help in the form of a massive cheeseburger, fries, and a coke :)*
**Corbin:** *Have you eaten today? I'm with Lucian. I can swing by with some food if you need it.*
**Me:** *No, but don't you worry, Grubhub is coming to*

*the rescue!*
**Corbin:** *Okay, enjoy that! See you Monday, Trouble.*
**Me:** *See you then! Sorry again about this morning.*

I really do feel like complete garbage. Who did I think I was drinking like that? Several seltzers, a fifth of liquor, and several tequila shots later, and I had totally forgotten about my plans today. I felt like such an asshole this morning when Frankie woke me up because Corbin was there to drive me to kickboxing. Once he saw the condition I was in, he was more than fine with dropping my ass at home on his way to class. There was no way in hell I was doing any sort of physical activity today.

Regardless, I had a fun night, from what I remember anyway. It gets a little blurry after that hot-as-hell shot-gun Greyson gave me, then the game of Circle of Death. The one thing I know for certain is that although I woke up with a massive hangover, I was enveloped in Greyson's scent. When did he give me his shirt and, most importantly, why?

Not going to lie, I haven't taken it off all day. I know it must make me some sort of masochist, but I can't help it. Having his scent around me makes me feel safe and protected.

I still haven't responded to his text. The fact that I'm even more confused after speaking with Frankie leaves me unsure as to what I'm going to say to him. If he wasn't with Amber that night, then why the hell would she have answered his phone... *maybe he did lose it.* My heart does a little flutter at the hope creeping through. *Don't be too quick to forget about that video.*

My brain hurts too much to think about it. I need to rest, and I'll text him tomorrow once my brain cells are functioning properly. *Yes, that's a good plan.*

***

Sunday brunch with Ethel is calm. She's busy talking my ear off about her upcoming fundraising gala for the Richmond Research Fund in November. It's a nonprofit she set up in memory of my mom. The RRF provides funds to doctors and scientists working on cutting-edge Leukemia research involving advanced treatments and maybe one day, a cure. It's probably the only selfless thing Ethel has ever done in her entire life, but that's beside the point. The gala is coming up in a few weeks and I need to start helping wherever I can.

Due to school scheduling conflicts in the past, this will be the first event I can attend in person. Supposedly, it's a really big to-do around here. Important people from all over will be in attendance. It makes me smile to know this foundation helps so many in their fight with Leukemia. My heart squeezes at the ever-present feeling of loss.

I'm brought back to our conversation when I hear Ethel pipe up. "The Roberts will be there. I expect you to behave accordingly. Besides, you owe it to Jacob after that stunt you pulled last time." I almost choke on my drink at her words. You have got to be kidding me.

"I don't think I owe Jacob anything... he's a friend, nothing more," I argue, my palms becoming clammy at the memory of that night.

"Oh Charlotte, always one for the dramatics. He's a fine boy and you could only be so lucky to catch the attention of a guy of his upbringing," she replies while taking a sip of her mimosa.

"Ethel, you know that means absolutely nothing to me. I don't want Jacob in that way. And, as of the last time we spoke, he was well aware of that fact," I say through a calming breath.

"Well as the sole heir of the Richmond Steel fortune, there is a certain level of class you are expected to uphold," she preaches with an iciness in her tone. I know she's still bitter about her parents' Will, but that had nothing to do with me. It was their decision and apparently, it was written a few years ago.

Besides, why does *my* inheritance even matter to her? Ethel is loaded. From what I've heard, husband number three left her with a hefty settlement after their divorce, *and* he was the third ex-husband to do so. In fact, I don't know if Ethel has ever worked a day in her life. She's always lived a lavish lifestyle ever since I could remember. It's crazy to think she's the offspring of Gigi and Papa.

Money was never the center of our lives in Gigi and Papa's house, it was love. Love is what we focused on daily, and you could feel it as soon as you walked through their front doors. I never wanted for anything growing up, they made sure of that. Gigi's smiling face would always welcome you in and make you feel at home and Papa's booming laugh could be heard from all corners of the house. *I miss them so much.*

"As the Richmond heir, I will do my best to ensure Papa's legacy continues on," is the only response I'm able to get out without causing a scene. Ethel certainly knows how to get under my skin.

A throat clears from beside us, causing us both to turn our attention. I peer up at a smiling Ford looking like the Pretty Boy he is in his uniform. I now understand why he works here. He has all the women young and old fawning over him. He must make a killing in tips.

"Hey Lottie." He smiles at me.

"Hey Ford," I say back.

He then turns his attention to Ethel, "Um, Ms. Richmond, the front desk is asking for you to swing by before you leave today."

"Oh, do you know what for? I already spoke to Claudia regarding the menu for the Gala," Ethel questions while finishing up her third mimosa.

"I'm not sure, to be honest," he replies while refilling our glasses.

Ethel looks to me. "Well I need to use the ladies room, then I will speak to them. I will be back shortly." As she stands, another waiter comes to the table to drop off a delicious-smelling basket of freshly baked pastries and croissants. My mouth instantly waters. Although brunch has been decent until moments ago, Ethel has a very strict diet she follows. Our meal consisted of fruit and yogurt, nothing more, and I'm fricken starving.

"Oh, that won't be necessary," she says to the waiter as he places the basket on our table, ignoring her statement. With that she steps away, leaving Ford and the intoxicating basket still lingering at my table.

"Our pastry chefs are some of the best around, you should try it," he says.

I look at him with a smile. "You know you can drop the Pretty Boy act with me."

"Aw you think I'm pretty?" he croons, placing his hands over his heart.

"Cut the shit, you know you are," I laugh at him.

He stands there with his stupidly handsome smile on his face as he rubs the back of his neck.

I nod my head in the direction Ethel just disappeared to. "What was that all about?"

"Beats me. I think it has to do with staffing or some shit," he responds, shrugging his shoulders.

"Have fun at the bonfire the other night?" he asks.

"Ha, you could say that. Probably a little too much fun." I laugh as I take a croissant from the basket. I can't help myself. It smells too damn good and although I've started to take care of myself more, I don't restrict myself either.

Biting into the tasty treat, I close my eyes to savor the flavor. I can't help the moan that escapes when I taste the chocolate melted inside. This is so damn good.

A blush erupts across my cheeks when I realize Ford is still standing next to me, witnessing my mouth orgasm from the pastry.

"Fuuuck," he softly groans. "Never knew eating could look so fucking hot," he says as he stares at my mouth.

As if being hit by someone, he quickly changes his tone. "Shit! Ugh, don't tell G any of this happened. Fuck, he'd kick my ass." He runs his hands over his face as if questioning what to do. "I—uh, I gotta go. See you later Lottie."

I laugh at his retreating form and finish my pastry and the last of my mimosa before Ethel returns to the table. My thoughts wander to Greyson as I mindlessly twirl my bracelet. The charm he gave me still hangs off of it as a reminder of what was. I hope like hell our conversation goes the way I want it to. We can put it all on the table and pray it helps us get back what we've lost. I have little time to dwell on my situation because I catch Ethel heading toward our table. I can tell by her tense body and clipped steps that something is wrong.

"Let's go, James is waiting for us," she says while aggressively gathering her things and tossing them into her bag.

"Is everything okay?" I ask as I stand and grab my clutch.

"Fine," she answers in a clipped tone.

Following her through the lobby, I glance at the staff buzzing around, some stand in close huddles speaking in soft whispers. I can't help but feel like those whispers have something to do with Ethel.

We slide into the waiting car. James greets us with a warm smile on his face. I don't know how this man works for her. He seems kind and trustworthy.

Definitely not someone I would expect to stay under Ethel's employment for long. He's been working for her for as long as I can remember, at least since my mom passed away.

"Is everything all right, Ms. Richmond?" he questions, his eyes reflecting in the rearview mirror.

She scoffs, "Can you believe they're complaining about their staffing needs and checks. Ungrateful, the whole lot of them."

"I told them they need to fix the scheduling and figure it out on their own. How dare they have the audacity to interrupt my meal for such nonsense," she says matter-of-factly, pulling out her makeup compact to powder her nose.

James' eyes meet mine in the mirror. I notice the way his eyes shift to her then back to me. Something weird is going on, but I'm not quite sure what.

Ethel mutters something under her breath but remains silent for the rest of the ride home. Once inside, she retreats to her corner of the house, and I retreat to mine. Brunch with her should fill my quota of Ethel interactions for a while.

I don't do much for the remainder of the day. I watch the new Spiderman movie and take a nap, ignoring my phone for most of the afternoon and night. There are several texts from Ashley, asking me if I'm alive and if she needs to call in people to hide any bodies. I laugh at her crazy ass and assure her I'm fine and no bodies need burying as of yet. There's also one from Corbin, telling me he'll pick me up for school tomorrow morning. Responding with a thumbs up, I pull up my last text from Grey and sigh.

**Greyson:** *Let me know when you're ready to talk.*

My fingers hover over the message, willing them to give me courage. This needs to happen, if not for explanations, then at least for closure. My heart constricts at that thought. *Stupid foolish heart.*

I take a deep breath, letting it out slowly. *You can do this.*

# Chapter Sixteen

I'm letting all my frustration out on the punching bag right now.

Right punch... Left Jab... Jacob... Snow.

Right... Left... Right... Jacob... Snow... Jacob

*Snow—that motherfucker.* I don't care if he is a trained fighter. I'll still whoop his ass.

*What if he's hanging with Lottie right now? Maybe that's why she hasn't responded to me. Or maybe she's with Jacob, visiting* his perfect little family.

I have never been so damn insecure and fucked in the head. *Well, maybe after I found my mom and learned the truth about her new life.*

But picturing either one of them with their grimy hands on Lottie has me going fucking crazy. Even more than that, I'm worried she won't ever be mine again. When I saw Lottie come out of Frankie's house yesterday and get in the car with Snow, I felt like someone was stabbing me with an ice pick in the chest. The night before had left me with so much hope for how Lottie felt about me, but then seeing that just shit all over my good mood. Then I realized she was still wearing my shirt... leaving me confused as fuck, which was turning into a normal state of being for me. Now I'm just down right raging. She still hadn't responded to my text about us talking and I'm fucking pissed thinking of all the things she could be doing with Snow.

I have never needed to let out so much pent-up anger as I have recently. On Sundays, Ford meets me and Lennox here after his shift at the country club. We've always gone to Lights Out weekly because it's owned by one of the Rebel Knights and it's where Nox trains, but lately it has been my refuge.

Friday was the best night I've had since the end of the summer. Every second with Lottie had me craving more. Once the alcohol took over her brain, I saw a glimpse of the girl who used to be in love with me. I just keep reminding myself of the phrase "*drunken words are sober thoughts*" and hoping like hell she'll come around. If she won't willingly talk to me, I'll have to corner her ass at school again and demand an explanation about what the fuck happened. We both deserve that.

Ford comes around the other side of my bag to hold it steady. He lets me get in a few more solid punches before he speaks up. "I saw her today." That has me stopping cold as he continues, "At the country club. Still can't believe she's Ethel *richie-bitch's* granddaughter. She looked pretty miserable, if you ask me. Sitting there in her perfect attire, acting all proper."

Knowing Ford would tell me if she was with anyone else, my anger is slightly eased, only to ramp back up when I think of her being paraded around by Ethel. Even with that shiny new confidence, she's still letting that woman get the best of her, and I hate that.

When I don't respond he says, "And I'm just going to go ahead and confess right now. I couldn't help but stare at her ass... damnnn that girl's got an ass. But I promise I'm working on it. I know she's off limits, brother."

With a slight jab to his gut, I say, "Today is not a good day to piss me off, Pretty Boy, keep your eyes and hands to yourself."

He fakes a wince and holds his stomach. I swear he should star in those romantic comedies he loves so much.

Ford may be a ladies' man but he's as loyal as they come. I trust him and Nox with my life. I know he is trying to get a brotherly rise out of me but I'm just not in the mood. Ford must be able to sense it. "I vote you spar with Nox today. You look like you need the pain to take your mind off shit." Knowing he's right, I head towards Lennox.

We all love to get in the ring and fight, but Nox is on another level. He trains daily to some degree. Either with us or a guy who comes in from Charlotte twice a week to coach him and Snow. Nox may be smaller than me at first glance, but his leanness makes him more agile. Plus he has a couple inches on me, giving his arm span even more of a reach when he throws a punch. And he throws a helluva punch.

Entering the ring, I tap gloves with Nox. "Let's do this. Don't take it easy on me either. Give me all you've got."

*Bring on the pain, brother.*

\*\*\*

After thirty minutes of one of the most intense sparring sessions we've ever had, I'm spent. I don't feel like a chump either because even Nox seems exhausted after that one.

"Don't let my coach see that side of you, he'll be recruiting you too." That has me smiling for the first time today. "Nah, I'll leave that to the professionals. Plus, you know I'm shit on the ground, that's why Ford is the one you wrestle with."

Nox has his first official fight coming up on New Year's Eve. He decided not to play football or wrestle for our school this year so he can focus on his fighting career.

"Okay Pretty Boy, your turn. I've been here longer than you two and I'm starving for Nana's home cooking," Nox says, managing to get Ford's head out of his phone. He jumps up and trades places with me. We always eat Sunday dinner at my nana's house. It's the best meal in town.

Watching these two grapple on the ground, I realize some of the tension has left my body. I needed to hit something and now that I did, I feel a little better. Now I'm considering going to the locker room to jerk off to the hidden folder of pictures I have of Lottie's ass and tits on my phone. The sexual tension in my body has only increased by tenfold since my close contact with her the other night in Frankie's room.

Instead of doing that, I look through the pictures I could never delete, even when I knew it was depressing to keep them on my phone. The ones of us happy as shit, smiling, laughing... in love.

She's so damn perfect. My favorite photo of her is from one of our many sunset rides. This particular night we took the truck out. Lottie was obsessed with the song "Sunroof" by Nicky Youre and Dazy. She said, and I quote, "It's just a vibe, it feels like sunshine and summertime in a song." We pulled over to one of the overlooks to watch the sunset, and I took several pictures of her as she sang and danced in her seat. At the end of the song she looked at me and said, "When I get my own car one day, it has to have a sunroof Grey. I want to hang out the top while you drive me around and I sing and dance to this song." For the first time ever, I wished Ol' Girl was a newer model with a sunroof, so I could watch her do just that.

The pictures only solidify the fact of how in love we were... *are.*

The couple I see would have never given up so easily on each other, which is why I can't give up on her... on us.

*** 

"Pass me the fried chicken again, please," Nox says to my dad.

"Damn boy, you eating for two?" We all laugh.

Nox chuckles as he says, "This is my last Sunday meal before I have to start my strict diet for the fight in December."

"I guess I'm going to have to learn how to cook some healthy meals for our future star," Nana speaks up as she walks around making sure everyone has an extra napkin and plenty to drink. I swear that woman never sits down to actually eat, she just fusses over all of us.

"Nah Nana you don't have to do that," he says, waving his hands around her big dining room table. "They'll have my head if you do anything different to your cooking. I'll come hang out after y'all finish eating. We can play dominos and I'll even let you win." He winks at her knowing she always whoops our asses.

Gunnar speaks up. "Yeah Mama Rex you better not change up this fried chicken recipe." He says before stuffing his mouth.

Nana just smiles and shakes her head at their antics. I know she loves having her house full. Since I was a kid, we always reserved Sunday nights for her. Normally a few of my granddad and dad's brothers from the Rebel Knights would join us. As I got older my boys started coming and they never stopped. Gunnar and Frankie are always here, even on weekdays. They're basically family. Nana is the main female figure in Frankie's life, so they are very close. Frankie comes here more often than most of us.

Now that Pop is gone, we all try to take turns coming over and checking in on her. Between my boys and the Rebels, she has someone to take care of every night of the week. I say take care of because there's no way in hell she'll let anyone help her. So, we have to trick her. She cooks us dinner or makes us baked goods, and we mow the lawn or fix things around the house. Lately, though, I haven't spent enough time here. My mind is a fucking mess and I know she'll see right through me. I need to get my shit together.

My heart skipped a beat earlier when I noticed Frankie was talking to someone behind her as she came into the house. As much as I wanted it to be Lottie, I was relieved when I saw Lucian. I want to be the one to introduce her to my Nana. *As soon as she's mine again.*

There's lots of chatter going on like always, you never knows what might be said. It's so loud when we all get together so it's not unlike me to sit back and just enjoy the banter.

"Greyson, my boy, are you okay? You're extra quiet today." I look up to see my Nana rounding the table towards me with more sweet tea in hand.

"I'm good Nana, just a lot on my mind."

She comes behind me and gives me a kiss on the top of my head as she refills my cup. "Yeah I figured you were busy since I haven't seen much of you lately." See, the woman doesn't miss a damn thing.

"Busy trying to impress Stacks." Ford's clown ass chimes in and I immediately give him a death glare.

Luckily my dad is at the other end of the table talking to Lucian, so he doesn't hear what Ford says. Knowing he will press me for answers like he did at the end of the summer when I came home a total mess. I really don't want to talk to my family about it until I get Lottie's side of what went down between us. With the look I'm giving Ford, Nana doesn't press me, and I speak up before anyone else can. "You're right Nana, I'll be by this week. Wanna go for a joy ride in Ol' Girl with me? I'll even take you down to the Dairy Queen for a Blizzard," I suggest, knowing it was a favorite treat of her and my grandpa's.

"Ooo big spender," Ford says as Nana whips him upside the head with her dish rag, which just makes him laugh.

"That sounds perfect. You know that's my favorite."

I smile at her. "It's a date then." I may be an asshole, but I'd do anything for this lady. She's one of a kind.

I thought I found my "one of a kind" girl too, but she was gone in the blink of an eye. I know my dad can relate but I also know he is thirty-seven years old and still lonely as fuck because he never got over "the one that got away," which is why I've been avoiding him. I don't want to talk about his reality being a possibility for me.

As I stand to take my plate to the sink my phone lights up on the table. My heart almost stops when I see the name on the preview.

> **Stacks:** *Okay, let's talk one day after school this week.*
> **Me:** *When?*
> **Stacks:** *Probably Tuesday or Wednesday. I'll let you know.*

I want to talk sooner, but I decide not to push her and to take what I can get for now. She's willing to talk to me and I plan to do more than that... I plan to get my girl back.

# Chapter Seventeen

*Lottie*

Walking out of my fourth-period science class, I sling my bag over my shoulder and carry my books to my locker. To my surprise, Corbin is leaning against it, looking all handsome. I don't even think he's aware of how many girls stop to stare as they pass him in the hallways.

"Hey Trouble!" he greets me with a sly smile, his dimple on full display.

"What's up?" I gesture for him to move so I can put away these heavy-ass books.

"You take Anatomy and Physiology, right?" he asks as he turns his body to lean his shoulder against the adjacent locker to face me.

"Yup. Just got out actually." I lift my heavy textbooks for emphasis.

"Sweet. So, um—I was wondering if you could help me out?" he questions.

Placing my books into my locker, I pull out my notebook for my next class. I turn to him and see him eying me.

"What do you need help with?"

"I was wondering if you could help me study for the quiz this week. I didn't do so hot on the last one and I heard you're some sort of science wiz." He lets out a small laugh at that last part.

I'm definitely not a genius by any means, but I do love science. So much so that I'm planning on going to college for Clinical Research. I've known this for quite some time, probably ever since my mother passed. I want to do my part to help others.

"Oh, sure. I can help... what day works for you?"

"Hmm, well I work Wednesday, and I believe he said the test was Thursday... shit, does tonight work?" he asks, looking quite desperate.

"Frankie and I have plans after school to watch the guys' practice, then we're all going for pizza. Would you be able to after that?" I hope that works for him. I don't want to cancel my plans with Frankie, but I also want to be there to help my friend in need.

"Shit yeah! That's perfect. Lucian told me about pizza tonight. I'll meet you all there, then I can take you home and we can study?" He beams, his face filled with hope.

"Perfect!" I smile at him just as the warning bell sounds.

He wraps his long arms around me, bringing me in for a hug. "You're a lifesaver. Honestly, thank you." I can hear the sincerity in his voice. "Now get to class Trouble," he says as he breaks away from our hug.

"I'll see you later," I wave over my shoulder as I make my way toward my next class. As I make my way down the hall, I lock eyes with Amber and her obnoxious group of friends.

Nope, not in the mood for their shit today, but unfortunately, my classroom is right where they're standing.

*Oh, this should be fun.*

As I approach the girls, trying my hardest not to look at their faces, which I know are all sporting serious sneers. I don't get it. I literally haven't done a damn thing to any of them. They're standing in a large group that takes up most of the hallway, leaving a small area for students to get through. As I attempt to pass them, I hear Amber tell the girls, "Oh ladies, make enough space for the new girl to pass." They all giggle, then pull back to line the sides of the walls. The smile that spreads across Amber's mouth has my hands clenching. "That should be enough space for her to fit," she says, enunciating every word to ensure I hear her.

*Do not engage. Do. Not. Engage!*

When I make it past the Jock Hoppers, as I've heard them referred to, I look up and see Frankie glaring at them.

She locks her arm in mine as she turns her head back in their direction. "Fuck off Amber!" she says, and I smile. It's really nice to have some genuine friends around here. Now if only Greyson and I can settle our shit, life will be somewhat normal again.

After our text exchange the other night, we agreed to get together and talk either Tuesday or Wednesday. Now that I'm helping Corbin tonight, I guess tomorrow will have to work.

\*\*\*

Sitting next to Frankie on the bleachers has been entertaining, to say the least. This girl has me cracking up over her lack of filter. The eye candy on the field doesn't hurt either. There's something to be said about watching sweaty guys play sports.

We're in the middle of reviewing our notes when we hear a whistle blowing repeatedly. Looking up to see what's going on, we see Greyson flipping out and being held back by some of the other players. His anger is directed at someone on his team. He whips his helmet off and throws it to the side. Breaking free from the hold they have him in he tackles another player so hard his helmet flies off too. Greyson lands two punches before more teammates pull him off. I can hear his yells from here. They're not clear enough to decipher what he's saying, but loud enough to hear the harshness in his tone. *What the hell happened?*

Frankie scoffs and shakes her head bringing my focus back to her. "I wonder if they're going to whip out their dicks to compare sizes next," she says, causing us both to chuckle.

Our attention goes back to the field in time to see Greyson sitting on the bench. His coach is yelling something at him, but he's definitely not listening.

Nope, not one bit.

He's too busy staring at me from across the field. I can feel the intensity in his stare. It sets my body on fire. Damn him and damn my body's reaction to him.

After what feels like an hour-long stare-off, Greyson goes back onto the field to finish practice. Frankie and I complete our assignments with what time we have left, and I draft a study guide for Corbin to use later.

Moments later, my phone chimes from my bag. Speak of the devil.

*Corbin: Have I told you what a lifesaver you are?*
*Me: Honestly, it's no problem. I'm glad I can help.*
*Corbin: What's your favorite snack so I can at least pay you in copious amounts of treats.*
*Me: You don't have to bring me anything. I'm more than happy to help a friend in need.*
*Corbin: Okay... so that means I'm picking up one of everything from the convenience store.*
*Me: Stahp! Not necessary lol.*
*Corbin: I'm going to do it unless you tell me.*
*Me: Fine... M&M's will suffice.*
*Corbin: Perfect... see you in a little bit.*
*Me: See ya soon.*

Tucking my phone back into my purse, I glance in Frankie's direction. "Mind telling me what has you smiling like that?" she asks as she gathers her things.

"Oh, it was Corbin. I'm helping him study for a quiz later. He was asking, no scratch that, demanding I tell him what kind of snack I'd like as repayment." I let out a small chuckle.

"He's a looker that one," she says from beside me.

"Yeah..." I answer nonchalantly.

"But—" she prods, knowing damn well there's more to my answer.

I let out a deep sigh, damn this girl. She really can read minds.

"Buuut, I'm still in love with your stupid friend," I say, shaking my head.

"Atta-girl! The first step to recovery is admitting you have a problem to begin with." We both laugh at that.

"In all seriousness, it seems like there's a lot of misunderstanding between the two of you. But I think it will all be okay once you air it out."

I wrap my arms around her. "Thank you. I really hope so. Honestly, it feels nice to have someone I can rely on here."

"No problem girlie." She stands, throwing her books into her bag. "Now come on, we're meeting them outside the locker room."

Leaning against the wall opposite the boys' locker room, I wait for the guys to get out. Frankie ran to her locker to drop off her books, so I'm by myself twirling my charm bracelet to pass the time.

"You going to tell me what you're doing here... in my town, Stacks?" His gruff voice startles me, but its familiarity soothes me to my core.

Why? Why is this so damn confusing. I just want to leap into his arms and wrap my body around his. To feel his love envelop me, making the horrible events of the last month and a half disappear. But even if what Frankie says is true about Amber and him, he still practically pulled that witch into his lap right in front of me as if to prove a point. The memory of the two of them is like ice-cold water being dumped on my head and has my anger flaring.

"Trust me, I didn't want to come here after the way things went down. I had no choice but to come live with Ethel," I say in defeat, contemplating just telling him why I'm here in the first place. He insinuated on my first day at school that I came here for Jacob. At the time I liked leaving him hanging on that thought but my resolve is fading and a big part of me wants him to know what's happened in his absence.

"What do you mean Lottie—" Before he can complete the sentence, I cut him off.

"My Papa died Greyson, he died. He's gone... just like every-one else who ever gave a shit about me," I say, trying with all my might not to let my voice crack.

Just as he goes to speak again, I spot Frankie and the guys walking our way. Not wanting to have this conversation here, I move to join them. We need privacy for this because I know damn well there's going to be a lot of emotions and tears.

He grabs my arm which has my gaze swinging his way. He just stares at me with a look on his face I can't quite describe, maybe it's shock, remorse, or pity. Whatever it is, I'm glad it's there. "Lottie... damn. I—I'm so sorry. I had no idea," he says with such sincerity it takes all I have to not break. I shake my head, keeping the tears at bay. "Not now Grey, later. We can talk later, I promise."

\*\*\*

## *Greyson-*

Vinny's is our favorite pizza spot in town but right now I could give fuck all about eating. Sitting here on my Harley, I still can't get over the fact that her grandfather passed sometime in the last month or so. He was the last living relative who truly cared about her. My heart aches for my girl. She has been through so much loss in her short life already.

Jumping off my bike, I see her entering the restaurant in front of Lucian and Frankie. I call out for Frankie to wait up. She hears me and thankfully stops, nodding her head to Lucian, silently telling him to follow Lottie inside.

"What's up G, Lottie seemed upset on the ride over. That have anything to do with you dickhead?" She says, giving me a tentative look as the door shuts.

"Look I know you don't want to get in the middle of it, but I am a mess right now. She just told me her Papa passed sometime recently. I can't believe I wasn't there for her. Did she tell you what happened and when?" I stop and shake my head, still in disbelief that he's dead. "Did she get to say goodbye to him?"

Frankie looks at me with pity, like she knows what she's about to say is going to fuck me up.

"Lottie got the call he was in ICU the evening you saw her with Jacob. She rushed back to New York and was able to say goodbye." She hesitates, "but he died right after she arrived."

I feel like my knees could buckle out from under me. If I wasn't wrestling with my own demons that day, I would have been with her when she got that phone call.

Frankie pats me on the shoulder. "G, you couldn't have known. I know you, don't beat yourself up over this."

"But why didn't she call to tell me? I would have flown there to be with her. Instead, she blocked me," I say desperately.

"Greyson, that's something you'll have to talk to her about. I've already said enough."

I nod, knowing that's all she'll give. Frankie hugs me before she heads inside.

Trying to wrap my head around everything, I take a second before following her. *Damn what are the fucking chances?*

The regret I've been carrying around for how the summer ended just increased by a thousand percent.

*Immature, insecure fuck.*

I was always so worried about Lottie's confidence and wanting her to understand just how amazing she was that maybe I wasn't looking in the mirror at my own insecurities. Obviously, I have some serious mommy issues that have caused me more problems than I like to admit, partially because I sweep those feelings under the rug.

I wish I could walk into this restaurant right now and carry her home with me. I just want to hold her all night and tell her how sorry I am. She adored her Papa.

Knowing the guys are waiting on me, I get my shit together and walk in. Instead of sitting at one big table, Nox and Ford are at a booth with Lucian's sister Emerson. Frankie and Lucian sit across from Lottie and Snow in the booth right behind them. As much as it fucking burns me up from the inside out, I take my seat beside Ford. Of course, I have the perfect view of Lottie, and she is looking right at me. There is so much emotion in her beautiful hazel eyes. I start standing to go to her, over this bullshit game we are playing with each other, but before I get out of the booth, I notice Snow sling his arm around her. She doesn't push him anyway either. Instead, she laughs at whatever he whispers in her ear.

*Way too fucking friendly for my liking.*

I will my ass to sit back in my seat, trying to keep my cool after what I just learned she went through. The guys feel the tension in the air and try making jokes to distract me, but nothing works. The waitress comes and I don't even order because I've lost my appetite.

Ford snaps me out of my trance when he puts his arm over the top of both my wrists. "Bruh chill. You're about to smash the parmesan all over the damn table." Looking down, I didn't even realize I was rolling the parmesan and red pepper shakers together in my hands.

"You're lucky this is all I'm putting my hands on tonight."

"Yeah, I know. It took five of us to get you off Matthews at practice before you landed another punch. I caught that he said something about Lottie, but what the fuck sent you over the edge like that?" Lottie's news from earlier had me forgetting about my prick-of-a-teammate. He saw her in the stands and started running his mouth about getting with her. I tried to stay calm and told him to shut the fuck up the first time he opened his mouth, but when he mentioned asking Snow how good her pussy was... I completely lost my shit.

"Put it this way, he's lucky I didn't kill him. It's one thing to appreciate a woman's looks, but it's another to say the shit he was saying... especially about my girl. Fuck him..."

Lottie gets up to go to the bathroom and I ignore whatever they say back to me as I follow after her. Giving Snow an "eat shit" look as I pass him. *He better not even think about following us.*

Not taking a chance on missing her coming out of the bathroom I park my ass right against the wall and wait. A few minutes later she comes out and does a double take as she sees me.

"Grey... wh—what are you doing?" she says as she stops in her tracks.

"Lottie, I need to talk to you. Please? This is driving me fucking crazy. Seeing you sitting there with him like you're his is killing me."

She doesn't come any closer as she says, "I don't belong to anyone Greyson. Not you, not Corbin, not Ethel... no one."

"All I'm asking is that you explain to me why you aren't mine anymore. I know I fucked up leaving that night and now knowing what you've been through during that time... I just need to understand everything."

Finally, she softens a little bit, "I want answers too, Grey."

Eagerly I say, "Then let me come by later or I can come get you. I'm on my bike and don't have your helmet with me."

"It's not my helmet and I'm sorry, but I have plans."

"Lottie you are the only person who has ever ridden on the back of my bike. Do I look like the type of guy who lets random bitches ride around with me? You know me better than that. I literally ordered it specifically for you this summer."

That seems to stun her "Maybe. But that was the Greyson I knew this summer... or the person I thought I knew." *What the hell is she talking about? I wonder what kind of shit her crazy grandma filled her head with. Regardless, I deserve a chance to explain myself.*

"Fuck that, you know me, Lottie. Better than anyone." I move toward her, and she doesn't back away.

"Cancel your plans," I say as I grab the back of her neck and make sure she is looking up at me. "You may say you aren't mine, but I am yours. Talk with me tonight. This can't go on any longer. You belong with me."

That longing and pain is back in her eyes. I knew I didn't imagine it the other day. "I'm sorry, but I can't back out on him now."

That throws fire on my emotions. "Who the fuck is him?"

She maintains eye contact with me. "Corbin, I'm supposed to help him study for Anatomy tonight. He was my first friend here and doesn't deserve me dipping out on him just because you say so."

"Are you serious right now?" I roar, no longer able to keep my emotions in check. "I guess I shouldn't be surprised, you have a habit of picking others over me. That's what got us in this mess in the first place, isn't it?"

She pulls away startled, taking her warmth with her, and I know by the look on her face I've fucked up. "Yeah, blame it all on me Greyson. I guess that's the only way you can sleep at night." Lottie starts to walk away as she says, "I'm not doing this with you right now. Not here for everyone to hear."

I don't even attempt to stop her. I'm so fucking pissed, I walk right to the booth, jerking my helmet off the seat, and tell the guys I'm out.

Maybe I'm delusional and she really doesn't love me anymore. No, what we had doesn't just go away like that. I refuse to believe that until those words come out of her mouth.

I practically begged her to talk to me and she still denied me. Fuck that. She's going to have to come to me this time.

# Chapter Eighteen

I sit in the passenger seat of Corbin's blacked-out Charger in silence. Normally I would be giddy over the fact that his car is fricken sweet, but no, I'm too busy dwelling on what just happened.

How dare he try to blame me for this. Yes, I admit him seeing me with Jacob was not ideal, but nothing happened. If he had given me one second of his time to explain that day, we wouldn't be in this mess. Instead, he ran off to Richmond Hills and did who knows what. But I'm the one at fault. Ugh!

My heart hurts and I already feel defeated. *Are we ever going to work this out?* I can see it in his eyes that he misses me, but his actions and words have my head a mess.

"You know Trouble, you can talk to me," Corbin says from beside me.

"I don't want to bother anymore people with my shit, but thank you."

"You and him are a thing, aren't you?" he asks, but he already knows the answer.

I shift in my seat to face him. I've been so distracted by my racing thoughts that I didn't realize we're already in my driveway.

"We met over the summer in Nori Beach, hooked up, broke up, and now we're here," I say, trailing off, not sure what to tell him and knowing damn well our relationship was more than those few little words, but I don't want to go into details right now.

"I knew you were too good to be true," he says, shaking his head.

"What's that supposed to mean?" I question him.

"The moment you walked through the doors at Lights Out, I knew you were different. Like a breath of fresh air. It didn't take long for me to pick up on the Greyson shit, but I couldn't quite figure it out. But now I get it," he says, smiling at me, but I notice it doesn't reach his eyes.

Shit, did I lead Corbin on? I mean he's fricken gorgeous and if I wasn't so hung up on Greyson, I would definitely be into him, but the heart wants what it wants.

"I'm sorry," I utter with sincerity, not really sure what else to say.

"Honestly, you did nothing wrong. Greyson is a lucky guy if he gets you back. But don't worry, I'll respect your fucked up relationship. Just know I'm here if you need me. If there's one thing for you to know about me, it's that I'm loyal as fuck, so when I say I got you, I mean it. And lucky for you, you now have an overprotective bestie," he says as he winks at me.

I lean across the console and give him a big hug, thankful for his understanding.

"Thank you," I beam, settling back into my seat.

"Alright, let's get this shit over with," he groans, reaching over to grab his backpack from the backseat. We both exit the car and walk to my front steps. "I hope you're as big of a wiz as they say you are because this shit's for the birds."

That has me chuckling as I punch in the code to enter the house. He nudges my shoulder with his. "There's that smile. Don't worry Trouble... it'll all work out."

I smile back at him. Everyone keeps telling me it'll all work out. Guess I just have to wait and see.

*** 

"You're kidding me, right?" I hear Ashley yell through the speaker of my phone as it sits on the counter.

"Tell me about it, trying to put the blame solely on me! Then he gives me the cold shoulder all week long," I say, walking around my room as I finish getting ready for school.

"I mean, it's been almost two weeks and you haven't had a legit conversation yet? What is wrong with you both?" she asks. I know she's right. If we let it fester any longer, who knows what'll happen.

"The timing is never right. Recently, our interactions have always been somewhere public and around our friends. Definitely not the right setting for what we need to talk about." I sigh as I throw my long hair up into a high ponytail.

"Tig, the timing will never be right. Sometimes you just need to let it happen. I know damn well you will feel a shit-ton better once you do," she says as she lets out a huge yawn.

"Ugh, I miss you so much. When am I seeing you? Are you able to make it to the fundraising Gala?" I ask her. I'm thankful she's only a phone call away, but I need to see my friend.

"I've been looking at my schedule, and I think I'm good for that weekend. I can come out that Thursday," she says through another loud yawn.

"Okay, clearly I'm boring you, so I'll let you go," I joke, knowing she worked last night and had only been sleeping for a few hours before I called her this morning.

"Oh, you shut your face. I'm always here to talk. But I do need my beauty sleep, I'm seeing Trent tonight." I can hear the smile in her voice.

"Love you Bitty, get some rest, and remember to stretch well before any physical activity," I laugh out at her.

"Love you too, Tig," she says and ends our call.

It's Friday and I'm happy to have the weekend ahead of me. Ethel is away, and Remi invited me to a party tomorrow night. I haven't made an effort to speak to Grey yet, considering he's been ignoring my existence since the pizza place. But I'm planning on staying sober at the party and asking him to go somewhere private with me—somewhere we can talk everything out without interruptions. I'm scared as hell to hear his side of things from that night, but I know we both need that or we are going to keep going in circles on this merry-go-round.

My day goes by without a Greyson spotting. He didn't even show up to lunch, much to my disappointment. Even though we're not talking, I still love admiring him from afar. As much as it pains me to say it, I crave his presence.

Closing my locker, I grab my bag and sling it over my shoulder. Placing one airpod in, I head toward the school exit. I'm halfway down the hall when I feel a tug on my ponytail. Not enough to make me fall, but hard enough to make me stumble backwards causing my bag to slip.

"What the hell?" I say out loud, at the moment not sure whom to direct it to.

"Oops, sorry," comes from behind me. I'd know that voice anywhere.

"You're kidding me, right? What the hell is wrong with you Amber?" I yell as I scan the ground for my fallen bag, but her words have my eyes jumping back to her.

"No, you're the one who's kidding yourself, you fat bitch! Thinking you can come in here like you own the fucking place.

I'm so sick of hearing your name everywhere I go. You're nothing but a spoiled fat slut," she spews at me.

I'm speechless right now. What in the actual fuck is going on? She doesn't know anything about me, I've never spoken a damn word to her. I feel the crowd forming around us.

"Oh, and stop throwing yourself at our guys, it's pathetic. I've already told you, they want nothing to do with you," Amber sneers as her girls snicker at her side.

It takes all the restraint I have not to punch this girl in the face. But I decide to use my words, and if what I've been told is true, they're going to hurt.

"No Amber, you want to know what's pathetic... it's chasing after a group of guys who don't give a shit about you. Throwing yourself at them day after day must be exhausting. Hoping they'll take you to an empty classroom, or the backseat of their car for a quick hook-up. Knowing damn well they'll never want anything more from you, you're just a hole for them, a way to quickly get off," I say as I shrug my shoulders, keeping my face void of emotions.

I hear the side commentary from the surrounding crowd, but I ignore them, trying to stay focused on Amber. I don't trust her to keep her hands to herself.

"Oh really, that's not what a certain someone said when I was last with him. If I recall correctly, he said I was the best he ever had and that's why he keeps coming back for more. But we'll keep names out of it," she sneers with a smug look on her face.

"Whatever you want to keep telling yourself, Amber. No one takes you or any of the Jock Hoppers seriously," I say, earning a big "Ooo" from the crowd.

"Jock Hopper?" she questions.

Feigning innocence as she did a few months ago, I answer, "Oh you didn't know? That's what everyone calls you and your friends... so desperate to hop from one jock's dick to another."

"You fat fucking bitch, how dare you!" she yells as she lunges toward me just as two large, tattooed arms grab hold of her.

"Oh Greyson, did you hear all the nasty things she was saying about me?" Amber says with a pout on her face that would almost pass as believable if she wasn't fake-as-fuck.

My eyes are locked onto his arms, which are slowly releasing her. I think I'm going to be sick. I go to leave but the sound of his voice stops me.

"I've heard plenty, Amber, and every word Lottie's said is the truth." *What?*

"Let's get one thing straight... Lottie is perfect, her mind, body, and soul. She's every guy's fantasy. You're only knocking her because you can't stand the way everyone wants her or wants to be near her. But trust me when I say, she is what *every* guy wants, not a petty ass bitch who can't take no for an answer. So fuck off Amber, and keep Lottie's name out of your mouth," he says as he gestures with his hand between the two of us.

I swear my knees buckle at his words. Did I hear him correctly? Chancing a look in his direction he looks pissed, and I'm not sure if it's because of Amber, or if he's still mad at me. Ford's hand clasps my shoulder, breaking my stare-off with Greyson. "You good?" he asks, and I nod my head, still unable to form any words. I notice he has my bag in his hand and Nox is standing next to him. Grabbing the bag, I mouth a silent thank you and they both nod in unison.

Amber and her cronies storm off in the opposite direction. She looked like she was about to cry. Serves her right for starting shit with me. I did nothing to her. She's the one who has instigated it since day one.

Greyson doesn't say a damn word to me as he walks past and out the front doors. This boy is a mind fuck, to say the least. He goes from giving me the cold shoulder to sticking up for me in front of everyone to not saying a damn word.

*What is going on in that head of yours, Greyson?*

# Chapter Nineteen

"Come on fucker, I don't have all night!" I yell at Lennox as he takes his sweet ass time talking to Emerson and his little brother Colton. I swear Nox has a soft spot for the girl, but he's too damn touchy about it, so we don't bring it up.

He walks towards me, flipping me off. I don't give a shit. Anticipation thrumming through me to get to this party, hoping Lottie will be there since Remi's friends are throwing it. It's on the east side of town near Ethel's house where all the rich kids in our area live. Our football game was away last night, so I didn't get the opportunity to catch her at the bonfire like last weekend. Even though I've been giving Lottie the cold shoulder at school all week, my need to catch sight of her any chance I can hasn't diminished. I did break my promise to myself about letting Lottie come to me when I heard Amber spouting off hateful bullshit to her the other day. *I better not see that bitch tonight.* I always knew she was a privileged little princess, but I didn't realize how much of a cunt she was until that moment. Hearing those words out of her mouth and the hurt Lottie tried hiding on her face made me hate the fact that I ever touched Amber.

"Chill dude, I was just looking out for them. Colton was trying to convince Em to go party over in Highland to see some chick he is digging. He thinks Emerson is his wing woman or some shit," Nox says as he opens the back door to my dad's Tahoe. I asked him if I could borrow it for the night because I was DD'ing and didn't know who would need a ride later. Of course, he offered to just drive us wherever we needed to go, but I told him I wouldn't drink tonight.

Ford decides to chime in as Lennox gets in the backseat and I pull off. "How Colton is only friends with her and those long, lean legs and perky tits... I have no idea. I wouldn't have been able to keep my dick in check."

A low growl comes from Nox before he says, "Don't talk about her like that motherfucker!"

"Oh, I forgot you're more protective of her than your little brother, her supposed best friend is. Wonder why that is, huh, Nox?"

For fuck's sake, I guess tonight is going to be that kind of night. Ford is feeling like testing the limits.

"Drop it Ford," Nox quickly says with a deadly glare.

Ford throws his hands up in surrender. "Okay, okay... damn, Coach must have gone hard on you and Snow in the ring today. You're touchy as hell."

Just hearing his name has me on edge.

Nox seems happy for the subject change. "He's been pushing us both a lot lately. Speaking of that though, I feel like it's my place to tell you..." He pauses and I meet his eyes in my rear-view mirror. "Lottie came with Snow to practice today to watch us spar. Coach jumped his ass about bringing a distraction with him, and Corbin told him it wasn't like that. So maybe it's not, but just wanted to prepare you because they both said they were going to the party tonight."

My skin starts to crawl just thinking about my girl hanging with him. I've seen how he looks at her.

\*\*\*

Stay calm... stay calm... stay fucking calm.

That's what I'm chanting in my head to keep myself from breaking Corbin Snow's neck!

By the time we get to the party things are in full swing and I spot Lottie almost instantly. Wearing a little red dress with her hair pulled up in a ponytail, she looks so fucking sexy it physically hurts as my eyes rake over her. The dress isn't low cut but it's short and fitted to her curves, showcasing them like the prize possessions they are. The dress shimmies up her thighs as Lottie dances, but she doesn't constantly tug at it like she would have in the past. No, she's carefree and having fun just like I've always wanted for her. Even the jealous fucker inside me is proud to see that. She has come so far from the girl I met at the beginning of the summer in that bunny outfit. Just like the first night I saw her, I'm easily caught up in the way she moves those perfect curves of hers on the dance floor.

I know she sees me standing here watching her like the obsessed fucker I am. Our connection is still so strong I always feel it intensify when we're in the same room. She can try to deny it but we both know it... we both *feel* it. That's why her eyes keep finding mine through the crowd.

After two songs straight of staring at her, my cock is throbbing in my pants—remembering the ways I taught her to put those moves on my dick.

I go from turned on to murderous in point two seconds when that pussy Snow puts his hands on her hips as she moves against him.

To top it off, Lottie is loving his attention. Grinding into him, laughing at something he's whispering in her ear.

*He's not that fucking funny.*

My fingernails are digging holes into my hands as I clench my fists, willing him to stop touching what's mine.

Right as I'm about to say fuck this shit and grab Lottie, Remi pulls her into a group of girls to dance. Snow makes his way over to the beer pong table with Lucian. I know he feels me staring at him, but he never looks my way.

I stay chill and let her have fun with her new friends. I may be pissed at her but seeing her smile like she does with Ashley makes me happy for her.

As these thoughts filter through my mind, she looks up at me and maintains eye contact with intention in her hazel stare. She is dancing sensually to this song as she rubs her hands all over her curves... still staring. Lottie may have toned up a bit, but my girl is still stacked in all the right places, and I need my hands on her so badly.

Adjusting my cock in my jeans, I watch her hips sway. *Fuck, she's torturing me.* Lottie has a smug smirk on her face, knowing exactly what she's doing to me. I realize Demi Lovato is singing about revenge and being a savage to her ex.

*Oh, fuck that.*

I know I told myself she would have to come to me, but I can't keep this shit up any longer. Before I know it, I'm moving towards her at the speed of lightning.

I grab her by the hips and pull her close. She looks up at me and gasps.

"You trying to tell me something with this song, Stacks?" I practically growl into her ear. "Have you gotten your revenge yet, huh? Has his cock been inside you... are you riding it just like I taught you?" She looks at me in utter shock.

"Tell me... does he make you melt under his touch? Can he make your body numb with ecstasy like it did under me? Do your toes curl and that pretty pink pussy of yours weep when he's deep inside of you?" I'm seething with rage and jealousy, no longer able to control anything that's coming out of my mouth.

Her eyes well up with tears and she smacks me across the face.

"You fucking asshole," she barely whispers and turns away from me to run down the hallway.

Shit! Rubbing my cheek and wondering what the hell I expected.

*That's exactly how to get her to talk to you... dumbass.*

Knowing I need to fix this, I get to the door right as she's about to slam it and use my boot to stop her.

"G... Greyson. Just leave me the fuck alone. Seriously, I can't deal with you being like this. How dare you speak to me like that and then to top it off, you have the nerve to ask me if I'm fucking someone else. Pot meet kettle."

"Listen Lottie—" I start as I move us further into the bathroom and lock the door.

She pushes into my chest and points in my face.

"No motherfucker, you listen. I loved you so much. I'm the one who deserves an explanation. On top of how the summer ended, I get to your school and the first time I see you, you're pulling that dumb bitch between your legs rubbing it in my damn face!" she says as she moves further into the bathroom, trying to put space between us.

"She doesn't mean shit to me, in case you couldn't tell that by the way I let her have it when I heard what she said to you at school Friday. I only pulled her into me that day to see if you even gave a fuck about me anymore, since you dropped me like a bad habit without any explanation." I continue, "Lottie, that was the one time you've seen me around her but yet I keep getting the privilege of watching you all over Snow. What is this, your way of punishing me? Or let me guess, Snow's just another bad boy to pass the time until you marry my fucking stepbrother!"

All the anger in her face drains and her shock is evident. Her parted lips are stunned to silence.

"Yeah, that's right Babygirl. Sherri Roberts is Mommy Dearest. At least you got to meet one of my parents before it ended. Jacob is the son she decided to raise. Even though he's not biologically hers and I am... she chose him over me. She chose that life over me," I say, pounding my fist on my chest.

"Greyson," Lottie whispers. Unshed tears fill her eyes as the realization of why I overreacted that day hits her. Covering her mouth with her hands, I can barely hear her say, "Oh my God, Greyson, I had no idea."

Lottie shakes her head in disbelief as I say, "I know you didn't."

The girl I love is still there. She knows my insecurities about my mother and how seeing him there with her that day would get to me. She comes to me and wraps her arms around my waist.

I embrace her. Holding her close I whisper, "I know baby, I just needed time to chill out and get my head on straight. Then I was going to come back and explain it all to you when we were alone. I just needed some time baby."

As she looks up into my eyes, I continue, "But then, when I came back the next day and Ethel told me you were gone for good... I started to question everything. I know she's a conniving cunt, so I didn't trust her word, but then you had me blocked from your phone and social media, so I had no choice but to assume you had a change of heart."

Looking up at me with her chin resting in the center of my chest, she shakes her head no. Relief floods through me.

She drops her head, putting her forehead where her chin was but all I want is to see her eyes. Leaning back and using my knuckle to tip her chin up to me, I whisper, "Hey, chin up Babygirl."

That gains me a teary smile as she says, "You don't know how many times I've told myself that over the past few months. Even when I didn't want your words in my head."

"Is that what you were telling yourself as you danced tonight? Were you showing off for me? I can't stand that fucker's hands on you." I grab her hips and bring her flush to me again. "Do you want him Lottie?"

"No Grey, I don't." She says, biting her bottom lip. I press into her for some relief. My cock has been half-mast since our stare down on the dance floor. Lottie lets out a little moan.

Leaning down, I lick her ear and whisper, "I've missed you so damn much. You going to let me kiss you, Stacks?"

Grabbing her ponytail and pulling back slightly to expose her neck to me, I take in her scent as I nip at her. She moans a yes. With no hesitation I move to place my lips on hers. Kissing her like I've been wanting to do for so long. Biting her bottom lip, unable to control myself from all the pent up need I have racing through me. She lets my tongue lap hers. Our mouths picking right up where we left off, like there has been no time in between. Lottie's body responds to mine just like it always has.

Trailing my hand down to the bottom of her dress, I graze along the inside of her thigh. I feel the chill bumps my touch brings to her skin. By the way her kisses become more intense, I take that as my okay to move my hand up to her panties. "Soaked, like always."

Moving the lace to the side, I groan, remembering the way she tastes. She whimpers into my mouth, "More." With that I start to fuck her with two of my fingers. I know exactly what she needs to let go completely. Taking my thumb to her clit as I move my mouth down to her tits, I bite her nipple through the fabric of her dress. That has her head falling back.

"Feels so good Grey. Yes... yes." Looking back up at me, she grinds herself down on my hand, moving in perfect rhythm with me.

"It's been too long since I've felt you." I feel the thrum of her body start to rise. "Fuck yes. Please don't stop."

"Never Babygirl, let me hear it. Let them all hear it... come on my hand." Knowing words always put her over the edge, she starts to spasm, moaning my name as she comes. Feeling her pussy throbbing against my fingers as they're buried inside her has my cock aching for a turn.

I don't remove my fingers until she pushes me back. My stomach instantly sinks until she drops to her knees and starts unbuckling my jeans.

*Oh, fuck yes.*

Helping her get my dick out, I feed it into her mouth. "Fuck me, I've missed this mouth." Letting it pop back out, she grabs my cock and licks every inch before slapping it against her tongue and pulling on my balls as she takes me into her mouth. Lottie hasn't forgotten a single thing I like either. Watching her beautiful face as she looks up at me through lust-filled hazel eyes has to be one of the sexiest things I've ever seen.

A knock on the door jolts us both apart. "Shit." I pull back, making sure the door is locked properly. I don't want anyone to see her like this.

"We're good," I say to Lottie as I walk back to her on her knees. I notice a weird look on her face. A million miles away from the seductive stare she was just giving me with my cock in her mouth.

She stands abruptly. "What the fuck am I thinking?" I try to grab her, confused as hell. "Shit... no, no, no. I'm not ready for this," she says, looking down at my still hard dick. "You are very capable of getting your dick sucked by other girls whenever you want. I've seen the video to prove it..."

Lottie gets out of my hold and has the door opened before I can even comprehend what just happened. "What the fuck, what video?"

"Look Greyson, I'm sorry about the Jacob situation. I truly had no idea. But the fact still remains... I didn't cheat on you and unfortunately, you can't say the same."

I pull my pants up and adjust myself before going after her. "Lottie! I never cheated on you. Don't run away from me," I roar as she continues to run down the hallway.

My mind is racing. What is she talking about? I may have my secrets, but that's certainly not one of them. I would never cheat on her.

By the time I get downstairs, Snow is comforting her as he says, "Okay, let me tell Lucian I'm leaving. Go to my car and I'll meet you out there."

I immediately grab his hand that's on Lottie's arm and throw it off her. "The fuck? You're not leaving with him." My eyes dart between the two of them, settling on her. "You owe me an explanation for what you just accused me of."

"Don't fucking put your hands on me." Those words come from Snow as he pushes at me, but Nox and Lucian are there breaking us up before anything can escalate. They're all staring at me like I'm a madman, and maybe I am. Truthfully, I don't give a shit about what any of them think right now. I need her, I need to talk to her.

"Baby please," I beg as I step closer to her. Taking both of my hands to her face, I hold her there to look in my eyes. "Stacks, I would never cheat on you." She attempts to push me away so I try to get through to her again. "I haven't touched another girl that way since the first night I met you in Nori Beach, I swear on my Pop's grave."

I can see it in her eyes and the way she relaxes in my hands. She believes me, or she wants to at least. "Please come with me, we can go wherever you want to go, but we need to talk all this out."

# Chapter Twenty

I place a calming hand on Greyson's arm and his eyes jump to mine when I say, "Okay, let's go." At this point, I just want to get out of here. We're surrounded by classmates and the last thing I need is to be the center of more drama than what I've already encountered this week.

We need this, to lay it all bare and see where we stand once it's all said and done.

Corbin is standing a few feet behind Grey and by the look on his face, he is fuming. I smile at him, hoping I can convey that I'm alright and that I'm grateful for his protectiveness. "I'm fine, Corbin, don't worry. But he *is* right, we really do need to talk. It's long overdue."

He nods, his face taking on a lesser pissed-off look as he says, "Okay Trouble, text me when you're home safe."

"Like fuck she will," Greyson practically growls from beside me. My eyes dart to Greyson's and I glare at him, hoping like hell he'll keep his mouth shut. Geez, can we just leave already without having more issues? He makes no effort to leave, just stays put and scowls as his eyes stay fixed on Corbin.

"I'll be okay, thank you," I say to Corbin as I turn to Greyson, pulling on his arm to get his feet moving toward all the cars parked along the yard.

"Aw man, there goes our ride," I hear Ford from somewhere nearby, followed by the sound of a smack.

"Ouch, what'd you do that for?" Ford whines.

"You're an idiot," I hear Nox's deep voice say.

Looking in their direction, I see Ford rubbing the back of his head and Nox looking disappointingly at his friend. Our eyes meet for a second and Nox gives me a knowing nod. *I wonder how much they know about us.*

*I welcome the crisp autumn air as we walk to Greyson's car in silence. There's so much to be said, yet how do we start?*

Needing to break the awkwardness surrounding us, I say, "We can go to my house, Ethel won't be there." He just nods his head in understanding as we continue to walk down the road.

He clicks the key fob in his hand as we approach a large SUV. I raise an eyebrow, wondering where this vehicle came from. Greyson catches my look and says, "It's Dad's, I was DD tonight and the three of us don't fit in my truck."

"Oh, that was nice of you," I say.

"Nah, not that nice. I really hoped they would be calling an Uber at the end of the night, since my mission was to take you home," he says with a smile as he opens my door.

I glare at him. "That was a little presumptuous, don't you think? Considering we've barely had a civil conversation since I've been here."

"Lottie, you forget how well I know you... you may talk a good game, but I see you, Babygirl. I know deep down, you're still mine and I will prove it to you every day. I'm tired of this bullshit chase." He runs his finger down my arm. The closeness of his body to mine and the feel of his hands on me once again has goosebumps running across my skin. The smirk on his face makes me want to hit him, not only because of his smugness but because he's right, and that fact bugs the hell out of me.

I climb into the passenger seat, and he shuts the door without another word. The silence is deafening between us, but I don't know what to say. He says he hasn't touched anyone since he met me. If that's the case, then why did Amber go out of her way to send me that? Well I know why... she's a dumb bitch. Clearly, he has no clue what she did. I wonder if he's aware the video exists.

We park in the driveway and head inside. He trails a step or two behind me. Chancing a glance in his direction, his head is low and for the first time, I see how much he truly is hurting from all of this. I walk through the kitchen, grabbing water for both of us, and walk out the French doors that lead to the veranda. We settle onto one of the numerous outdoor couches and just sit. How do we even begin? I'm so wound up I don't know if I can get my story out correctly.

The cicadas and crickets are loud tonight, helping me get lost in the symphony of them. The constant chirping eases my tension as I stare out at the stars. The night sure is something down here. The light pollution of Manhattan used to drown out the glow of the stars, but here, I feel like I'm staring at a completely different sky.

"I mean it Lottie, every word I've ever said. Nothing has changed for me. Now it's your turn to tell me what's going on in that pretty head of yours. Tell me what has you on your knees, eager to swallow my cock one moment, then ready to gouge my eyes out the next," he says, eyes still focused on the sky as well.

*Here goes nothing... or everything.*

"That night, after you saw me with Jacob, I got a call from my Papa's aide and family friend Sally. She told me he was being rushed to the hospital and that I needed to head home as soon as I could. I had been trying to call and text you for a few hours with no luck. I wanted to at least let you know I was leaving town and would come back as soon as I could," I say, facing him on the couch.

"When I called, a girl picked up the phone and said her name was Amber. I asked if you were around, but she refused to put you on. She was so mean to me Greyson, I don't think I have ever heard someone say such hurtful and nasty things to another person in my entire life." I pause, trying to maintain my composure. He reaches out to grab my hand and I let him, his warmth calming my hands that I wasn't aware were shaking.

"I lost my phone that night. Frankie and the guys wound up taking my drunk-ass home," he says, his blue eyes shining at me.

"I know... Frankie told me last week—"

"So, then what is this all about then, if you know I wasn't with her, and the guys took me home. You said I cheated on you Lottie, something I would never do, especially not to you," he says, his voice growing loud with frustration.

"Let me finish. Not soon after I hung up the phone, I received a text message from an unknown number. It was a North Carolina area code, so I opened it. It was a video of a girl with bleach-blonde hair giving head. At first, I wasn't sure what I was seeing, but then I heard your groans, and I just knew it was you. I didn't know what to do. My world was crumbling down around me. I blocked you and the number that texted me. I felt so foolish and betrayed. So used and devastated," I cry out as tears stream down my cheeks.

Greyson grabs my face, cupping it with his hands. "I haven't touched that girl since last spring, and it was a one-time thing. I was drunk at a party, and I let her go down on me. It was a stupid mistake because Amber then thought she had some sort of claim to me. I set her straight many times before, but you see how delusional she is. She continues to hang around, hoping I'll throw her a bone. I sure as fuck didn't know she filmed it. You have to believe me, Lottie. I swear to you." I can see it in his expression and in the depths of his eyes that he's telling the truth.

I exhale a shaky breath. "I can't get that image out of my head. The thought of her lips on you has me seeing red. I hate her, Greyson. I don't think I've ever hated anyone in my entire life as much as I hate her."

"Come here," he says as he pulls me onto his lap. I snuggle into his chest as he wraps his arms around me.

"I'm so sorry you had to see that. I didn't know she filmed it. I can't imagine what that must have felt like. If the roles were flipped, I think I might have gone off the deep end," he says, placing a light kiss on my head.

"Papa died shortly after I arrived at the hospital early that morning. I felt like my life was over. I didn't know what was real anymore." I sob into his chest. "All I kept thinking was how everyone I've ever loved leaves me."

"Shhh," he says, trying to calm my shaking body. It feels so good to be in his arms. "It's going to be okay; we're going to be okay," he whispers into my hair as his hand rubs soothingly up and down my back.

"I'm so sorry I didn't give you the chance to explain the video or why you ran away—" I say as he cuts me off. "Don't you apologize, I'm sorry I didn't reach out to you before I got so shit-faced I could barely walk. I just couldn't handle the fact that Jacob was sitting so close to you, that he had his hands on you. Deep down I know nothing happened, but in that moment, the fear that you were giving up on me took over. The possibility that you wanted someone that would fit into the lifestyle you're accustomed to. And now that you know who he is to me, I hope you can somewhat understand my freak out. It doesn't excuse why I fled, but it really was nothing you did. More of the possibility that someone I love could choose him over me again."

"Jacob is a family friend, nothing more. I've been around him numerous times, and it's always been platonic. After he made a move on me, which I don't think he would have done without Ethel's encouragement, I immediately pulled away and told him about you... about us. But it was too late, you already saw us and were storming off. And you know damn well I don't want or need any of this." I wave my hand around Ethel's obnoxious estate to prove my point. "I'd much rather have something that's real than something bought or bargained for. Besides in three months, I'm going to be one of the wealthiest eighteen-year-olds in North America," I say sardonically.

Greyson looks at me with a raised eyebrow. "Papa left me everything, even the Nori Beach house. Ethel walked away with nothing but a piece of paper," I say, answering his silent question.

"Everything?" he asks.

"Yes. Everything."

"So then why the hell are you even here? If you have the means to go anywhere with your new fortune, why are you in Richmond Hills?"

"Stupid New York laws... I'm not eligible to access my inheritance until I turn eighteen. So, my only living relative, who was omitted from her own parent's will, is now my legal guardian until then."

"Fuck..." he says understanding the situation.

"Has she said anything to you about it? Blame you for any of it?"

"No, not yet at least. Ethel's actually been on her best behavior around me. But I think something is going on that she's not telling me. Something is just not right."

"Shit Lottie, I'm sorry I was such an asshole to you when you got here. If I had known any of this... I would have been there for you. I hope you know that. I would have flown to New York to be by your side."

"I know you would have..." I say, snuggling a little bit closer to him.

Greyson holds me tighter and looks out at the night surrounding us, shaking his head back and forth as if he is still processing his thoughts, then looking back at my face. He takes in all my features with a sad, almost desperate look. "I was so lost without you Babygirl. So wrecked. I have been so angry, confused, and just fucking upset. I still can't believe this is happening to us. The fact that you just up and left without so much as an explanation, I knew right away that something was wrong. But then you blocked me, and I had no way of getting to you. Trent said Ashley refused to share any information about you, besides the fact that you were okay. Babe, I swear I've been so desperate that I was going to hire the Rebel Knight's PI for fucks sake. I just needed to find you. I was planning on going to Manhattan, finding you, and forcing you to tell me what the hell happened."

Feeling his body tremble with anger, I run my palm over his chest trying to soothe him. "I was a mess. I needed the time to heal, not only from my Papa's passing but from the devastation of losing you as well. We were so much so fast, that I don't think we even realized how attached we were. Coming to Richmond Hills was tough. I knew I was going to see you and I wasn't sure if I was going to be able to handle that. But I've met some really great people since I've been here."

I can see him tense up at my words. I'm not a fool, I know he still thinks there's something going on with Corbin. Tilting my head so I can see his face I say, "There is nothing between Corbin and me, he never tried to make a move, nothing. He said he knew almost immediately there was something between me and you and that he wouldn't do anything to interfere. Corbin's been nothing but kind, like an overprotective best friend. Something I really needed walking into school that first day."

His face calms and almost turns remorseful. "You don't know how much I regret not being the one to walk you through those doors the first day. All I kept hearing was how gorgeous this new girl was and all I kept thinking was how she didn't hold a candle to you. You could imagine my surprise when you strolled into the cafeteria, head held high, looking hot as fuck. I didn't know what to do. I was excited to see you, but still angry at the fact that you had just up and deaded me. Then you wouldn't even so much as glance in my direction. When I saw your interactions with Snow and my friends, jealousy raced through me. I couldn't think straight. Seeing you with him every day has had me raging... the only thing holding me back from punching him was fear of pushing you away more."

"Mmm, there's that protective, possessive man I've missed so much," I practically purr into his chest and his arms tighten around me once more. The candidness of this conversation and his feelings has me melting into him. His touch, smell, voice, heart, all of it. *Oh, how I've missed him.*

"Nothing has changed for me. You belong to me, Lottie Richmond. You're already anchored in here," he says, pointing to his chest. "Bone deep... soul deep. I am yours... completely and always." I can't help but let out an audible gasp at his words—realizing how long I've waited to hear him tell me that he still cares and that I'm still his. Because even through all my hurt, I've known. Known that my heart still belongs to him, it will always belong to him.

"I'll always be yours, Greyson. I love you so damn much it hurts. Even when my world was crumbling, I still thought of you daily," I sigh, staring up into his blue eyes. "But this has been a lot to take in and I think it's best if we take it slow. It's not that I don't want you, because god knows I do, but I need some time to process everything and get back to us, ok? I don't want anything to stand between us. Please promise me we will be open and honest with each other from now on. No more dodging tough conversations."

"I promise I will try my best," he replies with a pained look on his face. He leans down, pressing his lips to mine, deepening the kiss as I shift in his lap. Our tongues swirling together, eliciting a low moan from his throat. I can feel him hardening beneath me, the ache to feel him inside me thrums to life. But for now, I want to stay just like this. Wrapped up in all that is him.

We talk until the rays of the morning sun begin to peek over the trees of the foothills. We settled into a comfortable silence, watching the sky illuminate with the dawn of a new day. Its symbolism is not lost on me as I lie in Greyson's lap, his fingers running through my hair.

I lazily run my fingertips over the ocean waves on his newly inked arm. "This is beautiful, when did you get it?" I ask him, tracing the intricate lines.

"Thank you... about a month ago. Was a bitch healing with my football uniform and all, but I had to get it done," he says.

"I love the fact that you now have the beach and the mountains on you. Two of your favorite places." I sit up to inspect the artwork further. My hands roam all over his forearm and bicep. I turn his arm so I can see every intricate detail. When I flip his arm over, I stop and my eyes jump to his.

"Greyson—" is all I'm able to get out. The words lock in my throat as I take in the infinity rope design that intricately laces through the anchor tattoo on the inside of his forearm. Just like my charm. The placement is beautiful and the ocean scene around it looks like something out of a drawing. I notice two sea horses near the anchor, and I choke up.

"I told you *always* Babygirl, and I meant it when I said it," he says to me, cupping my face in his palms.

"Always," I say, barely able to keep the tears from falling. His arms wrap around me as my lips lock on to his.

I feel at peace, finally. I'm not completely sure where we go from here, but I haven't felt this at ease since the last time I was in his arms.

# Chapter Twenty-One

Cutting my bike off as I park in front of Ethel's massive house, I approach the front door with my nerves running wild. Even though we've been on plenty of dates over the summer, I know Lottie is keeping her guard up, so this feels like unfamiliar territory.

I told myself I would take it slow and not rush into things, but it's so fucking hard not having my hands on her. I'm trying my best to take it slow, which I am doing a shit job at as she reminded me mid-week after she found me waiting, yet again, to walk her to all her classes. That night when she agreed to let me pick her up from kickboxing after my football practice was over, I confessed to her that this was a hard transition for me but that I would back off some if she needed me to. Thank fuck she asked me not to. Lottie made a confession of her own, she said she was working hard on erasing the image that video of me instilled in her brain.

My chest ached at that. I couldn't imagine the roles being reversed and seeing a video of her with someone else. *Amber will pay for that shit, mark my words.*

Knocking on the large wooden door, James answers and welcomes me into the house. He may be Ethel's right-hand guy, but he's always been decent to me, so I reach out to shake his hand.

I see Lottie coming down the stairs, looking sexy as hell in tight black ripped jeans, little black biker boots that I have never seen before, and a tight burgundy long sleeve shirt. A total biker babe, and I love everything about it.

*Damn, maybe I shouldn't invite her to the Rebel Knights' cookout next week. They'll all be salivating like drooling dogs.*

"Look at you... are those boots new?" She blushes. *Fuck, I've missed that.*

I grab her and pull her into a hug as I whisper, "Sexy as hell, Babygirl."

"Oh Greyson, I didn't think we would be seeing you again after the summer."

*This bitch. Just the sound of her voice pisses me off.*

"Good to see you too, Ethel," I reply, not even attempting to smile at her. She was a big reason for our demise, and I don't take that shit lightly. I hope to keep our interactions brief, hating the fact Lottie has to live with this lady.

Lottie grabs my hand, pulling me towards our exit as she says to her grandmother, "Oh, I forgot to tell you, you'll be seeing a lot of Greyson again and please add him to my guest list for the Gala." Not sure what that's about, but if Lottie wants me to go, there's no question for me... I'll be there.

Before the door shuts behind us, Ethel huffs out, "We will talk about this later, young lady." I can't help but let her words worry me.

"I'm so done with letting her dictate my life." She pauses to smile up at me and says, "Let's Ride!" Lottie's statement eases some of the dread I feel.

Reaching into my saddlebag I hand her the helmet I bought over the summer. Giving her a quick kiss, I say, "Sunset rides are for us pretty girl. Now hop on!"

Having her warmth wrapped around me as we cruise down the road has me overwhelmed with peace. I have been in a constant state of anxiety since I drove away from her that day. The happiness she brings me is unmatched to anyone or anything else in my life. Knowing she was in the stands last night watching me play brought back some of the love I have for football. That's when I realized I have just been going through the motions without her.

I wish I could have introduced her to my dad and nana after the game last night, but I didn't want to push that on Lottie. I'm hoping like hell that she agrees to go with me next Saturday to the cookout my Dad and the club are having. He's noticed the change in my attitude since last weekend and is bugging the shit out of me to meet my girl.

Last night at the afterparty Lottie and I made out until Nox busted us up so we could go pick up Emerson. I'm so ready to sink myself inside her but I'm letting her set the pace. Can't say I hate the lead up either. The anticipation and little touches when I know exactly how good she feels on my dick are driving me crazy in all the right ways. I know when she does decide to open that side of herself up to me again it's going to be explosive between us. All the pent-up love, anger... desire.

As we get closer to our destination, I find myself not wanting the ride to end. Between Lottie's thumb rubbing soft strokes across my stomach and her gentle kisses to my back, this feels like what I want my heaven to be like.

When we pass the first entrance for Mountain Ridge University, I feel Lottie perk up as she points over that way. I look back and read her lips, "Can we stop?"

We pull into the beautiful campus that sits in the valley looking up to the vast ridge of the Blue Ridge Mountains, hence where the name of the college came from. They must have an away game today because the campus is quiet for a Saturday this time of year.

Finding an empty spot that has a great view of the mountains, I park the bike and Lottie hops off.

"This is so crazy. I was just looking this place up yesterday. I planned to talk to the guidance counselor about it," she says as she whips her helmet off and looks around.

Hope blooms in my chest at the thought of her staying close by for college. Especially the fact that it sounds like that's what she wants to do. "Holy shit, it's so beautiful here, Greyson."

I love watching her see things for the first time. Not taking my eyes off her, I say, "Yes, so beautiful." *Yep, I'm officially one of those guys.*

Pink cheeks smile back at me as I ask, "Why were you looking it up yesterday? Thinking about applying?" *Please say yes.*

She nods, "Yes, they have a great biology department, which would be perfect for my undergrad studies since I've decided I want to do clinical research for Leukemia."

"Wow, that's awesome. Your mom would be so proud. That sounds like the perfect job for you. I think it'll be very rewarding for you to see your work help others who you can relate to."

She smiles softly. "I think so too. I'm super excited. I really love North Carolina and I'm now the owner of some land on the outskirts of Richmond Hills. Something else I inherited after my grandfather's passing. Land I didn't even know he owned. In a weird way, I think I feel closer to my mother here."

"I'm glad you're loving it. I'm partial to it, especially now that you are here too."

She gives me a quick kiss and says, "Yes there are several perks to living here."

*This girl.*

"You know this is where Berkley got her early acceptance to. You should reach out to her."

By the smile on her face that excites her. "Oooo really? I need to text her. She reached out to check on me after everything, but I ignored her because I honestly didn't know what to say."

"She won't hold that against you. You know she isn't like that. Nathan's kinda freaking out because he committed to play football at NC State his junior year, but Berkley was waitlisted there."

"If anyone can make it work long distance, it's those two."

I nod my head. "That's what I told him."

I grab her into a hug. "I think we could have too. But I don't ever want to find out. I'll follow you to the ends of the earth if you'll let me, Lottie Richmond." Kissing the top of her head, she gives me an extra squeeze.

I pull back. "Okay, we better go so we don't miss seeing our sunset baby."

Twenty minutes later we make it to the spot that overlooks Fontain Lake. The leaves are turning, showing the early signs of fall. The sun is setting off in the distance, painting the sky above the lake with orange and pink. It's exactly what I wanted Lottie to experience.

In awe she says, "Damn I thought I had never seen anything more beautiful than a Nori Beach sunset... but I think this takes the cake." I pull her back into my front and hold her as we stand there taking it all in.

"I knew you would love it. I took a ride up this way last fall with my dad, Gunnar, and Frankie on our bikes. This spot was my favorite view. It was the first time I had really paid attention to the true beauty of the leaves turning before they die and start fresh. I guess as a kid those are things you don't care about as much."

"Autumn has always been my favorite, so this spot is beyond perfect to me." She lifts my hand up to her lips and kisses my palm before she continues. "I loved watching football on the weekends with my Papa, going upstate to the apple orchards and pumpkin farms with Ashley and her family. Halloween too, of course." She stops and gives me a wink. "You know how much Ashley likes to design outfits and dress us up."

Licking my lips, I think back to that sexy little bunny costume from this summer. "Yes. Oh yes, I do." She shakes her head and continues, "Gigi was always baking more during that time of year too. She even got us matching 'pumpkin spice and everything nice' aprons. I'll have to make you her famous pumpkin cheesecake."

"Yes, I'll eat anything you make, but cheesecake is one of my major weaknesses."

She smiles at me. "I didn't know that. But I guess this summer we mainly ate our weight in ice cream and cookies. I could definitely go for a scoop from Beaches and Cream right about now too."

We had so many good days on that boardwalk... just hanging out, enjoying each other, eating ice cream. I'm excited to make new memories with her though.

"Speaking of cooking. How do you feel about coming to a cookout with me next Saturday at the clubhouse?" That question brings back the memory of her rejection the last time I asked her, but I believe her when she says Ethel isn't controlling her life anymore.

She looks up at me with remorseful eyes, most likely able to read my thoughts, and says, "Yeah Grey, I would love that. I'm excited to meet them. Does your dad hate me after what happened at the end of the summer though?"

I shake my head. "No baby, I honestly didn't want to talk about it so I kind of just blamed it on the long distance and asked him not to bring it up. This week he did notice the change in me and asked about things. I told him we were taking it slow but you had actually moved to North Carolina and we were hanging out again. I promised to bring you around to meet him when you were ready, so he is far from hating you. He's looking forward to it. In his words 'I'm excited to meet the girl who makes you less of an asshole.'"

"Okay then, it's a date. I'll be there."

"Perfect. It smells like rain, I don't see a cloud yet but just in case let's get going. I want to show you one more spot a little further up the mountain."

She reaches into her pocket for her phone. "Okay I just want to take a few pictures of this view." Lottie snaps some pictures and then asks me to take a selfie of us together in front of the beautiful backdrop.

We get back on my bike and get to the end of the road in no time. I pull to the side but don't get off yet. Lottie speaks up, "Please tell me we aren't going through that pitch black tunnel Grey?" That makes me chuckle.

Several other bikes and cars are parked off to the side where we are. "So where is everyone, what is this place?"

"Kinda creepy huh?"

She shivers as she says, "Yeah it's weirdly quiet and just so strange the tunnel comes up out of nowhere and it looks like nothing but trees on the other side of it."

"It's actually called 'The road to nowhere'. Years ago they were building this road as a cut through and never finished it, so the road literally ends here at this tunnel. You can walk through the tunnel and there are cool trails on the other side."

I feel her shake her head behind me. "Hell no, that sounds like an awful idea." I laugh again and then I feel the first drop of rain. "Damn I swear when I looked this morning, they weren't calling for rain. Let me look on my radar."

Checking my weather app, it looks like a small shower is heading our way. I show my phone to Lottie. "I know you are going to hate this idea, but I have something we can do to pass the time." She looks at me skeptically. "Trust me?" She nods and I crank my bike back up. Slowly heading towards the tunnel, I feel her squeeze my torso. The light on my bike shows another couple walking this way with flashlights in hands.

"I'll keep my light on for now, okay?" We're barely inside the tunnel just enough to cover us from the rain. I reach into my saddlebag and take out the black can of spray paint. Shaking it, I say, "What should I write?" That seems to excite her because she jumps right off the bike and looks around at some of the other graffiti covering the concrete walls.

The other couple passing us speaks up, "Damn, I guess we didn't beat the rain."

"No but the radar doesn't look like it will be long," I say, not sure if they're on a bike or not.

"Okay thanks. Y'all have a good one. If the rain stops, the hiking trails on the other side have some awesome views."

"Thank you, we will definitely keep that in mind," Lottie responds before they make a run towards one of the parked cars. I give her a look that says you know damn well you won't keep that in mind.

Ignoring me she says, "Ooooh, I have a good idea."

"Okay, give it to me, Stacks."

"What about an anchor with "Grey" on one side and "Stacks" on the other... or is that too cheesy?" I love that idea, looking down at the charm bracelet as her eyes go to my tattoo.

"Cheesy or not, that's fucking perfect." I get to work painting. I may not be the best artist, but I do know a little something about painting bikes so I'm not half bad.

When I'm finished, she giggles at our corniness and snaps a few pictures of it.

"This just means we have to come back every so often and make sure it's still here."

"Deal, but next time, let's come when it's broad daylight."

"I can make that happen. The rain looks like it's slowing down."

"Yes, but you know what... I want to do something before it does." She steps out from under the shelter of the tunnel and pulls me into the rain. She goes up on her tippy toes and kisses me, then says, "Every girl should be kissed in the rain at least once in her life."

Smirking at her, I say, "Oh yeah?" Before she responds I am on her. My lips and body crashing into hers, heart thumping in my chest. Today is what I want every day. Her, all of her, no holding back. She gives back as much as she gets. Slow and sensual, yet hurried and needy. She wraps her legs around me when I pick her up. I can feel the heat from between her legs, lighting me up inside even more. I need to have some self-control. Pulling back, I put my forehead to hers. "Fuck Babygirl. I can only handle so much. Don't forget, I know what it feels like to have your sweet pussy squeezing my cock." She closes her eyes and lets out a little moan. I have to step back and adjust my cock in my pants.

"Greyson I'm..." I put my finger to her lips, knowing if she tells me she's ready, I may not be able to control myself. I really don't want to fuck her for the first time in what feels like forever somewhere that I can't take my time.

"When you're ready, I want to kiss and lick every inch of you. I want to see every part of you and not have to worry about someone walking up and seeing what's mine," I say, taking her chin in my grip. "I'm already jealous enough of other dudes riding by and seeing how perfect your ass looks on the back of my bike. Much less if anyone saw this beautiful face and body while I make you come."

Grabbing my hand, she pulls us back into the tunnel and pushes me to sit on the side of my Harley. The kickstand still holding it up, she reaches over and surprises me by turning my bike light off.

"Let's get these off of you, I'd like to finish what I started the other night." Turned on by the thought and the possessiveness in her tone, I unzip my jeans and do as I'm told. "I'm going to erase that bitch from our memory."

I'm a little stunned by her words but I know in a weird way she needs to do this for herself even if Amber doesn't mean shit to me and never has. "Babygirl, it never remembered her to begin with." Lottie pulls at my pants, silently telling me to give her more access. She jerks them over my hips as soon as I lift up. Quickly getting on her knees once she has me like she wants me. I almost feel bad she's getting down in the dirt for me but my dark and depraved side loves that she wants to get dirty for me. Just as my eyes start to adjust to the darkness, she licks me from the center of my balls all the way to the tip of my rock-solid cock.

"I want to be the only tongue..." Lottie starts kissing the head of dick like it's my mouth. When she gets to the sensitive underside, I feel like I'm going to lose my shit. "The only lips..." Then she moves to my heavy sack and takes them into her mouth. When she lets them go with a pop she says, "The only mouth that ever touches your beautiful cock again."

I moan her name and say, "Trust me, from the moment I saw you, you are all my cock has ever wanted." With that statement, she goes to town sucking me... wrapping those full lips around my length and gliding up and down. My pre cum and her saliva mixes and drips down her chin, creating the sight wet dreams are made of. I wish I could see her hazel eyes better as she looks at me while taking me down her throat. When she moans around me from her own pleasure, I feel my orgasm start to build.

Grabbing her head, loving the pace she's going at, I look past my cock and see the slight bounce to her tits and that does me in. Exploding into her mouth... she takes every drop. "Damn Lottie—" I say just as we hear footsteps. Both of us got so carried away that we didn't see the flashlights coming from the other end of the tunnel. She stands and I pull her to me to hide my spent cock. Thankfully the other people hurry out of the tunnel. Probably traumatized or turned on from the moans that echoed off the tunnel walls as I came down Lottie's throat. As soon as they're gone, Lottie busts out laughing, and I can't help but join in.

"See that is exactly why I won't be fucking you out in the open. If they would have seen you come, I would have to kill them," I say as I hand Lottie her helmet.

She giggles and says, "I love how possessive you are of me. I mean, I wouldn't want you to try to control me all the time, but it's a huge turn-on that you want me all to yourself."

Smacking her ass, "Damn Straight. You are mine pretty girl, and always will be, even if you don't want me. That little possessive stunt you just pulled turned me on beyond belief... now let's go get some food."

"You are mine, Greyson Rexwood, don't ever forget that. And food sounds great. I'm getting hungry, which in about thirty minutes will turn into hangry."

*Damn, I love this girl.*

I pray to God when I finally decide to tell her the one thing I know could ruin us, that she still wants me because my words are true... she is it for me.

# Chapter Twenty-Two

"Hell son, you have it bad. I know that look, you are so far gone for this girl, aren't you?" my dad says with a stupid grin on his face as I shove my phone back into my pocket yet again. I've been helping him set up outside for today's cookout. Lottie had Frankie come over to her place while she baked Gigi's famous pumpkin cheesecake to bring later. She told me it was stupid for me to leave to pick her up since Frankie was coming too. I only agreed when she promised she would call as they were pulling up. I'm a selfish bastard, and I want everyone to know she's here with me. Now I can't stop checking my phone, scared I'll miss her call. I'm not ashamed to admit to my dad that he is one hundred percent accurate.

"Honestly, I can't even describe how big my feelings are for her. I am definitely as far gone as they come." Dad smiles at my words, but I can tell his mind is far off thinking of the one girl who had him by his heart and soul years ago. My heart aches for him more now that I know what losing Lottie for over a month felt like for me. I can't imagine what a lifetime would be like.

"Well, I can't wait to meet her, G. I'm happy things are working out between you two."

"She should be here any minute and she is really excited to meet you. Since Nana doesn't come to the cookouts anymore, I asked Lottie to come to Sunday dinner tomorrow, too."

"Oh man, she's in for some eating then. Mama will be so happy to meet the girl who brings so much of you to life," he continues as I think about his last statement. "Okay, I'm going to go check on the food. Love you buddy."

"Love you too."

My dad is right. Lottie breathes a desire for life and my future into my lungs. The happiness she brings me is seeping out into all aspects of my life.

Gunnar and Casen walk out of the newly built Barndominium and head my way. As President of the MC, my dad is proud of the fact he was able to build a better place on the property for the club members. The new house has six bedrooms plus a meeting room for them to hold church. The middle of the clubhouse is a huge open layout with an enormous kitchen and an area where everyone can hang out and party. Since most of the brothers are family guys, you won't find any half-naked woman in there right now, but later tonight may be a different story. On the other side of the property is where our garage sits. There's a separate entrance for that to keep randoms out of their sacred space.

For the cookouts, we set up tents for the food and music outside. One of the brothers has his own band so they normally put on a little show for everyone.

"Yo, heard we get to meet your girl today?" The question comes from Casen... former cop turned PI and now a Rebel Knight.

"Yeah and keep your hands and eyes to yourself." That has them both laughing. What they don't know is I am fucking serious.

"Shit... you are your father's son," Gunnar says.

Casen hits my arm to get my attention again. "You know I'm only twenty-three. Is she eighteen?"

I know he's joking, so I shoulder him and say, "You better shut the fuck up..." as the sound of a car pulling into the compound takes my attention away from my threat. My phone rings.

I answer, "Hey, wait right there. I'm coming over to get you."

"Yes sir." She giggles. I can tell it's a nervous giggle.

I walk her way, ignoring the whipping sounds the guys are making behind me.

*Yeah, I'm pussy whipped... heart and soul whipped, and I don't give a shit that they know it.*

"Don't be nervous baby. I'm right here."

I hang up as I approach the car. Both girls are looking in the mirror, putting stuff on their lips as I open the door.

"I don't know why you're putting that shit on... I'm about to kiss it off." She looks up at me and smiles wide. "Well hurry up and kiss me then so I can reapply."

Leaning down with one hand holding on to Frankie's car and the other grabbing Lottie's face into my hold, I kiss the shit out of her.

Frankie interrupts, "Okay you two. I'm used to the PDA but we have another guest who may not want to see that shit."

I give Lottie one last peck before I look up to see who Frankie's talking about. I'm startled by another girl in the backseat. "Oh shit, I didn't see you back there."

She's looking at me with wide, knowing eyes. Like she's surprised to see me... like she knows me. She's a pretty girl... looks a little older than us but I can't place who she is.

Lottie speaks up, "This is Lola... Lola meet Greyson."

We exchange hellos and Frankie says, "She is connected to the Rebel Knights out in Texas. But goes to Mountain Ridge now. You remember JJ?" I nod, recalling him as my grandfather's sergeant of arms when I was a kid, he only comes around every so often now. "Lola is his niece."

"Cool, nice to meet you, Lola," I say as I pull Lottie out of the car.

"Come on Babygirl... a lot of people are excited to meet the old ball and chain." That makes her laugh. I reach for her hand as the other girls head toward the house. I check out every inch of her as she intertwines our fingers together. "Damn Stacks," I whisper because I'm nearly speechless looking at her right now. She is beautiful like always with her hair down and curled, she even wore the little black biker boots but her pants... her pants are what wet dreams are made of. I grab her waist and spin her around, checking out her ass in these deadly things. "Fuck me."

Lottie looks back at me over her shoulder. "You like? I bought them with you in mind."

The shiny, black-leather material clings to her curvy ass. She shakes her butt at me, and I can't help but reach out and smack it. "Don't tempt me... we can leave right the fuck now," I say as I pull her to me. Her top is long sleeved and made of black lace. It tucks into her leather pants accentuating her big tits even more. "I think I changed my mind; we should leave."

She playfully smacks me, "No way handsome. I'm ready to meet Daddy Rexwood."

"First off, I am well aware of my Dad's nickname around school, but you are never allowed to say that shit again." She lets out a deep laugh at that. "Secondly, I'm serious. You look good enough to fucking eat. I don't know if I want to even give these guys the privilege of seeing you tonight. You may give some of these old men a heart attack."

She gets up on her tippy toes and kisses me. I open easily for her, grabbing onto her leather-clad ass as she pushes into me. I didn't think my need for her could increase but kissing her like this every day has been the sweetest torture. Breaking away from me she says, "I'm ready Grey. If I could have you right now I would but I know this is important. Let's go in here so I can meet the people who made you, you." She trails her finger down the front of my torso and my dick twitches in my pants as she says, "But later tonight, I want all of you... every inch." I groan with the picture that creates in my head, but she grabs my hand again and starts dragging me towards the party.

"Hold on Babygirl," I say as I take my hand away and adjust my hard-on in my pants. "You know how to excite a guy. That's for sure. I need to think about my grandma for a few minutes." She laughs at me, and I really let my thoughts drift to Nana. "Speaking of that, are you still able to come to dinner at her house tomorrow? I haven't told her yet just in case this was all too much this weekend."

"No, I'll be there. How did Remi tell me to say it... I'll be there, Lord willing and the creek don't rise."

"Oh hell, they're teaching you southern grandma slang now huh?"

"Yep! Now come on."

My dick is finally calming down and I'm ready to show off my girl.

*Don't look at her ass. Don't look at her ass.*

Nodding towards the outdoor grill area, I tell her, "There's my dad. I want you to meet him first or he'll get jealous... I get it from him." I wink at her as we head his way.

"Hey Pop," I call out to him. He turns to me with an immediate big smile seeing my hand in Lottie's. In the blink of an eye, all the color drains from his face. I look to Lottie to see the smile slip from hers with my dad's reaction to her.

"No fucking way." I recognize Gunnar's voice and then Frankie asking him what the hell he's spouting out about.

"Dad, you okay?" I pull a now hesitant Lottie along with me.

He whispers almost inaudibly, "Leah?" like it's a question.

Lottie gasps... I look at her as shock forms on her face "Smith?" she questions my dad.

I'm confused as fuck. No one calls my dad by his first name but my grandmother.

"What the fuck is going on?" I say, looking between my dad and Lottie. "Who is Leah?"

"My mom," Lottie says as her eyes gleam with unshed tears and it all hits me at once.

Lottie's mom, Leah... is the love of my Dad's life.

The one who got away.

His anchor that sunk him so deeply, he's still at the bottom of the ocean with it.

*** 

## Lottie-

*It can't be him... can it?* The one I've read so much about. All the journal entries, notes, and keepsakes have all been about this one man.

Instinct takes over and I run to him, wrapping my arms around his stomach as a sob rips from my throat. I feel like a piece of my mother is here with us and I hold on to Smith for what feels like an eternity. His embrace is strong as he strokes the back of my head to help calm my overwhelming emotions.

Pulling back slightly to wipe my eyes and feeling a bit embarrassed, I say, "I'm sorry, I don't know what came over me. I just can't believe it's you. I feel like I know so much about you from my mom."

By the way he startles, I can tell my words surprise him. "Leah told you about me?" His warm ocean-blue eyes fill with what appears to be hope.

"She did, but I learned more about you from all the journals she kept and her notes from you. My Gigi gave them to me when she thought I was old enough to read them. I think I've read each one at least a dozen times," I say, smiling through the tears. He stands there in silence for a while, as if he's unsure how to cope with me being here. Greyson's hand rests on my lower back and for a few moments, I forget where I am.

"Dad are you alright?" he asks.

Smith nods in his son's direction, but his eyes never leave me. "You look so much like her, I thought I was seeing a ghost," his voice almost a whisper.

"My Gigi used to say that all the time, that I look a lot like her before she got sick." I'm trying my hardest to keep it together. I twirl my mom's bracelet to feel her presence, to silently thank her for leading me along the way.

My fidgeting causes Smith's eyes to catch on the bracelet, and his hand goes to it. His fingers touch the dangling charms so delicately. Smith's eyes meet mine as his hand remains on the charms. "Do you mind?" I shake my head, allowing him to look at it.

He twirls it a few times and stops on the ocean-blue colored seahorse. His breath catches and I can see tears well in his eyes. He releases a shaky breath and runs his hands under his eyes to dry up any wetness that might have escaped.

I wonder what this must be like for him. Seeing me, a spitting image of the woman he used to love... well, still loves, according to Greyson.

Smith reaches for the seahorse charm again, rubbing his thumb back-and-forth over it. He says so quietly I think I'm the only one who hears, "Seahorses mate for life," and I know immediately what he's remembering.

*Dear Journal,*

*We rode throughout the mountains today. I don't think I'll ever get over the thrill of riding in his large truck with the top off. It's so freeing, having the wind whipping*

*through your hair. Like you have the world at your finger-*
*tips.*

*Smith says after my next treatments are over, he'll take*
*me on a road trip over to Gatlinburg. Just the two of us*
*in his Bronco, stopping wherever we please, enjoying each*
*other's company and the beauty of the mountains around*
*us.*

*We stopped for a picnic at a lookout along the road today.*
*Always so incredibly thoughtful, he had delicious sand-*
*wiches and snacks packed for us. I'm sure Nana helped,*
*that woman sure is something special. Always goes out of*
*her way to make me feel welcome, like I'm part of their*
*family.*

*After we finished, he surprised me with a gift box. He told*
*me it was a year to the day that we met, and his life was*
*forever changed. Swoon!!*

*He gave me a beautiful seahorse charm to add to my*
*bracelet! It's the same color as his eyes too. Smith said*
*seahorses mate for life, and that he'll forever be by my side*
*no matter what comes our way. I literally jumped his bones*
*right then and there! (don't worry no one was around)*

*I can't help but stare at it. It's so perfect, he's so perfect.*
*I love him with all that I am, always and forever.*
*xox,*
*Leah*

"I can't believe you have this…" he says, shaking his head to clear
his racing thoughts. I can see all the emotions running across
his face. He gave her this charm; he was supposed to be her
seahorse. They really did have a tragic love story, but I never
learned how it ended.

He clears his throat once more, "I'm sorry, I wasn't prepared
for this. Greyson said he was bringing you, but I—. He said your
last name was Richmond. I wasn't expecting you to be Leah's

daughter. Wasn't aware she had a daughter. Doctors told her when she was hospitalized, when we were around seventeen, that she was unable to have kids."

I grab his hand to help calm him. I know this must be as overwhelming for him as it is for me. To think the love of my mother's life is the father of my Greyson. *My Love.*

I hear Greyson approach us. "Hey dad, can you excuse us for a second?"

"Sure thing," Smith quietly replies, but Greyson is already leading me a few steps away.

He spins me to face him, eyes taking in my face, gauging my emotions. "Holy shit. I can't believe this... are you okay?" he questions, looking as shocked by this revelation as I am. I nod.

"I think I'm in shock, to be honest." I'm not really sure what I'm feeling.

"This is crazy... almost like fate. I know you've been dying for that connection with your mom and now it looks like you get a chance to learn who she really was," he says as his hand cups my cheek. I love when he does that. The simple gesture makes me feel so cherished, so wanted and loved.

"I have so many questions. Do you think he'd be up to talking with me?" I ask, excitement now thrumming through me at the possibility of Smith sharing stories about my mom.

"I'm sure he'd love to," he says with a smile.

Wrapping my arms around his neck, I give him a kiss. Silently thanking him for his understanding. This cookout was supposed to be my opportunity to meet his Dad and the rest of his Rebel Knights family and here I am, a mess of emotions. "I love you," I whisper, as he leans down to give me another kiss.

We walk back to where his father stands, his face still filled with shock. I can tell he's lost in his memories. Greyson steps into his view. "Why don't the two of you go sit somewhere and talk? I'm sure you both have a lot of questions for one another. I'll take care of the rest out here. Are you okay with that, babe?"

I look at Smith, hoping I'll see the same eagerness to talk that I know is written all over my face.

Smith gives me a smile and then turns to his son. "We'll be over at the shop. Come find us in a little while."

"No problem, Pop," he responds, giving me one last smile then turning to face his family, all of whom are staring at Smith and me.

"Those two—" Smith motions with his chin in the direction of two men who are talking with Greyson. "They knew your mom well. I'm sure they're as stunned as I am."

We walk across the grounds to a side entrance of the motorcycle shop. I'm in awe of this place. Now I understand why Greyson wants to take it over. It's impressive. This is no run-down shop one would expect when they think of an MC's place. No, this place is pristine, with a fifties vibe with its black and white tiles along the floor and red trim along the ceiling. There are tin signs and motorcycle collectibles lining the walls and shelves. Several display cases are scattered around the space showcasing what appear to be custom-made bikes. This place looks like it could be in a magazine.

How did I not put this all together from her journals? I literally have every page memorized. I would have picked up on any hints of Smith being a part of an MC. It just doesn't make any sense. The collection of books I have is not complete, but it's like all traces of him being a part of the Rebel Knights were erased.

"I never knew. I mean, I've read about you, but I didn't know about the MC or all of this. The journals did seem to end abruptly, and some pages were ripped out. The pieces of the puzzle I did have made it obvious how much she cherished you and I always wondered what happened that would end such a love story."

Smith leads me to a small seating area, where I sit on a black leather couch, and he takes a seat in one of the two matching chairs across from me.

"Our love story never really ended, Lottie. Honestly, I will love her till my last breath, but I know she felt like she was doing the right thing by leaving me."

He's quiet for a moment then looks at me with sincerity. "I'm sorry for your loss Lottie, your mother was an amazing woman."

I hold back my tears. "Thank you, I'm sorry for yours, too. I can tell how much you meant to her and she to you."

He cups his face in his hands and drags them both down slowly, releasing a loud sigh as they fall. "I can't believe you're here. That Leah had a daughter, and my son is head over heels in love with her."

"What are the chances?" I ask but not expecting an answer.

"Do you mind me asking why your last name is Richmond and not DeMoine?"

"Well from what I was told, my mom got pregnant with me not long after she started dating a guy at college in NY. Being so young, he wanted nothing to do with the pregnancy or my mom for that matter. Knowing what a blessing it was for her to become pregnant, my mom raised me with the help of my great-grandparents. She hated her own father and clearly wasn't going to give me that asshole's last name, so she decided on my great-grandparents' last name, Richmond."

I see tears form in Smith's eyes and I reach my hands out to hold onto his. "You're a miracle, Lottie. She always thought she couldn't have kids. I'm sorry that sack of shit had no idea how special you truly were, especially to Leah."

"Thank you," I say, my voice just above a whisper.

"Shit, this is supposed to be a party and here I am crying like a fool. Seeing you brings back so many emotions I thought I had locked away for good. But it really is great to meet you, Lottie. I've heard so much about you."

"I'm so glad I finally got to meet you too. Although, I feel like I've known you for a long time through my mother's words."

"She was such an amazingly loving person, strong-minded and independent. It destroyed me when she left, but if leaving me gave her you. It was worth it."

"Do you mind me asking what happened between you two? Her journals just end abruptly and pick up once she's living in New York and those entries are few and far between."

Smith's expression turns solemn. "That's a conversation for another night, there's too much to dig into."

"I understand, I was just curious," I say, a tad disappointed, and I really *do* understand. Seeing me opened wounds that had since scarred over, possibly even long forgotten. Right now is not the time to dig through all of that.

"I can tell you that from this little time together, you're just like her. Heart and all."

That has my eyes welling once again. *Geez, I can't keep it together for more than five minutes.*

"I can't wait to share my stories with you. You'll have to come over one night soon. I have a bunch of things I'd love for you to see. You're coming to family dinner tomorrow, right?"

"Yes!" I say with a smile, "Greyson asked me to come a few days ago."

Smith beams a smile at me. "Oh man, I can't wait to see the look on my mother's face when she sees you. She loved your mom so much, so get ready cause she'll probably fawn over you all night long. I think I still have a bunch of photos and stuff at her house from when your mom and I were young. We'll have to rummage through it together."

I let out a light chuckle. "I can't wait."

"Now, come on." He stands, shaking off the remaining emotional fog that surrounded us. Stretching out his hand for mine, he says, "Let's go have some fun tonight. There will be plenty of time for us to share stories later."

There's a genuine smile plastered on my face as I take his hand. We leave the shop and head across the way to where the party seems to be in full swing by the sounds of the booming voices and laughter.

I look to the sky and send up a silent thank you. To my family watching over me, making sure the cards aligned and I found my way... home.

# Chapter Twenty-Three

Bliss, pure bliss. That's how I would describe how perfect this weekend has been. After my heart-to-heart with Smith, we returned to the cookout, and he introduced me to several of the brothers in the Rebel Knights MC. At first, some were just as shocked as Smith about who I was, but that faded quickly, and they welcomed me into their family circle. Greyson, being the sexy, possessive man I love, made sure he reminded the brothers to whom I belonged every chance he had. Stealing passionate kisses and intimate touches all day and night had my body on fire.

I don't think I've ever seen a party like that, and I've been to plenty of parties. The Rebel Knights can go all night long. Seriously, at one point I could tell the evening was taking a turn towards debauchery and Greyson signaled it was time for us to head home. I was more than willing to leave with him; he had me on edge all day. The way I was feeling, I couldn't care less about taking it slow. I was ready to be with him again... I *needed* to be with him again.

To my disappointment, once we arrived at my house, he didn't stay. He tucked me into bed and left me with a very ungentle-man-like kiss. I was about to beg him to sleep over, but his phone rang out several times. It was Gunnar, asking Grey if he could return to the clubhouse to pick up Smith. He said something about them all being banned from Uber and everyone being too wasted to drive home. So, I can now say I've been officially cock-blocked, and by my boyfriend's dad, no less.

Needless to say, I'm a bit high-strung today sitting around Nana's dinner table. Especially with his hand rubbing small cir-cles on my thigh. I swear I must sound like a bumbling idiot in my attempts to answer his nana's questions. Greyson is certainly enjoying this torture, or at least my reaction to it, because he's smiling from ear-to-ear next to me.

Smith was right. Nana was stunned when she first saw me. Took her several moments to get her bearings. But now recov-ered, she's been chatting up a storm ever since.

"This meatloaf is absolutely delicious," I say to Nana Rex as I finish my plate. "I haven't had a meal like this since my Gigi passed." She went all out for dinner tonight. There's homemade garlic mashed potatoes, green beans, and fried okra, and fresh cornbread. Greyson said this is how she usually cooks for every meal and to save room for the dessert. What a far cry from the salads I'm served at Ethel's house.

"Thank you. Please, there's plenty where that came from," she says and scoops another helping onto my plate. "You're welcome here for dinner any day of the week. Just make sure you get here early enough otherwise these hooligans will leave you with scraps." She motions to the table full of smiling faces, all deep in conversation. Frankie is in a deep conversation with Smith, and Ford is showing Gunnar pictures on his phone of a bike he's interested in. She smiles at the rag-tag family she's acquired, and I can feel the love radiating off her. Although I will always live with the grief of losing my closest family, I feel somewhat at ease at this table. Like I'm meant to be here.

Nana reaches across the table and places her hand on top of mine. "My door is always open," she says with such an endearing smile. "Your mother knew that too. I was devastated when Leah left without saying goodbye. Then Smith let me read her letter to him and I understood why she felt like she had to," she adds, choking up slightly towards the end. *Why would she leave without saying goodbye? She left him a letter... I wonder if that's what Smith was referring to last night when he said it's a story for another time.*

The sentimental moment is disrupted when Greyson's hand slips higher up my thigh and pinches me lightly, causing me to let out a small yelp and jump in my seat. My cheeks flush with embarrassment as all eyes turn my way. *Bastard.*

Nana Rex must be aware of her grandson's antics because she stands and asks him to help her clear the table. He grumbles a response along the lines of "why can't Ford do it" but does as he's told. Loving the dynamic, I stick my tongue out at him. Childish I know, but it felt necessary.

I'm having such a great evening. I haven't stopped smiling and laughing since I walked through her door.

After we finish with dessert and all help clean up the kitchen, we make our way to the living room. Greyson mentioned it's been recently re-furnished to accommodate their large "family". Ford turns on the football game, and we all settle into the incredibly comfortable couches, Greyson taking up the corner seat with me nestled into his side.

Smith disappears down the hallway for a bit, returning with a box in his hands. I know immediately it's the box of memorabilia he mentioned yesterday. He places the box next to me and sits on the other side. Sitting up quickly and re-adjusting my position, I wait patiently for Smith to open it. Even though I'm dying to rip it open, I'm letting him take the lead here. I can only imagine what this must feel like. How often does he rummage through these memories?

He opens the box lid and smiles at its contents. I sit up a little taller to peek inside. "Leah loved to keep busy, we were always doing something together," Smith says as he pulls out a stack of concert tickets.

"She had quite the eclectic taste in music, she loved it all. We would go to the amphitheater at least twice a month."

Gunnar pipes up from across the way, "She would drag us to every show possible, even if we didn't know the artist performing. Our asses were there." That makes us all chuckle.

The stubs are pretty worn and faded, but I shuffle through the stack regardless. They weren't lying, they've seen literally every type of musical genre there is. I see a Tim McGraw ticket, one for Blink 182, and a K-Ci and Jojo stub. I'm in awe of the amount there are, and for the fact that Smith kept them all. The tickets remind me of the few she had in her box as well... *those must have been her favorite memories.*

He then hands me a small photo album. Definitely looks like something my mom made, almost like a scrapbook. I tear up at the images inside. Quite a shock seeing my mom and Smith when they were our age. Even crazier are the similarities to Greyson and me. It's overwhelming.

Greyson is looking alongside me and there's one photo of my mom on Smith's bike and I still. It looks almost identical to the one that's set as Greyson's phone wallpaper.

"Holy shit," he says, not needing to say anything more. The similarities are uncanny.

Then as we flip further into the book, you can see the changes in my mom. From the looks of her, I'm guessing this is when she started to get sicker. Her frame is much, much thinner, and her face looks different too, still gorgeous, but definitely different.

I haven't seen many photos of my mom during this time in her life. I now understand why, she looks frail and weak, not anything like she would want to be remembered as. My mom told me about her first bout of Leukemia. She was seventeen when the doctors discovered it and started treatments. There was a period when she was hospitalized from the strain on her body from the treatments. But to know she had Smith by her side through it all makes me even more thankful for him and solidifies the type of love they shared.

Greyson's hand swipes at my cheek to dry my tears. "You okay, Babygirl?" he says as he kisses the top of my head, his arms wrapping around me and pulling me closer.

"I am, just a lot to take in. I've never seen her like this." I motion toward the picture of the frail girl. "I was young when she passed away. The Leukemia had come back aggressively, and she was gone not long after they found it again. I don't recall her ever looking this sick."

"Fuck babe, I'm sorry," he says, squeezing me a little tighter to him. Staring at the photo book for a bit longer.

"Dad, did Aunt Natalie meet Leah?" Greyson asks his dad. "I'm only asking because she met Lottie this summer and never mentioned anything."

"She did... but if I recall correctly, it's when Leah was really sick. Nat probably wouldn't have put two and two together if I'm being honest. Not many people recognized Leah for a while." Smith says with a saddened look on his face.

"Yeah, she really looked like a completely different person there for a while," Gunnar says, reminding me we're in the middle of Nana's living room surrounded by people. *Wow, I really zoned out there.*

Looking around the living room I notice Ford and Frankie are in their own world watching the Panthers game. It seems quite intense by the looks on their faces. Gunnar is busy scrolling through his phone, when he's not peeking through the memorabilia Smith passes his way.

Nana is in her recliner, the only piece of furniture that doesn't look like it was replaced during the remodel. The color doesn't match, and it appears to have seen better days, but I can guarantee it's her favorite thing in this place. She looks content as hell, lounging and reading her trash magazines. I'll have to remember to pick up some next time we come, I love a good gossip mag.

Smith is digging through the box once more, then pops his head up once he finds what he's looking for. I can see the unshed tears in his eyes, but there is a smile on his face and I'm assuming it's because of what he found.

He hands me a piece of paper that's been folded in some sort of origami-looking way. He motions for me to open it and I do so carefully as to not rip the worn-out piece of paper.

I can't help the small laugh that escapes when I read it.

**Hey Hot Stuff,**
**So, I'm thinking you're pretty cool and I like spending time with you. I was wondering if you'd like to be my girl. We're basically together every day anyway so I can't see any reason for you not to say yes.**


**JK- please say yes!**
**-Smitty**
**P.S: Gunnar says this is stupid, but I don't give a shit what he says.... So, what do you say?!?**

*Wow when you put it that way, how can a girl say no?!?*
*Tell Gunnar to shut his pie hole- and yes, I'd love to be your girl...*

*My only requirement is constant snacks-*
*-Xox-*

Greyson grabs the letter when I'm done and reads it as well, letting out a chuckle when he finishes. "Damn Dad, real smooth."

"What can I say? I'm a natural Casanova." He winks at us.

"I mean, how could she say no to that?" I laugh.

"Let me see whatever this is that has you laughing away the tears," Gunnar asks, reaching for the letter in Greyson's hands. He reads it quietly, then smiles.

"Shit, I remember this day. You were so damn nervous..." he says, smiling at Smith. "Feels like it was just yesterday... now look at us, with grown-ass kids and shit." He laughs.

"Ain't that some shit," Smith nods.

We hear a loud snore break through, and we all turn to glance at Nana, who is passed out with her magazine still in hand.

"Guess that's our queue to pack it up," Greyson says to the group.

"Guess so... you heading to the clubhouse Gun?" Smith asks.

"Yeah brother, you coming with?"

"Think I will," Smith replies, then turns his attention to me.

"I know there's a lot you still want to know, but I promise we'll get to it all someday." Then he turns his gaze towards Greyson. "I'm staying at the clubhouse tonight. I'll catch you in the morning." With that, he loads up the box and takes it back down the hallway.

After saying our goodbyes and tucking Nana into bed, Greyson and I are on our way to his house.

I'm excited to get him to myself tonight. He sure knows how to drive me wild.

My phone buzzes from my purse beside me. Pulling it out to check who it is, I see Ashley's gorgeous face on my screen.

"You going to answer her?" Greyson asks from beside me. I nod and smile, then accept her call.

"Hello, Beautiful!" I say as he turns down the radio.

"Ahh, Tig, I've missed your voice. What are you doing?"

"Riding to Greyson's house. You're on speaker and he's here with me." Greyson gives me a look, but I know my bestie and her mouth needs to come with a warning label.

"Hey Ash," he yells from the driver's seat. Luckily, after I explained everything that went down between us, she was totally supportive of us getting back together. Now, only Amber remains on her shit list.

"Ooooh, okay, hi G! I won't keep you two for long. I just wanted to ask you something. It's about the Gala weekend."

"Oh no, are you bailing on me?" I ask, unable to hide my disappointment.

"Hell No, I was actually wondering... well, since you and Greyson are back together... can I invite Trent too? I mentioned I was coming to see you and he seemed interested, but I wanted to run it by you first."

"Of course, you can! The more the merrier. Eeep, this is going to be awesome. Did you still want to go to Nori Beach for a night or two before the Gala?"

"Abso-fricken-lutely I do! I'll look at flights and let you know our schedule."

"Hell yeah, this is going to be fun," Greyson says.

"Okay love, I'll let you guys go. Have fun and wrap it up! I'm too young to be an auntie."

We all laugh as I end the call.

"I'm so excited," I say to Greyson as we pull into his driveway.

"Want to know what I'm excited for?" he asks with a devilish glint in his eyes.

"Hmm, I don't know. What are you excited for Mr. Rexwood," I say in my sultriest of tones.

He doesn't respond with words but with his body. His arms wrap around me, and he pulls me onto his lap with my legs straddling him. I lean in and take his lips with mine, sliding my tongue teasingly at them for him to open, which he does instantly. His large hand grips the back of my neck, and a shiver runs through my body. *I need him, now.*

"Fuuckk, Babygirl. I need to get you inside. I want you sprawled out across my bed so I can worship every inch of you."

My only response is the moan I release when I grind down on the hardening length in his jeans.

Moments later, after practically running through his house, we burst through his bedroom door. He picks me up over his shoulder and tosses me onto his bed. Reaching behind him, he swiftly removes his shirt with one hand. *Fuck he's hot, and all mine.*

Greyson eyes me on his bed, eyes wild, like that of a man starved and about to feast for the first time in years. He leans over and kisses me gently, then sits me up so he can remove the long-sleeved shirt I'm wearing. I go for the button of his jeans as soon as my shirt is off. He steps out of them and then goes to work on removing my jeans.

Pulling back, his lust-filled stare roams over my nearly naked body. "You're so damn beautiful. Every single part of you is perfect," he says, taking my lips in his once more. His mouth starts to trail along my jaw and then to my neck. His expert fingers release my bra clasp from behind me, freeing my chest.

He wastes no time, taking a hand to one of my breasts as his mouth takes the other. The warmth of his tongue swirling along my sensitive nipple has my body quaking beneath him.

"God, that feels good," I moan when he switches positions and takes the other in his mouth. Greyson continues his path down my body with his warm, loving kisses. He slows his journey around my belly, which in the past I would have shied away from, or pushed his head further for him not to linger too long in that area, but now, I know how much I mean to him. And when he says he loves every single inch of me, he means it. Stretch marks and all.

I freely give my body to him, no longer afraid of its size. He wants me for me, and I absolutely love that about him.

Greyson's hands grab the sides of my panties and slide them down. I lift my hips to help him slip them all the way off. He moves to the end of the bed, taking each of my legs in his hands and pulling my body down towards him. Wasting no time, I feel his tongue run along my slit and my legs fall wide open. I can feel him smile at my eagerness. *It's been too long since I've had him like this.*

"You're dripping for me, pretty girl," he says and pushes a finger ever so slowly inside. His tongue goes back to circling my throbbing clit. I let out a long moan when I feel another finger join the first, stroking softly in a rhythmic motion.

"Holy shit... please don't stop," I beg. Knowing it won't take much to push me over the edge.

A few minutes later and my body tenses and that oh-so-familiar heat courses through my body.

"Mmm that's it, come for me," he growls into my pussy, not slowing down his fingers as he lazily licks at me. It takes a while for my body to come back down. Little shivers of after-shocks trail along my limbs.

"Damn baby, you have no idea how much I've missed you. How much I missed the taste of you. The sight of your body writhing beneath mine," he says, crawling back up my body, licking along my neck and taking my mouth in his.

My toes curl when his hand locks into the hair at the back of my head. Our tongues twirl with one another as his body settles on top of mine. His hard cock is still covered by his boxer briefs.

Wrapping my soft thighs around his muscled body, I'm desperate to feel his length press against me. He grinds down hard, causing us both to moan-loudly.

"Fuck Grey, I've missed you so much. I need you. I need to feel you. Please," I beg when his mouth returns to my neck and collarbone.

"Mmm Babygirl, I feel like I've been waiting forever to hear those words." He grinds down harder to emphasize his need as well.

"Please."

There's some shuffling along the bed, no doubt Greyson is ridding himself of his boxers. Then he aligns himself back between my thighs.

"You ready for me baby?"

There is no reason to respond, but I shove my hips in his direction. That earns a soft chuckle from him. "So eager," he says, then thrusts inside.

I can feel every glorious inch of him. Finally placing together the last piece of our broken puzzle.

Kissing along his neck as he moves above me, I take in the way his muscles move with each slide of his hips. Unable to stop myself, I grab hold of his large back. My fingers trailing light, almost teasing, strokes along it. I need to feel every part of him. Every piece.

I feel his body shift ever so slightly, but I'm too distracted watching where our two bodies meet.

"I love you, Lottie Richmond. Your heart and soul. Every piece of you was made for me."

Tears well in my eyes, and I shift my body so I can kiss his lips. "So much Grey. Love you so much." *I've missed him and the way he makes me feel. Always loved and protected.*

His pace begins to quicken like he can't hold out any longer and I'm more than ready to feel him fill me. I lift my leg further back to give him easier access to my aching core. It's exactly what he needed because within moments, he goes from firm, contained thrusts to a wild man.

Greyson leans back onto his knees and takes my ankles in each of his hands, as if they are handles to help him along the way. A growl comes from deep in his chest as he begins to pound into me. My large chest bounces wildly with every thrust.

"Fuck, oh yes... fuuuck!" I yell as his motions hit that special spot deep inside repeatedly.

"Yes. That's it. Give it to me. Fucking come on my cock. I want that tight pussy of yours squeezing my cock as I cum inside of you."

*Holy Shit!*

His words alone could set me off, but he releases one of my ankles. Letting it fall to his shoulders, he finds my sensitive clit with his thumb with his free hand.

"Oh shit, I'm going to come. Grey... Aaahh!" I scream as I climax, clamping down on his long, hard cock inside me.

"Fuck yes," he roars as his climax follows closely behind. His motions still as he allows my throbbing pussy to milk his release from him. It's so fricken sexy I swear my orgasm lasts for what feels like forever.

Greyson collapses on top of me, both of us covered in sweat.

"That was... that was—" I stammer, unable to choose the right words to describe what just transpired.

"Indescribable..." he says as he kisses me.

I smile at him because he's right. There are no words for how that felt.

Utterly exhausted, we don't bother cleaning up. We just cuddle into one another and enjoy the sounds of our calming breaths. His lips peppering light kisses along my shoulder as we drift off.

Before sleep overtakes me, I hear Greyson whisper, "You're it for me Babygirl. I'm yours always."

I swear I respond with an "Always" of my own, but my eyes close moments later.

# Chapter Twenty-Four

Smiling like a loon when I spot Lottie getting out of Frankie's car, I see exactly why she had me pissed this morning when she texted me to just meet her at school.

Stacks has her hair in two French braids, looking cute as hell. Taking my eyes down to the shirt she has tied in a small knot right above her jeans, showing a sliver of that soft skin I love to kiss. My football number "55" is stretched across her front in garnet and gold, with a little anchor hanging off the bottom of one of the fives. Lottie must have made it last night during "girl time" with Frankie. She feels my stare and looks up with a wide smile. Letting out a whistle showing my appreciation for her, she turns her back to me, lifting her arms up and using her thumbs to point down at the back of her shirt. I read REXWOOD as her head turns towards me and she smirks.

"Get your fine ass over here!" I shout.

I pull her in for a kiss as soon as she gets close enough. "I missed you," I say because damn if it isn't the truth. Not caring how pathetic it sounds... I can't stand going more than a few hours without laying eyes on her.

"I know baby but isn't this..." she says, pointing to her DIY shirt, "worth it?"

Grabbing her hips to turn her around again, I say, "Seeing my name on your back is priceless, Babygirl. I didn't know you had it in you. I thought Ashley was the costume designer."

She nods her head back towards Frankie, who is heading this way with Lucian's number painted across her top. "Luckily, my new bestie is also creative and artistic. Come on... you know I can barely draw a stick figure."

Only two weeks of having Lottie back as mine and it's... indescribable. I have spent this past week inside of her every chance I can get, both of us making up for lost time. I love feeling that connection with her, as close as any two people can be, and watching her fall apart in pure pleasure. It's the best fucking sight in the world.

There are really no words that could fully express the way she makes me feel. I remember thinking the same thing over the summer once I realized just how special she was to me. But this is next-level compared to that. Maybe because I know what it's like to lose her and I can't imagine that again. Or maybe because a big part of this feels even more like fate after hearing about our parents.

*I am still a little mind-fucked from that revelation.*

My dad seems to be somewhere between peaceful and a cluster fuck over the news. I haven't told Lottie that part because I don't want her to feel like it's her fault, and even though he's trying to save face, I can see some of his demons coming out to play.

Gunnar called me to pick my dad up after I left the cookout because they were all drunk and he insisted on going home. When I got back to the clubhouse, he was outside with the Lola chick that Frankie had introduced me to earlier in the night. There seemed to be a familiarity between the two of them, but I have no clue how.

Once we got him in the truck, I realized he wasn't in a good head space. He was slurring and telling me he thinks Leah brought me into Lottie's life to love her forever and finish what they started. In a weird way, I think he's trying to find his peace in that, and I sure hope he does. His heart deserves to move on, and I feel like Leah would want that too.

After he showered off some of his drunkenness, he found me on the couch and told me to stay far away from Lottie's grandmother. I assured him I had my eye on her and that I know she's a calculated woman. My guess is she tried controlling Leah all those years ago just like she does with Lottie. I already planned to avoid her at all costs. If it was up to me, Lottie wouldn't live with that woman.

Sunday seemed to be better for my dad when he was talking to Lottie and reminiscing about the past, but the rest of this week he appeared to be in a fog. Gunnar said I just need to give him some time because the situation has stirred up a lot of old feelings, including some things I don't even know about.

Even as close as we are, I know my dad has his secrets just like I have mine and I respect that.

***

By lunchtime, I'm so ready to bend Lottie over in nothing but the little handmade jersey she's wearing in support of tonight's big game. Seeing my name on her back has me thinking all kinds of shit.

*We may be young, but I can't help hoping she will wear that last name one day as her own. I know if it's up to me, she will.*

When we make it over to our lunch table, Lottie sets her stuff down and tells me she'll be right back. I watch her as she walks over to Snow, and he gives her a big smile that makes me lose my appetite. She wants us to all hang out sometime, claiming it will help me get over my issues with their friendship. As right as she may be, I'm just not there yet. Every smile she gives him has me raging inside. I trust her completely but I'm still not sure about him. He has to prove himself to me first. I need to know that he understands she's mine.

Lottie gives me a kiss on the cheek as she sits back down and snuggles into my side. Unable to help it I look Snow's way to see if he's still watching her and am surprised to see a genuine smile on his face as he watches our exchange. *Not enough to lower my defenses completely, but can't say I'm not happy to see that reaction.*

"One more week and we get to see Ashley and Trent," Lottie says, grabbing my attention.

I smile at her excitement and say, "I know you are ready to see your girl... and we get to go back to where it all started. Glad Trent gets to come too. I'm not entirely sure what their deal is but he seemed eager to get out of New York and spend a weekend with her."

"Is Ashley hot as fuck too?" Of course that comes from Ford.

"So hot. You'll be obsessed but... she's taken though, sorry," Lottie replies.

"Yeah dipshit, she's my cousin's girl so keep yourself in check." I know he's just being Ford but I have to give him a hard time. It's what we do.

"I'm just saying... I want to go to Nori Beach. That seems to be where you go to find a girl this perfect." He gestures to Lottie.

She blushes as she says, "Ooooo. I have a great idea."

"What Babygirl?"

"What if Nox and Ford come spend the summer at the beach with us? I own that property now so you guys can all stay with me."

*That actually sounds like a damn good plan.*

"Hell yes. For real?" Ford chimes in. Lottie nods her head excitedly as she looks to Nox.

"You know what, yes. I'm going to need a break from training at some point. Maybe not the whole summer but I will take you up on that invite for a few weeks at least. Thank you."

He nudges Ford, who then says, "Oh yeah. Thanks Stacks, you're the best!"

"Don't call her that or you'll be uninvited," I growl.

The guys laugh at my shit.

We finish eating our food, and Lottie leans over to whisper to me. "I'm going to go to the bathroom. My period came on today, so I need... ya know. Ugh, sorry TMI, but that's what you get since you have a girlfriend now." She lets out an awkward giggle.

Speaking lowly to her, "I don't care about that baby. Do you need anything? I could go to the school nurse and get you a heat pack. I remember the heating pad and a good back rub helping you over the summer."

"No, I'm okay Grey. It's not too bad. Thank you, though. You're the best." Her eyes are so full of love and adoration.

I give her a kiss on her head. "Okay, I'll meet you after next period. Text me if you need me."

A few minutes go by and since I'm done eating, I go check on her, just in case.

Waiting outside the women's bathroom. I hear high heel clicking as someone else approaches. Feeling her hand run down my arm sends an uneasy awareness through my body.

"Hi G. I'm glad I found you alone. I wanted to talk to you." Jerking my arm away from Amber's touch, her voice is like nails on a chalkboard.

I've been on such a high having Lottie back in my life, but I haven't forgotten about what she did.

"Me too Amber. It's about time we talked about the little stunt you pulled."

Feigning innocence, she asks, "What do you mean?"

"For starters, you videoed us without my consent. I was drunk as shit that night and finally gave in to you begging for my cock. Did you ever think maybe there was a reason I kept denying you?" I pause for emphasis, "I didn't want you. But that night you thought you had the right to take advantage of the opportunity and be sure to record it, huh? Well, guess what... you didn't and you're lucky I don't pres

s charges on your ass, especially after the pain you caused Lottie over that." I seethe just thinking about it.

"Oh, poor fucking Lottie. I thought she was just another one of your fuck buddies, obsessively calling your phone that night. A phone you left out in the open without a lock on it. I thought I was doing you a favor by erasing her from your life," Amber sneers.

"Are you fucking kidding me Amber? I can't believe you would stoop so low as to erase her from my phone like some crazed psycho." I run my hands over my face. It all makes sense now. Why I didn't see her calls or any of her later messages. Amber erased them all.

"Lottie is the love of my life, and you played a huge part in taking her away from me. Thank God she found her way back. You think you played me so well that night? What, were you pissed I wouldn't let you touch me again even when I was so drunk I couldn't see straight?"

She scoffs. "What the fuck ever, Greyson. Your dumb girl-friend was so easily manipulated. I wouldn't have given up on you so quickly."

"You don't know her at all. What... just because I let you suck my dick at the end of junior year you think you have some type of pull over me? You don't have shit on me. I would never want someone who treats people the way you do." *Fuck using a filter with her. She doesn't deserve a sugar coating.*

"Keep Lottie's name out your fucking mouth. Delete that video from your phone and that night from your memory because it didn't mean shit. You need to grow up and have some respect for others... hell even yourself, or you're going to live a miserable life." I look her directly in the eyes, making sure she understands every word coming out of my mouth.

She's crying as she huffs and turns on her heels. I would say I feel bad but I'm actually happy to see some emotion out of her. I want her to realize her actions are fucked up.

*Glad that shit show's over.*

Checking my phone before I bust into the girl's bathroom to make sure Lottie is good, I see a text from her.

> **Stacks:** *Made it to class... I'm okay, promise. You just focus on winning tonight and then I'll take you up on that heating pad and back rub later. Maybe some chocolate too =]*

She must have gone to a bathroom closer to her classroom. I head to the vending machine knowing exactly what she needs.

Rushing to her classroom right as the bell rings, I walk past her teacher, not caring.

"Hey pretty girl," I say, and she looks up, stunned by my voice.

"Greyson, what are you doing here?"

Holding up my full hands to show a few of her favorite treats, "I brought the goods."

Sitting down the pack of peanut M&M's and a bottle of coke before I lean down and kiss her, I add, "Sorry, there's no pop-corn to mix in with the M&M's but I thought this might make you feel a little better."

Her smile reaches her beautiful hazel eyes as she says, "Aw, Thanks babe! You know me so well. This is exactly what I needed. You're the—"

"Mr. Rexwood. I suggest you get to your next class."

"Okay, that's my cue to get my ass outta here. Love you Baby-girl."

She reaches out to grab my hand. One last touch before I go. I give her a wink and head out.

Thinking how much I can't wait to cuddle with her tonight.

*Who the fuck am I?*

I'm the guy so madly in love with Lottie Richmond, he can't see anything else. Not even the destruction around the corner.

# Chapter Twenty-Five

"Try one more on, please Tig! I saved the best for last."

I hear Ashley pleading to Lottie as they try on dresses for the Gala tomorrow night.

"Well, why the hell didn't we start there... five dresses ago," Lottie responds.

Smiling to myself because Lottie only gives her sassy side to me and Ashley. I secretly love it.

Since it's my bye week for football, the coach gave us a three-day weekend to rest up. With no practice, I convinced Lottie that we should skip school and spend Friday at the beach with Ash and Trent. They flew into North Carolina last night, and we all met at Lottie's beach house.

Ashley had several dresses for Lottie to try on for the big Gala tomorrow evening. I know Lottie is a little nervous about the event because this is the first one she's attended. Even though she says this is the one good thing Ethel does, she still feels uneasy because you never know what Ethel's ulterior motives are. On top of that, I'm sure the event will bring up some of the pain from her loss. Thankfully, she'll be surrounded by her big support team, including my dad, who apparently has been coming to these things for years, even though Ethel hates it.

According to him, she will always see him as the no-good riff-raff from the wrong side of town. He and Gunnar, along with several other small business owners, have sponsored a table and donated to the auction ever since he discovered what the cause was for. Ethel will really hate it this year when she sees more of our crew at the event. I don't really give a fuck. We bought an expensive ticket just like everyone else did, so we have every right to be there. Honestly, I'll enjoy the look of disgust on her face when she sees us. Just like I'm enjoying this beach house without Ethel anywhere near it.

All of us being back together in Nori Beach just feels right. It has me even more ready for next summer. Not quite sure how I feel about Lottie's inheritance, but I know who she is as a person and her money doesn't change that. She knows me well enough to know I would never feel right living off of her. I still have a lot I want to accomplish in life. Lottie still wants to pursue her dreams, which just shows the type of person she is. Most *almost*-eighteen-year-olds would take a gap year for the rest of their lives with those assets.

The house may have fewer items inside it than it did last summer, but it feels more like home already. All of Ethel's things have been removed, and the evil left the building with it. Some of the furniture, including Lottie's bedroom, was purchased by her great grandparents, so she wasn't given a completely empty house.

Trent's snores pull my attention across the room to his long legs hanging off the beige couch and the drool on his chin. We all made it here with enough time to go to the boardwalk last night and eat at The Shack. Even for a Thursday in November it was busy enough that when we saw the manager running around, she jokingly asked if I wanted to take some tables.

When we got home the girls had the bright idea to make Jell-O shots for day drinking by the pool today. Apparently, Trent went a little harder than the rest of us.

We plan to have a bonfire on the beach tonight. I did threaten to tear down the gazebo and throw it in the burn pile after a flashback of Jacob touching Lottie crossed my mind. But Lottie told me that was "absolutely ridiculous" and basically that she didn't light my dick on fire so we can call it even and move on.

*Tou-fucking-che.*

Can't argue with her there.

"Ohhhh hell yes, Lottie! That's the one." I hear some excited movements and more from Ashley. "Damn I'm good. I knew with those banging curves of yours this was going to be the one. You're rocking that thing babe!"

Curious, I start making my way over to the room they are in. Right as I turn the doorknob. Ashley shouts, "Greyson... don't even think about it. You don't get to see her fine-ass until tomorrow night, buddy."

*Damnit.*

"I was just checking on y'all. Come get your man up so we can eat. And give me my girl back."

"Hold your damn horses, cowboy. You're the one who gets her all the time now!" Ashley yells and I hear Lottie giggling at our banter.

\*\*\*

Two hours later we're back on the couches in the entertainment room grubbing on take-out from El's Diner. Trent couldn't shake his tiredness from day drinking and Lottie had a headache from all the sugar in the Jell-O shots, so greasy food was exactly what everyone needed. Deciding to skip the bonfire, we try to agree on a movie.

"We should watch *It Chapter Two*!" Lottie chimes in on the movie choice. "Grey and I watched the first one on Halloween night. Well not the OG one but the newest version and it was really good. Scary, but good."

Trent says, "That's very different than the Halloween we had last week." At the same time Ashley says, "You actually enjoyed that creepy clown movie Tig?"

Lottie looks to her best friend first. "Yes, I'll take that any day over screaming people running from a guy with a chainsaw. You know I think those things are ridiculous and since Halloween was on a weeknight, all our friends went to a haunted forest instead of partying." Then her eyes flit to Trent like she just realized what he said earlier. "What did y'all do for Halloween... do tell?"

I smile to myself, hearing that she's picking up on the word "y'all".

Realizing he probably said more than he should have, Trent looks to Ash for permission. "Well, it's not like they don't know about the club."

That's true. We both know about their first official meeting almost a year ago at the club Masqued in New York.

Trent elaborates, "We went to the club and had some fun dressed as a masked Harley Quinn... and the Joker, of course."

"You did? I thought you guys could only see each other on Fridays?" Lottie says with curiosity in her voice.

"We occasionally find other ways. Cass got us in for their annual Halloween costume party," Ashley answers as she looks to Trent and swallows. "It was very... interesting."

*I bet it was.*

"Ooooh did you go in one of those back rooms?" Lottie asks excitedly.

"Have you been there?" I practically growl in Lottie's direction. She quickly shakes her head no and relief rushes through me.

Ashley rolls her eyes at me as she speaks to Lottie, "Maybe... let's just say we played out a little fantasy of Trent's that started on his first night at Masqued. Now subject change please... let's watch this demon clown do weird shit."

Lottie laughs and Trent eyes Ashley, probably replaying their Halloween night in his head.

The entertainment room has three couches. Each are wide enough for two people to comfortably lay beside each other. I pull Lottie down on the couch opposite of Trent and Ash as she searches the *Firestick* to find the movie.

As the movie begins to play, every time we see the clown, Lottie burrows further into me under the blanket. Every brush of her ass across my shorts has my dick hardening. After the third time I know she feels what she's doing to me because she purposefully shifts her ass from side to side against me.

"If you want to finish this movie, you better stop," I whisper, moving my hand down the front of her sleep shorts. "Don't think I won't take you right here on this couch, they can't see us, but they could hear us." I slide my fingers through her wet center. "I saw how intrigued you were by the club talk. Do you want to get fucked in front of everyone Lottie?" She softly moans and lifts her hips into my hand, showing me what she wants. I start fucking her with my fingers. Slow then fast just like she wants it. I drag my fingers out and rub her wetness from her ass to her clit before I plunge back into her. "Did you secretly wish that couple had seen you sucking my cock in the tunnel, Stacks?"

She doesn't answer with words, instead she turns towards me with my fingers still inside her pussy and starts to devour my mouth. I love it when she gets like this... so needy for her orgasm. I keep up my rhythm, fingering her as she grinds her clit onto the heel of my hand. Our kisses are sloppy, teeth clashing. Both of us chasing her orgasm until I take her over the edge. Swallowing Lottie's moans, I continue to kiss her.

When Lottie comes down from her release, she kisses my throat and whispers, "How loud was I? You can lie to me if it was bad."

I look over to Ash and Trent, seeing him over top of her as they make out. "Trust me, they don't give a shit. They're in their own world too." I kiss the top of her head. "But I'm not done with you yet. Fuck this crazy clown. Let's go take a shower." She giggles and nods into my neck. Just as I go to pick her up, I see Trent carry Ash out of the room.

*Who knew Stephen King got people so horny.*

# Chapter Twenty-Six

"Shit, yeah, I needed this," Ashley moans from beside me. I look over at her reclining in the pedicure chair next to mine as her legs and feet are being massaged.

"Damn girl, if you moan any louder, people are going to get the wrong idea about this place," I say, swatting at her arm. We both burst out laughing.

"I'm so excited for tonight. I cannot wait to be all dolled up. The guys are going to be so hot. I don't know if I should even bother with panties," Ashley rambles as the ladies next to us giggle.

"You have no filter, do you?" I ask.

"Who me? Fuck no. Never have, never will. And that's what you love about me."

"You're right. That's one of the many things I love about your crazy ass." I blow a kiss in her direction.

"Are you ready for tonight? I mean, with all that comes with it," she asks, concern filling her eyes.

"It's definitely going to be an emotional evening, but I think I'll be okay. Especially now that I'll have you guys with me. Thanks again for coming this weekend. It means a lot to me," I say, trying my best to keep my feelings at bay.

"Aw babe, of course. You know I'm here when you need me."

"This really does feel so fricken good," I exhale, leaning further back into my chair.

"Yeah, you need it after all the physical work you put in last night." Ashley giggles.

That has me blushing a bit. I guess Greyson and I were louder than I thought. He swore the sound of the shower would drown out our noises.

"No need to be all shy now... I'm just happy you're happy again," she says.

"I really am, and you're one to talk. I don't think Trent's hands have left your body for more than a few minutes this weekend." I grin. Her reply is a silent, dreamy smile, and the look on her face says more than words can. She's in deep.

As we sit at the drying station, my phone vibrates in my lap with a text from Grey.

> **Greyson:** *You two heading back? We have to hit the road.*
> **Me:** *Soon, just finishing up.*
> **Greyson:** *Good... see you soon, pretty girl!*
> **Me:** *PS- they totally heard us last night... the shower hid nothing!*
> **Greyson:** *Would you be mad if I said I didn't care... I enjoyed you screaming my name, and I'd do it again. You didn't seem to care either when my cock was deep inside you.*
> **Me:** *You're incorrigible.*
> **Greyson:** *Love you too, Babygirl.*

The drive back to Richmond takes us longer than usual, so by the time we arrive, we're rushing to get ourselves ready.

Ethel keeps her comments to a minimum as we scurry around the house. However, she informs us she will head to the Gala ahead of us so she can ensure everything is set to her standards.

Trent and Greyson get themselves ready in a guest room down the hall while Ashley and I take over my room. It seriously looks like a glam squad took over my space. There are numerous garment bags hanging around the room. Multiple hair tools and sprays sprawled along my bathroom counter, and makeup spread from one end of my dresser to the other. Thank God for my bestie.

We lose track of time amongst the hair spray and shimmering fabrics, and it's not long until we hear the booming of the guys 'voices telling us we need to get going.

"Damn Tig, I think I'm ditching Trent and taking you as my date," she says as I take a final twirl in the full-length mirror. Not going to lie, I love the reflection staring back at me.

My dress is a light champagne full-length gown with a draped neckline. Its mermaid style and shimmering fabric accentuate all my curves. I feel amazing. Ashley styled my hair in long loose curls and one side is pinned back with one of Gigi's ornate hairpins. My makeup is done in a neutral smokey eye, and the false lashes Ashley put on make me feel like a total vixen. *I can't wait to see Greyson's expression when he takes me in.*

Ashley's reflection joins mine in the mirror. She looks absolutely stunning in her tight red slinky dress. The low back looks amazing on her with her blonde hair in a loose up-do. I loaned her one of Gigi's elaborate pairs of earrings and I think they really pull the whole look together.

Walking down the stairs of Ethel's house feels like something out of a princess movie. The slight curve to the staircase, the feel of the dress behind me. Not to mention the handsome as sin suit-clad Greyson waiting at the bottom. His expression is everything. The way his eyes roam over every inch of me has me grinning from ear to ear.

Greyson's arms immediately encircle my waist and pull my body flush with his. No words are exchanged as he just stares at me with love and lust in his eyes. I can't help but crash my lips into his. We're entwined with one another for several moments before I hear Ashley.

"Okay, you two. I can see where this is heading, and it's definitely not towards the front door."

Greyson ignores her completely and pulls back just enough so he can look at my face. "You look absolutely stunning. If it was up to me, we'd be skipping out on this whole thing, and I would spend hours worshipping you."

I slap him playfully on the chest. "Well, it's a good thing it's not up to you. Besides, there's always later."

"You bet your fine-ass there is," he says, swatting my behind as I walk past him to grab my clutch.

"Come on, the car is waiting outside."

I hear a yelp coming from Ashley, and I turn to see a devilish smirk on Trent's face. "You better behave, mister," I say, wagging my finger at him. Trent just smiles at me and draws a cross over his heart. *Liar.* I know those two will sneak off the first chance they get.

"Wait! Before we go, can we get a pic with all of us?" I put down my bag and rummage through it for my phone.

"Fuck yeah, we look hot. Set it up over there." Ashley points to the entryway table as a good spot to set up my phone. I set the timer and we take a series of photos. Some serious, some goofy, and of course some lewd ones.

My nerves get the best of me on the car ride, since I'm unsure of what I'll be walking into. I've been to many fundraisers with Gigi and Papa, but never one that supported a cause so dear to me. I hope I can make it through with my wits still intact. Greyson places his large hand on my thigh, squeezing lightly. "I'll be there for you all night, wherever you need me." I guess I'm not doing a good job hiding my anxiousness.

"Thank you. I didn't realize how nervous I was."

"I get it, but you got this. You're one of the strongest people I know Lottie Richmond." That puts a smile on my face.

Leaning over I give him a light kiss. "Let's do this."

I'm in awe at the splendor of the grand ballroom. The room is filled with women in gorgeous gowns and men in their finest suits and tuxes. The smooth strumming of the string quartet fills the space along with the light chatter amongst the guests.

I've lost count of how many hands I've shaken and how many introductions I've had. All give me condolences once they're made aware the Richmond Research Fund was set up in honor of my mother.

Within an hour of my arrival, I've had just about enough of Ethel parading me around, but I understand the importance of tonight. I'm doing this for the foundation, my mother's legacy. Not Ethel. At times, it becomes a bit overwhelming meeting and making small talk with so many people, but I'm thankful for all the familiar faces I see in the crowd. They're always there to make me laugh or smile, or hand me a shot of liquid courage when I need it. There must be several hundred people here, most of whom seemed enthralled with my grandmother.

Through it all, I never lose sight of Greyson, or better yet, he never loses sight of me. He's by my side when I need him and knows when to let me be on my own. Especially when it comes to discussions with some very important people in the clinical research community. My rock, my *anchor.*

During one of my many social breaks, I find myself sitting amongst Smith and Gunnar. Trent and Ashley are lost in each other's arms on the dance floor. I love the fact that they get to enjoy this time together out in the open.

"So, what do you think the big-ticket item this year will be?" Gunnar asks.

"Oh, you know, probably one of the usual. Some fancy all-expenses paid weekend away... last year wasn't it a week-long yacht cruise around the Keys?" Smith responds.

I turn my focus to the two. "How long have you guys been coming to this?"

Gunnar looks to Smith then back to me. "We started in its inaugural year, so maybe four years now?"

"Yep, this is our fifth event. But it's funny how up until this year, Ethel never mentioned Leah's daughter. And now you're the center of every interaction," Smith mentions with a sour look on his face. We both gaze in Ethel's direction where she's currently talking to a large group of people. They all seem to be laughing and enjoying their time. *She really knows how to turn on the charm, doesn't she?*

"Wow, I didn't realize that." Surprise is surely written on my face. I mean, it makes sense why a few of the people I was introduced to seemed stunned at first. Why wouldn't Ethel have mentioned me? Was she embarrassed that I was being raised by her parents and not living with her in North Carolina?

"But you bet your ass our table is the best one at this thing. No others can compare. Not only are we the best looking, but our dance moves are unmatched." Gunnar laughs.

"Keep telling yourself that!" comes from a man I recognize from the cookout the other weekend. The whole table starts laughing.

"Lottie, they're all jealous, they know I'm the best. I'll have to show you my killer dance moves later," Gunnar winks at me.

Smith grabs my hand. "Ignore that moron... in all seriousness Lottie, I'm so happy to be here for you... for her. Whatever I can do to help."

"Thank you, that means a lot to me."

"I've been watching Greyson all night. His eyes haven't left you for a minute. I'm glad to see you two together. He's so protective over you, I'm actually surprised he's not here now."

He's right, I haven't seen Greyson in a bit. I wonder where he is. He probably saw I was with his dad and felt comfortable leaving me to get some air for a few minutes. I know this type of event probably has him feeling stuffy.

"If you'll excuse me, I'm going to go look for him," I say as I stand to leave.

"Hey! You better warn Greyson. We'll be on that dance floor before the night is over." I hear Gunnar call out before I disappear into the crowd.

While making my way through the ballroom, I freeze in place when I hear the crooning of Ethel's voice nearby.

"Oh, there she is... Charlotte, Charlotte darling there you are. Mr. Roberts and I were just talking about how splendid you look this evening. I told him how hard we've been working on your image and diet." I feel my skin crawl in disgust. How dare she act like she had anything to do with it?

Walking over to where they're sitting at one of the large round dining tables, I politely greet Mr. Roberts. "It's so nice to see you, thank you so much for coming this evening. It really means a lot to us."

"It's my pleasure, honestly. You look wonderful as always Ms. Charlotte." I smile kindly in response to his compliment.

"Charlotte, please sit. Speeches will begin soon. I believe the seating chart has you here at table two with me, Mr. Roberts, and Jacob." I'm so sick of her incessant disregard for my relationship with Greyson.

"Oh, that's funny, I could have sworn it said table four," I say with false uncertainty.

Ethel ignores me and focuses back on Mr. Roberts while patting the seat next to her, discreetly commanding I sit down beside her. "I'm so sorry to hear Sherri wasn't feeling well."

Ethel ignores Mr. Roberts' response as her eyes shoot to mine. Her face sporting a look that's somewhere between 'what has gotten into you' and 'sit your ass down'. I just smile at them both.

Mr. Roberts, of course, is oblivious to Ethel silently losing her shit at my disobedience. The mention of Greyson's mother has me wanting to get the hell away from this table, even more than I already did.

"Mr. Roberts it's been great seeing you, but I must be going. My boyfriend, Greyson, is looking for me. Hope you enjoy the rest of the night."

I leave them both without a second glance. I've had enough of Ethel. I will no longer allow her to dictate my life.

# Chapter Twenty-Seven

Turning the corner to re-enter the ballroom, I run right into a black tux.

"Sorry man I didn't—" He stops as we look up and make eye contact for the first time tonight. *Jacob Roberts.*

Now I'm even more thankful I turned down the shots of tequila Trent was doing with Ford in the staff lounge. Originally, I said no because I know how important this event is to Lottie. Lucky for Jacob because liquor would have thrown my self-control out the window.

I move to walk past him, not wanting to cause a scene, until he grabs my arm to stop me. With his hands on me, all bets are off.

"Don't touch me Roberts," I snarl. I believe Lottie that they were just friends, and he was respectful to her, but that doesn't mean I like the guy.

"Look Greyson. I've been wanting to talk to you for a long time. Way before I ever knew you were with Lottie. Can we talk for a second... in private?"

His words surprise me, as does his tone. No malice, no deceit. Making a split-second decision, I nod my head towards the balcony.

We stand there in silence, leaning against the white railing on the second floor.

"Alright, you got me out here. What do you want?" I say bluntly.

He turns towards me. "I know you think I'm the enemy, but I'm not. She is..." The confused look on my face has Jacob continuing, "I remember the first time I saw you come by our house. I overheard the conversation you had with your mother. I already had my opinions of Sherri, but after that, I knew she was a piece of shit. I never even knew you existed."

Shaking my head, I'm overcome with more emotion than I want to be at the thought of my mother not acknowledging me.

"I'm not saying this to hurt you," Jacob says before continuing. "But I confronted my dad soon after and he told me that you chose to stay with your father. When I suggested it might be untrue, he told me to forget what I heard, that he couldn't handle losing her too."

He pauses, seeming to get emotional himself. "You see, my father had already buried his first wife, my mother. It absolutely wrecked him. So for him, he was going to do whatever it took to keep Sherri around for my brothers. Even if that meant hiring nannies who were ten times the mother figure she ever was."

"Damn," is the only thing I can muster as I look out at the night sky. I never in a million years thought I would relate to this guy in any way. This just goes to show that money can't buy you everything.

"Yeah." Jacob sighs.

He's quiet for a minute and then says, "That day in Nori Beach was the first time I had ever given in to Ethel's persistence about me pursuing Lottie. Which, by the way, she's even been in my ear tonight, telling me to sit with Lottie or asking me to go talk to her. But I see through Ethel, just like I see through Sherri." He eyes me, expecting a reaction but nothing Ethel does surprises me anymore.

Jacob continues, "The moment I touched her in the gazebo she told me she had a boyfriend. I had no idea, much less that it was you."

Nodding I say, "I believe you."

"I'm happy to see you two have moved past that, but I just needed you to know my side of things," Jacob says, relief in his voice.

Deciding to be uncharacteristically vulnerable like he has been with me, I say, "I appreciate you telling me that. I remembered you from that day in your backyard with my mother. I wasn't expecting Lottie to be sitting there with another guy and definitely not you."

"Yeah, after the dust settled, I realized that and felt really bad. I even thought about reaching out to Lottie to tell her why seeing me there probably sent you over the edge, but I wasn't sure how much of your personal life you had shared with her, so I didn't want to overstep."

"She knew but she didn't know it was you." I appreciate him thinking about that because he's right. If it were anyone other than Lottie, I wouldn't have shared my mommy issues with them.

"Man fuck... I didn't want to like you." We both chuckle at my admission.

"Well good because the reason I've been wanting to reach out has to do with our brothers."

*Our brothers.*

"Are they okay?" I say immediately.

He nods. "They're fine, other than having a crappy mother. But I think they would benefit from knowing their other brother. If you're up for it, I'd like to arrange for us all to hang out. They are both cool little dudes who know how to keep a secret."

I've never given it much thought but now knowing more of the situation, I definitely want to be a part of their lives. The fact they would have to keep our relationship a secret should piss me off, but I find myself not caring. At this point I don't expect anything from my mother and I would rather her not know.

"Yes, I want to officially meet them... have a relationship with them."

He smiles and nods his head at me. "Listen, I don't know you super well but from what I've gathered... Conner is a lot like you. He loves cars, sports, and at eleven he's already a ladies' man. Aden is smarter than all the other fifth graders in his class, which tends to make him a target. He could use some of those fighting skills from his big brother."

Hearing Jacob talk about them has me feeling hopeful at the chance to build something with them.

"Let's plan something." I pause trying to find the right words. "I'm not always the best with words but... thank you. This is not at all how I saw this conversation going."

"I'm glad you didn't punch me when I grabbed your arm earlier. I saw the thought flash through your face as you flexed your fist."

That has us both laughing again as the balcony doors open and a confused-looking Lottie appears.

"Grey... there you are. Wait, what the hell?"

I look to Jacob and smirk at Lottie about to shit a brick before I say, "It's all good Babygirl. No one's thrown a punch... yet."

Still stunned Lottie says, "I feel like I just walked into the Twilight Zone. But you'll have to fill me in on it all later because right now they're about to start the speeches. Come on." She grabs my hand, pulling me into the ballroom. "Good to see you Jacob," Lottie calls over her shoulder as he follows us inside.

"Come find me before the end of the night and I'll give you my number, so we can set that up," I say before breaking away from him.

Lottie looks at me with a furrowed brow. I kiss the top of her head and say, "We're good, nothing bad." Nodding towards the ballroom, I add, "I'll explain everything after."

Several speeches and accolades later and I'm ready to get out of here. I know Lottie is exhausted too after such an emotionally draining day. Her head resting peacefully on my shoulder throughout most of the silent auction. After the last number is called, I lean over to Trent and let him know we're heading out soon. Ashley and him both nod saying they're ready to head out as well. He has a separate car picking them up because they decided to stay at a hotel tonight since they don't get alone time back in New York. Unfortunately, their flight leaves early tomorrow morning so we let the girls start their long-winded goodbyes.

Not too long later we're headed home. Before I could even sling my suit jacket to the other side of the limo, Lottie was asking me about my conversation with Jacob. I understood her concern after our history involving him, so I fill her in as we drive.

She places her hand on my arm. "Grey... I'm so proud of you for hearing him out. Your brothers will be lucky to know you."

"Thanks Baby," I whisper.

"You should tell Jacob to bring them to your game against Highland in a few weeks since it's close to their house," Lottie says quickly, like she always does when she gets a new idea.

"That's a good plan. I'll mention it to him. I'm sure he'll have to see if they can get away with it behind Sherri's back."

Lottie shakes her head. "Such bullshit that you have to be treated like their dirty little secret. I really don't like that woman."

"I agree but enough about me. What did you think of tonight? Seemed like the auction went smooth and raised a lot of money."

The auction seemed to be a big hit. Ethel and James are still there with the event planner handling the money transfers and awarding the winners their items. I never realized how hands Ethel was with everything. She seemed genuinely invested in the success of tonight's event. I still don't trust the lady.

I'm glad the first event Lottie was able to attend went so well but we're both more than ready to get back to her place. Thankful we'll have the house to ourselves for a bit before her grandmother finishes up, I need to take care of my girl. Wish we were heading back to my place, but we have more privacy at Ethel's.

"I was blown away with the support and generosity of so many. It was inspiring hearing the speech from the president of the North Carolina Leukemia Research Foundation."

"You never know, that could be you one day Stacks."

She smiles shyly. "I don't know about that, but she did give me her card so we could discuss my goals regarding clinical research. I mentioned Mountain Ridge to her, and she said that's a great choice for my undergrad."

"That's awesome. You know I won't complain about you being thirty minutes away and getting to follow your dreams. Sounds like a win-win to me."

Picking her dress up enough to straddle my lap, I say, "It sounds perfect to me, too. I don't ever want to be far from you again."

I gently squeeze her bare thighs and massage them. "Have I told you how gorgeous you look tonight in that dress? I'll give it to Ashley, the fact she hand-picked that without you trying it on first... the girl is good."

The champagne-colored dress fits her curves like a glove. It's sexy yet classy... exactly like Lottie.

"She is the best." She smiles at me as she continues, "when I first put it on, instead of being self-conscious about how tight it is, I thought... holy shit, Greyson is going to love my ass in this thing."

Hearing her openly admit that proves she's finally seeing the same beautiful girl I always have when she looks in the mirror.

"Pretty girl, I more than love it. Right now, all I can think about is the first time I bent you over my truck-bench and fucked you, watching that beautiful ass bounce back on me. And how much I would love to take you in this limo right now."

"Okay Grey, I'm about to tell the driver to step on it. Or you whip your dick out right now," she says, trailing her hand back and forth at the waistband of my pants, making me even harder. I would take her up on that offer if I didn't see the iron gates to Ethel's community out the window.

*Thank Fuck.*

We crash through the front door of Ethel's mansion, already ripping at each other's clothes.

I pin Lottie to the closed door behind us, grinding into her. Coaxing her tongue with mine and loving the sensation. Her taste, her moans, the way she feels in my arms... all of it drives me so fucking crazy for her. Not taking my mouth off hers, I reach down to pull the dress up over her hips. Lifting her up, she wraps her legs around me, allowing her hot, wet center to rub against my suit-clad dick. I groan as I look down and realize she doesn't have on any panties.

"You walked around bare all night?" I growl in her ear.

"I didn't want any panty lines," she whimpers as I bite her neck.

The only thing keeping me from being inside her right now are my clothes. She reaches between us to undo my pants.

Letting them drop to the floor, I step out of the suit and spin Lottie around. She follows my lead, placing both hands flat against the door above her head, intentionally pushing her exposed lower half towards me. Unable to help myself, I smack her perfect ass and watch it jiggle back at me. The sight makes me harder than steel. Lottie moans... "More—"

That spurs me on, and I give her two more good smacks. "This ass is mine." She writhes under my touch as I slide my finger down her ass to her forbidden puckered hole. "You going to give this to me one day, Stacks?"

I keep sliding my hand towards her pussy, feeling her wetness as she whispers, "Yes, everything. I'll give you everything."

"One day baby." Turning her so her back hits the door again, I push my fingers inside her. "But right now, I want this pussy. I want to taste it, I want to feel it squeeze me as you come on my dick." Lottie is moaning and riding my hand so hard her body is moving up and down against the door. When I know she's getting close, I stop fucking her with my hand. She groans as I pull out of her. Placing my fingers to her lips to shush her she licks them clean, tasting herself.

"Fuck me." I moan at the sight, loving how bold she is becoming.

"Get that dress all the way off. I want to spread you apart so you can come on my tongue."

She doesn't waste any time taking it off as I pull her into the sitting room off the foyer.

"Sit down and open up for me Babygirl."

Lottie leans up on her tiptoes, licking my neck as she shoves her hands into my boxers and strokes my dick. We start to make out again. Our lips always wanting to touch the other's. Loving that spark, the connection we feel. Licking and sucking, so much passion... so much want. She pushes my boxers down and pulls me on top of her on the couch. With her hand she puts the tip of my dick at the entrance of her soaking wet pussy.

"Eat me later baby, I want your cock now. I don't think I can wait another second."

Without hesitation I slam into her. Fucking out all of the pent-up desire I've had for her ever since I saw her coming down that staircase earlier. Her fingernails dig into my ass as I rut into her. "Yes Grey... fucking yes." Knowing her orgasm's on edge from earlier I keep going. I'm going to explode with her. Ripping her strapless bra down so I can see more her... the sight of her big tits exposed still pushed up by her bra almost makes me blow right there.

"You are the sexiest fucking thing in this world Stacks." I lift her leg, shifting myself even deeper inside. Her head falls back, and she moans incoherently. I see the moment her eyes open again and roll back in her head as she squeezes my cock so tightly and lets go completely. I empty myself inside her while moaning her name.

I come back to with her brushing her thumb across my lips. "I love you so much Greyson Rexwood. Thank you for tonight, for being by my side."

"I love you... you couldn't get rid of me if you tried." *And I mean every word, because one day she may want to.*

That thought has my stomach turning sour. Trying to push it out of my head, I feel our juices leaking out of her. "As much as I want to leave a 'fuck you' to Ethel on her couch, we better get up and get you cleaned off."

I rip my undershirt off over my head and shove it between her legs to keep her from getting messy. Picking her up, I carry her to her room.

Upstairs, we fuck two more times until we are both sated and exhausted.

Even with being as tired as I am, I still find myself tossing and turning with that gut feeling.

*My guilt is catching up to me and I know I need to tell her before someone else does.*

\*\*\*

Unable to lie in bed with my thoughts any longer, I take the opportunity to make Lottie breakfast in bed.

I hear a throat clear as I turn the stove burner off. Looking up from the omelet in the frying pan, I see the bane of my existence has entered the kitchen.

"Rexwood, your time is up. You need to end things with my granddaughter by the end of next week. I have plans that need taking care of and I need her to ensure they happen," she says in her snarky voice.

"Over my dead body Ethel, I won't lose her again. I don't give a fuck if you tell her about our arrangement. I was planning to explain it all to her soon anyways. I won't let you take her away from me," I growl at her. My elder respect for this lady went out the window a long time ago.

An evil smile creeps onto her face. "Oh, but I will. You see, I know things... have evidence of things that would put your precious father and his biker buddies away for a long time."

That gives me pause. Unsure of what's she playing at, I remain silent and let her continue.

Ethel moves closer to me like a predator. "You were almost perfect until you became a problem when things didn't end for good. The exact reason why I keep some of my cards in my pocket. Just ask Daddy dearest... he knows how I play." *What the fuck is she talking about?*

"I knew Lottie would fall for you just like her mother fell for your loser-of-a-father. The minute I overheard you talking to that other punk at the club about spending your summer in Nori Beach, it was like my plan fell perfectly into place. Get rid of Jonathan quickly so that by the end of the year she could be engaged to Jacob. Until my father went and croaked, leaving me no choice but to bring Lottie to this town, closer to you, before she had time to forget about you altogether."

I clench my fists at her words.

With a sly smirk I would love to smack right off her face, she continues, "I wish I could have just skipped you all together, but I knew the Roberts boy didn't have it in him plus I didn't want him to tell his father my plans. It would have all worked out, but you did something I didn't expect you to do... you actually fell in love with my granddaughter."

Rage courses through me as I slam my fist down on her kitchen island, snarling at her, "I'm madly in love with her and I don't give a fuck what bullshit you have over my head, you won't take her away from me."

*I hate this woman with every fiber of my being.* Wishing I could forget that day—the day I made one of the worst decisions of my life, not understanding the consequences.

"Tell me Greyson, what did you do with the money I paid you this summer to woo and date my granddaughter?" she asks as she taps her fingers on the counter, not one bit ashamed of her actions.

A new voice echoes in the room. My favorite voice... the sweetest voice on earth... but right now, there is hurt and anger in that voice I love so much and it's because of me.

"Yeah... tell us, Greyson. What did you do with the money dear ole Grandma here paid you to date her naïve granddaughter?" Her words confirm she heard the majority of our conversation. She shakes her head in emotional disbelief. "Was that what you were paid to do... make me fall for you?"

Ethel's game has never had any effect on my feelings for Lottie. I just need to make sure she understands that.

I go to her, unable to hold back. Scared to death to lose her again... my anchor. She isn't leaving without dragging me through the sand with her.

Grabbing her chin, making her look me in the eyes to see all my truths, I tell her, "I wasn't paid to make you love me."

# Chapter Twenty-Eight

Greyson

## *Beginning of summer-*
## *Richmond Hills*

Needing to cool off, Ford finds us a spot in the shade to sit. I took him up on the chance to make some extra cash by helping clean the country club's pool today.

"Damn, it's hot," I say as I take a big swig of my water.

Ford uses the bottom of his shirt to wipe the sweat off his forehead. "At least you get to work by the beach this summer with that nice ocean breeze, while I'm stuck here sweating my ass off."

"True, I'm ready for the beach life. But don't even act like you work outside every day, Pretty Boy. Your ass is normally in the air conditioning, serving the rich folk."

He laughs at that comment, knowing it's the truth. He only occasionally does work on the club grounds and when he does, he always recruits me or Nox. We get it done in no time and split the money.

"Yeah, I'm trying to be like Patrick Swayze in *Dirty Dancing*. Find me a sugar mama and an innocent rich girl this summer."

I roll my eyes at him and his damn chick flicks.

"This is probably my last summer in Nori Beach, since Trent is going to college in August. We always have a good time, but this summer I'm more about making money."

Smirking at me, Ford says, "I'm sure you'll find a surfer chick to warm your bed in that fancy guesthouse." It is a pretty sweet set up I have staying in my aunt's pool house with my cousin.

"It's North Carolina, not Cali dipshit. Plus, most surfer girls don't have enough meat on their bones for me."

"Well, you know I don't discriminate either way," Ford replies... and he really doesn't. Homeboy just loves pussy. As long as she has pretty teeth, he's down.

Standing, I say, "Okay, go check with your manager to make sure we're good before we head out."

Ford goes inside and I look out at the beautiful acres of grass-covered foothills. The country club may not be my type of place, but it does have beautiful views.

"Excuse me, Mr. Rexwood, is it?" A polite, proper voice interrupts my thoughts. I turn around and see Ethel Richmond. She is "big money", as we would say, well known in town for her bank account, not so much for her personality. She's never spoken to me until right now.

"Yes, ma'am, can I help you?" I was raised to respect my elders and since she owns the club, she may have found something else she needs us to do.

"I couldn't help but overhear that you're going to be spending your summer in Nori Beach," she says, and I nod my head in response.

She moves closer to me. "I have an opportunity for you to make some extra cash, and I want to run it by you."

*Does she have a place there? Maybe she wants me to be her pool boy?*

"Okay. What are you looking for?"

She gives me a smile. I'm not sure if it's genuine or not, it's hard for me to read her. "Well, my granddaughter is about your age and she's dating this young man who is quite awful to her. I don't think she understands that there are other fish in the sea. I want you to ask her on a date and treat her well. Show her there are plenty of other people out there who could make her happy."

Okay, that is not what I was expecting her to say. She continues before I can answer. "I'll pay you two grand up front to take her on three dates. Then if she breaks up with him, I'll give you another two grand."

I almost choke on my tongue at the money she's offering for something that's so simple. *Typical rich people shit.* At least she seems to have a good cause behind it.

Normally I'm a blunt and honest person, so deception is not in my nature. It's not like I'm going to make the girl fall in love with me. In the end, it will help her see the punk she's with is no good and she can go find someone much better than either one of us. Plus, four grand will get me a hell of a lot closer to purchasing the machine I want for the shop.

Ethel interrupts my pondering, "If you are unable to do the task, I understand—"

"No, I'll do it. A few dates. I'll treat her good, but not good enough for her to catch feelings. I don't want to hurt her in any way." I want to be clear about that because if she's asking me to be more than just a distraction, then I am out. I won't stand by and hurt an innocent person.

"Of course not, I appreciate you considering that." This lady gives me weird vibes, but she seems to care about her granddaughter.

"I leave for Nori Beach next week. How will I know where to find her?"

Ms. Richmond takes her phone out of her purse, handing it to me with a blank contact already pulled up. "My assistant, James, will be in touch to get you your first check before you leave. He will correspond with you in Nori Beach as well."

I enter my cell number into her phone, and she gives me an eerie smile as I hand it back to her. I should be happy about this easy cash but for some reason, I feel like I just signed a deal with the devil.

# Two weeks later–
# Nori Beach

Heading into work, my brain has never been so preoccupied with a chick before. I came here for the summer to make money. Of course, I planned to get laid at some point but within my first week, I didn't expect to meet a girl so intriguing. I mean, I want to fuck her, yeah but there's something more between us. I don't know how to describe it, but I just feel the need to know more about her.

*I hope this arrangement I made with Ethel Richmond doesn't fuck up my plans of getting to know Lottie.*

I received a phone call yesterday from Ethel's assistant asking about my work schedule. Ethel herself called back a few minutes later and said she would casually bring her granddaughter by my work for lunch the next day. I was to flirt with her, plant the seed, and then ask her out when the opportunity came. If this girl has any common sense, she will automatically be skeptical since a woman like Ethel Richmond typically wouldn't be caught dead in a place like The Shack.

Lottie and I have been texting, but I don't want to make plans with her until I know how today will go. The last thing I want is her seeing me out with another chick right after I ask her on a date.

An hour into my shift, I spot the gorgeous girl who has been taking up so much of my head space walk through the door.

*How did she know? I haven't told her where I work yet.*

My stomach does a nose-dive when I see none other than Ethel Richmond in front of Lottie as she follows the hostess to my section.

*No fucking way.*

*Can't be.*

*Okay, Greyson chill... chill. This could work in my favor. I actually like Ethel's granddaughter... as in Lottie. And if that pussy, Jonathan, from the other night is who Ethel wants her to break up with, then sayonara motherfucker.*

*How the fuck is this my damn luck right now?* My heart is racing and not in the way it just was when I first noticed Lottie walk in. No, in the I'm scared way. Realizing I may have fucked up any real chance with Lottie by agreeing to her grandmother's scheme.

Getting my shit together, I head over to their table. I see the minute she realizes I'm her server... her eyes widen with shock.

I'm still stunned and now I'm thinking about how I hope she doesn't hate me when she finds out about the arrangement I made with her grandma. Even though it has nothing to do with my interest in her.

Hearing her say my name, I recover quickly. "Lottie, it's great to see you again."

"So crazy! I didn't know you worked here," Lottie says, and Ethel makes a noise to get our attention.

"Oh, I'm sorry, G, this is my gran—Ethel. This is Ethel Rich-mo—" Lottie starts.

"Nice to see you, Mrs. Richmond," I interject. I refuse to pretend I don't know her. It's one thing to leave out the arrangement but I'm not going to lie about not knowing her grandmother.

"It's nice to see you too, Greyson. How do you know my Charlotte?" She eyes us both.

"Wait, a second... you two know each other?" Lottie blurts, surprise on her face again.

"I'm from Richmond Hills. Everyone knows of the infamous Ethel Richmond," I say, telling the truth.

"Yes, I've run into him several times at my Country Club," Ethel says in a straightforward tone.

"But please, do share how you two know each other?" a skeptical Ethel questions.

"I met her this past weekend at my cousin's house," I say with a big smile directed toward Lottie. "We had a really good time," I add with a wink. A night I haven't been able to stop thinking about.

Trying to change the subject of this awkward situation, I ask for their drink order. Of course, Ethel orders a fucking sparkling water with lemon at a beachfront shack.

I look to Lottie to get her order. "Uhm, I'll have a sweet tea—" she says in an unsure tone.

Her grandmother chimes in, "You'll have the sparkling water, dear. Remember it's summer, which means fewer clothes to hide behind." Her words piss me the fuck off. I nod my head and leave the table. One sparkling water and one sweet tea coming right up, *bitch*.

This whole thing is starting to seem fucking fishy. A memory from the other night pops into my brain. Lottie mentioned something about being paraded around by her grandmother. I could tell she wasn't very fond of said grandma. Now I am wondering if there's more to this whole setup. I mean, I saw first-hand through his text message that her boyfriend is a douchebag. Lottie seemed ready to break up with his ass on her own though. Maybe Ethel underestimates her granddaughter or there is something else going on.

Honestly, I don't know what to believe about Ethel, but I do know I don't like the way she just spoke to Lottie. I won't stand for that shit.

# End of summer– Nori Beach

I've been calling Lottie since I got my phone back this morning. We tracked it with the find my iPhone app and luckily it was in the house we partied at last night. Nox ran over to get it for me while I drank some coffee and sobered the hell up.

I was a fucking disaster last night. No matter how much the rational part of my brain kept trying to intervene, my destructive side was winning out.

Today my need to get to Lottie is outweighing my hangover.

Pulling up to Ethel's mansion feels like a slap to the face after yesterday. I was so happy just twenty-four hours ago parking in this exact same spot. Now I have no clue where we stand and it's killing me. I drove my truck today in case she tried to call me back. My calls keep going straight to voicemail. I even tried from Ford's phone just in case. It rang all the way through but no answer. The guys think she might have blocked me. She wouldn't do that to me... but maybe I'm in denial. I don't blame her for being pissed at me, I shouldn't have taken off like that last night.

Within thirty seconds of knocking on the door James answers. He tries to greet me, but I waste no time. "Hey James. Is Lottie around?"

"What are you doing here Mr. Rexwood?" Ethel says, appearing quickly as James opens the door for me to come in. The sound of her voice is another sign of my unlucky day.

"I came to speak to Lottie. I can't get her on the phone. Is she in her room?" I say, eyeing the staircase and considering barging up there without their permission. I need to see her.

A sly smile appears on her face. "Oh well no such luck here. She left to go back to New York late last night. Said she realized she had been living in an unsustainable fantasy this summer and needed to get back to reality."

*What did she just say?*

"She left? No, she wouldn't do that, not without talking to me," I say, my words sound surer than I feel at this moment.

Needing to see for myself, I dodge past James up to her room. Busting through her door, the hope that Ethel was lying deflates right out of my chest.

Everything is gone... the bare minimum remains. The unicorn I won her sitting on her perfectly made bedspread is the only sign of the summer we spent together.

I rush back downstairs to demand answers. *I know Ethel had something to do with this shit.*

Ethel walks back into the foyer when I make it to the bottom of the staircase. I notice she has something in her hand as she says, "Well do you believe it now, Mr. Rexwood? As you can see, she is gone. What did you expect? You knew this was a means to an end. She would never end up with someone like you. After yesterday, I think she finally sees that Jacob is better suited for her."

Like a ton of bricks, it hits me... this was her plan all along. It wasn't about caring for Lottie and getting her away from Jonathan. This was about getting in good with the Roberts family. She's using Lottie just like she used me this summer. Money and greed rule every decision Ethel Richmond makes.

She drives the nail into the coffin with her next words, "Your mother just adores her. Sherri thinks she would be a great fit for Jacob." My chest aches with her words, with the thought of Lottie meeting my mom and having no clue who she was to me. Just that she was Mrs. Roberts, Jacob's mother... *stepmother.*

"Now here... take this and move on with your life," she says, reaching her hand towards me.

Completely ignoring her, I snarl, "You are a manipulative piece of shit!" I can't see straight I'm so pissed at this spiteful, calculated woman.

"You're entitled to your own opinion Greyson, but you didn't seem to mind when I was writing you a check earlier this year. I suggest you let Lottie move on or she will be hearing about the role you played in her falling for you this summer."

Her hand stretches out toward me again. I look down, realizing it's a check she's trying to hand me. I snatch it. My vision starts to cloud with black as she says, "A deal's a deal." Pulling myself together and ripping the check into tiny pieces, I throw it at her. It lands around her on the shiny porcelain floor.

"Fuck your money. I was planning on giving you this yesterday... but here," I say as I hand her the envelope from my jean pocket. "I don't give a fuck about anything but Lottie. You know good and well us falling for each other this summer had nothing to do with the deal we made. This is what you gave me at the beginning of the summer. Every cent of it." Shaking with rage, I hand her the check for two thousand dollars.

Refusing to take my money she says, "You made your bed, now you have to sleep in it." Not looking the slightest bit remorseful, she turns her back to me and walks away.

*FUCKING BITCH.* If she wasn't a sixty-year-old woman I would drag her ass back here right now and shove this check down her throat.

Still fuming, I feel like I have so much to say to her. I held a lot back this summer once I saw how she treated Lottie.

As I fell for Lottie it became very clear to me that Ethel didn't have her best interest at heart and had done a number on her self-confidence. Part of me held out hope that there was a caring bone inside her body, one that genuinely thought Jonathan was a bad dude and wanted Lottie away from him. But over time it became clear that wasn't the case.

I need to find a way to get Lottie to talk to me and explain everything to her myself.

"Tell me where she is? Give me your parents' address at least, Ethel!" I holler after her.

James steps to open the door. "Son, it's time to go. She won't hesitate to call the cops and I don't want to see you get in any trouble. Just trust that everything will work out for you and Ms. Lottie."

"Fuck her. Let her call the cops," I say, trying to reign my anger in, but I want to punch a hole right in her foyer wall. My fists flexing, feeling the need to let my anger out on something.

"If you end up in custody, how are you going to find Lottie?" he says, still standing with the front door open.

Considering his point, my phone begins ringing in my pocket. *It's her.*

I walk out the open door without another word as I pull my phone from my pocket. Disappointment floods me when I see Ford's name flash across the screen.

*Maybe she called him back.*

"Did she call you?"

I hear the thud of fists pounding the punching bag in the background as he says, "What? Oh, no she didn't. I was just calling to check on you. We're up at the gym and wanted to make sure you made it to her safely."

"She's fucking gone!" I roar.

"Gone... where?"

"I don't know but far away from me apparently." My words come out with a growl. I'm not mad at Ford, I'm just fucking pissed at the world right now.

"Damn Brother. You okay... need us to come get you?" There's concern etched in his voice.

"No." Not sure which question I'm answering as everything runs through my mind.

*She really left me. I must be missing something. Lottie wouldn't do this to me.*

Hanging up on Ford, I continue to try her number my whole ride home. Every call going right to her voicemail. Her sweet voice killing me each time.

Pieces of our perfect summer together burrow themselves into my bones with every minute she doesn't answer.

*How did we get here*

# Chapter Twenty-Nine

"Please Lottie, let me explain," he begs.

"Oh yes, do explain Greyson," Ethel croons from behind him, the sound of her voice sending an icy shiver down my spine. How could she do this to me? We're family. I should have known better. Should have known that she always has an ulterior motive... but what do I have to do with any of it?

I step into Ethel's view with so much fury I feel like I might combust.

"I don't want to hear a word from your mouth right now!" I yell at her, causing her to flinch at my outburst. She had to have known this would catch up to her. Secrets can't stay hidden forever.

"Better yet, leave Ethel. I can't stand to even look at your face right now."

"This is my house, young lady. You cannot speak to me with that tone," Ethel practically snarls back.

"Fine, I'm leaving. I can't stand the thought of being around someone as miserable as you."

Ethel just scoffs, acting unaffected by the current situation. Greyson's head ping-ponging between the two of us.

"I always knew you had a black heart, but do you even care about me at all?" I question her bluntly.

With that, Ethel walks away. Just fricken walks away without another word.

"Shit." The curse is almost a whisper out of Greyson's mouth.

I whirl to where he's standing there like a lost soul whose world is shattering around him. His pleading eyes beg me not to run from him. We've been down this road before, and we promised to listen to one another. *But then why not tell me when he had the chance to come clean?*

"Why didn't you tell me? We laid everything out there and yet you still didn't come clean."

Greyson winces slightly as he takes in my words, my voice void of emotion. I don't know if it's because of shock, or if it's because I was waiting for the other shoe to drop. I always knew Ethel wasn't to be trusted, but to think her manipulation and games went this far and that Greyson fell for it.

"I fucked up and I'm so sorry, Lottie. I was going to tell you.. I was just waiting for the right moment. But you have to believe me. I made that agreement before I knew who you were. I didn't put two and two together until that day at The Shack when you came in for lunch," he says, his hands running through his already tousled hair.

"You could imagine my surprise when you showed up. The girl who had me entranced from the moment I saw her on that dance floor. I knew right then and there that I needed to return the money to Ethel, but by that point, I had already put the money down towards the CNC machine for the shop. So, I decided I would work my ass off the rest of the summer and pay Ethel back every cent. The day after I saw you with Jacob, I went to your house. After she told me you were gone, Ethel had the nerve to try and pay me the second half I was owed from our original deal. When she tried to give it to me, I basically spat at her. I went there intending to pay her back and then I was going to tell you everything. I knew it had gone on too long. Instead of accepting the money, Ethel refused. She told me I now had to live with what I did and let you go, or she would tell you about our deal before I got the chance to." Greyson paces the length of the hall.

All I can do is stand there and listen as he continues. "Clearly once we got back together, I was scared as shit to say anything to you. I just got you back and was not ready to face this when our relationship was just on the mend. There was still the issue with the money as well. I didn't want to tell you until I had returned the funds back in some way. So, last night I made a hefty donation on behalf of me and the guys at the Gala. Knowing at least in doing so it was going to a good cause. I know none of this excuses me from what happened, I just hope you can understand. It doesn't change anything that happened between us, everything was real... *is* real. I love you, Lottie, with all that I am," he finishes and storms up to me, waiting for my reaction or some sort of response.

I let out a long breath. That's certainly a lot to take in. I don't know what to think anymore. I mean, I believe him and am grateful he donated it to the RRF, but I'm still furious. All I can think about is why he would have ever agreed to something like that in the first place.

"What kind of person agrees to be paid to date someone? Did you think it was funny, a game? Was it some sort of challenge to you? 'Let's see if I can get the lonely rich girl to fall in love with me?'" I can feel my tears streaking down my cheeks. Finally... some sort of reaction instead of the numbness I felt moments ago.

"It was never like that. I was just supposed to show you a good time in Nori Beach. Try and get your mind off the asshole you were dating. Ethel convinced me he wasn't good for you and that she wanted you to be happy."

"Oh, so you thought you were a better match for me than him? You deserved to be with me?" Thinking back to Jonathan, I didn't even like him that much. I played up our relationship to Ethel because I could tell it pissed her off, but I never thought she would pay someone to get me away from him. And all so I could get in with the Roberts family. *Nothing she does surprises me anymore.*

"Fuck Lottie, no—I mean yes! I do deserve you. Jonathan is an asshole. From the first moment you mentioned him, and then again at the boardwalk, I knew that he wasn't good enough for you. When I met you and Ethel at lunch, I realized he was the guy I was supposed to get you away from and to be honest, it didn't seem like such a bad idea."

"But you are? You're good enough?" I question him, staring into his loving eyes. I can see the anguish in them, the fear that he may have lost me yet again.

"I am, and I told you I would prove it to you every day if you'd let me. I know I fucked up, and I am so, so fucking sorry."

I run my hands over my face. Where the hell do we go from here? To think the man I love was originally paid to date me. *Geez when you put it that way, it's pretty fucked up.*

But I believe him when he says we met before he knew who I was, and I know damn well our love is not something that was fabricated. I just need to figure out if I can get past all of this.

Looking at Greyson's tense form in front of me I reach out my hand to grip his, which currently has a small tremor to it. "I believe you, all of it." He wraps his arms around me, pulling me close.

"Thank fuck. I'm so sorry Babygirl," he whispers to the top of my head.

Pulling out of his arms I look him square in the face. "But that does not mean I'm ready to forgive you. The fact that you kept this from me for so long hurts. Hurts really fricken bad... I don't know what to do right now, all I know is I need to get out of this house."

"Okay, I get it. Let's get some of your stuff, then I'll take you wherever you want to go."

He makes like he's going to follow me upstairs, but I stop him. "Wait here. I'll be back in a few minutes." He looks disappointed but nods his understanding.

Pulling out two large suitcases from my closet, I start to throw the contents of my room in them. I try calling Ashley to see if she's still in town. I need my bestie. She mentioned they had to catch an early flight, but I don't even know what time it is. To my disappointment, the call goes right to voicemail. I send her a quick text to call me when she lands.

Where am I supposed to go? I can't go back to Greyson's. I need to get my thoughts in order without him clouding my judgment. Ugh! I wish I had a fricken car, then I could go wherever the hell I want to. Maybe I'll try Frankie, unless she knew about the deal all along? Would she have told me if she did? Well, I guess there's only one way to find out.

> **Me:** Hey, are you home?
> **Frankie:** *Yeah Girl, what's up?*
> **Me:** *Do you mind if I crash there for a little...*
> **Frankie:** *Not a problem, whatever you need.*
> **Me:** *You're amazing. I'll be over soon.*

When I approach the stairs, suitcases in tow, I peer down at the foyer below. James is there with Greyson, handing him his suit jacket from last night. They exchange a few words, then peer up at me. Greyson smiles and then meets me to carry down my heavy-ass bags.

James gives me a solemn look when I reach him. He gives me a quick hug and says, "I'll check in soon, Ms. Lottie." I give him a quick smile and a nod as we head out of the door.

When we reach the front steps, I turn and ask the one question that's been bugging me. "Do any of your friends or family know about the deal with Ethel?"

"Fuck no. Like I told you, this wasn't a game or a contest. No one knows about any of it, not the boys... not even Trent." I let out a long breath I wasn't aware I was holding. Him not telling anyone helps me relax just a little.

"Okay, then please take me to Frankie's house. I'm going to stay there for now." He eyes me for a long moment. "I'm not running away, Greyson. I just need time to digest today and get my head straight."

"I understand," he says in almost a whisper. Our ride to Frankie's is quiet, but I don't mind as I stare mindlessly out of the truck window at the changing colors of the leaves.

He helps me get my luggage into Frankie's house but doesn't linger too long. Frankie gives me a look and I just shake my head. I don't know if I want her to know. Actually, now that I think about it, I don't think I want anyone to know.

She doesn't press me for more, which is also why I decided to come here. She respects people's privacy and right now, I couldn't be more grateful.

"Thanks again for letting me crash here. I had a huge blowout with Ethel and couldn't stay there any longer." At least that's somewhat the truth.

"I get it, and please, it's not a problem at all. You're welcome here anytime." I smile at her as we walk down the hall towards the room I'll be staying in.

"Throw your stuff in there and come find me on the couch when you're done. My plan was to smoke a joint, veg-out, and watch movies all day. I hope you're game," she says. I wrap my arms around her, thankful for her kindness. She tenses at first then wraps her arms around me. No words are exchanged, there's no need for them. She knows I appreciate her.

We spend the rest of the afternoon and evening eating take-out and binge-watching movies on Netflix. We don't discuss what happened today, just laugh and enjoy each other's company. By the time Gunnar arrives home, we're both passed out on the couch. I briefly hear him talking to someone, but I'm too knocked out to care. I feel a warm blanket being draped over me as I settle in for a well-deserved night's rest.

I'm awakened by the smell of fresh coffee brewing. I sit up surveying the mess we made of the living room. Wrappers and empty containers litter the coffee table, along with drink cups and gossip magazines. Frankie is still passed out on the other end of the couch, her wild hair hiding her face. I look to the bright front windows and see Gunnar outside on the front porch in deep conversation with somebody. I peek around to see Greyson sitting in a chair sipping on a cup of coffee. *What is he doing here?*

I open the front door with the blanket wrapped around me and both men stop and turn in my direction. Who knows what I look like after yesterday, but regardless Greyson smiles as he takes in my disheveled self. He on the other hand, looks like complete shit as if he hasn't slept at all. *Was he out here all night?*

"What are you doing here, and so fricken early too?" I ask as I settle into one of the outdoor chairs, pulling the blanket tighter around me. Gunnar excuses himself and goes back inside, leaving just Greyson and me.

Greyson looks at me with concern in his eyes. Does he not understand I'm not running away? He doesn't have to guard the door for fucks sake.

He gathers a stack of papers he had next to him and hands them to me. I look at the stack in my hand and then back up to him for any explanation.

314 MAKE YOU LOVE ME

"James snuck these into my coat before we left yesterday. I read through them all, several times. You need to read them, then we're going to meet up with him in a little while." Is this what kept him up all night? How important could it possibly be?

I look at him a bit confused, still shaking off my sleepiness. "What is all this?" My eyes barely registering what I'm reading.

"It's our chance at revenge."

***

To say the ride to meet James is a confusing one would be an understatement. I shuffle through the stack of papers for what feels like the hundredth time. All the statements, notes, and money transfers. Then there's the note from Papa. I can't wrap my head around it.

"I know, it was a hell of a lot for me to take in, too. Shit, it kept me up all night," Greyson says while placing his hand tenderly on my thigh. Not sexually, but to comfort me.

"I just can't believe it. How could she do this? How did she get away with this for so long?"

"Honestly, I have no clue. I'm hoping James can help shed some light on all of this," he says as we pull into the parking lot of a diner on the outskirts of town.

Staring through the windshield, lost in a daze, I hear Greyson's body shift in the driver's seat. I look over to see him staring at me intently.

"Listen, Lottie, I know things are fucked up between us right now, but I want you to know I'm here for you throughout this whole thing. I will be by your side." I reach over and grab his hand in mine and squeeze it lightly.

"Thank you." It's all I can really say at this point. He's right, things are a mess between us right now, but I still need him. Still want him by my side for this.

We walk towards a booth in the far back corner. James is already there sipping a cup of coffee. He stands and gives me a big, very un-James-like hug. A little stunned by his affection, he motions with his hand for us to sit.

"I'm so glad you could meet me on such short notice. I had my morning schedule blocked out for errands, and this worked out perfectly," he says.

Placing the stack of papers on the table, my eyes go to James. "Please, help me understand, and most importantly... how did you get all of this?"

"Ah yes, well as you know, I've worked for your grandmother for many years now. But what you don't know is that your great-grandfather is who actually hired me for the job. Unfortunately, he and your grandmother never really got along. I believe he saw who she was deep down and never truly trusted her. I can't say I blame him."

My eyes go wide at the mention of Papa. He knew all along what a witch Ethel was. It would explain why she never came to visit for the holidays and why with my mother's passing, I was left in their custody and not hers.

"As you see, your grandmother is completely broke and has been for some time now. She can no longer afford the upkeep on her house, the salaries at the clubhouse, or her lavish lifestyle. But I know a woman like Ethel does not go down without a fight. So, a few years ago, when I started to see her life returning somewhat back to normal, I was perplexed as to where the money was coming from. That's when I began to take note."

"I can't believe this... I mean, I see it. It's here, right in front of me, but I still can't believe it. She's always so concerned with keeping her image and how we're perceived and this whole time it's been her who's been the stain on our family," I say, more to myself than to the two with me.

"I've always known Ethel to be a manipulative and deceitful woman. But it wasn't until this past summer that I started to see the full scope of what she was doing. Of course, I told Mr. Richmond what I suspected, and he started an investigation of his own. So, I can't take all the credit for this." He waves his hand over the pile of papers. "Most of that was thanks to your papa." I give James a sad smile. My Papa, poor man must have been riddled with disgust at what his daughter had done, what she had turned into.

"From what I gathered, Ethel opened a line of credit against the Country Club property around ten years ago to help catch her up financially. Looks like it was all working fine until about six years ago when she stopped making her loan payments. I believe they closed the line of credit at that point, and she had no more money or source of income. That's when she created the Richmond Research Fund and skimmed from the donations in order to pay her employees, and whatever else she pleased."

"How—how did you figure this all out?" Greyson asks, both of us hanging on to every word.

"Well, it definitely took some time to piece together the whole puzzle. For the last two years of the research fund, I made sure to obtain a copy of the total donations after expenses versus what was deposited into the fund's account. At first, everything seemed legit until I saw the invoice for event expenses. By using her own country club as the location, she was able to inflate the cost of every service provided. She would take the difference in cost, store it in an offshore account, then use it when she needed it. Just look here at this comparable." James says while shifting through the papers to find the document he's referring to.

"You see here." He points to a document labeled Willington Wedding. "This wedding was hosted last November for five hundred guests." Greyson and I scan the document, noting the extensive invoice totaling sixty thousand dollars. From what I can see, the item list is comparable to what was seen at the gala the other night. The white glove servers, top-of-the-line passed hors d'oeuvres and sit-down menu, high-end linens, house string quartet, and DJ, the similarities go on and on.

"Now look at what Ethel's event cost for three hundred guests on a similar weekend, with an almost identical itemized list," James says while pushing another invoice over to us.

After several moments I hear Greyson say, "Holy Shit!" Holy shit, indeed. Like James said, Ethel's event mirrors the Willington wedding. However, Ethel's invoice is more than double the cost. She claimed the event cost the foundation a whopping hundred and thirty thousand dollars to host.

"But how did this pass the events coordinator and manager?" I question, holding the questionable document in my hands.

"Because this document is what the country club has on file," he says, sliding another document our way.

This one is almost identical to the Willington's, cost and all. I knew it, I fucking knew it. To think Ethel started that foundation out of the goodness of her heart. No, she has no heart. She started it so she could somehow find a way to skate along.

"I just can't believe this... No, I can believe it, I just can't believe she would stoop to this level to maintain appearances. If she was that hard up for the money she could have easily gone to her father. Even with their strained relationship, he would have helped her, I'm sure of it.

I look at Greyson and see pure rage written all over his face. His eyes are locked on the papers below, his jaw tense, and his body is tight beside mine. I give him a nudge with my shoulder, trying to break him out of his stare. He gives me a sad smile and squeezes my hand that's resting on the booth seat between us.

"How long has she been doing this?" Greyson asks, taking the words right from my mouth.

"As long as the foundation has been active, so five years now," he says solemnly.

"Papa knew of this, of the money laundering?" I ask, turning my attention back to James.

"Unfortunately, yes, he did. I'm sure you've read his note by now. It was the one left for her at the reading of his will. He was devastated when we realized what she was doing."

Papa's note was a warning letter to Ethel. He had said he knew what she was doing and rather than call the cops, he was giving her a chance to right her wrongs. He didn't want me to know what she had done and didn't want any of the backlash to fall in my lap.

"His note mentioned something about consequences if she didn't fix this..." I say, recalling that specific part.

"I was the consequence. I was to do with this information as I saw fit. And seeing what Ethel has done to you and your family, I thought it was best for you to decide."

Just then a phone rings, startling us all out of our haze of revelations. James shifts in his seat and shows the screen to us. It's Ethel calling, I'm sure to summon him back home and order him around.

"I have to go, but please call me once you decide what you want to do with all of this. I want to help however I can."

"Thank you so much, James, you've done enough already. I truly appreciate this."

"Please, it's my pleasure to see that wicked witch go down." He goes to leave our booth but stops. "Oh, before I forget, I want you to give this to your dad." He hands Greyson a sealed envelope with 'Smith Rexwood' written on it. *What the hell?*

"I think your father would like to see this," he says, then tips his head and leaves us.

Greyson and I just stare at one another, unsure of what our next steps are. He gathers the paperwork and scoots out of the booth, extending his hand to help me stand up.

"I didn't get to talk to my dad last night and I'm wondering if this envelope has anything to do with what Ethel was spewing about having evidence on him and the club. I honestly just thought she was saying shit to get into my head, but now I'm starting to second guess that," he says with worry in his tone as we walk towards his truck.

"We will figure all this out. If she has anything on him, it can't be anything worse than what we have on her. You know your dad, he's a good man," I say, and he nods at me knowing I'm right, but it doesn't take away that uneasy look I see on his face as he shuts my door.

"What's our plan?" I question him as he gets in on his side of the truck.

"Not really sure, but I think we need to go see my dad," he says as he throws his truck into reverse, and we speed off towards town.

# Chapter Thirty

*Dear Journal,*

*I can't get the shrieks out of my head. I thought I had been through so much in my short life, but the sight I saw last Friday night made me realize someone always has it worse.*

*It was a beautiful fall evening, so my love and I went for a walk. As the sun began to set, we headed back to his bike. Smitty can never say no to me, so when I asked him to make one last stop on the trail, we did. This spot has always been one of my favorite views. It looks up to the expansive blue ridge mountains. Sadly, I hope to never see that view again. Too much grief is held there now.*

*Even as I write this, my heart tugs at this admission.*

*I am so thankful I made us take that detour because it saved two innocent people, but I also hurt for my soulmate because he did something that night that will live with him forever.*

*The trails had been quiet for quite some time because they're supposed to close at dusk, so most people clear out way before that. So, when we heard screaming and pleading, we knew we were the only people nearby to help whoever was in trouble. Following the screams, we ran through the trail. When we found them, the sight in front of us had Smith stopping in his tracks, trying to shield me from what was ahead... but it was too late. I had already seen it.*

*A young man a little older than us was bloody and lay-
ing on the ground motionless. Another man dressed in all
black under his Savage Sons' cut was wrestling a young
woman on the ground as she begged for mercy. With all
the commotion, they hadn't noticed us. Shock had taken
over my body. Smith picked me up and put me out of sight.
Handing me his phone and told me to tell his father where
we were. Tell him to bring the brothers, he had said. I
didn't even question him when he handed me the phone
and it was calling Papa Rexwood's number and not 911.
I'm usually kept in the dark when it comes to MC business
but I do know Smith, his father, and the rest of the Rebel
Knights don't trust the Richmond County Sheriff especially
when it comes to the Savages—the only motorcycle club
the Rebels have bad blood with.*

*Smith took off to aid the helpless woman fighting for her
life. I didn't even attempt to stop him because I knew there
was no use. He isn't the type of guy to let something like
that go. I watched as he caught the man by surprise as he
was trying to get the woman's underwear down. I can still
taste the acid in the back of my throat as I realized what
that lunatic was attempting to do to the woman.*

*My shock turned to horror when the blunt force of the
rock that Smith slammed into the attacker's head knocked
him off the woman. She was pregnant... I had forgotten I
was even holding the phone to my ear until I heard Pop's
voice through the other end. As I watched Smith pound his
fist into the guy's face, I knew I had to snap out of it and
speak. So, I did. I told pop everything that was going on
and where we were. He reassured me he and the guys were
on the way and to be strong until he got here. Keeping his
words in my head, I went towards Smith. My sweet man, I
had never seen him this way. So determined to make sure
this evil man got nowhere near any of us again.*

*I knew better than to grab him in the heat of the moment while he was in fight-or-flight mode, so I called his name. After several times he finally looked up to me. I assured him he was a hero, and that sack of shit couldn't hurt us. I told him we had to get moving because the Rebels were on their way.*

*When we looked back to the woman, she was cradling what I'm assuming was her love's lifeless body against her very swollen belly. Her face was tortured with tears pouring down her cheeks. Smith looked down to the man's limp body underneath him and finally snapped out of his rage. I went over to the young woman, and I reassured her that help was coming as I stroked her hair. I saw the dreaded look on Smith's face when he came over to us, he knew her. Renee.*

*He told her the Rebel Knights were coming which most likely meant her uncle as well and they would take care of her. Putting two-and-two together I realized Smith knew her from her uncle's involvement with the motorcycle club. He reassured her that her husband would be taken care of, but we needed to get her to the hospital.*

*Renee had started feeling cramps right before Smith's dad and everyone arrived. I wanted to go with her to the hospital. I was so worried, but I knew it would look suspicious.*

*As I went back to Smith's and showered off all the sadness from that day. I prayed and prayed for her and her unborn child.*

*A few hours later when I was laying in my own bed trying to decompress from the most awful day of my life. Smitty called me—Lola Rebel Daniels was born 3 weeks early at 4 pounds 7 ounces. A healthy, beautiful baby girl.*

*My heart ached that night and still does for Renee and Lola, a huge piece of their world was no longer walking* with them. Lola would never know her father. I hoped that as she grew her mother would tell her many stories of him and their love story. I didn't have that same luxury from my own mother. I knew more than most the need to know where you came from and who helped create you.

I made a wish for little miss Lola that night. That she grows up to be strong, loyal, and kind. But also true to her namesake... a little rebellious.

My sweet guy was all over the place with his emotions. I even snuck back out that night so I could hold him in his bed. He said he didn't regret what he did but ending a life is a tough thing to wrap your head around. I can imagine, which is why I am glad he won't have to recall it in a courtroom. Justice was served that day and now Renee and Lola have relocated to Texas and are safe and sound.

I can't tell a soul about this since things had to be handled behind closed doors because our sheriff's department can't be trusted. Not to mention the war it would cause between The Rebels and The Savages if this information was to ever get out. But I had to get my thoughts out of my head. Thank you Journal for always being my faithful confidant. We have been through a lot over the years. Love and loss, but this has been one of my most therapeutic entries. I already feel much better.

xox,
Leah

# Chapter Thirty-One

## Smith

If Ethel's afternoon tea spilled across her desk isn't enough evidence that me being here is a surprise, then the shock displayed on her face sure is. James was true to his word, and Ms. Richmond had no clue I was going to be paying her a little visit on this fine day.

When Greyson and Lottie came to me earlier with a folder regarding Leah's mother, I had no idea so much of it would involve me.

"Smi—Mr. Rexwood, what are you doing in my study unannounced?" she says, unmoved as hot tea continues to spread across the large piece of mahogany furniture.

"I think the minute you started blackmailing me twenty years ago, all rules and customaries went out the window for us," I say while I take a seat across from her. Calm, cool, and collected... at least on the outside.

Twenty years ago, was a different story. I came to this very house, guns blazing, wanting to know what she did to convince Leah to leave me. To my shock, she actually told me the truth.

**_Back then:_**

*"Where the fuck is Leah? What did you do to finally convince her to leave me?"*

*I'm met with an amused silence from Ethel. "Tell me!" I yell.*

*"It was quite easy, actually. Your perfect little Leah isn't as smart as we all think she is," Ethel crooned.*

*"What the hell are you talking about? Tell me where Leah is!"* I'm losing my patience with this woman.

*"She loved you, I'll give her that. Even when I told her she wouldn't be able to give you a family, she said she didn't care. That you guys could just adopt. She said she would never give you up... until I gave her no other option."* Why does she get so much enjoyment out of hurting her only child?

*Leah and I had talked about that scenario. We knew it was a chance she wouldn't be able to have a baby, but I told her without any hesitation that no matter what, I wanted her. We would find a way to have a family of our own.*

*I grab her by the shoulders.* "Stop playing games with me. Tell me what the fuck happened?"

*Laughing in my face, not scared at all, she says, "I know you're a killer, Smith. But you won't kill me. You don't have it in you. You could barely handle killing that Savage."*

*Immediately, I drop my hands from her shoulders like she's on fire. How the fuck does she know that? My stomach churns with anxiety.*

*Ethel lets out another venomous laugh.* "See, not so smart after all. She wrote about that night in her journal. Even though it was in a lockbox in her closet, I had been going into it every so often since you two started seeing each other. I knew she would slip up, I just never thought it would be something quite that useful. I knew threatening you and your family would get Leah to agree to anything... even leaving you."

*Too stunned by Ethel's knowledge of that night to speak... it's not only me who could go down for the things we covered up. I've been told ever since I was a kid that if anything ever went down to call my dad or a brother first. The cops in our town have it out for anyone and anything related to the Rebel Knights. I know the few deputies we can trust, but you never know who may show up when you call. I just hate Leah was even the slightest bit involved that night.*

*Damn baby. I should have let her talk about that night more, but it was hard enough to live through it. I know writing her thoughts and feelings out in her journal was always therapeutic for her.*

*"Look Smith, it's just business. My daughter was never meant to be with a low life like you. She's the granddaughter of a steel tycoon, not a biker princess. The best thing you can do is just forget about her."*

*That snapped me out of my shock-filled daze. "It's not just fucking business... it's our life! I could never forget her. She deserves to be with me. She deserves to be happy, especially after everything she's been through. NO ONE will love her the way I do. How can you do this to your own flesh and blood? You are a sick fucking bitch!"*

*She shrugs her shoulders without a care in the world. My words having little to no effect on her whatsoever. "She'll get over you eventually. Money talks, she'll find someone who can take care of her. Don't worry," she says nonchalantly.*

*That thought has me feeling rage like I never have in my life and punching a hole in the foyer wall. "Fuck you!" I yell at her as my hand starts to bleed. No amount of pain could surpass what I feel right now with the knowledge that she has truly found a way to keep the love of my life away from me.*

*How can I go on without her? We were supposed to be for life... forever. Seahorses.*

*"Smith, I suggest you leave before I call the cops, and let's be honest... I have a lot I can tell them. The Rebel Knights and your daddy sure know how to cover up a murder, don't they?"*

*Fuck, I would never want my dad to take the fall for that night. He did what was best for all of us without starting a war with the Savages or taking a chance that the dirty cops in our town would try to turn something around on me. She knows exactly how to play me and right now she's holding all the cards. I have no moves left.*

*Her voice is like nails on the chalkboard. "Oh, and one more thing Smith. If I find out you have tried to contact my daughter in any way, shape, or form, there will be consequences. Don't think I won't take her down with you. Sounded to me like she was an eyewitness who intentionally withheld evidence from law enforcement. I would rather her go to prison than witness her marry you."*

*My soul burns for Leah with this knowledge. Not just because I know this truly means it's over but also the fact her own mother would do something so cruel to such a beautiful person. A person she created.*

*Heading towards her door before I do something I can never take back, I say, "You may think you're better than me Ethel. You have more money... a bigger home, but Money can't buy you everything and you certainly can't take it with you to hell."*

Ethel gets herself together as she finally stands to address me.

"Now Smith, I wouldn't call it blackmail. I was looking out for my daughter's best interests."

I laugh as I throw the copies we made down on her desk. "Don't worry if they get wet. We have plenty more where that came from." After G and Lottie came to me with all the paperwork that James had given them, I shared what was in the envelope James had addressed to me, feeling it was right they heard the whole story from me. Once it was all out on the table, we made a plan to confront her together and I asked to speak with Ethel alone first.

I see her trying to decipher what the papers mean and I take joy in elaborating for her. "Did you have Leah's best interest in mind when you created a fund in her memory so that you could launder money for yourself?"

I see the minute her facial expression changes and she puts my words with what she's seeing on the papers. "Yep, that's right. It's all there from the last several years. Hell, just last week's Gala has thousands unaccounted for."

I chuckle spitefully as I stand and say, "Well, that's not true. It is accounted for. It was moved into your offshore account and then transferred into the country club's checking account. Isn't that right Ethel? You ran out of funds to get that club going years ago so instead of making an honest living you did the unthinkable."

I move closer to get into her sullen face. "You used your dead daughter's name and disease to keep you up. And to think you once called me a low life. YOU, Ethel Richmond, are the scum of the earth," I say slowly and sternly, hoping she hears every fucking word.

I remember when I first started dating Leah. She would tell me little things her mother had said or done, and I was always shocked because there was really no better person than Leah. She was smart, classy, fun, kind, focused, and loyal. Even when she started living on the wild side with me, she was still a parent's dream. It wasn't until Leah left me that I realized how truly evil the lady she had grown up with was. I am beyond thankful that after she passed away her grandparents raised Lottie.

Ethel's demeanor suddenly changes after a few seconds of looking like a fish out of water. "Where did you get this information?" she says angrily.

"Certainly not out of someone's personal journal," I say sarcastically.

"You aren't going to turn me in because if you do there is nothing stopping me from doing the same to you," Ethel says confidently as she picks up her phone, most likely to call James. *Joke's on her.*

My comeback to this reaction is ready and waiting because I expected her to say that. "Oh, I know, and I am fully prepared for it. First off, twenty years later do you really think a piece of paper is going to hold up in a court of law? But if that's what it takes, I don't care... you are going down for this Ethel Richmond." I smile because it's going to be a sweet day when justice is served. "I'll share my damn cell with you if that's what it takes."

\*\*\*

## Lottie-

The anticipation is killing me. I don't know how much longer I can listen to Ethel spew such nonsense. The fact that she has denied nothing gives me a sense of satisfaction. But I still want answers. I want to know why. Why did she let it get this far? What role was I supposed to play in all of this?

Greyson is stoic beside me, letting me take the lead when I want to burst through the doors and raise hell. I want to give Smith his time to hash things out.

I hear Smith say something about sharing a cell with Ethel, and I take that as my queue to enter the room. He's certainly not going to jail, not over this woman.

Turning the knob to the study, my hand is halted when Greyson lays his on top of mine. I look up into his green eyes, seeing his concern.

"You got this," he says, encouraging me and filling me with the strength he knows I'll need to face her. "There's enough fire in your eyes to tear down this whole fucking house but know I'm here if it becomes too much to bear." He places a gentle kiss on the top of my head and then removes his hand from mine.

"Thank you," I say, straightening my back and lifting my head high. I can't help but smile at the look of pride Greyson sports as we enter Ethel's study side by side.

Ethel's stare cuts to Greyson and me as we cross the threshold. Smith stands there with a smirk on his face as if he's had fun playing with Ethel so far. She still seems fairly composed, all things considered.

"Oh Charlotte, darling, please help me find James so he can escort this riff-raff out of our home." I have to hand it to her, she really knows how to turn it on.

"Well, considering he let the riff-raff in, I highly doubt he's going to be helping you," Greyson practically sneers from beside me.

Ethel scoffs as if she refuses to believe James would have played a role in all of this. She looks to me, then to the Rexwood men who flank my sides. My disdain for her is written all over my face. There is no talking herself out of this one, and I think she just came to that realization. Her body sways ever so slightly, but she quickly recovers and straightens her back.

"Charlotte, please let me explain. They're lying. All of this is just their attempt at revenge."

"That bullshit might sound legit to someone else, someone like your accountant who you have obviously been lying to for years, but it won't work on me. After discovering the deceit and finagling you have done to keep this charade going, I wouldn't put anything past you at this point." I pause to make sure she is hearing me before I continue.

"So please, just be straight with me. For once in your life, cut the act and the façade. Because we all know you've been stealing from the research fund, you're ass-up on your loan on the country club, and basically broke. But what was my purpose in all of this? How did you think I was going to help you get ahead because we all know you weren't going to touch my inheritance."

Ethel snaps at the mention of the inheritance. "Stupid, fucking man. How dare he give a seventeen-year-old what's rightfully mine."

"He was still alive when you started having money trouble... why wouldn't you have just gone to him instead," I say, grabbing the folder of all the copied documents from Smith.

"Please, that old bastard wouldn't have given me a cent. He despised me, probably because of your mother... the apple of his eye. You know she could do nothing wrong in his mind. He worshipped the ground she walked on. Even when she got knocked up by some loser who left her immediately after finding out, he made sure you and her would want for nothing. Then you came along, little chunky thing that you were, and he could see no wrong in you either. I was pushed out by my own legacies."

My jaw hits the floor hearing the hate Ethel harbored towards her own flesh and blood.

"Shut your damn mouth Ethel. You don't get to talk like that about Lottie in front of me. You're done feeding her mind with stupid insecurities based off your own jealousy." A pissed-off Greyson growls beside me. I love how protective he is of me but for once I'm going to say exactly what's on my mind.

"You never even tried! You cast yourself out. There were plenty of opportunities for you to show you had some shred of humanity inside that black heart of yours," I yell, no longer able to contain my frustration.

"I didn't want his pity money."

"That's bullshit and you know it! Papa and Gigi hoped like hell you would show up one day. Show up for your family who had suffered enough. Show up for me, the stupid seventeen-year-old who has lost everyone she ever loved. The one that kept holding out hope even when Papa and Gigi told me I didn't have to go to Nori Beach in the summers if I didn't want to. But I kept going because a stupid part of me thought maybe one day I would be good enough for you and you would finally see me."

I wipe the tears from the corners of my eyes, trying to regain my composure. I feel Greyson's large hand press against my lower back, urging me to continue, to get the answers I need.

"I'm going to ask again. Why me? What role did I have in your plans?"

"Well, once lover boy over there got you away from the horrid Waterbury's son, I was hoping to set you up with Jacob. The Roberts family comes from a long line of money. They're an original railroad family. Did you know that? They basically swim in it...Jacob's father has been the biggest sponsor of the fund for years. He lost someone very close to him to cancer."

"So, you mean to tell me you exploited this man's grief and loss for your own personal gain? What kind of person are you? Wait don't answer that, we're all well aware of what you are," I say, waving my hand to the three of us standing as a united front.

"How did you think Lottie being with Jacob was going to help you?" Greyson asks.

"She just wanted to ensure the cash never stopped flowing," Smith answers.

"Is that all I am to you? A means of securing a lifelong donor? I wonder how Mr. Roberts would feel knowing it was you he was supporting and not the fund," I spew at her as she just stands there unmoved by anything we're saying. She really is a black-hearted bitch. Has only and will only ever care for herself.

The snarl on Ethel's face says what she won't say herself. She knows she's caught, and we have enough proof to put her behind bars if we really wanted to.

"How does it feel... knowing you've ruined any last shred of a relationship with your only living family member? Because I can guarantee there is no coming back from this. I am no longer a pawn in your sick and twisted games. I am done with you."

"So, what now Charlotte?" Ethel asks without a shred of remorse in her tone. Nope, still the nasty old woman I'm used to.

This is something Greyson, Smith, and I spent quite a bit of time talking about. What did I want to do with Ethel once this was all over? I've thought it through and I think I came up with a plan.

"Now Ethel, you're going to find a realtor and list both the country club and this oversized trophy-of-a-house. With the ridiculous amount of money you will make with the sale of these two properties, you are going to pay back what you owe to the foundation and the bank. You are going to resign as head of the Richmond Research Fund and disaffiliate from anything pertaining to it. Then you're going to take whatever remains and move far away, somewhere that no one knows your name or who you are. Because I don't ever want to see your face again. And if for some reason you don't do as I'm telling you, I will not think twice about dropping this folder off at the police station. So please don't test me," I say with a steady, detached voice, one I wasn't aware I possessed.

"You wouldn't dare report me to the police. You don't have it in you!"

"Try me, Ethel. You have a month to get it sorted."

Linking my arm with Greyson's I look up at him and say, "I'm ready to go now." Greyson looks past me at his dad and then, with no further words exchanged, we walk out the door.

Leaving it all behind... all the hurt, the betrayal, and most importantly the devil of a woman who I once called family.

# Chapter Thirty-Two

"No babe, it's clutch then shift," Greyson yells from the passenger seat as I hear Ol' Girl's gears grind.

I slam on the brake and turn to him. "How am I ever supposed to learn if you keep yelling at me?"

"I'm not yelling at you, just wasn't sure if you could hear my instructions over the destruction of OL' GIRL'S GEAR BOX!"

"Keep that up and I'm just going to ask your dad to teach me instead," I grumble.

A week of driving lessons with Greyson has been interesting, to say the least. Although he's an excellent teacher, he's shit at keeping his cool. After mastering driving an automatic, Greyson thought I should practice on Ol' Girl to learn a stick shift. It's not going great.

"You go right ahead Babygirl... you think I have no patience? Just wait." He winks and squeezes my thigh. I stick my tongue out at him like a petulant child.

Leaning across the bench seat, Greyson pulls the brake and grabs the back of my head to pull me in for a kiss. A kiss I feel all the way to my toes.

It's been a crazy month, but I think I'm finally coming to terms with everything that's happened.

Being that Greyson was also a victim of Ethel's manipulation and schemes helped me move forward in our relationship. It took me a bit, but ultimately, he knew what he did was wrong and tried to make it right. I couldn't imagine going through all that without him by my side. He is my rock, my anchor.

A few days after the blowout with Ethel, I moved into Nana Rex's house. Smith is the one who originally suggested it, and I couldn't have thought of a better place for me to finish out the school year. Greyson, being the possessive man he is, wanted to move in there along with me, but Nana refused. Saying we have the rest of our lives to live together. It's been such a positive experience to live with someone who genuinely cares about me, which is something I've been missing these past months.

Being part of a big family means even bigger holiday feasts. Thanksgiving was unlike anything I've ever experienced. Nana, of course, outdid herself, so much so that Gunnar had to make her a second table to fit all of us and the food. The love and laughter that filled the room from our rag-tag group was heartwarming.

We had a lot to be thankful for, well, me especially. James had called us early that day to let us know Ethel was officially out of her house two weeks earlier than expected. Not sure how she pulled it off, but James confirmed a check was written to the RRF and the bank in the full amount owed. I don't care where she moved or what she did with all of her things. I'm just happy to put that chapter of my life behind me.

Today, I'm taking Greyson on a date. He doesn't know it yet but we're celebrating. Even though it's only the beginning of December, I just got my acceptance letter to Mountain Ridge University. Since I haven't taken my driver's test yet, Greyson still needs to drive us to the surprise I had Frankie help set up.

There's a slight chill to the air today but I'm not going to let it ruin this.

We drive down the long tree-lined dirt road for quite some time. The confused look on his face only makes my smile grow larger.

"I've lived here my entire life and I don't think I've ever been on this road. How'd you find it?" he asks just as the thick trees start to thin out and the end of the road approaches.

"It's so pretty here," I say, ignoring his words.

Once we're parked, he looks ahead spotting the balloons bunched together on top of a grassy hill. Greyson exits the truck first and then walks to my side. I can't help the giddy squeal I make when he scoops me into his arms, spinning me around and then putting me back on the ground, kissing me deeply.

"What have you been up?" he questions, his lips mere inches from my own. I lean up on my tiptoes to close the space and take his lips with mine once again.

"It's a celebration," I tell him once we pull away. Taking his hand in mine I lead him up the hill to where the balloons are tied to a basket resting upon a blanket.

"And what are we celebrating, might I ask?"

I hand him the envelope I have tucked in my purse, practically bouncing up and down as he opens it and reads the letter inside.

His eyes scan the written words and a huge smile spreads across his face.

"You got into Mountain Ridge! I'm so proud of you. I knew you could do it," he says as he pulls me in for a hug, kissing the top of my head.

"I got the letter two days ago. I've been dying to tell you, but I wanted it to be special."

"This is such great news, but why are we here?" He looks around us. It really is gorgeous here. In the distance, the mountains peek out just beyond the dense trees giving us the most picturesque backdrop.

"Well... I wanted to show you where we're going to be living. This was Papa's property."

Greyson does a full slow spin to take in the vast hills and wooded areas around us. "All of this?" he asks.

"Yeah, I believe it's around thirty acres... do you like it?"

"Like it? I fucking love it! This is amazing babe." He pauses for a second as if recalling something. "So, the road we came in on...?"

"That's our road. I don't think the street sign was there, but in the paperwork it's called Leah Drive."

"Leah, as in your mom?"

I nod, smiling at him. "It's all ours, I want us to build the house of our dreams... and grow old together in the home we create here."

He grabs my hips and pulls me in close. We stand back to front with his head resting in the crook of my neck, looking out at the property before us.

"I can't think of anything I'd want more than to grow old with you by my side," he says and places a kiss on my neck.

"Eee! This is so exciting. I can just see it now... a large garage for you, a garden behind the house filled with rows and rows of flowers. We can even make our own little kickboxing gym for nights we can't make it into town..." I point to different spots in front of us as I continue to discuss some of my visions.

"Sounds perfect to me," he says, listening intently to my grandiose plans. I turn in his hold wrapping my arms around his neck.

"This is our project. I want you to have just as much say as I do."

I can tell by the look on his face that he wants to say something. I know what he's thinking, but I have a plan to ensure he feels like he's sharing the responsibilities too.

"What?" I ask, already knowing what he's going to say.

"No, honestly, I love it all. I just... I just want to contribute to it, however I can," he says.

"Good!" I smile at him, then continue, "I was thinking of asking Gunnar to be the general contractor on the project. And you know damn well he'll put you boys to work."

"You bet your fine ass we will work on it. Have I told you how amazing you are?" He leans down and takes my lips in his.

"Mmm, maybe a time or two." I giggle when he attacks my sides, tickling me until I can barely breathe.

"I fucking love you, Lottie," he says as he grabs two large handfuls of my ass.

"Love you more..."

We make our way to where the picnic is laid out. Once we finally get ourselves situated on the blanket, Greyson opens the basket, allowing the delicious smells from the feast Nana packed for us to fill the air. "Now let's eat, I'm fricken starving."

\*\*\*

Greyson's hands haven't left my hips since we've been back at his place. Smith is out with the guys for the night, so we're on his living room couch attempting to watch a movie. But by the way Greyson keeps touching me and grinding his already semi-hard cock into me from behind, I know we won't make it through much more of it. I wasn't expecting to finish the movie, we rarely do. The loose pair of sleep shorts and Greyson's over-sized t-shirt that I'm wearing aren't providing much of a barrier between us, nor are they preventing his hands from wandering.

"Guess you're not too interested in the man in the iron suit, huh?" I say, pushing my ass into him.

"I don't give a shit what's on that TV, Babygirl. All I have is a vision of you bouncing on my dick with these big tits in my face." His hand snakes up my shirt and grabs my chest for emphasis.

Wiggling myself out of my shirt, I sit up and he soon follows. My legs straddle his lap and I kiss him deeply. I love this guy so much, every touch of his is like an electric current straight through me.

"Fuck, you're perfect. I can't wait till we have a place all to ourselves. I'm going to fuck you on every damn surface there is," he says, pushing his hips upwards.

I lean back to allow him room to slide his sweatpants down. Quickly removing my shorts, I then settle myself back over his lap. His hands grab my ass and drag me over his rock-hard erection. Greyson's mouth teases me with small kisses along my neck, causing my breath to become heavy with want.

"Get on this dick baby. I want you to ride me."

"Oh, how romantic." Faking a swoon, I grind down on him, eliciting a groan from him.

"Oh, I can give you romantic... I can give you all the flowers, thoughtful gifts, and dinners you want pretty girl. But I know damn well you prefer screaming my name as I make you explode with ecstasy because that... that is romance baby. That's my soul anchoring itself to yours."

With that, he lines up the head of his cock and pulls me onto him. "Fuuuck," we both moan once I'm fully seated on him.

I move my hips, ever so slowly groaning at the feel of him. "I love the way you ride my cock. The look in your eyes when you feel me pressing along that sweet spot deep within you."

My hands go to his shoulders to give me more stability as I pick up my pace. Rocking my hips back and forth with just enough sway and control that I feel my orgasm creeping up already. *Fuck he feels so good.*

I'm lost in him, in his scent, in the way his muscular shoulders feel beneath my hands, and in how perfect he feels when he's deep inside of me.

He leans back into the couch and brings his arms behind his head. "I have the perfect show right here... damn Lottie, you ride me so well. Show me how much you love my cock inside of you," he says with that sexy-ass grin of his. His commanding tone sends me into a frenzy, and I ride him without any inhibitions.

"Aah Grey, I'm going to come soon," I moan, feeling the tingles rise.

"Mmm, that's right. Use me, baby... come for me," he commands, his hands abandoning their relaxed position behind his neck and grabbing onto my hips. Taking a firm hold, he helps me find my release.

"Oh shit! Yes please... yes." My moans and his fill the space around us. Just a few moments later, my toes begin to curl as heat radiates throughout my body.

"Fuck, yes," he groans, and I feel his orgasm release deep inside me. I collapse onto him, the sound of our breaths a soothing melody. We stay that way for who knows how long, just enjoying the feel of our bodies on one another. My head on his chest and my legs still straddling his hips. Greyson's arms draped lazily over my body, one of his hands drawing small circles on my back.

"Thank you..." he says in almost a whisper. Leaning my head up to look at him, I raise my eyebrow in question. "For believing me... for seeing the undeniable love I have for you instead of my numerous mistakes. You make me so happy I don't know what I'd do without you."

Kissing the spot directly over his heart and placing my head back on his chest I say, "I love you, Greyson. You don't have to worry about that... you're never getting rid of me."

# Chapter Thirty-Three

Tonight is turning out to be one of those nights. A night none of us will ever forget. Nox fought in his first big showdown. It was surreal seeing my best friend walk out into the ring. When he won by knockout in round two, our crew went crazy. He beat the local undefeated welterweight fighter.

With Lennox being the new buzz of the town, by the time he had showered and met us in his dressing room we had an afterparty to go to. There was a guy in a suit who came in and introduced himself as Eric. He invited all of us to a club here in Charlotte to celebrate Nox's win and bring in the New Year. According to Eric, the door will let us in if we were with him and not to worry about IDs.

The club is on top of the Epi-Center, right by our hotel and the venue. It's partially outdoors, with an open terrace where the DJ is set up. Eric got us a roped-off area with couches right on the edge of the indoor portion of the club.

"I have exactly thirty minutes to find my New Year's eve kiss," Ford pipes up as we all settle in.

"Dude, get a drink first," Nox says with the biggest smile I've ever seen on his face as he moves to sit beside Emerson.

Nox's brother, Colton, and his girlfriend of the week went back to the hotel for some "alone time". We all knew what that was code for, but Nox looked slightly relieved when his brother told us his plans didn't involve coming with us. I'm almost one hundred percent positive that had to do with Emerson, since her brother also wouldn't be with us. Lucian and Frankie were staying at the venue with Snow to watch the main event that wouldn't happen until closer to midnight.

"Speaking of a drink, Ford licks his lips when the cocktail waitress arrives with two bottles of champagne.

She smiles at him but addresses Nox, "Eric had these sent over for you guys to celebrate your victory."

Staring at me, she bites her lip and asks, "Do you want me to open one for you?" Before I can answer, I feel Lottie's hand possessively on my thigh.

I glance at Lottie as I say, "Nah, we're good. Thanks though."

Looking back to the waitress who suggestively says, "Okay, well let me know if you change your mind."

"He won't," Lottie says sternly beside me. Thankfully, the chick realizes it's a good time for her to leave.

Ford chuckles, "I guess she's into beards."

"Well, my fingernails are about to be into her eyeballs if she doesn't stop looking at my man," Lottie says aggressively to Ford as he holds his hands up in innocence.

I laugh and grab her chin. "Babygirl, as much as I love this side of you, either chill or you're going to get yourself fucked in the bathroom."

Tugging her lips between my teeth... nipping at them before I say, "She can look all she wants, but she'll never have me. No one else will. You know that, right?" Her lust-filled eyes look at me as she nods. I give her a hard kiss to drive my point home. I feel her shifting against the couch, needing relief. That's my sign I need to stop or we won't make it to midnight. Before I can make myself pull away, a piece of ice hits me in the cheek.

"What the hell?" I growl and look directly at Ford.

"Y'all were making me jealous. Save some for the rest of us."

Lottie giggles as she reaches for the champagne. "Let's pop this!" Looking to Nox she exclaims, "In honor of the future welterweight champion and his KO tonight!"

"How you feeling about everything?" I say to Nox as the three of us watch Emerson take a boomerang video of Lottie popping the champagne.

"Honestly, pretty fucking amazing. Being in that ring was unlike anything I've ever experienced. I thought I would be nervous as hell but fighting for a crowd that large was such an adrenaline rush. It felt like I was there to entertain, and I thrived off that." That smile still stretched across his face from his win earlier.

"Well, I'd say you did just that." It's the truth too. We weren't the only people going nuts when he won tonight.

"Yeah, brother you were a crowd favorite... and the ladies loved you," Ford says to him, but Nox looks to Emerson who is laughing with Lottie. Looks like he only has eyes for one lady.

I give him a look that says *I know the feeling buddy.*

We continue to talk about Nox's plans for his fighting career. I've always believed in him but after seeing how well he handled himself under pressure tonight, I have no doubts about him making it big one day.

I tell him about the prideful look his mom had on her face as he won. I also let him know my dad texted to tell me he and Gunnar just dropped her off at home, since they all decided to head back tonight.

The girls pass around the champagne glasses and demand we all make a little toast to the next year.

Ford goes first, "To turning eighteen and becoming a prospect for the Rebel Knights." His aspirations don't surprise me at all.

He's always known he wanted to be a part of the club, which is one of the reasons he's so close with my dad.

Emerson lifts her glass next. "To winning my own fight this year. And to surviving Richmond Hills High without you guys."

Nox puts his arm around her and says, "If you keep that right hook, there's no doubt in my mind you're going to win... My jaw can attest to that." Emerson takes a knuckle and barely taps his chin, staring up at him a lot like Lottie looks at me. Ford and I exchange a knowing look.

"Here's to watching the "Lights Out" Mermaid," Nox says as he touches a piece of Emerson's blue hair. "Kick ass in the ring next year." He looks at all of us. "And here's to you guys for always being there for me. I'm ready to see where this year takes everyone."

We all nod and cheer to that.

Now it's my turn. "Here's to never going a day without calling this girl mine again," I say as I pull Lottie onto my lap. "And to a year of learning how to make business boom for our shop with our new customizing machine." After all the shit with Ethel, my dad wanted an explanation as to why I agreed to a deal with her in the first place. He was furious but understood my need to try to contribute instead of being handed everything. Two weeks later the machine I wanted for custom work arrived at the shop. My dad made a deal with me that I could pay it back like a loan as I brought business in. I beat myself up for a good week after that, knowing if I had of just gone to him with a loan proposition to begin with then I would have never hurt Lottie. Luckily, I opened up to her about what was going through my head and she reassured me. She said we all make mistakes but it doesn't define me as a person or us as a couple.

Lottie kisses the side of my head. *I love her little affectionate kisses.*

Holding her glass high she says, "Lastly here's to me being an official North Carolina resident with a driver's license." She smiles widely at that accomplishment. "And never living too far from my guy again." Everyone cheers and chugs their glasses. *We ain't the sipping type.*

Ford excuses himself to go prowl with only a few minutes before the ball drops.

"I have to go to the bathroom," Emerson says, standing up shortly after Ford leaves.

Lottie looks to the TV countdown as she says, "Crap it's three minutes till midnight. I hate to ask but do you think you can wait till after? I don't want you to have to go by yourself."

*My girl isn't missing out on her New Year's Eve kiss.*

She told me earlier this was her first New Year's having anyone to kiss and I told her it was my first too. I didn't do that shit in the past... knowing it would give the Ambers of the world false hope.

Before Em can answer, Nox steps up. "Nah it's okay I'll go with her. You lovebirds stay here."

When Big Sean's "Bounce Back" ends the DJ announces the countdown for the New Year. Our waitress reappears and quickly puts some party horns on our table. Not giving her a second glance, I continue to stare at Lottie who's still sitting on my lap.

*How did I get so damn lucky?*

"Ten, nine... The crowd gets louder with each number eight, seven..." The numbers fade as Lottie moves herself to straddle me. Looking into those *need-you* hazel eyes of hers. The same eyes that have had me sucked in from the very first moment they met mine, I remember instantly knowing there was something about her.

My explanation... she was made for me and I for her. We were always meant to be. No question about that.

Lottie kisses me as I hear the crowd erupt with cheers. Moving my hand to the back of her head I pull her into me, searing my lips to hers as she opens up for me. I never want to let her go... never plan to. This kiss is a promise. A promise of the new year, new adventures, new plans... but within all that new there will always be us.

She grinds down on my hard dick.

"I'm so ready to have these legs wrapped around my beard..." I say skimming my hands along her exposed thighs.

Lottie reaches up and tugs on my beard, I see the lust in her eyes at the thought. Biting my bottom lip, she groans, "Later Baby."

"You love getting me all worked up, don't you Babygirl?" I say, adjusting myself in my jeans.

She giggles, not denying it. "Happy New Year's Grey. I love you so much."

"I love you Stacks. This is going to be our best year yet," I say, giving her one more kiss.

Smacking her ass when she stands and adjusts her black, backless dress, I lightly run my hand down her spine, which is cut out to right above her ass. I can't help but skim my fingertips under the material, feeling her thong. "Greyson." She warns me with a look.

Nox and a flushed Emerson rejoin us as the DJ cranks the music back up.

"Lottie you wanna go dance?" Emerson asks.

"Hell yeah!" Lottie turns to me grinning, "Come find me on the dance floor in a bit," she says seductively.

"Yes ma'am," I say while she stands. Grabbing her arm so she makes eye contact with me again, I add, "I'll have my eye on you guys... I don't want to kill anyone tonight."

Lottie smiles and shakes her head at me. Giving me a quick peck on the lips, she grabs Em's hand and heads to the dance floor.

The DJ is on fire. Song after song, the girls sing every word as they dance with each other.

"There y'all are!" a familiar voice says. Turning around, I see Frankie and Lucian coming into our sitting area.

She hugs us and asks where the girls are, heading their way as soon as she spots where I'm pointing.

"Hell of a fight," Lucian says to Nox as he daps both of us up.

"Thanks man, when are you going to get in the big ring?" Nox offers him champagne with his question.

He chuckles. "Nah I'll leave that to you and Snow. You know I just do it to stay in shape for football and baseball."

We both nod and Nox says, "Speaking of, where is Snow?"

"He's close behind us with some of the other fighters the coach trains around here. The main event ended up fighting earlier than we thought, and they only went three rounds." That explains how they got here so soon after midnight.

Ford walks back over to us with a shit-eating-grin all over his face. "I'm guessing you found a New Year's Eve kiss Pretty Boy?"

He shakes his head. "Nope." Smiling he says, "Not *A* kiss... I found two. They both had pretty teeth, I couldn't turn either down, so we made it a thing." *This guy.*

We all laugh, shaking our heads at his typical shit. I can't wait till the day a girl brings him to his knees.

Looking back over to the girls, I notice a guy has moved in on Emerson. Frankie and Lottie dance with each other. Em tries to smile and keep distance between her and the stranger. I see Nox watching them intently, gripping the railing that separates us from the dance floor. When the guy takes Emerson's hand and spins her around, she smiles until he pulls her flush to him moving his hips into hers. Nox jumps over the railing, heading their way before Lucian and Ford even know what's going on. I go after him before he does something stupid.

Before I even get there, the guy is gone. Nox and Emerson are talking in hushed tones as Frankie and Lottie look at me like *What the fuck.*

Emerson storms off, followed by a pissed-off Nox, as her concerned brother joins us asking what the hell happened.

350 MAKE YOU LOVE ME

To my surprise, Lottie chimes in... more perceptive about the situation than I realized she was. "A random dude came up dancing on Emerson. Nox must have seen the guy was really drunk so he told him to get lost, but Emerson was annoyed saying she can take care of herself."

"Sounds like her," Lucian says, seemingly satisfied with that explanation. "You think I should go make sure she's good?"

"I'm sure Nox caught up to her. She's probably telling him how she'll show him who the boss is next week at the gym." I say and we all laugh.

Nox has been giving Emerson one-on-one training lately. Since they're both lefties, everyone thought he would be the perfect fit to teach her. I think it's pretty obvious there's a lot more going on than training, even if they're trying to deny it.

Snow and a couple guys I don't recognize spot us and head our way. His first official fight is next month, so tonight he was just a spectator.

Lottie goes over to give her friend a hug. We've come a long way in the last couple of months, and I think our mutual respect for each other is growing into a sort-of friendship. I still watch closely. Not because of Snow, but the big guy beside him. I see him eating up Lottie's ass with his eyes. Something my jealous mind has to get used to because she has a great ass. But the minute he touches her arm to get her attention, I'm walking over there.

Snow taps him on the chest to stop him as I quickly approach. "This is one of my best friends, Lottie, and her boyfriend's that big motherfucker heading your way."

"What's up Snow?" I say, wrapping my arms around Lottie from behind as I glare at the newcomer.

"My bad," the guy speaks up. "Your girl is beautiful, you can't blame me for looking. I didn't know she had a boyfriend."

"Now you do," I say bluntly as Lottie squeezes my arm wrapped around her, silently telling me to chill.

My mind battles within itself. Even the jealous fucker I am is confident enough in my relationship that a part of me likes Lottie hearing what this guy just said.

For a long time when I first met her, she didn't realize she was so fucking perfect. In her mind, because she was curvier than most girls her age, she wasn't desirable enough. She finally sees the falsehood behind the lie that had been fed to her most of her life.

Not only are her curves what most men want, but she's also always the most beautiful girl in the room. I'm the lucky fucker who gets to call her mine and know just how pretty her heart and her pussy are too.

Wiggling out of my hold she grabs my hand, "Let's dance Baby... see you later Corbin!"

I know she's just trying to distract me, but I don't mind, I've been wanting to have her to myself.

At first, she shimmies and shakes, dancing around me to some techno dance music. I take her in... the sound of her laugh as she teases me, her long brown hair in a high ponytail leaving her exposed back on perfect display, the way her eyes shine at me. There is no better feeling than knowing she loves me.

The song changes to "Love Nwantiti" by Ckay, the perfect beat to feel her body on mine. I pull Lottie to me, and without hesitation, she starts rocking her hips back and forth against me. So in tune with each other and the beat of the song as we dance. Holding on to her hips and grinding into her as she continues to sway her ass against me. She reaches back, grabs the back of my neck, and pulls me down to her. I lick the exposed part of her collarbone up to her ear.

"I can't wait to feel this ass bounce back on my dick when I get you back to that hotel room. Do you feel how hard you have me right now?" I huskily whisper into her ear.

She moans and turns to face me, still grinding into me. "I'm so wet for you," she says, going up on her toes to kiss me. The kiss immediately turns to licking, sucking, moaning... needy. *I need her.*

"I'm past want, I NEED you, Babygirl." Instead of responding, she grabs my hand and starts to pull me off the dance floor, calling out to our friends that we are leaving... they all laugh at us.

"Wrap it up," Ford calls out.

*Fuck that. Thank God for trust and birth control.*

Walking the two blocks to our hotel, Lottie says, "My first New Year's sex and my first hotel sex all in one."

"I'm the proud owner of all those firsts and I plan to continue to be."

She squeezes my hand. "I can't help but selfishly want more of your firsts too."

"Baby you may not be my first, but you are the only one that's ever mattered to me." I know she knows this but I'm sure it's not easy knowing I gave a lot of my firsts away to meaningless people either. "There is one fantasy I never had until you and it's something I've never done before."

"Really, what...a threesome?" she asks nonchalantly as she continues to walk down the sidewalk.

"Fuck no. You know I wouldn't share you." I growl. "Wait do you want that?" I think she's messing with me but now I need to know.

"No Grey, I was just messing with you. I knew it wasn't that but for real, what?" she says in an amused tone.

"I've never done anal." Grabbing a handful of her ass, I add, "But this ass. I know it would look so fucking good spread open for me."

She stops on the sidewalk, that same lust in her eyes from the dance floor. "I always assumed you had done that too."

"Nope," I respond matter-of-factly.

"Can we try it tonight?" she asks curiously.

"We can start getting you ready for it. How about that?" I answer honestly.

"Really, how?" Her eyes wide with intrigue.

"Just let me handle that," I say placing my thumb on her bottom lip. She takes it into her mouth and sucks. *Fuck, she's sexy.*

"Yeah..." Now I'm the one pulling her. "Let's go. I need to be inside you right fucking now."

"Instead of my usual chin up, tonight it's going to be... Ass Up, Babygirl!"

# Epilogue

## *Six Months Later*
## *Greyson-*

"Oil me up, Lennox," Ford says, standing in front of Nox's lounge chair by the pool attempting to stir the beast.

"Fuck off, Pretty Boy," Nox says as he smacks the tanning oil out of Ford's hand.

"Damn, G. I can't believe you are actually going to leave me here with this moody bitch." Ford and Lennox are both in Nori Beach with us this week. Well, Ford is... Nox is here physically but not mentally.

"Nox, you know it would be better if you opened up and at least told us what the fuck is wrong with you," I say to him because his misery is obviously not getting any better.

"Okay pot meet kettle. Do you not remember *you* at the end of last summer? I'll talk about it when I'm ready." *Well damn, he has me there.* But that confirms my thoughts that it has something to do with Emerson. He's right though. We need to let him talk when he's ready.

The back door to the house opens and the prettiest girl in the world walks out.

"Grey, you ready?" Lottie says with her beach bag slung over her arm.

"Yep, trucks loaded. Just waiting on your fine ass." I stand up, flicking the guys off. "Bye fuckers! Behave while mom and dad are away." They return the one-finger salute.

"See you guys tomorrow. There is plenty of food in the fridge!" Lottie calls out to them.

"Babe, they are grown-ass men. They can feed themselves," I say, squeezing her hip as I approach her, still unable to keep my hands off her.

"Our mommy likes to take care of us," Ford says, waggling his eyebrows at her, using my words from before in his favor. Lottie giggles. She's used to his antics at this point.

"Shut up... dumbass. Y'all just don't tear anything up," I say as I follow Lottie out the side gate towards my truck.

Grabbing her hand to bring it to my lips, before I say, "You excited for camping?"

*I know I am.* The house has been full lately—between the guys, Ash and Trent, even my brothers have been down for some day trips with Jacob. As much as we love having everyone here, I am in serious need of some alone time with Lottie.

With a big smile, she says, "I can't wait! I love having the guys in town, but I'm ready to have you all to myself tonight." She traces her free hand through my beard and down my throat to the top of my chest, sending a jolt of electricity to my cock.

Always killing me with those little touches.

When we reach my truck, I toss her the keys and say, "wanna drive, Stacks?"

She catches the keys and beams that gorgeous smile of hers. "Hell yes, I do!"

*My girl finally learned how to drive my truck and watching her work that stick shift is sexy as shit.*

***

I wanted to do something special for Lottie in honor of one year of loving her. Nathan let us borrow his boat so we could anchor out off Shackleford Banks for the night. Since it's getting close to sunset, most people have cleared off the island by the time we arrive. Lottie got her first experience at being First Mate when we anchored down for the night. Now we're sitting in our beach chairs as the waves come in and gently crash against our feet. Our tent's set up behind us, far away from the tide. There are a few others scattered throughout the beach. Luckily, we aren't near any of them... I plan to have my girl screaming my name all night long.

"Wow. I swear sunsets here never get old," Lottie says as we look out over the water to the pink and purple sky. There's even a dusting of orange right above the horizon.

It really is something special. The view, the location, the person... my person. It doesn't get much better than this.

Jogging over to our stuff, I grab the little gift I got her.

She eyes me curiously as I come back towards her. "Here open this," I say as I hand her the little box.

"What's this for Grey?" She starts to open it.

"Just a little something I wanted to give you for our one year. Sitting here with the waves all around us, I thought it was the perfect time."

Holding the small charm up, she examines it first. Then she looks at me with tears in her eyes. "It's perfect."

"I love you—" I start, but she finishes my sentence.

"—more than all the waves in the ocean."

Standing from her seat, she kisses me softly. "Greyson, you never cease to amaze me. And to think you used to not be good with emotions and words," she says, looking down at the wave charm. I take it from her to help place it with the others on her bracelet.

"Babygirl, it's still hard for me to find the right words to express the love I have for you. Sometimes I'm overwhelmed by how much I feel now that you're in my life." I get a little choked up but continue, "No matter what ups and downs life throws at us, I want you to know I will always be right there with you to ride them out. Like a wave to the shore."

She beams at me with so much emotion in her eyes. "Absolutely baby, and just like the anchor to that boat right there, I will always be there. Even through the storms. I love you, Greyson. My best friend, my family... the love of my life."

"Look." She points over my shoulder excitedly. I turn to see what has her suddenly hyped up. "Greyson, it's them! They're coming this way. Holy shit, how perfect is this?"

Four wild horses are coming our way along the sand. Beautiful, light brown with blonde manes, they are amazing creatures.

Lottie grabs my hand, and we walk a bit closer to stand near the path they seem to be on.

"They are so beautiful." They get a little closer and her squeal tells me she notices the little one. "Greyson, there's a baby one!"

"I know baby, don't scare them." I chuckle. She's so damn cute over these horses.

Covering her mouth, she says, "Sorry, I'm just in awe right now."

"I'm glad you're getting to see them up close and personal, pretty girl."

"Oooh hold on, I want to get my phone and take a picture." She runs over to our stuff and hurries back, snapping a few pictures of them as they slowly make their way towards us.

"I want to get this blown up for our house. How perfect would that be in the living room?"

The mention of *our* house brings an overwhelming sense of happiness to me. I am more than looking forward to making the house we're building a home for us. A place we can have a family of our own and give our children the love they deserve from both parents.

*One day.*

I know some people will say we are too young, but I can't wait to experience everything the future holds for me and Lottie... together. I know what it's like to be without her and I never want to feel that again.

Wrapping my arms around her, we take in the moment, and I finally respond, "That would be pretty perfect. Almost as perfect as loving you forever."

Lottie looks up at me, rubbing her thumb across my forearm she says, "Even forever wouldn't be long enough."

*** 

## Five Years Later
## Lottie-

*Dear Baby Rexwood,*

*I can't believe tomorrow is your Daddy and my wedding day. It feels like I've waited my whole life for this. As a little girl, I used to dream of what my perfect wedding day would be like. Now, all I care about is the man that will be waiting for me at the end of the aisle. Your handsome, loving, and protective dad.*

*This past month has been a very busy one for us. I graduated from Mountain Ridge University and start my clinical research assistant internship at the end of June. I'm so excited to start this journey, and to hopefully help so many others one day.*

*Our wedding, which we're having at our house in Nori Beach, is this weekend. All mommy's and daddy's closest friends and family will be there. No one knows about you yet. So, for now, you're still my little secret. Oh man... I can't wait to tell everyone. Auntie Ashley and Auntie Frankie are going to freak out when I tell them. Don't even get me started on your Pops. I think we may have to limit his visitation. He'll try to hog up all of your time. I know Nana will certainly spoil you rotten any opportunity she'll get.*

*Not sure how I should tell your Daddy. He's been praying for you for months now, so I want to make your announcement special. I'm so damn proud of him. You will be too. He's been working so hard these past few years to get the shop to where he wanted it to be, and his dedication has certainly paid off. So much so that a top motorcycle magazine did a feature on Rebel Customs a few months ago.*

*I'm thinking I'm going to surprise him after the ceremony but before the party. That way, we will have so much more to celebrate walking through those doors together.*

*I can't wait to hold you in my arms and shower you with love. You're our precious gift and I know my angels above are smiling down on us.*

*I'll love you always...*

*xox*

*Mommy*

THE END

# Sneak Peek

## Reckless Abandon

### 8 years ago
### Sloan

My back is pushed up against the bedroom wall when his lips find the sensitive spot on the nape of my neck. I moan at the contact of his soft, luscious lips. Wes' knee presses between my locked thighs, begging for me to open. I slowly spread them apart as he quickly fills the space. Strong hands make their way up my shirt as a low growl escapes him. Grabbing onto his broad shoulders, I have the urge to drag my nails down his back.

"God, how long I've waited to taste your skin," he whispers into my neck, causing my blood to ignite. His mouth makes its way to my jaw as his fingers tease my hardened nipples. I grind my hips onto the large bulge forming in his pants, taking pleasure in the way his body wakes my inner siren. She's begging to be touched, needing the release only he can give me. Finally, his lips lightly brush against mine. I can no longer wait for their connection and grab the back of his head and press our lips together. His kiss is unlike anything I've ever experienced.

Needy.

Hard.

Desperate.

His lips devour mine and our tongues swirl together.

A sound I wasn't quite sure I could create escapes my mouth. "Please, Wesley," I beg him.

"Mmm, what do you need Lo," he responds as he moves his mouth back to my neck. Still grinding my body onto his, I feel a rush of heat between my thighs. I know one brush of his hand on my clit, and he'd send me over the edge.

"Please touch me, oh god... I need to feel your hands on me," I moan softly to him. He growls at my plea, grips my thighs, and hoists me up so I can wrap my legs around his firm body. Taking a few steps, he gently guides our entwined bodies onto my bed. Wes' lips find mine once again, thrusting his body to match my grinding hips. I moan loudly, no longer trying to keep my desire quiet.

"Shhh," he whispers. "We can't risk anyone hearing you." I groan in return, not caring if the entire house hears us. This moment is exactly what I've craved for what feels like my whole life.

Wes' hands make their way into my sleep shorts, sliding his fingers across my slick opening. I jolt forward at the connection. Dipping his fingers into my wet sex, he spreads it along my clit, swirling his fingers.

"So fucking wet for me, Lo," he says with a predator-like growl. I feel my orgasm build, teetering on the edge of pure bliss. Our breathing is labored, and I'm panting uncontrollably, desperate for release.

I need him to push me over the edge.

I need it to be him.

Ignoring the light knocking sound I hear, it seems as if my heart is trying to escape my chest. Grabbing his head, I pull him into a kiss once again. The feel of a familiar tingling sensation starting to take over in the tips of my toes. I rock my hips into his touch, hearing the confirmation of my own desire. The light knocking sound appears again and possibly a voice. Our lips break apart and Wesley's eyes shoot to the door.

Our bodies still, hoping we're just hearing things. Then I hear the voice again, "Sloan it's time to wake up."

What the hell?

"Come on chica! We're going to be late." My eyes pop open, recognizing the voice of my older sister. I lie there panting, looking around and realizing I'm alone with my fingers on my throbbing clit.

"Geez, it was all a dream." I sigh to myself and throw my arm over my face.

I hear a knock again. "What the hell Lo? Wake up!"

"I'm up, I'm up," I yell back, trying to calm my racing heart.

I drag myself out of bed making my way into the bathroom. One look in the mirror and the aftermath of my wet-dream bliss is written all over my face. Smiling to myself, I touch my cheeks that are still flushed crimson.

Wow, what a dream, it felt so real. As if Wesley was really there with me. Oh, how I wish that were true. He seems to be a staple in my dreams lately. My mind starts racing and I run my hands down my body, enjoying the flushed color of my skin, my sex still throbbing.

I snap back to my current situation when the auto-start of my brother Eli's truck roars to life. I hurry to get myself together, ensuring my cheeks return to their natural color before leaving my room and facing my family. Is it possible for a chick to have blue balls? If so, I'm going to have a serious case all day long.

# Acknowledgments

First and foremost, we want to thank our readers. From the bottom of our hearts, we thank you.

Thank you to my ride or die, LOML, my husband, for always supporting me and loving me through everything. Also, for the writing inspo :)
Shout out to my toddler for entertaining herself when I needed to fit in some writing and for inspiring me to be the best version of me.
I also want to thank my best friends for their support and love throughout this dream of mine.
Thank you to my book bestie now co-author for riding this wild roller coaster with me and being the other part of my brain. Let's make magic together, babe!
-A
I want to thank my husband for dealing with my many late nights filled with writing and unwatched shows. Thank you for encouraging this crazy dream of mine.
Thank you to my children for understanding that "I need just a few more minutes" really means "until I get this scene finished." You two are the reason I'm shooting for the stars. I want to make you proud.

Eeep! My other half, thank you for doing this with me. We make one kick-ass team and I'm so proud of what we've accomplished so far. Let's show em' what we're made of!

xox - L

Cindy, thank you for every encouraging word and piece of advice along the way... Your ability to decipher our crazy babble is top-notch. Thanks for being our O.G. ride or die! We love you!

Shannon, thank you for being as direct & honest as you are supportive & excited throughout this journey! Your proofreading and keen eye play a major part in our writing adventure. We appreciate you and all the encouragement.

Author Jessica Grace, thank you for your guidance and feedback! We are thankful to know amazing authors like you.

To our wonderful Editor—Brandi with My Notes in the Margin. Thank you for your hard work and flexibility.

To our Beta team—Sara, Corinne, Trisha, Melissa, and Jennifer... Thank you for dedicating the time to read our book and giving us feedback to make sure Lottie & Greyson's story was told in the best possible way.

Thank you to our ARC team. We appreciate each and every one of you for taking the time to give us honest reviews and promote our book. Reviews help authors more than people realize and we are so appreciative.

TL Swan, not only would we not have met because of your readers' group, but we also wouldn't have been so encouraged to be authors. Thank you to Tee and the fellow cygnets for all the advice and constant motivation to go for it!!

Last but certainly not least, we want to give a shout out to our Book Obsessed Babes community...

Each of you inspires us to continue this crazy journey.

Thank you all for being a part of something that we cherish. We're truly grateful.

# About Author

A New Yorker and a Southern Belle.
Two Book Obsessed Babes that became lifelong best friends
over their love for a good romance novel.

When they're not writing, they're devouring a good book or
spending time with their family and friends.

Total opposites in some ways and exactly the same in others,
making them a dynamic author duo.

## Keep in touch with us...

### Follow us on Instagram
https://instagram.com/Book.obsessed.babes

### Join our Facebook Reader Group
www.facebook.com/groups/bookobsessedbabes/

### Laugh at us on TikTok
https://www.tiktok.com/@Bookobsessedbabes

# Also By L.A. Shaw

## *Make You Series*

#0.5  Make You Miss Me
(Trent & Ashley)
#1  Make You Love Me
(Greyson & Lottie)
#2   TBD
(Emerson & Nox)- 2023

## *Reckless Hearts Series*

#1 Reckless Abandon
(Sloan & Wesley)- December 2022